Advance Praise

"A family and step-family struggle worthy of Shakespeare, a tense courtroom drama, unforgettable characters... *Trial by Family* kept me up all night! Roselee Blooston is a novelist to follow for years to come."

—Alice Elliott Dark, author of *In the Gloaming*

"Roselee Blooston puts characters on the page that are as real and raw as you or I. *Trial by Family* pairs a trio of adult siblings and their aging father with one heckuva antagonist—a scheming, conniving second wife who's trying to assure her own healthy retirement while supporting a failed-to-launch kid and her spouse. Blooston allows the reader a kind of literary eavesdrop, an intimate peek at a battle no neighbor could keep from opening the window to overhear, and no passerby could help stopping to gawk at. Then, with kindness and wisdom, she gives us hope that we would do as well."

—Jenny Milchman, *USA Today* bestselling author of *Cover of Snow* and *Wicked River*

"A fractured family comes together over a contested inheritance, only to reopen the wounds of deep sibling resentments. Masterfully told through tense courtroom drama and a shifting point of view that gives each player their turn on the stage, *Trial by Family* explores the complexities, the pitfalls and moments of clarity, that define the web we call love."

—Marina Antropow Cramer, author of *Roads: A Novel*

"Roselee Blooston's *Trial by Family* is a devastating tour de force about a family's slow-motion explosion, triggered by anger over an inheritance but really about the jealousies and losses within that have been festering for years. It may be too familiar to many, too honest and true, but Blooston lays it out for us with such insight and compassion—and, at times, humor—that we emerge shaken but wiser, disturbed but enlightened. We are thankful it is not our family, yet the power of the story-telling warns us that it very well may be."

—Martin Golan, author of *One Night with Lilith*

"Roselee Blooston's *Trial by Family* is a tale of a family in crisis. It touches on many issues that we come across in our elder law estate planning practice. The raw emotions stirred up when a family fails to plan for the future, courtroom drama, and ultimate resolution are not only entertaining but act as a reminder that "getting your affairs in order" should be a priority… all of the characters are thoroughly engaging. We recommend Ms. Blooston's novel not only as a good read but as a cautionary tale as to how vital proper planning can be."

—Michael Ettinger, President & attorney, *Ettinger Law Firm*

"Blooston shows a deep understanding of the complexities of adult sibling relationships. *Trial by Family* is a story of modern day family dynamics many of us will recognize, and many of us will relate to."

—Gail H. Goodman, founder of *Talking Alternatives*, a family mediation firm

Trial by Family

Trial by Family

a novel

Roselee Blooston

First Edition

Paperback ISBN: 978-1-62720-208-4
Ebook ISBN: 978-1-62720-209-1

Printed in the United States of America

Design by Lillian Lane
Editorial Development by Margaret Jenkins
Author Photograph taken by Maureen Gates

Published by Apprentice House Press

Apprentice House Press
Loyola University Maryland
4501 N. Charles Street
Baltimore, MD 21210
410.617.5265 • 410.617.2198 (fax)
www.ApprenticeHouse.com
info@ApprenticeHouse.com

In memory of my parents,
Leone and Arthur Blooston,
and
of my brother, George,
who encouraged me to write this story

Family is a mixed blessing.
You're glad to have one,
but it's also like receiving a life sentence
for a crime you didn't commit.
—Richard Pryor

PART I

Mother's Day

1

Alvin Segal inched his way down the hall past his first wife's paintings. Fay had hung them to make him feel at home, but set against her flocked wallpaper, the abstract sweep of Estelle's brushstrokes shook his equilibrium and made him feel all the more displaced. He found himself walking with blinders, looking neither left nor right.

Alvin planted his shaking foot on the first step. It would take him a while to get down the stairs, but he was determined not to call for help. Fay would send Consuelo and grumble that she wasn't getting her work done, and it would be his fault. He didn't want to start the morning with trouble. Not today.

At the bottom of the staircase he loosened his grip on the banister and straightened his jacket. Alvin prided himself on dressing well, even in retirement. It made him feel stronger and more able. The process took longer than it used to, what with his blurred vision and tremors and the confusion that sometimes overcame him in the middle of brushing his teeth. On Tuesday—or was it Wednesday—he'd brushed until his gums bled. This morning—it must have been Friday—he entered the bathroom twice, and couldn't remember what he'd done until he ran his tongue along his upper teeth and tasted the mint film.

"ALVIN! WHERE ARE YOU?" Fay's screech shot through him like an air raid siren. He had trouble with his hearing, but he wasn't *that* deaf. She was so much louder now than when they met.

"Coming! I'm coming," Alvin called back, knowing his voice wouldn't carry. He adjusted his trifocals and headed for the kitchen. He liked the sunny room, the way the light from the window bounced off the white tiles, but even after two years, he missed his home on Essex Street in the quiet Maryland suburb of Dorset, and Estelle's copper pot collection. He was glad Alyssa had kept the display intact. Fay was a collector, too, though not with Estelle's taste, or Alyssa's for that matter. Tourist tchotchkes from their honeymoon year sat on every surface: Eiffel Towers in half a dozen sizes on the wooden shelf above the stove; Bahamian shells rested on oval platters; dishtowels scrawled with *Palm Beach* draped the deep porcelain sink. Alvin appreciated the sentimental tokens, though the honeymoon seemed a long time ago.

Fay bustled back and forth from the chrome and laminate kitchen table to an old-fashioned standing desk she used for bills and mail. Her thinning platinum hair, exposed in the streaming sunlight, looked to Alvin like a fuzzy halo. She had a pen in one hand and a pad in the other. "There you are," she said eying him while writing something in large strokes. "Don't you look spiffy."

Alvin was pleased she noticed. Maybe he would take her to that new bistro on K Street for lunch after they completed the business at hand. He loved wearing this suit, the Burberry Estelle had picked out on their last shopping trip together, just before she went into the hospital. He hadn't wanted to go. "I don't need anything, sweetheart," he pleaded while she steered him by the arm through the mall, dragging her oxygen tank behind her like a reluctant toddler.

Fay tilted her head and studied him through her enormous dark-rimmed frames, which magnified her tiny eyes into giant black marbles. "But the tie is a bit much, don't you think? Oh, of course, you can't tell, can you?" Fay laughed.

It was true; he was colorblind. Estelle used to put blues on the left, reds on the right. Alvin thought this was the special rep tie he had worn for his last District of Columbia court appearance. Oh well. He dressed himself by pattern now, and mockery was the result.

Fay stabbed the pad with what must have been a period, then steered him to a chair. "Here. Sit." She shoved a huge bowl onto the Tower of London placemat. "I made your favorite."

Alvin peered down at the cereal; the steamy mush pooled in gray lumps. He didn't know how Fay managed to ruin oatmeal, but she must have neglected to measure the water. Why did she bother anyway? Why didn't she just ask Consuelo?

Their housekeeper had been standing at the sink all this time, her back to him, scrubbing last night's dishes. Alvin found her continued presence in his life a comfort. Consuelo Marti hadn't changed much in the thirty years she'd worked for his family: same thick Dominican accent, same solid frame, only wider and grayer.

Fay swished her caftan-covered form past him. The paisley design threatened to give him vertigo. "Eat," she ordered. "He'll be calling any minute." She was in a dither. Something had changed since their first year together when nightly foot rubs were the norm. Fay seemed preoccupied lately, less available. She stayed up all hours watching ridiculous British sitcoms. Wouldn't come to bed, even when he begged.

When they did talk, it was usually about money. "Alvin, let's sit down with your lawyer. Discuss the estate plan." Over and over again until he relented. They met with his long-time attorney, Martin Patras, a dear friend, almost a son, who reminded him of Kenny. If only he hadn't pushed the boy so hard. "I don't like the way Alyssa treats you," Fay said, more for Martin's benefit than Alvin's. He had heard it all before. "She didn't even come to our wedding." Then

Fay shocked Alvin with a suggestion that prompted Martin to ask her to step out of the room.

After Fay left in a huff, Martin whispered, as if she might be listening at the door. "Alvin, do you really want to cut Alyssa off?"

Alvin pictured his troubled youngest child: her round pale face, thick hair, and short neck so much his mother's that the war flooded back just looking at her. No matter what Alyssa had or hadn't done, he couldn't punish her like that. Alvin said, "No."

He hoped his firm rebuff would quiet Fay, but it fueled even greater demands. "We need to talk to the broker. Soon." Alvin didn't understand her concern. Hadn't he taken care of everything they needed? But Fay continued to push, so here he was, about to do her bidding.

Alvin stirred the murky goop. It reminded him of the flour and water paste Estelle used to mix for the children's papier-mâché projects. Too bad he couldn't make anything out of this.

"Now don't forget, it's Mother's Day this weekend." Fay pointed to the wall calendar Alyssa had given them, the one with the oversized numbers. Today was May 12th. "Gretchen, Pablo, and the girls will be here for brunch on Sunday." Alvin got along well enough with Fay's family. Her son-in-law was a bit creepy with his oily solicitude, and her daughter was respectful, if remote, but the little girls charmed him with their hugs and kisses.

He missed his own grandchildren. Every morning he looked at a picture on his dresser of the Roosevelt Monument—a bread line of bronze men, with him and then nine-year-old Jamie leading the way. Lorraine had sent the boy down from New Jersey. The first year without Estelle, had been Alvin's loneliest, worse than 1941, when the letters from his parents in Poland stopped coming. Seeing his oldest grandson had helped. It took some persuading to get Fay, whom he had just begun dating, out of the car to snap the shot. Alvin loved showing Jamie around the nation's capital, just as he had done with Lorraine, Kenneth, and Alyssa decades before. God willing, he would do the same with Ken's babies. The monuments still retained their power to thrill Alvin. "Roosevelt was our greatest President, next to Lincoln," he told the boy, proud to say "our." Then he added, "A government of laws, not men. *Men* are fallible."

In the photograph, Jamie's head almost reached his. Alvin looked below the kitchen table at his pants, the cuffs covering his shoes. He was shrinking. His grandson must have surpassed him by now. Since his wedding, he hadn't seen much of Lorraine or Jamie, or Ken's family for that matter. Oh well. They have their own lives. He would call Lorraine on Sunday.

Alvin watched Fay bend over the desk. The felt pen tip squeaked as she wrote. She was the first woman to take notice of him after Estelle died. A friend of a friend set them up at a dinner party. Fay sat next to Alvin the entire evening, and engaged him on books, the theatre, presidential peccadilloes, and art. Fay was no artist, but she loved museums. Good enough. He listened to her babble on, and felt at ease. Estelle had been a talker too. He needed a lively companion and Fay fit the bill.

"Alvin!" Fay snapped her fingers. "You're drifting." She pointed to the congealed mass still in his bowl. "Eat up. We have work to do." Then she tittered in the high-pitched girlish way he hadn't been able to resist. No one had ever flirted with Alvin like that before. Certainly not Estelle, who had been an innocent nineteen-year-old when they married, and grew into a strong, willful woman. Alvin found feminine force in any form irresistible.

Fay looked at her watch, then at the wall clock, then back to her watch. Impatience hardened her face. She wasn't beautiful like Estelle, but at eighty he couldn't afford to be choosy. He liked that she was Jewish, short—he didn't want a woman towering over him—and close to his age. She wouldn't tell exactly how old, an absurd vanity Alvin humored. No matter. Fay had aroused Alvin from his widower's coma, and for that he would be forever grateful. And hadn't Estelle begged him to find someone? She had said so, or rather scribbled, after the operation robbed her of speech. "Find someone," she wrote. He wished he had kept every scrap.

Alyssa told him that she had seen Lorraine, in the hospital, stashing her mother's notes. It was obvious from the way Ally bit her lip that she didn't approve. This made no sense to Alvin. Didn't Alyssa keep a lot more than mere paper? Alvin couldn't understand why his youngest and oldest didn't get along. Estelle had tried to reconcile them, but it didn't take. Now, he was too tired to make the effort. They would have to work things out for themselves.

He comforted himself with the thought that he had done what Estelle had asked. The children wondered why, at this stage, he would get married. "Fay wants to," he told them. They fell silent, except for Lorraine, who was very like her mother—pretty, sharp, and opinionated. She warned him to "be careful," though he couldn't remember exactly what she meant.

Alvin brought the soupspoon to his mouth and sipped the gruel. Fay turned her head without looking at him. "Finish up, Alvin." He put down the spoon. He had lost his appetite. "And drink your juice, or your voice will sound dry." He hadn't said a word, but did as he was told. It was simpler that way.

"Consuelo, clear Mr. Segal's dishes, and then go upstairs and scrub our bathroom—floor, toilet, everything. Roll up the oriental too." Fay scowled at Alvin. "It'll have to go to the dry cleaners."

Fay was still fuming about his "accident" the night before, especially about the rug. She had screamed her head off about that. He couldn't help it if he sometimes missed the bowl. But he hadn't defended himself when it happened, and he wasn't about to now. Not in front of Consuelo, who looked at him with sympathy. He considered mentioning the tie tack he'd dropped on the carpet that morning and was too stiff to retrieve. He pictured the vacuum sucking the pieces into its metal tube. He sat between the two women—one subservient, one in command—and sank into paralysis. If he said something, Fay would berate him all over again. He couldn't bear more shouting, more indignity.

Consuelo removed his dish. "Yes, Mrs. Fay."

"And Consuelo?"

She turned slowly and faced Fay. "Yes, Missus."

"I'll be going out shortly, for the rest of the day. Watch Mr. Segal." As if he were the family dog.

"Fay, no. Please. Let me come with you. We could have lunch at that French restaurant you love."

"Don't be silly, Alvin. I'm meeting my *friends* for lunch and shopping. You know you aren't comfortable with girl talk." Alvin sighed. He still wanted Fay's company even if she no longer wanted his. He was partly to blame. He had given Fay charge accounts, and put her in touch with Estelle's personal shopper, a jolly man who had attended the funeral and was eager to oblige.

"Watch him," Fay barked. Consuelo nodded and turned away from Alvin, saving them both embarrassment. Then she went upstairs to clean up his other humiliation.

Fay handed him the paper she had been writing on. "Use this when you talk to Stackwell. I don't want you getting confused." She had written out a script for him to follow in huge block letters. Alvin read the note and rubbed his forehead. They had made a plan. He had agreed. Still, he had the distinct sensation he was missing something, something more crucial than brushing his teeth. But he couldn't force the bit to the surface. If he felt around, dipped down into the sediment, he'd force it further into the muck. That was what his mind had become. Oh well. If it was important enough, it would come back to him. He read the note again. Yes, it was a lot of money, but if he did what Fay wanted, maybe she would stop harping.

The telephone rang. "Yes, Jimmy, he's right here." Fay handed Alvin the receiver, stood behind him and pressed down on his shoulder, holding him in place.

Alvin read the words into the phone, and answered the broker's kind inquiries about his health. "I'm fine," he said, clearing the sludge from his throat. He would be better when this was done. He sounded far away, even to himself.

Afterwards, Fay clapped her pudgy hands and kissed his forehead. Her saccharine perfume choked him and he coughed. "You've made me very happy, darling," she said, and slung her gigantic handbag—ripe for stuffing—over her shoulder. She blew him another kiss. "See you later, dear. Be good."

Alvin stared at Fay's wake. Alone again. He willed himself to move and walked slowly into the living room. He lowered his aching body into his favorite chair—the Eames with the ottoman that Estelle had given him when he made partner. It didn't fit with the overstuffed sofas Fay preferred, but it fit him. He listened to the thrum of Consuelo's vacuum. Its monotone blast couldn't drown the disquieting fusion of uneasiness and reprieve that rumbled inside him. Alvin had done what he had to, he told himself, not entirely convinced. He had made his new wife happy. He hoped her contentment would last. Maybe then he would have some peace.

2

In the parking lot of the Bethesda Neiman Marcus Alyssa leaned against her car and stared at the imposing white building. Tomorrow was Mother's Day, a fact that tricked her into a shopping spree in Mother's honor. But looking up at the marble exterior of a building so familiar it could have been her second home, Alyssa was losing her nerve. The structure loomed like a landmark backdrop in one of the live shots she regularly produced. The monuments transmitted an impersonal grandeur asking nothing of her. This structure taunted, *go in, what's the big deal?* She had done it a million times.

It was Saturday, four years to the day since Mother's death. In all that time Alyssa had not set foot inside the store. Up until Mother's illness, their Saturday ritual had been to browse, buy, and lunch. Alyssa missed the picking and choosing, the trying on, and most of all, Mother's peremptory tone with clerks, all in the name of getting Alyssa exactly the right piece to go with her jacket or dress or shoes.

The morning sun bounced off the shiny walls and ricocheted at her like in squash, a game she had played only once, at Zeke's request. The ball was too fast, the walls too white, and the court too claustrophobic. Get back in the car or stand in the shade under the store's front awning. Come on. In or out. Decide.

Alyssa exhaled, tightened her grip on the purse in her right hand and plowed through the revolving doors. On the other side of the moving glass she stood suspended, blinded by the store's artificial light, brighter than outside, until two women coming from behind bumped her free hand. She flinched, and pulled the purse closer. Their unison "sorry" jolted her out of her head. This wasn't her imagination. She was really here. Alyssa took a deep breath and ordered herself to browse.

She started down the main aisle. But it was no good. The minute she hit the cosmetics counter with its rows of lipsticks, face powders, eye shadows, and night creams she reeled. Floor to ceiling mirrors reflected her rapidly blinking eyes batting the long Zsa Zsa Gabor lashes Mother had loved. Alyssa was startled by her own image. Once she adjusted, she couldn't help focusing on her deficits—broad shoulders and boxy torso. And she would gladly have traded her stature—five inches taller than Lorraine's—for her sister's delicate throat, elegant collarbone, and tiny waist.

Alyssa turned and took a sharp left towards the perfume aisle. Well-dressed women lifted tester bottles to their wrists and sprayed. Some wafted scented cards back and forth under their noses. The clashing fragrances choked the air. Alyssa's stomach heaved. Was that *Joy*, Mother's signature scent? Alyssa's hand flew to her mouth. A tall clerk leaned over mocking bottles of *Eternity*, *Opium*, and *Poison* and asked, "Are you okay?"

Alyssa shook her head. She was not. Beads of perspiration broke out across her forehead. Her chest contracted. She couldn't catch her breath. The animated voices—buying, selling, laughing—rebounded off the glossy surfaces, their surreal echo a noxious reminder. Mother's not here. Alyssa lurched towards the door and stumbled, out of rhythm with the rotating panels. Outside she shuddered in her spring jacket, soaked with sweat. Breathe. Count. 3, 6, 9, 12, 15, 18, 21, 24. What had possessed her? How could she have thought this excursion would end any other way? Had she really expected to leave, shopping bags in hand? What a fool she was. Go, she told herself. Go home.

Alyssa rolled over, and tossed the quilted duvet to the floor. She squinted at the alarm clock. 8:30. She'd overslept. She prided herself on rising every morning at 6:00. But after yesterday's fiasco, she was too drained to move. Alyssa dreaded Sundays. Especially this one. Maybe she could call the station, log some extra hours. Her workplace's familiar expectations and known parameters kept anxiety in check. No danger of panic attacks there. Or she could stay in the house. The safest place.

Alyssa blinked and looked around the bedroom. She was still acutely aware, that she slept in her parents' bedroom. Though not in her parents' bed. She had replaced it with her own. It would have been too weird to sleep on the bed in which she was conceived. She kept many of Mother's canvases splashed across the mango walls. An odd color for a bedroom, but Alyssa hadn't had the heart to change it. Every decorative decision had been an inner dialogue with Mother. Could she move the green cut floral rug? Did she have permission to give away the Waterford bowls or to carpet the unused dining room, since she didn't cook and never had guests?

Zeke called her "crazy" for turning the dining table into a permanent laundry station. "What will we eat on?" he asked.

"The kitchen table," she answered.

"You're really nuts," he said, and packed his duffle bag and left.

Alyssa kept the engagement ring. She figured it was the only one she'd get.

She was forty. She wouldn't have another chance. She had the diamond reset into a locket around her neck. After Zeke moved out, Alyssa began sleeping ten hours at a stretch, rising only to shower, eat a hard boiled egg, and go to work.

With Dad at Fay's, this house was Alyssa's to do as she pleased. And she began to mark every inch of it. Since she didn't want to throw anything away, she changed the space by adding to it, first in small ways—piles of magazines and newspapers she might need to refer to someday; she was in the news business, after all—then in bigger statements. She went to flea markets, and yard sales—something Mother would never have done, so no danger of flashbacks or meltdowns. Alyssa picked out objects in threes: three chipped china bowls, three chenille shawls, three glass bud vases, and placed them throughout the house on any available surface. The more she amassed, the more she felt safe and at home.

On the one day a week Consuelo came, Alyssa didn't let her touch anything, even when she gave Alyssa a long look—dust rag in hand—and begged to clean up the mounting collections. "Later," she told Consuelo, meaning never. She didn't want anyone moving her special things.

Alyssa kept the mail addressed to Alvin Segal on a table by the front door in case he dropped by. This was still his house, and he could come back to stay whenever he wanted. Now that he was married to that woman, Alyssa only saw her father when she visited him—a couple times a month—to deliver said mail and to see how he was doing. She didn't stay long. Fay's house made her uncomfortable with its shoddy furnishings and tacky doodads. She had a hard time being civil to this person who had so quickly and so permanently attached herself to her father.

As for the junk mail addressed to Estelle M. Segal, Alyssa didn't have the heart to toss it. Her mother's name in print comforted her. Her beautiful, warm, all-knowing Mommy was even now in the world, if only by virtue of the credit card promotions, cable offers, and catalogues, which covered the desk in foot-high stacks.

And then there were the letters in the desk drawer. Lorraine's letters. Every once in a while, Alyssa would take one out and look at the return address. She didn't have the energy to open them, let alone send them back.

Alyssa got up, put on her robe, padded into the bathroom, and splashed water on her face, dabbing it with a towel: cheek, cheek, forehead. Her stomach growled. After she got home yesterday, all she could do was crawl into bed. No lunch. No dinner.

She walked down the stairs, careful not to knock over the piles of *National Geographics* she'd unearthed from the attic. She liked having them in plain sight. They reminded her of her childhood, when she and Mother would leaf through the glossy photographs and dream of traveling to the exotic locales. Alyssa resolved every time she ascended or descended the staircase to reread them at her leisure.

In the kitchen she contemplated scrambling a couple of eggs, but she didn't want to have to clean a skillet or risk spilling yoke on the counter, so instead she toasted a slice of whole wheat bread and spread it with a generous spoonful of peanut butter for protein.

She brought her plate into the living room and carefully stepped over the secondhand books with torn covers that she had grouped on the floor to resemble controlled rubble, like the post-modern art installation Mother had once admired on one of their gallery walks.

Alyssa sat in a tapestry-upholstered chair she had purchased at an estate sale. The stitching, a crimson and gold floral, looked like needlepoint, a hobby Mother had taken up in her last month, when she was too exhausted by chemo and radiation to paint. Alyssa scanned the room. She loved the folk toys on shelves high and low: wooden acrobats, nesting dolls, miniature clowns. Alyssa had rearranged them into triangles, along with the lacquered Chinese tables guarding the corners, the crystal candy jars filled with ancient bonbons, and the Kachinas on the mantel overlooking a vista of leather sofas. "The Museum of Mother," Lorraine called it the last time she'd been here. After the funeral. Before everything came apart between them.

When Alyssa permitted herself the fantasy of a reunion, she pictured Lorraine waltzing into this room and assessing every inch of it with her eagle eye. Her sister had a photographic memory and would notice every change, no matter how small, and she would disapprove. She wouldn't understand why Alyssa needed what she needed. The power Lorraine had to infuriate and shame her extended from interior design to Alyssa's very being. A condemnation of her furniture choices could easily morph into dismissal of her entire way of life. Hadn't their big falling out started with an argument over blinds? Alyssa liked them down; Lorraine liked light, and never the twain...No, Alyssa wasn't ready to see Lorraine, and she wasn't ready for Lorraine to see her. She didn't know if she ever would be.

The distressing image of Lorraine in the living room forced Alyssa to move. She prompted herself to stand up, shower, get dressed. She passed the playroom—she still called it that—though it hadn't been one since she, Ken, and Lorraine had left for college, and Mother turned it into her studio. Alyssa almost never entered the artistic sanctum, except to toss another bag of old clothing, or linens, or dishtowels. Things she meant to give to the Salvation Army. One of these days. When she got around to it.

The phone rang. Who would call before noon on a Sunday morning?

"Alyssa?" A man's voice with a familiar hint of accent.

"Who is this please?" Alyssa never acknowledged her identity until the caller did.

"It's Martin, Martin Patras. Sorry to call you so early, but it couldn't wait." He sounded rattled. Martin, the charming Greek her father trusted to handle his affairs. Alyssa liked Martin, a younger version of Daddy with the same courtly European manners. She'd even gone out on a date with him, at Mother's urging, but it hadn't led anywhere. Now Martin was married with a second baby on the way.

"That's all right. I was up," Alyssa said. "How have you been?"

"Uh. Fine. No. Uh." It wasn't like Martin to stutter. "I don't want to upset you, Alyssa, but you're the only one of Alvin's children in town. And I don't have Ken's or Lorraine's numbers."

Alyssa squeezed the phone harder. Her knuckles turned white. "What? What is it?"

"I care about your father–"

Alyssa's stomach sank. "Is he okay? What's wrong?"

"I'm not sure, but I'm concerned. His broker called me–Jimmy Stackwell?"

"I know Jimmy. He's my broker too." Alyssa had invested her retirement account with his firm.

"Jimmy called yesterday–"

"On a Saturday?"

"He didn't want to call during office hours."

"Why not?"

"He told me that he was alarmed by a conversation he'd had with Alvin on Friday."

"Alarmed? Alarmed how?"

"It seems your father directed Jimmy to transfer a large sum to Fay—a very large sum—and Jimmy said Alvin didn't sound like himself."

Alyssa's temples began to throb. "Why didn't you call me right away?"

Martin paused. "I had to think. Whether or not to cross that line." He paused again. "How has your Dad's health been lately?"

"He's had a couple of episodes, some confusion, but nothing lasting. The doctor thinks he had a small stroke in March, but assured us that he is still capable. He's taking blood pressure medication."

"Did he say anything to you about the transfer?"

"No." Alyssa began to gulp air. "How big a transfer?"

Martin cleared his throat. "Too big."

Alyssa pulled her robe over her chest. "The house? What about the house?" Fear strangled her voice, which came out in a hoarse blurt, breathy and small.

"I don't want to scare you–" Too late. Martin's measured tones told Alyssa that he was handling her. "The whole estate is at risk. I wouldn't break confidentiality if there were any other way to protect his interests. I tried calling him yesterday, but Fay wouldn't bring him to the phone—said his hearing wasn't good enough."

Alyssa had wanted to have her father fitted with hearing aids months ago, but Fay delayed the appointments. "Been there done that," she said, referring, Alyssa supposed, to husband number two. "Alvin hears what he needs to hear," Fay added in that shrill piping laugh of hers.

Martin continued, "Then I went over to the house. Fay wouldn't let me in. Said Alvin wasn't up to having visitors. You're going to have to call Ken and Lorraine. The three of you have got to get your father out of that house so we can discover what his intentions were in transferring the money. If he meant it as a gift, and if he gets sick, there won't be enough for his care, or anything else. After his death she'll get the prenuptial money too. "

Alyssa began to hyperventilate. "Prenuptial money?" She didn't know there was a prenup.

"Yes." His voice dropped. "It's the same amount as the transfer."

"Martin!" His name flew out of Alyssa's mouth. Too loud. Her mind raced. She couldn't catch her breath. Would Daddy cut them all off? For Fay? "Do *you* think that's what he intended?"

"I don't know. I hope not. Call your siblings. Get them down here. Depending on what Alvin says, it might be possible to stop the transfer. Jimmy will try to hold the paperwork a couple of days."

Alyssa shuddered. "I'll take care of it." She'd call Ken. Ken would call Lorraine. "Thank you, Martin. I know you've gone out on a limb here. Thank you so much."

"I love Alvin like a father," Martin said quietly. "I couldn't stand by and watch him being taken advantage of. And Alyssa–"

"Yes?"

"Don't go over there alone. Wait until Ken and Lorraine get here. Don't try to do this by yourself."

Alyssa didn't like being told what to do, being talked to like a child. Her fight instinct had already kicked in. "I'll do what I have to do, Martin."

After she put down the phone, Alyssa surged up the stairs, scattering the most recent stack of *National Geographics*. Martin's phone call had transformed her early morning inertia into furious action. She threw on a pair of jeans and a t-shirt, and sprinted out the door. She would call Ken from the car. That fucking bitch. Thinking she can pull a fast one. In her rage Alyssa forgot to turn the handle three times before locking it behind her. 1, 2, 3. There. Now go. A bearded jogger glanced up at her. Who was he? A neighbor? She wasn't sure. Alyssa didn't participate in the biannual block parties that filled the tranquil street with noisy children, skateboard competitions, and smoky barbecues. He tipped his head in greeting and looked back at her over his shoulder. Her hand shook as she jammed the key in the car door. It wouldn't open.

"Goddamnit!"

The neighbor backtracked. "You okay?"

Alyssa nodded furiously, and waved him away. She didn't need an audience; she was agitated enough. But the man ran in place and continued to watch. On the third try she opened the door and jumped in. She backed out of the driveway in a jolt, forcing the runner to hop onto the opposite curb. He put up his hand, a cautionary salute. Alyssa tried to smile an apology, but her mouth refused. She slammed the accelerator. In the rearview mirror, the jogger had thrown both hands in the air. He was shouting at her like she was going to run him down. Sorry, but this was an emergency. Alyssa clenched her jaw and tore up the hill. It's Mother's Day and she was going to rip that woman's face off.

3

Ken pushed open the creaky screen door and stepped outside. His eyes were almost albino-sensitive and it hurt to look up. He refused to wear the sunglasses Priscilla not so subtly pressed into his hand. He hated the way they slipped down his nose the minute he moved. Ken bent over and stretched his left hamstring. The blood rushed to his face and he wiped sweat from his brow and cheeks. He'd shaved the night before and stubble had already formed. Ken used to grow a full beard in less than a week, but not once since he returned east from Texas over a dozen years ago, his body changed forever. Before, facial hair said free spirit, rock star; now, it screamed disturbed veteran or borderline personality. No, he wouldn't give the world the chance to misjudge him. Ken vowed to keep his face clean, and his body—what remained of it—in marathon shape.

He leaned right and checked the strap on the state-of-the-art leg Dad had insisted on buying him. When Ken announced he was taking up running, his father said, "Let me help you. It's the least I can do." Ken appreciated the offer—he couldn't have afforded it himself—but he cringed at the guilt lacing every syllable out of the old man's mouth. What happened wasn't his fault. And Dad's misplaced sense of responsibly did nothing to assuage Ken's own remorse. It doubled it.

The only cure turned out to be running itself. And the leg *was* spectacular—a combination of carbon fiber, aircraft aluminum, titanium, and plastic, powered by lithium batteries, so efficient he didn't have to think about running let alone walking. It put his everyday prosthesis to shame and looked cool as well. Three-year-old Josh liked to hold it over his head and race around the house calling, "I'm Robo Dad, the fastest leg on earth." To Josh and to the rest of the world—everyone, it seemed, except Priscilla—Ken *was* his leg, or its absence.

On weekdays Ken ran at dawn, before the baby Stella alarm went off and Josh came marching into their room to pounce on the bed. That left plenty of time to shower and change before he was expected at school. On weekends he allowed himself an extra hour of shut-eye. Priscilla tolerated the regimen—she knew he was addicted—even though it meant she never got to sleep in herself. Even on Mother's Day.

Not to worry, he told himself, as he sprinted down the block and past the identical brick and clapboard houses that defined this pleasant Philadelphia suburb, he would make it up to her with a gourmet family picnic in the park. Ken loved to cook. He would have been perfectly happy to be a househusband if money permitted, which it didn't. So he contented himself with cooking on Saturdays and Sundays, concocting his own version of James Beard classics. He had stayed up last night finishing the duck cassoulet, Priscilla's favorite, and so much better the second day.

Ken sped past the high school where he taught, and, if they stayed, his children would attend. All weekend he had been preoccupied with the work he would have to finish this evening—comments on his A.P. European History students' final papers. So far, the essays reeked of senioritis; the students had gotten into college, and could barely drag themselves through their last assignments. He empathized; he could barely drag himself through grading them. He'd been at the high school for four and a half years, the longest he'd spent at any gig. Correction. He needed to stop thinking of the job as a gig.

It wasn't working part-time as a research assistant in Michigan or as the editor of a now-defunct history journal in upstate New York. This was a real job with good benefits and a yearly bonus as department head—a coup for someone not yet tenured—and as close to a career as he was likely to get. But it wasn't where he'd thought he would be at forty-three: teaching spoiled kids in a town he could barely afford. His modest, lovely wife didn't seem to mind the strain. Her quiet forbearance diffused the constant pressure of his legacy. Then again, relaxed acceptance was easy for her. She hadn't been raised a Segal.

Ken approached the entrance to the park, and pumped harder as he reached the top of the winding road. This far into the run his body fused and for a few precious minutes he forgot what was missing. In his endorphin-fueled bliss he was neither fractured human nor invulnerable machine. He was whole, inside and out.

Circling the plateau, jogging in place, Ken ran his hand through his kinky curls and across the thinning patch on top. Baldness came from Mom's side, but he identified with his father's pate, not to mention large skull. "Big head, big brain," Dad used to say. Ken's scalp burned. Priscilla had reminded him to use sunscreen, but he promptly forgot.

Ken wanted to stake out a picnic spot overlooking the town center. Next to a majestic willow at the far edge of the expanse was a clear flat patch that would be just right for their feast. Ken slowed to a trot and approached the tree. Chilly sweat washed his arms. His thigh hurt. He could see the pristine spire of the Presbyterian church and the tops of cherry trees puffing like cotton candy. The blossoms reminded him of Washington's Tidal Basin. He had loved growing up near DC. It would be wonderful to raise his children there, but he didn't see how he could swing it. No. Better to stay put. Make this work.

Ken leaned against the back railing and untied his shoe. Under his foot the crack on the top step was getting wider by the day. If the place was theirs, he would fix it. But it wasn't. He would have to call the owner, a careless widower who would wait months to take a look.

"Your sister's on the phone," Priscilla called from inside the house.

Ken stood up. "Which one?"

"Alyssa. She wants to speak to you." Since their mother's death, Alyssa made a point of calling Priscilla on Mother's Day. But she didn't usually want to talk to him.

"She sounds upset."

So what else was new?

His wife craned her swan neck around the door. "She says it's an emergency."

4

Fay Tabor Cohen Segal went to the bottom of the stairs. "Alvin!" Where was that man? She didn't have the energy to make the climb. Fay yawned and shook her head. She couldn't stand this much longer: her sleep interrupted night after night by Alvin's tossings and turnings, his trips to the bathroom at 2:30 in the morning, and then there was that awful incident when he fell out of bed and she had to call Alyssa and her redneck boyfriend—Zach, or was it Zeke? Too bad that didn't work out. It might have alleviated Alvin's worry, and put Fay front and center.

Since that night, she had made some decisions. Friday's transaction was a start. One thing Fay knew for sure: she wasn't going to let this marriage go the route of the last one. Barney Cohen had been a fine companion until Alzheimer's robbed him of himself, their savings, and any semblance of a life together. She visited his nursing home four times a week and endured the discomfort of witnessing him dance through the hallways with nurses, orderlies, and patients, blissfully unaware that *she* was his wife. Sometimes he would smile and wave like he was perched on a parade float. She acted the adoring fan and waved back. He was lucky. All of her husbands were. They didn't have to carry on, make the best of it. They could waltz out of her life, oblivious to the wreckage they'd left behind. Even Simon Tabor, her child's father, who had died suddenly in a Beltway car crash, had it better than Fay. He didn't know what hit him.

She did. Then years of supporting—by herself—a little girl, working horrible sales jobs, on her feet all day.

"Alvin, come down!" Fay called again, louder this time, straining. She couldn't, she just couldn't go through this again, not without some assurance that she would end up with something substantial. And she wouldn't play nurse. No, Alvin's children would have to step up and take care of their father, if it came to that. Fay Tabor Cohen Segal had been through enough, and she deserved a reward.

Fay deserved whatever Alvin Segal could give her. She had been a bargain hunter her whole life. After meeting Alvin she could finally breathe a little, splurge, treat herself. He was a dear man with delightful old-world manners, a bit passive, but that was a good thing. Alvin let her plan their days, schedule their vacations, fill their lives with errands and engagements. As long as there was plenty of money and they were both healthy, Fay happily took on the role of social director on the good ship Segal.

But ever since Alvin began to show his age, Fay resented his presence in her house—all that was left from Barney, and not nearly enough. This used to be a decent neighborhood. She couldn't take a walk in the evening anymore. She thought about selling, getting an apartment, maybe in one of those assisted-living communities. But why move to a condo when the Georgian that Alyssa inhabited was perfect for their needs? Alvin said he wasn't interested in moving again. Fay tried to persuade him that going back to Dorset wasn't exactly a move, just a return to his rightful place. And hers. Alvin didn't want to uproot his daughter though, and with Martin at his side, he wasn't inclined to budge. It was complicated, emotional. Alvin had so much guilt about that girl. Nevertheless, Fay was determined to find a way. The two flights in her colonial, not to mention the incline down to the garage, were ruining her knees. She'd just have to mull it over a bit longer, keep at him, and eventually he'd cave.

Fay stood on the landing under Estelle's ridiculous painting with the yellow and purple swirls, a sop to Alvin's comfort, and shouted, "Al-vin! Darling! Please come down!" Still no answer. Fay turned towards the kitchen. "Consuelo, would you go upstairs and tell Mr. Segal that Gretchen and the children will be here shortly?"

Consuelo peeked out from behind the swinging door. She nodded, averted her reproachful brown eyes, and headed upstairs. Fay couldn't escape the sense that Consuelo tolerated her for Alvin's sake, that the woman's allegiance would always be with the dead Estelle. Consuelo softened her voice for Alvin, and soldiered through the chores without so much as a look in Fay's directions. But since she was willing to work Sundays for special occasions, like today's Mother's Day brunch, Fay put up with her.

"Mrs. Fay!" Consuelo's heavy alto voice sounded down the stairs. "Mrs. Fay, I finishing Mr. Segal's buttons."

Fay shrugged. "Hurry up. They'll be here any minute." No sooner had she stepped off the landing and veered towards the dining room to check the table setting than the doorbell rang. Goodness, they're early. Well then, Gretchen could help, and the kids could play in the yard—it was such a gorgeous day.

Fay opened the front door. Before her stood Alvin's difficult youngest daughter looking like she hadn't combed her wild thick hair or washed the sleep off her sad eyes. In the past year, Fay and Alyssa had spoken only to negotiate the transfer of mementos from one house to the other. And then Alyssa was borderline rude. Her mother had spoiled her baby rotten. "Oh! Alyssa! What a surprise! We weren't expecting you. We were just about to have Mother's Day brunch, as soon as Gretchen's family gets here. You're welcome to stay and eat with us."

Alyssa pushed her way into the hall and started for the stairs, almost knocking over Fay in the process. "Where's my father?" Surly, as expected.

Fay blocked Alyssa's path and stood eye to eye. "He'll be down any minute." The girl was seething with pent-up...what? Fay didn't care. She would not tolerate disruption. Not today. It was her house, her Mother's Day, and no one was going to spoil it, least of all Alyssa Segal. "Consuelo's with him."

Alyssa took a breath. "I need to see him."

"Is something wrong? Kenny's okay? Lorraine?" Alyssa glared at her. Fay knew that Alvin's girls didn't speak and enjoyed poking the sore spot.

"Everyone's fine," Alyssa answered through gritted teeth. "I have to see my father. Now!"

"Ally! Sweetheart!" Alvin paused at the top of the stairs. Then he leaned on Consuelo, and walked down, one painful step at a time. Fay hated seeing him so feeble. It meant the good times really were over. He wore a blue silk vest with ornamental buttons, and the gray slacks with the tomato stain on the leg that Fay hadn't bothered to send to the cleaners—he'd just soil them again. Alvin glowed with parental concern. "What are you doing here, sweetheart?"

"I thought we could take a drive, Daddy, maybe go to the cemetery, put some flowers on Mother's grave. I could take you to lunch." Alyssa's suggestion sounded more like an order to Fay. The girl barked like a rabid dog. What had gotten her so riled?

"Oh Alvin, dear, I'm sorry. I didn't realize you and Alyssa had plans today." Fay took Alvin's free hand. "Thank you, Consuelo. Would you check the quiche? It should be almost done. And cut the melon?" Consuelo nodded, with a slight tip of the head in Alyssa's direction. Fay winced. Invaded by mercenaries.

Uncertainty passed over Alvin's face. "I'm not sure. Perhaps I forgot. Did we have plans, Ally?"

"No, Daddy. I just decided since it *is* Mother's Day, that it would be nice to visit her." Alyssa moved to her father and pecked his cheek. The kiss had a magical effect on Alvin, and he looked imploringly at Fay. He wanted to go with his daughter. Yes, it would be easier, and more pleasant not to have to deal with Alvin's needs. How could she bask in her own celebration when he would demand constant attention? It wore her out just thinking about it. Good. Alyssa could take him off her hands for a few hours.

The doorbell rang again and Gretchen, Pablo, and their two girls entered, bearing a bouquet of pink roses, a bottle of pink champagne, and boxes of presents, wrapped in pink paper.

"Gretchen, Pablo, you remember Alyssa!" The two sets of children had met only once, at a joint Thanksgiving last fall, at the Mayflower hotel. No way was Fay going to cook for both families, and Alvin had been happy to treat. Alyssa managed an appearance—the hotel dining room was neutral territory—though she excused herself before dessert. Something about breaking news. Fay had difficulty imagining how Alyssa could function in such a high-pressured job, but Alvin's children were smart. She'd give them that.

"Hello, Alyssa. I didn't know you'd be joining us?" Gretchen was her big strong girl. Tall like Simon, with curly brown hair like hers used to be. Fay was so proud of her. She just wished she had married someone steadier. Pablo was certainly good-looking—the proverbial tall, dark, and handsome—but he couldn't keep a business going. First the chain of liquor stores, then the Mexican restaurant that went bankrupt. Why not Puerto Rican, something familiar? Now he needed money to start a dot.com venture. Fay didn't understand anything about computers. All she could do was write a check and pray that this time he'd succeed.

Pablo put his long arms around Cara and Sabine. The little girls leaned into his legs. Cara had Gretchen's hair and Sabine was the image of Pablo. Whatever his shortcomings, Fay had to admit he was a good father. And he had agreed to raise the girls Jewish. Fay had waited a long time for grandchildren, and she would do everything possible to make sure they had it easier than she and Gretchen.

The children skipped around their father. Fay watched Alyssa take in the assembled family and noticed her cheeks turn blotchy and her eyes narrow. She seemed to resent their presence. The nerve.

"No," Alyssa spat, then turned to Alvin, "Please, Daddy. I really need to spend some time with you. Today." Something in her voice gave Fay pause. But she dismissed Alyssa's overly insistent tone. It was understandable, considering her morbid attachment to her mother. Of course she needed Alvin, today of all days.

Alvin looked from his daughter, who had backed into the front door, to Fay.

"Go on Alvin darling. We'll be fine here. Spend some time with Alyssa." Alvin seemed relieved to have the decision made for him. No sooner had she spoken, than Alyssa grabbed Alvin's sunglasses off the hall table and shuffled him out. The shuffling was literal. Alvin had trouble lifting his feet. It drove Fay crazy.

"Happy Mother's Day, Fay!" Alvin blew her a kiss. Sweet.

Just before she closed the door behind them, Fay said, "Don't forget to call Lorraine. Wish her a 'happy' from me!" Alvin didn't answer. He probably couldn't hear her. She could have sworn that Alyssa darted her a nasty look.

When they were gone, Pablo ushered the girls outside. Gretchen followed her mother into the kitchen where Consuelo was filling the breadbasket with croissants.

"Consuelo dear, would you make sure the powder room has soap and finger towels?" Consuelo mumbled her assent and trundled out.

Fay turned to her daughter and smiled.

Gretchen picked up an empty champagne flute and smiled back. "What's up?"

Fay put the pink champagne in the refrigerator and took out a bottle of Dom Pérignon. "Good things. On Friday, Alvin gave me the most marvelous early Mother's Day gift."

"Oh?" Gretchen stretched her arm and held the glass while Fay poured. "I'd love to see it." Bubbles foamed over the crystal's lip.

Fay laughed. "You can't."

"What do you mean?" her daughter persisted, "Where is it?"

Fay chuckled again. She poured herself a glass and inhaled the sweet effervescence. Gretchen tapped her fingers on the counter. Fay enjoyed teasing her daughter, prolonging a delicious moment. "With the broker," she said, and took a long satisfied sip.

5

Ken met Dad and Alyssa at Judean Gardens as she had requested, though he didn't understand why, considering what loomed. Something about not wanting Dad to forget Mother, she said. Not possible. But Ken knew not to argue with his little sister. He still thought of her as the nervous infant Mother had warned him and Lorraine not to disturb. He missed his own family. Driving over the Delaware Bridge on the way down, Ken mulled how he'd make this up to Priscilla. His supportive spouse had said go, but he felt bad. This was supposed to be her day.

At the graveside, Dad, vibrating with tremors worse than Ken remembered, knelt on one knee, more like a suitor proposing than a widower mourning, to place a single bloom. The somber tone was broken when Ken asked Alyssa whether she had called Lorraine.

Alyssa bristled. "You *know* I didn't. Why didn't *you*?"

Typical. Ken was sick of being in the middle of the war between his sisters. He loved them both. He accepted Alyssa's quirks and Lorraine's stubbornness. He'd vowed that he wasn't going to take sides. But there he was: stuck as the go-between in a standoff he couldn't comprehend. Ever since Alyssa reached puberty, they'd fought. And then there was the big blowout, when he had to pry them apart. They were more work than his children.

By the time they got back to the house Alyssa was in full caged animal mode, pacing the living room floor, three steps right, three steps left. Ken found it painful to watch, not only because she was counting, but because three steps was all there was space for. He walked into the dining room. Oh my God, what happened here? The table was invisible under mounds of clothing, and the rest of the room was filled with old playroom furniture that had been stored in the basement for ages. Had his sister really lugged all of it out by herself? Zeke must have helped. A real shame when that ended. Ken worried about Alyssa. And this chaotic jumble of household effects didn't ease his mind.

Dad didn't seem to notice. He wandered into the kitchen with Alyssa close behind like he might topple backwards at any moment. She shoved deli sandwiches, wrapped in wax paper, onto a butcher block table barely big enough for two, and jerked her head in a silent order to sit and eat. Ken complied, but found that he couldn't stretch his leg. He was still stiff from the drive. Oh well. Better get down to business.

Ken addressed his father, who stared at the pots on the wall and then down at the food. "Dad?" The old man looked up through smudged trifocals. "Dad, may I ask you something?"

His father nodded in slow motion. Everything about him had slowed down in the past year. Ken hoped that the brilliant legal mind he had been so in awe of as a child, was still there. "Dad, this past Friday, the twelfth, did you call your broker?"

"My broker?"

"Yes, Jimmy Stackwell. Did you call him about a transfer of funds?"

"Yes. Actually he called me. But yes, I did speak to him." Ken detected pride in his father's precise answer and in the lengthening of his spine against the hardback chair.

Alyssa sniffed, and took a huge bite of her sandwich. Ken leaned in, and rested his elbow on the table. He tried to catch his father's cloudy eyes. Focus Dad. "And what, if you don't mind my asking, did that transfer entail?"

"Oh, boychick, I don't mind at all. You children should know everything." Alyssa's eyes widened. Ken sat back in his chair. They smiled at each other. This, from the man who had never, ever mentioned, let alone explained, his will or estate plans to either one of them. "I transferred our general fund to Fay. She had wanted me to for some time."

"I'll bet!" Alyssa exclaimed. Ken shot her a look and she fell silent. It was important for Dad to tell his own story without comments from the peanut gallery.

"Dad, there's some question in the mind's of Mr. Stackwell and of Martin–"

His father brightened. "Martin! Martin is a wonderful lawyer and such a nice man. Trustworthy. Your mother always said so–"

"Yes, Daddy," Alyssa interrupted. "Martin's concerned that there's not enough money to cover the transfer–"

"Alyssa!" Ken wanted to tape her mouth. Why couldn't she control herself? She made a face at him. They could have been five and eight, fighting over the last brownie.

Alyssa bit her upper lip. "What did I say?"

Ken did not want his exasperation with his impulsive sister to derail them. Dad sat quietly, his brow etched with concentration. He seemed oblivious to his children's disagreement, like old times. Ken put his hand over his father's. The small square palm, the short, thick fingers, the prominent blue veins, cool in his much larger hand, gave Ken the same visceral message—protect him—that he got whenever he walked his little boy across a street.

"Not enough money?" Dad shook his head. "How could that be?"

"Dad, we want to make sure that your needs can be met. We need to know what you intended in making the transfer to Fay. Was it a gift *in addition* to the prenup?" Alyssa's lips were pursed. She seemed to be holding her breath.

Dad pulled his hand away from Ken's. "The prenup?" Dad paused. "Oh, I–" He closed his eyes and rested his chin on his chest.

Ken leaned in. "Dad?"

His eyes opened, and drew himself up in the chair, once again the esteemed attorney about to make an objection. "NO! It *was* the prenup!"

Alyssa exhaled, "Thank God!"

"So you intended to give Fay an advance on the prenuptial amount?"

When Ken had spoken to Martin on the phone, the lawyer made a point of asking him to find out if his father understood this distinction.

"Yes, an advance," his father repeated. "Otherwise, there won't be enough for the grandchildren." Dad slumped back in his chair.

Ken gave Alyssa a pinch. "Good," he said. "That's good, Dad. Martin is going to make sure your intentions are clear. To everyone." Then turning to Alyssa. "Where *is* Martin?"

"He'll be here," Alyssa said. She bit into a nail.

His father sighed. "I'm sorry. I'm sorry."

"There's nothing to be sorry for, Dad," Ken said.

"There is. Sometimes–" Dad halted. "Sometimes. I don't remember things. Important things." Shame flooded his father's face. Ken wanted to look away. "I forgot. About the prenup."

Ken rubbed his father's forearm. "It's okay, Dad. This will all get straightened out." His father closed his eyes again. His face relaxed. Had he fallen asleep? Ken tapped his sleeve. "Dad, would you like to lie down for awhile, take a nap in the study?"

"Yes, I think I will." Dad got to his feet, took tiny labored steps down the hallway separating the kitchen and the study. Then he stopped and turned his head from side to side. What was he looking for? Ken took his father's arm and steered him towards the foldout couch. "No." He pushed Ken away. "But first I have to make a call."

"To whom?" Alyssa darted a warning at Ken. He knew she was concerned that their father would tell Fay before they got a chance to fix things.

Ken preferred to believe, until proven otherwise, that this was all just a mistake, that Fay hadn't realized the repercussions of the transfer, that she would agree it had to be reversed, but his last conversation with her gnawed at him. When he mentioned Dad's symptoms, she dismissed them. "Your father has lived a long life. He's survived so much." A cryptic remark that sent a chill through Ken. And she rejected his suggestion to try a new specialist. "Alvin's been to doctors, many. Age. Nothing to be done." Fay's cool disregard for his father's health threw him. It didn't jive with the jolly amiable woman who seemed so crazy about Dad when they first met. So in case Alyssa's paranoia turned out to be justified, he would rather that Dad didn't speak to his wife. Strange to even think the word. Ken still couldn't wrap his head around the concept of his father married to another woman.

"Who do you want to call, Daddy?" Alyssa asked again.

Ken watched his father retrieve someone from deep within himself. "Lorraine," Dad said. "I have to speak to Lorraine."

6

Through the airplane window's dirty glaze Lorraine spotted the familiar landmarks of her long ago home city. As the jet circled for landing she saw the Washington Monument, its reflecting pool crimson with sunset. The glassy water conjured Daddy, skates on his feet, holding her well-wrapped toddler body by the waist. He glided around the rink with her aloft on his shoulder in the shadow of "the giant pencil," as she had called it. Alvin Segal was an effortless skater from his childhood in Poland. Lorraine never did learn to skate. She hadn't imagined when the day began that she'd be anywhere but home this evening, snuggled up against Brad on the family room couch, listening to Jamie practicing the cello.

Lorraine used to love Mother's Day. Back when Jamie floated inside her, Brad started what became a Warner family tradition: breakfast in bed with all her favorites—French toast, bacon, blueberries, super-strong coffee, and freshly squeezed orange juice. Later, postpartum, she sipped Champagne. This morning Jamie had croaked, "HAPPY MOTHER'S DAY!" in his changing voice, just as the door burst open with her two guys carrying the tray of goodies, the Sunday paper, presents, and cards. Lorraine praised the addition of kiwi to the menu and kissed her son, who plopped down next to her.

Then Brad picked up the camera, ordered, "Smile, you two," and took the annual shot. Lorraine loved the ritual and them, but the last few celebrations, she couldn't shake haunting images of her mother's final shrunken form: her healthy sensuous face turned skeletal, the rippling gray hair, feathery wisps, and the overfull lips thinned and rendered useless once her mother ate through a stomach tube and spoke on a pad. Only the prominent nose kept its integrity. And the green eyes like bluegrass.

But it wasn't her mother's ghost who had dampened today's festivities. Lorraine and Brad and Jamie were at the garden center—another tradition—loading carts with flats of annuals and looking forward to an afternoon of digging, planting, and mulching, when Daddy called and Ken got on the phone to summon her.

On the ground, in the airport taxi, Lorraine felt a dull pang as the driver, a thin Croatian smelling of cigarette smoke, rounded the long curves of Rock Creek Parkway. She couldn't help but be aware that the Segals only came together under duress—illness or death. She didn't know what to label this latest crisis, but it seemed serious enough to risk a reunion.

Lorraine peered at the darkening trees. No matter how many parks graced her father's alabaster capital, she found it off-putting. "It represents justice," he often intoned.

Then Mother would add, "Its industry is paper." For Lorraine paper meant writing poems and plays. She never fit into this world of civil servants and lawyers. Neither did her artist mommy, who sent herself and her eldest mixed messages: shine, conform. Lorraine fled at the first opportunity. Then Kenny followed suit. Only Alyssa wanted to stay. Lorraine didn't think this was healthy, but she was relieved that Mother had had one daughter near, since it couldn't be her.

Streetlights flickered on as the cab sailed over Dorset's speed bumps. Her parents had moved here, only a mile from the District line, when Lorraine was almost five, a few months before Alyssa was born. Lorraine loved Essex Street, though she hadn't lived there since she went off to drama school, decades before. It wasn't Washington. It was *her* street.

The taxi slowed. She directed the driver to the top of its four hills. On snow days the Mayor used to declare it closed to traffic and Dorset's children would gather at the top and race their Flexible Flyers down the slopes. She and Ken and Alyssa had spent their happiest hours together sledding, screaming wildly, noses running, eyes watering, fingers numb, Lorraine on the bottom, Ken sandwiched in the middle, and little Ally, who had to be reminded to hold tight, but not strangle her brother, on top. A big storm, rare for Washington, produced enough snow to last for days. By the third day, with the street a raceway of polished ice, Lorraine and her siblings would zoom down all four hills without stopping. As they gathered momentum barreling over their private mountain range, they sang out, "Segalia forever!" Until the day they hit a parked car, and Ally split her lip so badly she had to have three stitches.

"You're supposed to take care of your sister," Mother said, and banned them from the top two hills. The beginning of the end of childhood.

The driver crawled past stately colonials and expanded capes. "Second red brick house on the right," Lorraine said.

Maybe it was the impending threat, or simply riding down these hills again, but yearning welled inside Lorraine. She wanted her family whole. What was left of it. Alyssa had ignored every message and invitation. Nevertheless, Lorraine was determined. She wouldn't give up hope. Her efforts pleased her father, though Brad wondered why she bothered. Ken just expected her to accept Alyssa's withdrawal. "She'll come back to you when she's ready," he'd say, whenever Lorraine called to bemoan the separation. She couldn't understand how Alyssa could bear to lose her, not after Mother. Then Ken would remind her, "Alyssa doesn't think like you and me." Still, Lorraine believed that if she tried hard enough, kept at it long enough, Alyssa would come round.

The taxi stopped. Lorraine got out and looked at the lone light over the front door, aware that she was about see the sister who had rejected her for reasons she still didn't fully comprehend.

Ken ushered Lorraine inside. "We postponed Martin until tomorrow. Dad's been napping for hours."

But when she tiptoed into the study, her father was awake. Lorraine was shocked by how small he seemed. "Daddy?" And she was shocked by the state of their childhood home. The place looked like an overstuffed storage container.

He turned towards her and brightened. "Sweetheart, I didn't know you were coming!" Lorraine sighed. He didn't remember their telephone conversation. He tried to pull himself up, then sank back against the cushion. "I'll just lie here for a little while longer," he said.

"That's all right, Daddy. You rest. I'll be right back." Lorraine motioned Ken into the hallway. Alyssa followed at a distance. "He's too worn out to leave." Lorraine was careful not to direct this at her sister, who from the moment Lorraine arrived, had avoided all contact by vacating whatever space she entered. Out of the corner of her eye, Lorraine studied Alyssa. She looked bloated, but her perfect skin shone over her cheeks. Lorraine, scarred from adolescent acne, had always envied her sister's complexion.

"He can't go back anyway. At least not until this is resolved." Ken said. Lorraine had never heard her brother so adamant.

"And after that, then what?" Alyssa flattened herself against the wall in a controlled implosion. She almost knocked down the tiny pen and ink drawing of a parrot that their mother had made in high school. "God knows what that woman will do once she finds out. I don't see how we can let him go back at all." It was no surprise to Lorraine that Alyssa leapt to the worst-case scenario, but she wasn't about to try to soothe her. Anything Lorraine offered would be interpreted as criticism. She knew from experience that she was lighter fluid to Alyssa's fire.

"It might not be so bad. Let's get him settled for the night and we'll deal with tomorrow *tomorrow*," Ken said. Lorraine loved her brother. And pitied him. No one chooses his birth order, and it seemed to her that the middle was the worst place to be. Certainly in this family.

"Daddy still keeps clothes here. I'll see if I can find some pajamas." Before either Lorraine or Ken could acknowledge the offer, Alyssa was gone. When she returned with a navy pinstriped nightshirt, Alvin complied.

"Please call Fay. Tell her I'll be back in the morning."

"Yes, Daddy."

"Sleep, Daddy."

"Don't worry, Daddy."

One by one Lorraine and her siblings kissed his bald spot in a bittersweet replay of their long ago bedtime ritual, when he used to sit in his favorite chair, reading the newspaper. Each of them would peck him on the head, and he would mumble good night and go on reading. Now he was already snoring. Lorraine shut the door behind her.

"I can't call her, Ken," Alyssa hissed. Her arms crossed, straightjacket style around her waist. Lorraine took a conscious breath to resist Alyssa's contagious tension.

"You have to, Ally. Fay doesn't know *we're* here." Ken included Lorraine in spite of Alyssa's continued attempt to look right through her. "If I call or Lor does, she'll know something's up. It's crucial that tomorrow morning go off without a hitch."

Alyssa released her arms. "All right." Then she plodded down the stairs. When she returned, her face was red.

"What did she say?" Ken asked.

Alyssa spit the answer, "To bring him back in one piece!"

Lorraine huffed, "As if she cared." Ally grunted her agreement. The moment of unity startled Lorraine. It had been a long time since they'd agreed on anything.

It struck Lorraine that not since adolescence had all three of them stayed together in the house. Ken slept on a futon in his old room. Lorraine wanted to sleep in her old room too, the one next door to Ken's that she'd shared with Alyssa, but when she peeked inside, she was confronted with floor to ceiling books, cartons and accordion folders, every surface covered, including the beds, with barely enough space to enter. Lorraine often attributed their problems to this tiny room—too small for one girl, let alone two. Ally had always been a collector. In this cramped space she spread out whenever possible, and Lorraine would trip over her stuff. But this. Lorraine shook her head and closed the door. Her sister had transformed their room into a cave. Or a cave-in.

Lorraine walked down the hallway to the spare bedroom. Maybe she could sleep there. When she opened the door she found a bed-less room lined with their vast foreign doll collection: each costumed doll stared at her with blank hard eyes asking, where had she been? Baby dolls wrapped in musty blue and pink blankets lay jumbled together in a corner, head to pudgy plastic toes, like unborn children in an overcrowded womb.

Two card tables stood in the center of the room. The one on the left held Lorraine's dollhouse, a simple two-story colonial with blue siding and a gray-slatted roof. The one on the right supported the same house, only pink with a brown roof, Alyssa's.

Lorraine was pulled towards the blue one, as if by a long-lost friend. She loved this dollhouse, should have taken it with her when she moved out after college, but she had no use for such a thing in her single life, and when she married and had Jamie, it didn't seem appropriate for a little boy, a conformity she couldn't shake.

Seeing its roof covered in dust, the contents topsy-turvy, saddened her and brought back the hours spent decorating its six rooms. When Alyssa was two she would play alongside Lorraine, handing her teensy books, foil wrapped cheeses, fingernail-sized utensils, and glass perfume tops, which, when turned upside down, became perfume bottles themselves. On Alyssa's fourth birthday Mother and Daddy gave her a dollhouse of her own. Lorraine made curtains, pillows, and bedspreads for her out of scrapes from their mother's sewing basket. She showed Alyssa how to create a picnic table out of Popsicle sticks for their yards, how to hang postage stamp art on the wall, and how to fashion frames from toothpicks. They had such fun together. Eventually though, Lorraine outgrew their pretend homemaking, and her doll family stopped visiting Alyssa's.

Lorraine righted the overturned dining chairs, but she couldn't fix the unraveling rugs she'd painstakingly knitted so long ago. Upstairs, the handmade sheets, yellow with age, lay crumpled against the peeling bedroom walls. Her house was a shambles, and where was her family?

Lorraine looked over at Alyssa's house. The pipe-cleaner Dad with his green velvet suit and the Mom with her yellow yarn hair in a ponytail were propped on the bed, side by side. Weren't those *her* doll parents? The baby in the rattan cradle, the boy in rust corduroy pants, and his sister with the beaded necklace and rubber Mary Janes stared at her without recognition. They lived in Alyssa's dollhouse now, which was, unlike her real one, in perfect order. Triangular arrangements had been carefully placed throughout: three candle sticks on the dining table, three brass goblets on the sideboard, three terrycloth towels on the bathroom rack–three of everything.

Lorraine got up. She had the urge to start cleaning, reclaim her dollhouse and her doll family with it, but she knew it was too late; she had deserted, and Alyssa had every right to the contents.

"Need anything?" Alyssa stood outside the entry of Mother's old art studio, her face in silhouette. This was the first time Alyssa had addressed Lorraine since they'd stopped speaking. Lorraine bolted upright from the daybed, startled. The voice was her own, only tighter. And Mother's. That was how she had sounded when she first brought Ally home from the hospital. She was a colicky baby, and whenever she cried, Mother blamed Ken and Lorraine.

It was dark. The room spooked her with its piles of mohair blankets, as if this were an emergency shelter. The huge black portfolios dared her to open them. "No. Thanks," Lorraine said, and craned her neck to see, but Alyssa had already retreated like a shadow puppet leaving the proscenium. "Good night!" Lorraine called, and then waited for the answer that never came.

In the morning, Martin took Lorraine into the study alone, while Ken, Alyssa, and Daddy met with Martin's replacement. Having broken confidentiality, he had decided to resign. "I encouraged your father to talk to you and Ken," Martin said. Lorraine sighed. Of course, Daddy hadn't. "With what is going on, I don't want you to be surprised." Martin's consideration impressed Lorraine. She tossed a stack of throw pillows on the floor and pulled up an armless chair next to Martin, who jotted down numbers on a legal pad. There on the yellow sheet he enumerated the stark truth: Fay or no Fay, Lorraine was pretty much an afterthought. She had expected something like this. Though born first, she knew when it came to the real reckoning—and what was a last will and testament, but an ultimate reckoning of family accounts?—she'd come in last. Still, the accuracy of her intuition shocked her.

"There are trusts for each of the grandchildren, and the now disputed prenuptial amount to Fay." So Daddy had taken her suggestion. When she made it, Lorraine thought a prenup would protect her and her siblings in case Daddy died first or Fay decided to move on to husband number four. Martin continued, "If the remainder is not needed for your father's care, or drained by legal bills, you and Ken will split it 30/70." Martin looked up at Lorraine. "Alvin figured that since you have Brad and are fairly well off, you wouldn't need as much as Ken, who has had a rockier time."

Lorraine hung her head. Of course, Ken was more deserving. She looked up, avoiding Martin's gaze, and stared at the wall of law books, atlases, and encyclopedias. She and Brad had struggled, but they'd kept their difficulties to themselves. There had been times when they were afraid of losing their home. After her parents' initial negativity—her husband was alien from his beanpole physique to his roots in Iowa's farmland—she hadn't wanted Daddy to know that Brad was anything less than perfect. And now it was apparent that she'd pulled this pretense off too well.

"I'm sorry," Martin said, putting down his pen. He stood.

Lorraine raised her hand, a schoolgirl in a family tutorial. There was another question she needed answered. "What about Alyssa?"

Martin paused and cleared his throat. "I thought you knew about that." Lorraine shook her head. No, she didn't know any of it. Martin looked down at her and said, "She gets the house."

Lorraine opened her mouth. Her lips formed an o, but no sound came out. All at once her self-blame receded and a wave of anger, a decade and a half old, crashed over her. When she had insisted on marrying Brad over her parents' objections, her mother said, "Don't expect any help from us. You're on your own." She may have intended only a swift kick into adulthood, but Lorraine interpreted this rejection as much more sweeping, something just short of banishment. Her parents' absence from the wedding devastated her. On her honeymoon Lorraine couldn't shake the feeling that someone had died. Not someone, something—her relationship with her parents. She never quite trusted them again.

Lorraine found her voice. "So Alyssa inherits the lion's share of the estate?" She had to say it out loud.

"Yes." Martin rose and adjusted his jacket sleeves. He seemed suddenly uncomfortable with the intimacy of his role. "I hope you understand."

Lorraine wanted to fling a volume of case law through a window, Alyssa's window. "Thank you for telling me." She should have known when Alyssa moved in as soon as Daddy went to Fay's that more than her father's kindness was at work. They had an agreement.

Martin placed his hand on her shoulder, patted it in a futile gesture of comfort, and left. "I'm sorry. I have to go. Mr. Grayson will take over from here. Call if you need anything."

In the next room Lorraine could hear her father and the new lawyer. She got up and moved to the doorway. Ken and Alyssa stood over Daddy, whose knees were covered in a green throw. Todd Grayson, a burly man about their age, sat next to him, and patiently explained the paper he had placed in her father's lap.

Daddy nodded and whispered, "I see." Then he took a pen from Ken and signed. Lorraine could tell, even from a distance, that her father was having difficulty. His hand shook and his fingers gripped the pen too tightly.

"I'm witness to his signature," Grayson said, "and his competence in regard to the document."

When he left, Lorraine entered the room and her father rose from the chair and headed towards the door. "I have to talk to Fay," he declared.

"No, Daddy!" Alyssa said.

Lorraine wasn't sure if her father had heard Alyssa's objection, but she knew that once he had made up his mind it was futile to try to change it. Alyssa and Ken rushed forward to support him down the slippery slate steps. It had rained overnight, an early thundershower that foretold a muggier than usual Washington summer. Lorraine grabbed her purse and followed. She dreaded what was about to happen, but she was glad to get out of that house. *Segalia*—the land of the Segals. She had been queen, Ken king, and Alyssa a lady-in-waiting. It was one thing for Lorraine to cede her dollhouse. It was quite another to relinquish her childhood home. Lorraine could no longer think of the trim brick structure with the deceptively modest exterior as home. No. It was foreign territory. And she was trespassing. It was Alyssa's country now.

7

"The prodigal husband returns!" Lorraine tensed at Fay's piercing greeting. Ken and Alyssa flanked Daddy like bodyguards and ushered him through the door. Then Lorraine brought up the rear. "And Kenneth!" Fay pecked his cheek. Ken flinched, but Fay didn't seem to notice. Lorraine inhaled her stepmother's choking scent, and suppressed the urge to cough. "Lorraine too!" She swerved to avoid Ken's fate, and then somehow managed to give the woman a perfunctory grin. Fay spread her billowy sleeves like a gospel preacher. "My, my, it's the whole Segal clan! What a surprise! We certainly haven't seen much of you these past few months."

Lorraine wanted to call her a liar, but she couldn't. She hadn't spent enough time with her father this year, much less than before his marriage. Back home in New Jersey, she had pictured him well-fed and content, and figured that she no longer needed to hover the way she had when Mother died. Seeing her father's current condition gave her pause. She had neglected him, turned him over to this woman, this stranger, without a second thought. Guilty as charged.

Daddy pushed past Fay into the living room. "Hold on, Dad!" Ken grabbed his arm and walked their father over to the black leather chair in the corner, adrift among Fay's gaudy collection. Alyssa lingered in the hallway, distancing herself from Fay. And Lorraine.

Fay fluttered around Daddy. "You look exhausted, Alvin dear. Didn't you get any sleep?" She dipped her chin in a coy pin-up pose she was fifty years too old to pull off. "Would you like some tea?"

"No, no I don't need anything," he called after her. But Fay was already gone. Lorraine was certain she was putting on a show, playing the attentive spouse for their benefit.

Fay returned, tray in hand, followed by Gretchen and Pablo. Alyssa contracted. Ken straightened up beside Daddy. "Consuelo's off for the day. Or is she at *your* house Alyssa?" Fay asked. Alyssa didn't answer. Not a chance, Lorraine thought. Not the way that place looked. Fay set the tray down on the cobbler's bench coffee table. "This is very simple. Tea and cookies. Help yourselves." No one moved. "Lorraine, Ken, you know my daughter and son-in-law."

Lorraine forced herself to speak, but stayed fixed on the faded mauve carpet. "Yes. Gretchen, Pablo, hello." Pablo extended his hand to Ken, not to her—handsome as hell, but a bona fide sexist. Gretchen's mouth twitched a silent response. Lorraine had met them at the wedding. But damn it, why do they have to be here now?

"Please sit down, dear." Her father managed to summon his most authoritative voice. Lorraine loved his elegant accent. She associated it with moral rectitude, and a touch of intimidation, which cast its spell on Fay, Gretchen, and Pablo, who lowered themselves onto the worn couch opposite him. Lorraine and her brother and sister remained standing.

"There's a situation we need to address," Daddy said. Ken cleared his throat. Alyssa hugged herself. She was barely holding on. Like Lorraine. But it reassured her to see her father in charge, at least for the moment.

"Oh Alvin, so formal." A hint of apprehension colored Fay's trill. "Did you have a nice day together?" She picked up a strawberry tart cookie and nibbled its scalloped edge.

He ignored or didn't hear her question. "We made a mistake," he said. Lorraine saw her father's fingers curl into fists on the arms of his chair. The strain worried her. He was making an enormous effort. "This morning I fixed it."

Lorraine resisted a grin, and the urge to look at Ken. She had to let this play out without interfering. Her siblings must have been thinking the same thing. They studiously avoided eye contact, while Fay and her children stared directly at them. Fay tittered and smoothed her lap, flicking crumbs on the floor. "Mistake? I don't know what you are referring to, dear." Lorraine was sure from the woman's overly firm tone that she was trying to shut him up.

"Uh, uh," her father stammered. In an instant, Fay had rendered him a bumbling old man. So much for restraint. Lorraine signaled her brother with a flick of her forefinger.

Ken took her cue. Lorraine knew this was not what he had hoped to find: Fay playing dumb, her family in attendance. "Dad is referring to the transfer made to you on Friday, Fay," he said, his voice quavering. "You remember."

"Oh yes!" Fay exclaimed. "It was a lovely gift. And so unexpected! Your father is so generous." Lorraine detected a simper in Gretchen's pursed lips and cool arrogance in Pablo's long look around the room. My God, they were in this together.

Daddy took a heavy breath and bowed his head. "I'm sorry, Fay. Please. Forgive. Me." He labored over each word. "I didn't realize. That you thought. It was a gift." Then he sank. For a moment Lorraine feared that her father was going to cry. He hated to disappoint anyone, especially someone he loved. Lorraine tried to swallow the bitter metallic taste in her mouth.

She'd eaten nothing that morning and felt woozy from hunger and nauseating realization: her father loved Fay.

"Well, what else would it *be*, dear?" Fay dared him to answer.

"An. An. An advance–" His voice trailed off. Lorraine held her breath and willed him to finish on his own, but his energy was fading. Ken took a step forward, about to catch the ball their father had launched into the air. Daddy opened his hands to wave her brother back and to place the fact before them. "On-the-pre-nup-tial-a-gree-ment." Then his hands dropped to his lap, only half-covering the red stain on his left pant leg. The woman didn't even keep his clothes clean.

Fay stood. "I don't remember any prenup." There it was: the brazen denial.

Ken took a document out of the folder he'd been carrying. Lorraine recognized it—the one Martin had brought with him that morning. "To refresh your memory," he said, and slid the paper across the glass coffee table. Fay, Gretchen, and Pablo reached out in unison. Gretchen lifted the sheet between finger and thumb like it was contaminated. Then she scanned the text, and handed it to her mother.

Fay held the paper at arm's length. "I don't have my reading glasses," she said.

Ken looked at her and in a firmer voice said, "I can tell you what it says. It says that you receive a lump sum, when the will is executed—the same amount as the transfer." Lorraine watched Gretchen's eyelids flutter at the word "lump." Pablo smacked his broad lips. They could hardly contain themselves.

"Well," Fay said, regaining her flourish. She began to waltz around the room, commanding everyone's full attention with one expansive gesture after another. "I never understood why that paper was necessary." So she did remember. "I only signed it to please Alvin. And I don't see what's to prevent him from giving me an additional gift. After all," she paused, dropping her voice along with her double chin, "when a woman of no means marries a man of means, he usually gives her gifts." Lorraine wanted to slap her. She was lecturing them on the ways of the world—the world according to Fay. Alyssa had turned her back to face the front hallway. Her shoulders heaved. Please God, don't let her be sick.

Ken nodded to Lorraine. Her turn. "As our father just told you, that wasn't his intention."

"How do *you* know what his intention was?" Fay asked.

"He told us."

"And a lawyer," Alyssa hissed, her face in profile.

Fay towered over Daddy. "Is this true Alvin? You spoke to a lawyer about this?" Ken lowered himself onto the ottoman in front of their father. Lorraine could see that he was positioning himself as a buffer.

"Yes, Martin and–" Her father searched each of his children's faces. When his eyes rested on hers, Lorraine realized that he couldn't remember the name of the new lawyer, and wanted her to fill in the blank. No. She wasn't going to give Fay any more information than necessary. The woman was already on the warpath.

"Martin Patras?" Fay scoffed. "Why? This is none of his business! Why shouldn't I have twice the amount if it comes to that? I'm your wife!"

At this, Daddy shriveled. "Yes. You. Are. But. But–" He stopped. Lorraine saw her father's energy vanish.

Then Alyssa swirled into the center of the room. Gretchen and Pablo shrank back against the sofa. Fay recoiled, like she was avoiding a beggar on the street. With her thick mane of red-brown hair and her flashing dark eyes, Alyssa looked supernaturally mad. Lorraine found herself both horrified and in awe of the avenging whirlwind that was her sister. The last time she'd seen Alyssa like this, Lorraine herself had been the target.

"Don't!" Ken warned.

"Sweetheart!" Daddy pleaded.

But it was too late. Alyssa sprayed words and saliva in a gusher of rage. "How dare you! Who do you think you are? You can't double your money! There isn't enough to hand you gifts *and* a prenup, *and* cover the college funds for Jamie, Josh, and Stella–"

"College funds! Since when is that Alvin's responsibility?"

"He and my mother wanted to provide them–"

"Well, I'm sure that's not necessary. Ken's children are just babies. He's got plenty of time to put together a college fund. And Brad's doing so well these days, isn't that right, Lorraine? You're in that lovely big house. A Queen Anne isn't it? You don't need help from your father. I do think it's marvelous that Alyssa is defending your part in all this, seeing as how she doesn't have any children of her own. Does this mean you two girls are back together? Wouldn't that be an answer to your father's prayers!"

Lorraine didn't say a word. Fay knew just how to get to them. Alyssa's purple face tightened like a prune. Lorraine could feel her own head thrumming in concert while her sister pressed on. "YOU'RE NOT LISTENING! There isn't enough money for what he intended *and* for his care–"

"As if you've paid any attention to *that*," Fay spit.

Alyssa barreled towards her. "So Dad signed a paper stopping the transfer–"

"ALYSSA!" Ken barked. Lorraine sank onto a nearby footstool. They'd discussed this very scenario in the car on the way over, and had all agreed not to mention the stop order. Ken had still been hoping that Fay would understand and suggest reversing the transfer herself. Lorraine found this naïve, but she respected her brother. We have to give her a chance, he had said. Too late now.

"Stopping the transfer?" Gretchen asked. She turned to her husband. "Can he do that?"

"This is outrageous!" Pablo chimed.

"Call Izzy," Fay ordered. Pablo raced out of the room. Must be their lawyer.

Alyssa paced. Her face contorted. She wasn't finished. The words tumbled out. "Yes, he can do whatever he wants! It's *his* money."

"And call Jimmy. I want to know what's gone into my account." Fay was all business now.

"Any money that has gone through already is an *advance* on the prenup, the *total* of which you will get LATER!" Alyssa froze. She was done. Her wrath sent a charge through the room. No one moved, except Daddy, who keened like an autistic child. Alyssa breathed hard and fast. Lorraine watched her sister glance furtively from wall to wall. She didn't know what to do with herself. If they had been close, Lorraine would have put her arm around her, but she couldn't. Instead, she backed into a corner to give Alyssa space, almost knocking over one of Fay's island pots. Alyssa turned and left. Lorraine jumped as the front door slammed shut.

Fay sniffed and collected herself in record time. "Well," she said, "there certainly *has* been a mistake. But I'm sure it will all work out for the best. There's plenty of money for everyone. Right Alvin?"

Ken had his hand on their father's shoulder. Daddy shook his head. Fay paid no attention. It was evident to Lorraine that the woman heard what she wanted to hear. Then she turned and addressed her with an inclusive nod to Ken. "You may not realize, since you see so little of your father, but he has not been well."

"Fay!" Daddy protested.

"I know you didn't want to worry your children, but they're here now, and so concerned about *the estate,* they ought to know the whole story." She was sticking it to them once again. "He's been more ill than you know, and forgetful. He wants to be sure I'm taken care of should anything happen to him. *Right dear*?" The last two words, unlike her previous question, struck Lorraine as non-negotiable.

"Yes," her father complied, but did not look up at Fay.

"So enough of this morbidity. I'm sure after Alvin gets a long rest cure, we're going to have many, many wonderful years together."

"Rest cure?" Lorraine asked, afraid to hear more.

"It was going to be a surprise, but we've had quite enough surprises for one morning. Alvin darling, Pablo's family has offered their home to us for as long as we want."

Lorraine's chest tightened. She hated her own helplessness against Fay's scheming. He father stared uncomprehendingly at this person in charge of his life. He was drowning and a mere daughter could do nothing to save him.

Ken pulled himself up to his full height, wobbled slightly, and then pinned Fay under his gaze. "You're taking him to San Juan? That's ridiculous. He needs medical attention. We have to get to the bottom of what's wrong with him."

Fay nodded and stared back. "Actually, Ken, that's taken care of. Alvin's seeing Dr. Cabot this afternoon. It's all planned. I've already spoken with him, and he gave the trip his blessing." Lorraine was struck by the false cheer in Fay's voice, which failed to mask her steely resolve. She *had* been planning. This and so much else.

Lorraine wanted to throw herself over her father like a net. "For how long?" she asked.

"Don't worry, he'll be back before Father's Day. That's your next visit isn't it?" Fay's jabs had lost their impact on Lorraine. Whatever her sins of omission, they were nothing compared to this woman's machinations.

Pablo called out from the kitchen in his deep basso, "Fay, Izzy's on the phone."

"In a moment, dear." Fay sneered at Lorraine and Ken, daggers drawn. Lorraine looked at her brother, whose face drained of color.

Gretchen rose and said in a tiny voice too small for her frame, "Come on, Mom. Your lawyer's waiting." Fay started towards her daughter.

"Please, Fay! Listen to reason." Ken sounded like Daddy, begging for this person to temper her natural tendencies.

"Reason, Kenneth? After today's display I won't be lectured about reason by *any* of the Segal children."

"You can't take him now! He's too ill!" Lorraine protested, though she knew it was futile.

"Of course, I can." Fay smiled. "I'm his wife!" Then she picked up the tea tray and sailed out of the room.

PART II

Island

8

The drive up to El Yunque in Pablo's Jeep was excruciating—all bumps and jagged turns. Alvin kept one hand on the cane and the other on his trifocals, which threatened to slip down his nose at every twist in the dusty road. By the time they reached the forest he had such motion sickness he couldn't stand. Pablo and a Park Ranger had to lift him up and out of the vehicle.

"Maybe I should stay here while you three walk," Alvin said.

"No," Pablo answered, handing him a bottle of water. "Fay wants you to get some exercise."

Ever since Alvin arrived in San Juan, Fay justified a relentless round of sightseeing with the mantra, "It'll be good for you. Build up your strength." The pace was too much. Alvin begged her not to overdo, for her sake, as well as his own.

"I'm fine, Alvin, dear. Don't you worry about *me*. I have energy to spare," she said, shimmying with a shake of invisible maracas.

"I've seen it all before," he pleaded.

"Not with *me* you haven't!" With that she dragged him off to Old San Juan, up and down the endless steps of Fort San Cristóbal, around the walled city, and through the cobbled streets. At restaurants she salted his food despite his protestations.

"My blood pressure!"

"No Alvin, at your last check-up you had *low* sodium. Dr. Cabot said salt is *good* for you." Fay nudged his plate closer to the edge of the table and pointed to the mound of beans, rice, meat, and runny cheese. "Eat!"

Both ravenous and revolted, Alvin swallowed what he could and reminded himself that she was only trying to take care of him. After one of these meals his head throbbed. No matter. They went shopping anyway. Fay couldn't seem to get enough of tourist trinkets. Alvin felt like a prisoner on a forced march. By the end of each day he wanted nothing more than to sleep for twelve hours.

Today Fay, Gretchen, and Pablo insisted that he come on a tour of Puerto Rico's famed tropical rain forest. Together they echoed Fay like a chorus of cheerleaders, "It'll be good for you."

Then at the last minute, with Pablo and his girls already in the car, Fay and Gretchen bowed out. "Been there, done that," Fay said. A phrase she repeated often. Instead, the women were going back to Old Town. "Can't have too many goodies!" Fay exclaimed and handed him her latest purchase, a carved walking stick in the shape of a serpent ready to strike. Then she and her daughter left, without a backward glance.

Pablo continued in his silkiest tones, "We'll skip El Toro–too steep–and take the Big Tree Trail. It's an easy walk. And so beautiful. You'll see." Then he and the children began down the marked path. Alvin felt his resistance slip, replaced by a familiar determination to rise to the challenge of the day. He wasn't an invalid yet. If Fay and Pablo thought he could do this, then he could. Alvin resolved to put one shaky foot in front of the other.

The forest was indeed magnificent. Cedars and satinwood draped in webs of knotted vines. Birds piped along the trail. Alvin imagined that he heard only some of the symphony—his ears were not what they used to be—but the muffled trills and squawks buoyed him along. Pablo told the girls to listen for the coqui, a tree frog known to reside in the forest.

Cara, doing her best imitation of the amphibian, hopped at every new sound. "I hear it Daddy! I hear the coqui."

Then Sabine trumped her sister. "That's not so great. *I* saw a parrot!" This amused Alvin. Just like Lorraine and Alyssa, ever competitive.

Despite his resolve, Alvin had trouble keeping up. The combination of sultry wet heat, the inclining pebble-strewn trail, and a steady stream of hikers, who passed him in both directions on either side, made him dizzy.

"Steady, Alving, steady," Pablo instructed, using Sabine's added 'g.' Once they heard her call him "Papa Alving," everyone in Pablo's family started to call him *Alving* too. He didn't protest; after all, he couldn't speak a word of Spanish. French and Latin were the only languages taught in Polish schools before the war.

Pablo grabbed Alvin's elbow and guided him towards the falls. The man's huge hand on his arm frightened Alvin. Pablo was behaving like a nightclub bouncer about to throw out an unruly customer. He deposited Alvin on a bench facing the waterfall, La Mina. "Rest here until we come back," Pablo said and pressed a bottle of water into Alvin's palm. Then Pablo steered Cara to the path and called, "Come along, Sabine!"

Sabine had wrapped her arms around Alvin's neck. She ignored her father and asked, "Why aren't you coming with us, Papa Alving?"

"I'm tired," he told her and patted the tiny fingers, which dug into his throat. She shrugged, let go, and skipped towards her family, her tiered miniskirt bobbing like a piñata. Her piccolo chirp sang out to Cara and her father, "Wait, wait for me!"

Alvin watched the three disappear up the trail. Then he tried to focus on the screeching children, nubile teens, and doughy middle-aged bathers who drenched themselves in the cascading shower. He envied them their cool soak. Alvin loved the water, but he hadn't thought to wear his trunks.

By the time Pablo and the girls returned, it was noon. The shady seat on which they had left Alvin had dissolved under the blazing sun, which baked his bald spot and melted down his face in salty rivulets of perspiration. All Alvin wanted was to leave.

"Papa Alving! Guess what we saw?" Sabine's face probed her step-grandfather's, her nut brown nose almost touching his. Alvin felt like a store window with enticing but unreachable merchandise on the other side.

"I don't know. Tell me." Alvin's mouth was dry. He'd long since finished off the water. The bottle in his right hand was sticky with sweat. For a fleeting moment he thought about simply releasing it, letting it drop to the already garbage-strewn ground. Coke and Pepsi cans, bottles of 7-Up, paper plates, plastic forks, and spoons surrounded his bench. The trash can a few feet away overflowed with debris. On the way in from the airport, Alvin had been shocked by the rubbish lining the highway. He gripped the bottle tighter, his palm slippery hot. He wouldn't litter.

"We saw another waterfall!" For emphasis, Sabine pressed his left hand, which rested atop the cane's snakehead. Her fingers were damp. Alvin reached out to pull her closer and noticed that the little girl's dress was soaking wet.

"Did you jump in?"

"Yes!" she squealed.

"Me too!" Cara bounded onto the bench. Her hair and clothing dripped over him. Alvin welcomed the cool rain.

"Time for lunch." Pablo lifted Cara off the bench and took Sabine's hand. "You ready to go, Alvin?" he asked, and walked away before Alvin could answer.

Of course he was ready. What kind of question was that? He had been ready for hours. Alvin shoved the bottle into his pocket, and pulled himself up by pushing hard on the cane. As he rose to vertical, the bottle popped out onto the ground, and bounced a few feet, like a jumping bean. Alvin considered what it would take to bend and retrieve it.

He could hear the girls shouting from a distance, "Papa Alving! Come on!"

Alvin took a step and reached down toward the bottle. Something metallic crumpled beneath him. Another step. Then a stab. Right through his shoe and the ball of his foot. His inner medic ordered: pull it out. Alvin placed a hand behind him to lower himself back onto the bench, but missed and landed in the dirt. Two teenaged boys, who had been laughing at him, like he was their own private joke, suddenly knelt beside him, and fired concern in rapid Spanish. Alvin couldn't summon his voice. What difference would it make? They wouldn't understand him.

"Pablo," he whispered. "Pablo." His foot throbbed. The pain shot up his leg.

The boys repeated, "Pablo, Pablo."

A long shadow passed over him. Pablo, Cara, and Sabine peered down. Alvin couldn't see their faces, only the sun's halo, which transformed them into a fiery three-headed dragon. Two high voices cried, "Papa, Papa."

Then a large impatient one boomed, "What now, Alving?"

Alvin tried to focus, but his bandaged foot pulsed and his bad eyes made it impossible to actually see the sand and water in front of him. Every day since his fall, Pablo's mother, Marisol, propped up Alvin's leg on pillows, and seated him in the rocking chair on her porch, with a glass of iced tea on the wicker table beside him. She waved toward the hazy cream-colored blur merging with an aqua sky, which must have reflected the blue-green waters below, and encouraged him to enjoy Dorado's view. Half-blind though he was, Alvin nodded and thanked her.

He might not have been able to see the beach, but he remembered. Estelle had loved this part of Puerto Rico—the elegant Dorado Beach Hotel, just down the road—the warm Caribbean waters, the festive rum drinks. How strange that this wife had brought him here, where memories of his time alone with Estelle, after Ally went off to college, shaded every moment.

And how different this visit was. Carlos and Marisol's home invited relaxation with its stone terraces, earthen pots filled with birds of paradise, and cushioned rattan loveseats both inside and out, but it was no hotel. Alvin missed the air-conditioning, and even before his mishap, had spent every possible minute that he wasn't traipsing after Fay, seated inside under a ceiling fan, or here on the veranda, catching the air like a sail in the Atlantic breeze. The thick, salty humidity was more bearable than Washington's, perhaps because he wore a Hawaiian shirt every day, instead of his usual suit and tie, but its heaviness was just as relentless. Alvin had more trouble tolerating the scalding sun and the wet air on this trip than years ago. Age spoiled everything. Well, at least he was done with sightseeing. In his hobbled state, nothing would be expected of him.

Marisol was kind. She had met them at the emergency room and talked with the doctor in whispered Spanish about his aftercare. She was a jolly round woman—mid-sixties, he guessed—with a bun of still-dark hair, probably dyed, something Estelle hadn't done. Marisol had large brown eyes, which even to his eclipsed vision seemed merry. Each morning she brought him fresh papaya—he loved the juicy sweetness, part orange, part mango—and reminded him with a tap of her watch that it was time to take his antibiotics. Too bad their exchanges were limited to "gracias," "por favor," and "si." Fay rarely sat alone with him anymore. He missed the engaging conversation of their courtship. He missed talking with a woman.

Alvin rubbed his arm. After removing the rusty nail from his foot, the doctor gave him a tetanus shoot. The site swelled into a hot red bump. Alvin shifted from his bruised left hip onto his right buttock.

"Purple, yellow, and green. Like one of Estelle's abstracts," Fay chortled when she saw the eggplant-sized welt. "You're lucky you didn't break it."

"Lucky, yes," he answered.

"Now Alvin," she went on in a darker tone, one she employed when she wanted to lay down the law. "Don't think we're going home early. I need this vacation. And besides, you're better off here, where I have help."

"I understand," Alvin said, though he didn't. The more complicated things got, the less he understood this woman.

Alvin turned his head to avoid the pungent smoke floating his way. Marisol's husband Carlos had entered the porch with a cigar. Alvin hated the smell, but he knew he wasn't in any position to complain. Carlos nodded. Alvin coughed. The man continued puffing. He was as lean as Marisol was plump, and sported a graying mustache. Alvin disapproved of facial hair; it smacked of sexual vanity and the unsavory. He hated it when Ken grew a beard during his Texas years. His son looked like the hippie he was. When Ken shaved it off after the accident, Alvin was pleased.

He watched Carlos flick ash on the sand. Pablo's father spoke rudimentary English, but didn't speak to Alvin. He felt his host's disdain almost as deeply as Fay's, meted out daily. Unlike Marisol, Carlos took sides. Alvin assumed that Fay,

Pablo, and Gretchen must have told him what had transpired in Fay's living room. Alvin didn't regret the confrontation—Fay needed to know his mind—but he did regret Alyssa's outburst, which inflamed an already difficult situation. Fay vented to Carlos, dropping snide remarks, catty jabs about Alvin and his children. "You should have heard the way Alyssa spoke to me–no respect, no respect for me or her father," she said, well within earshot of Alvin, for his benefit he was sure. "But it was marvelous to see them all together. I guess blood is thicker than water where money's concerned!"

When Fay found out that the stop order had gone through, she was furious and needled him to do something. "My gift! What about my gift?"

Alvin held his tongue and tuned her out. If only she would let it go.

But Fay never let anything go, not when she was unsatisfied. She and Gretchen huddled with the men and murmured, "travesty-outrage-betrayal," just loudly enough to annoy him. They didn't realize their obvious carping only further hardened Alvin's resolve.

When she looked over at him to gage his reaction, Alvin intoned, "What's done cannot be undone." Fay turned her blank face to him. "Macbeth," he added. Fay shrugged and walked out of the room. Standing up to her to rectify his lapse had taken every ounce of Alvin's strength. That effort and his battered body had left him drained and lonely. He wanted to go home to Washington. Home to Dorset. Carlos exhaled another gray plume. Alone under his host's cold and studied guard, Alvin felt like a hostage.

"Alving? Alving?" Carlos tipped the rocker to such an awkward angle that Alvin thought he would fall. "You okay?" Carlos rubbed Alvin's forearm to shake him out of his stupor. Alvin wondered how long he'd been asleep. Carlos lifted the iced tea to Alvin's lips. "Drink this."

"Give him a virgin Piña Colada. He needs calories!" Alvin craned his neck to see Fay trundle towards him carrying the frothy pineapple concoction.

"Fay, no. My cholesterol!"

"Nonsense. Carlos says you were woozy, muttering to yourself. That's blood sugar. Drink!" Alvin took one sip and pushed the glass away. He was sick of being ordered to drink non-alcoholic beverages. Where was Puerto Rico's famous rum? "Don't be that way, Alvin. We have a big night tonight. A surprise, just for you."

"You like music, Alving?" Carlos asked.

Before he could answer, Fay volunteered, "He loves the cello. His grandson plays."

Carlos clapped his hands. "Then you will love the Festival!"

Alvin sighed. He was not up for anything, including culture, but once again, that didn't seem to matter to anyone but himself. Carlos and Fay smiled, which made him feel no better. Why did they care to entertain him? Another puzzle he didn't have the energy to solve. So he decided to make the best of it. After all, a concert would not demand much. It might even be a relief. He had only to sit and let the music carry him away.

That evening at the Luis A. Ferré Performing Arts Center, Alvin's spirit lifted for the first time since he had set foot on the island. The Festival Casals with its strains of Dvořák's Concerto in B Minor bathed his increasingly feverish body in soothing melancholy. He loved music and fought the overwhelming urge to let it lull him to sleep. He sat on the aisle, leg extended, in a wicker wheelchair Marisol had borrowed from an infirm neighbor. Fay sat next to him, stone-faced, a Kabuki mask of scarlet lips and white powder. Beside her, Gretchen posed in an Indian sari, and the girls fidgeted in their layer cake dresses, with their other grandparents between, patting their beribboned heads and bare legs to calm them. Pablo had absented himself earlier in the evening. "A previous engagement," he said.

Surrounded by Fay's extended family, Alvin suppressed his loneliness—where is *my* family?—and let the strings transport him back to the Casals Museum where he and Estelle had poured over its posters and tapes, to bring back to Jamie, their then seven year old grandchild, already a budding cellist. The tiny modest 18th century house with its display of the maestro's cello, his photographs, and videotapes had a humble quality at odds with Casals' reputation. Yet it was somehow fitting. It told Alvin that genius was human after all, and didn't need grandeur to assert its gift.

His head hurt. The lights of the concert hall flashed on and off. The orchestra echoed between his ears. A hand, Fay's, reached out and felt his cheek. "My God, Alvin! You're burning up." She stood and threw her shawl over her shoulders, brushing Alvin's brow with its fringe. She turned his chair around and rumbled it up the aisle. His glasses slid down his nose.

Their entire row followed, accompanied by little girl voices asking why, and angry shushing from the row behind. Alvin heard his voice sing atop the cello solo. "No, no! I want to stay. The music, I need to hear the end of the music." He must be dreaming. Alvin sang with Casals, the bald cellist resurrected, his long-lost twin.

Tiny fingers played his piano keyboard arms. "Papa Alving, wake up." Yes, he *was* dreaming. Someone rolled him out into the lobby. He listened to large figures, who spoke too fast, and then lifted him up into an over-bright container. Alvin couldn't remember the name for it. Then Dvořák sirens screamed into the night taking him he knew not where.

9

Pablo Luis Diaz brought his wife and daughters down to visit Papi and Mamá three times a year. In between, he took day trips to Atlantic City and weekends in Vegas. Gretchen didn't seem to mind as long as he held the limit, a number they always agreed upon before he went out the door. This time though, she was uncharacteristically strict. "A thousand, that's it for the week," his wife reminded him, lips tight, while she painted them in front of the vanity mirror earlier that evening, before she and the rest of the family left for the concert hall. Fay wanted to cheer up Alvin after the disastrous trek to the rainforest. Pablo felt bad dragging the poor man around in the heat, but he was in no position to argue with his mother-in-law.

He ran his fingers through Gretchen's sandy curls and bent to inhale her musky gardenia scent. Then he whispered in her ear, "Unless I win. No limits on *that.*"

She swiveled to face him, and pulled him down by the lapel to meet her eye to eye. "I'm serious. We can't afford to lose any more this month." No kidding. He hadn't told her about the business. If the evening went as planned he wouldn't have to.

A week before, his partner, Louis, a pudgy computer genius with no social skills, whom he'd met stateside in engineering school, slapped him with the bad news. "The dotcom's still-born, man. Going nowhere."

After graduation Pablo's father had asked, "Why you not becoming an engineer?" Pablo didn't want to design sewer systems, but an honest answer wouldn't satisfy Diaz Senior, so disappointment became the reliable code between them. Pablo drifted from job to job, until his twentieth reunion, where he and Louis commiserated over beer and sketched out a business plan on cocktail napkins. They joked about calling it Louis-Luis.com. The next morning the two got serious. Info-red.com was born—software alerts, virus protection, anti-spam strategies. Pablo borrowed the start-up capital from Fay, who'd hit the marital jackpot on her third try. Louis created the programs. Pablo handled money, sales, PR. Their unspoken pact: failure, not an option.

"Give it time," Pablo told Louis.

"I'll give it time, if you give it money." Louis sat in Pablo's living room, elbows on knees, rubbing his hands together. The guy was a nervous wreck. If he'd held a stick he would have started a fire.

"I'll take care of it," Pablo promised. He knew this was their final shot at gold, before middle-aged fatigue benched them forever.

Gretchen waved her brush at him. "Pablo! The girls' tuition is due in three weeks."

"You worry too much, mi amor." Pablo knew her mother's money would take care of that. It always did.

This time though, he insisted on calling the amount a loan, but Fay laughed and said not to trouble himself about it. "There's more where that came from," she assured him. Pablo admired her certainty. Despite the stop order Alvin's aging brats had masterminded, Fay managed to hand Pablo a hefty sum. He told Fay the money was for Sabine and Cara, and asked her to keep the exchange just between them, not to bother Gretchen. Fay agreed. She knew how panicky Gretchen was about all things financial. With luck, Pablo would pay Fay back, cover the bills, save the business, and Gretchen would never have to know.

"There's plenty to worry about," his wife said, and handed him her necklace, a string of island coral. "This mess with Alvin and his family–"

Pablo kissed her nape and fastened the clasp. "Nothing listening to a little violin–"

"–cello–"

"Nothing listening to a little *cello* music won't fix." He put his hands on Gretchen's knobby shoulders. "Your mother will turn him around in no time!" She shook her head. He withdrew his hands. Pablo didn't get why she had less faith in her mother's powers than he did. He figured Fay was tough and smart, and had managed to wrangle that first chunk from the old guy, exposure notwithstanding. Here, with the Segal progeny out of the picture, she'd have a second chance. Pablo believed in second chances. He'd had so many.

Pablo sauntered through the main lobby of the Sands Casino—his favorite among the island's gaming establishments. He adjusted his white linen jacket, primped the collar of his lucky blue designer shirt, and caught a glimpse of his lanky frame in the mirrored walls, approving the snappy cufflinks, perfect tailoring, and confident stride. Looking good helped him play the conquistador. The Sands was his regular Saturday night battleground, oozing a grandiosity that fed him. Pablo looked up at the Murano glass chandeliers, longer than his parents' casa. Their reflections animated the polished marble surfaces and silenced all doubt. For tonight at least, this was a palace and Pablo was king. He patted his breast pocket. Fay's money padded him like armor.

Pablo steered around hundreds of slot machines and the beefy tourists in loud t-shirts, tank tops, tight shorts, and flip flops, who took advantage of the lax dress code outside the main rooms. Older ladies with bluish helmets—twentieth century versions of powdered wigs—prayed and shook their quarters in ritualistic routines. The supplicants flapped their upper arms, kissed their fists and plugged the slots, while murmuring seduction to the mechanical sugar daddies. Pablo pitied them. This was no way to make a killing.

Then he passed under the arched opening into the inner sanctum, relishing the contrast: vacation players at the gaming tables as overdressed as the slot aficionados were under. Women in sequins, necklines down to their cinched waists, men in tuxes and heavily moussed hair crowded table seven—Pablo's home base. Its purple sign flaunted the betting limits for high stakes Blackjack, his game of choice.

Tina batted her false eyelashes in his direction. She had a thing for him. Pablo was sure of it. She was a terrific dealer and not bad to look at. The white satin halter, with the fuchsia cummerbund and the snug skirt beaded in black jet emphasized her impressive cleavage, bronze shoulders, and resplendent hips.

He surveyed the table. Tourists, he noted with rising smugness. They placed sloppy, extravagant bets, the kind he could have taken full advantage of in poker. Blackjack was all about the dealer. Still, it was more fun to play surrounded by inexperienced nouveau riche than by his jaded peers. He'd set a tone, dominate the table.

An hour later Pablo amassed his winnings in a mound, gave himself a moment of satisfaction, and then, without hesitation, pushed them back into the box, riding the wave. He was over Gretchen's limit—way over—but to hell with caution. In minutes though, his streak ended. He had to stand, walk off his jitters. He looked back at Tina, and pointed at his chair. Save it. Was it wishful thinking or did she return the wink with more than professional encouragement? Then he returned to the cashier window. One of his tablemates, the guy with the slick toupée, sneered at him, stage whispering to the line, "Poor sucker. Lost all his winnings from the first round."

Who's he calling a poor sucker? Pablo turned and walked toward the table, trying to block out the guffawing. He needed to concentrate. He wasn't through. He would stay, all night if necessary.

Tina waited while he pulled another wad from his breast pocket. Then she counted out his chips. Pablo plotted a new strategy. Count the cards. Don't crack. Don't sweat. Be the man.

10

Fay and Gretchen ushered Alvin into the emergency room of the nearest San Juan hospital, Los Madres. Gretchen went for coffee, and left Fay alone with the masses, men and women with injuries and ailments more minor than Alvin's. Saturday night was the island's peak party night. The triage nurse took one look at her husband—flailing and disoriented—and called for attendants, who lifted him onto a gurney and rolled him behind closed metal doors.

Fay kept to a far wall, away from the contagion and middle-of-the-night misery, which permeated the humid air. She waved a crumpled concert program across her face while huge industrial fans blew the rancid smell of drunken vomit around the room. Fay had a strong stomach; she hadn't flinched when her little girl got sick or a dead animal had to be removed from the crawl space under their porch. But this was more than she could bear. She turned her nose away.

Fay yawned and glanced at her watch. 1 a.m. It had been four hours since they'd arrived and still no word on Alvin's condition. Her mind raced. He'd better be fine. What if he's not? This couldn't be happening. Not here. Not yet. She wasn't ready.

Fay pressed her palms together, not in prayer. Though she attended temple, she didn't pray, not since Simon's death. She had no faith, only ritual. Somehow that was enough, a pattern to cling to, a heritage, a communal bond. She loved her

Wednesday mornings breakfasts with the Jewish women of B'nai Sharon. The rest—prayer, faith, spiritual healing—were out of reach, like a language she had no aptitude for. Instead, Fay clung to realism, a philosophy grounded in practical assessments, concrete decisions. It was safer, she concluded. Nothing surprised a realist. Not even the terror of her third husband collapsing in a foreign concert hall. For a realist, everything life had to offer was expected in the fullness of time: terror, catastrophe, pain, loss.

Was it too late to call Izzy? No. He'd understand. Necessity bore down on Fay. She counted the minutes on the large wall clock above the nurse's station. 1:13. How many time zones away were they? She wished circumstances were different so that she could be patient, and wait for Alvin to return to a receptive, companionable state. But it was not to be. Izzy would have to act quickly. No more holding hands with Jimmy Stackwell, that incompetent broker whose excuses about the aborted transfer had so far succeeded in keeping her from her due. He told her he was sorry. "This was how Mr. Segal wanted it." Fay hung up on him. What grown man calls himself Jimmy?

She hoped that a few weeks by the beach would bring Alvin back to his senses, restore their understanding, but she had miscalculated. She thought treating him normally was the best strategy. But the jaunts into the city, the busy itinerary backfired. Alvin was too sick. She'd pushed him too hard. Day by day she felt him retreat further into himself, to a place she could not reach. The more he withdrew, the more she pushed. Then the fall in the forest. Now this. Fay feared he might not come back. She needed Alvin conscious, to clear up this mess, to sign the power of attorney, to reverse those ridiculous "advance" papers. How could she have been so stupid? She would have to salvage the situation somehow. There was no more time to waste.

Gretchen returned and handed her watery coffee in a waxed paper cup.

"Call Izzy," Fay said.

"It's too late. I'll wake him up."

"Call him anyway. Tell him it's an emergency. He has to have all the paperwork ready to sign when we land."

"We're going back?" Gretchen cocked her head. Sometimes her daughter wasn't the swiftest.

"Of course. Alvin's sick. He can't be treated properly here. Besides, the vacation is spoiled. We won't be able to enjoy ourselves now."

"Did you call his children?"

Fay sipped the bitter brown liquid and scalded the tip of her tongue. "No. I did not." She fumbled through her purse for her address book. "Gretchen, would you please call Alyssa? Have her meet the plane." Maybe take Alvin home with her for a few days, or as long as it takes. But she didn't say this to her daughter. Fay couldn't be a nurse. Not again. Not at her age.

"Has the doctor spoken to you yet?" Gretchen asked. "We should wait. At least until we have a diagnosis."

Gretchen was right. Fay could hear Alyssa scream accusations of neglect and abuse. Why had Fay dragged her father all the way to Puerto Rico? How could she be so callous? There was no way Fay could explain her behavior to Alvin's youngest. *It seemed the right thing to do at the time. Your father liked to travel. The doctor said it was okay.* None of this would suffice. "I'm going to the ladies room," she said.

Gretchen pointed to the *Señoras* sign on the green door down the hall. Fay entered with trepidation. The bathroom was spare and dirty with rough paper or none at all in the stalls. She checked her face in the smudged, distorted mirror over a rust-encrusted sink. The lipstick she'd applied earlier had faded into an orange stain, spreading into the fine lines, which encircled her mouth. Her eyes were ringed with coal. She looked like a clown after the crowd had gone home. Only her hair, a perfect platinum shell, had kept its integrity.

Fay splashed her face with water and patted herself dry with a sandpaper towel. Next to her, a woman, brown-skinned, heavy-set, typical of island ladies past fifty, stood over the adjacent sink, sobbing into a wad of toilet tissue. Fay knew no Spanish, though this was not her first trip. Sabine and Cara were fluent, but she was too old to learn. Even had she been able to speak to the woman she would not have. Grief was private—too private for a stranger to address. Fay felt the weight of almost fifty years of marriages, deaths, and spousal abandonment. Layers of mourning had settled in her, changing her fundamentally. She was not the buoyant, trusting young woman who had married Simon Tabor and had a child with him, nor was she the middle-aged career woman who had joined with Barney Cohen for a life of dinner parties, professional conference weekends, and great sex. She was not even the elderly woman who had eased a kind gentleman lawyer past his own recent grief and into a companionable twilight. The woman looked over at her. Fay looked away. She was done with grief.

Gretchen entered and checked her reflection, brushing the tired curls away from her forehead. Fay noticed that the lines between her daughter's eyes had, in the past few months, deepened to a permanent scowl. Pablo. Always a new venture. A surefire scheme. And then he was often out at night. Fay hoped that the money she gave him would lighten the load, at least take the girls' tuition off the list of their worries, but no matter how much she gave, he always needed more.

"Mother, the doctor wants to speak with you."

"Call your husband," Fay said. Gretchen nodded, but didn't move.

"Señora *See*gal–" The doctor's accent landed heavily on the first syllable of her last name. His smarmy presence—all shellacked hair and over-manicured sideburns chased with a dash of cheap after-shave—disturbed Fay. If this weren't a hospital, she would have sworn she was meeting a dance instructor at Arthur Murray's.

"Your husband, he is *verry* sick," the doctor went on. "His foot is infected, causing high fever and delirium. In addition, his blood pressure is too high. I suspect a stroke. He has a *heestory*?"

"Yes. He does." Fay was not about to discuss this further with an island quack. "When can I take him back to the States?"

"Not for at *leeast* two or three days."

"Too long." Fay swung into command mode. "We're going. Immediately. Gretchen, find Pablo, have him drop whatever he's doing and get over here. We'll need help moving Alvin. Then call Alyssa."

"Mother–"

"Call her. Tell her we'll be home on the next available flight." Fay watched Gretchen fly down the hall to do her bidding. Good girl.

"But Señora, he should not be moved!"

Fay folded her arms in front of her. Every muscle in her body ached. She was old enough to be this subpar doctor's mother and too old to stand there, in the wee hours, arguing. Fay pinned the doctor with her eyes until he had to avert his. "May I see him now?"

The doctor motioned for Fay to follow him past the rows of faded blue curtains separating one sad case from another. The doctor stopped at the fourth set and parted them with a flourish. "Señor *See*gal? Your wife is here to see you."

Fay stepped into the space occupied by a metal hospital bed, a side table, and monitors attached to Alvin's fragile frame. It was a shock seeing him, only hours ago dressed to the nines, swaying to the strains of the symphony, now shriveled in this filthy hospital, gray as his remaining strands of hair. Fay looked behind her for something to sit on. There was no chair.

"My wife?" Alvin asked, scanning her without focusing. They had removed his glasses and Fay knew he couldn't see a thing without them. He continued to look around and, it seemed to Fay, past her. Beads of perspiration dotted his forehead. Good. The fever must have broken.

"I'm right here, dear," she said, taking his clammy hand in hers.

Alvin looked at her, puzzled. "The doctor said my wife was here. Where is she?"

Fay withdrew her hand. "Alvin, you've had a difficult night. I'm taking you home to Washington."

"You're not taking me anywhere. Doctor!"

The doctor, who had been lurking outside the curtains, reappeared at the end of the bed. "Señor?"

Before Alvin could ramble any further, Fay interjected, "He doesn't know me."

The doctor took Alvin's pulse and peered into his eyes with a light. "He is still feeling the effect of the *feever* and perhaps of a stroke. Does he suffer from *deementia*?"

"Not usually." Fay wasn't about to give this pseudo-practitioner any excuse to keep Alvin a moment longer. She sat on the edge of the bed and leaned in, this time holding both of his arms. He had to recognize her. "Alvin. It's Fay. You remember."

Alvin thrashed his upper body side to side, as if he were avoiding a collision on a bumper car ride. "I don't know you. ESTELLE! Where is Estelle? I need MY WIFE!"

Fay wanted to run—or failing that on her swollen legs—walk, step by painful step, away, leave him to fend for himself with the tubes, and the machines, and the disorientation of his misfiring brain. After all she'd done for him, to be dismissed like she never existed!

Gretchen entered behind the doctor, looking more drawn than ever. "Izzy's not picking up. I got his service. I'll try him again in the morning." She paused. "Alyssa will be there."

"Good. And Pablo?" Fay knew the answer, but had to ask. Her daughter said nothing and bit her upper lip. Fay took Alvin's hand again, and stroked the thick blue veins. "Quiet, quiet now."

He didn't respond. His cloudy eyes stared past her. "Estelle?"

Fay felt the doctor's judgmental presence. "No dear–" she said, careful to speak in low soothing tones,"–it's Fay. *I* take care of you now."

PART III

Father's Day

11

The soaring glass and concrete arches of Dulles International—Alyssa's favorite Washington area airport—had a spiritual lift to their long heavenward lines. The terminal held itself in perpetual takeoff position. Alyssa stood and faced the sign for American Flight 473 from San Juan. Flight 473 wouldn't leave until her father's plane—number 474—landed. The two flights were part of the endless shuttle that brought families, singles, old and young, to and from Puerto Rico. Alyssa had never been there and had no desire to go. She preferred the Virgin Islands—no language barrier.

Alyssa looked at her watch. 1:40 p.m. Twelve hours since Gretchen's alarming wake-up call. All she knew from the brief, cryptic phone conversation was that her father had fallen and needed more medical attention than San Juan could provide. When Alyssa pressed for details Gretchen demurred, saying only that she'd call back with the flight number. But even with so little to go on Alyssa knew things must be very bad for Fay to cut her vacation short and for Gretchen to call her in the middle of the night. Just to be safe, Alyssa had arranged for a private ambulance.

"Daddy should never have gone down there in the first place," she told Ken, who was rushing back to DC.

"What were we supposed to do? Kidnap him?" her brother snapped.

"Maybe."

"That's Fay's M.O., not ours," he said. "I'll see you at the hospital."

Alyssa checked and re-checked her watch. The flight was late. She had no idea what she'd do or say when she saw Fay and her progeny. She'd try not to lose it, not in a place as public as this. Besides, her venom was long spent. The blowout three weeks ago made her shudder now. She had frightened herself.

When Alyssa discussed the incident with Terry, her therapist since Mother's death, she asked, "Is it normal, behaving like that?"

He smiled kindly—Terry was kind—a quality that kept her coming back, even though seeing a shrink made her feel like more of a failure. Still, his gentle manner mitigated her self-inflicted battering. "How did you feel?" he asked, and passed her a cup of tea. Terry reminded her of Mother, albeit gay and skinny. She would have offered Champagne instead of chamomile, but the effect was the same. Alyssa felt cared for and safe.

"Enraged and miserable."

"Enraged at?"

"Fay, of course."

"And miserable why?"

"Because we're in this situation."

"We?"

"My father, Ken, me." She paused. "And Lorraine." Alyssa sipped the hot liquid, while her words settled around them. When something new happened in therapy she and Terry would "sit with it" before either one would make any comment.

After the requisite absorption period, Terry said, "I don't think I've ever heard you refer to the members of your family as 'we'. You're in this together?" Half question, half statement.

"Yes," Alyssa said, "I guess we are."

"So you're not the only one facing the situation."

"No."

"You're not alone."

"No, but–"

"But what?"

"I feel alone."

The door to the ramp opened and passengers streamed into the waiting area. First class travelers came first, loaded down with shopping bags, their expensive shoes and linen pantsuits distinguishing them from the masses. Fay and her father should have been among them, but weren't. Then the coach passengers poured out. Children whined and jumped. Alyssa bristled at the sound. She didn't want children, one of the few things she was sure of; she didn't want to take care of anyone smaller, weaker, or more vulnerable than herself. Young women ran past her and threw themselves in the arms of burly men in tank tops—the offensive term was "wife-beater"—appropriate for the gruff, thick males who slapped their women's backsides with proprietary verve. A young couple embraced an elderly man and woman in straw hats—parents, grandparents, great-grandparents—Alyssa couldn't tell. Then she spotted a raised hand.

"Alyssa! Thank God!" It was Fay, glad to see her for once. She sported a large aqua sunhat, matching tunic, and Jackie O sunglasses. Blood red lipstick streaked her mouth. Her siren voice wailed over the buzzing crowd, "Home at last."

Gretchen, very tan, trailed behind her, followed by Pablo, dark circles under his eyes, and the little girls rubbing theirs awake. They all smiled and waved—no hint of animosity. The only person missing from the family tableau was her father.

"Where's Daddy?"

"Right behind us," Fay said with her usual bravura.

"No he's not," Alyssa shot back, anxiety rising within her. She kept her eyes on the trickling flow of passengers. "Don't you think one of you should go back and check on him?" They all turned towards the opening, but no one moved to reenter. More travelers passed them. Still no little old man. No Daddy.

"I'll go," Sabine said. The little girl volunteered with an enthusiasm Alyssa would have found touching, if she weren't so worried.

"You'll do no such thing," her mother said, and grabbed the child's upper arm. "You'll stay right here." Sabine made a face, and wriggled out of Gretchen's grip and over to her father.

An attendant ran up to Fay. "Your husband. He must have tripped in the aisle. They're getting a wheelchair for him now. He'll be out any minute."

A wheelchair. My God. Alyssa felt short of breath, on the verge of a panic attack. "One of you needs to go back into the plane," she said. "I can't. I wasn't a passenger." She said this out loud to stop her legs, their muscles contracted, ready to sprint up the ramp.

"Don't worry, dear. Let the professionals handle it," Fay said.

Alyssa's insides churned. "They're stewardesses, not doctors," she blurted and tried to slow her breathing. She knew she was letting this woman get to her.

"Neither are we," Fay said. Alyssa thought she caught a smirk between Fay and her daughter.

Alyssa positioned herself between Fay and the exiting passengers. She had to be the first to greet her father. "I have a private ambulance standing by to take him straight to the hospital."

"That won't be necessary. Rest is all he needs." Alyssa had whiplash from Fay's changing signals. First, an emergency wee hours phone call, now, minimizing her father's condition.

She would have to stand firm. "I insist."

Fay paused, opened her mouth to reveal crowded pointy teeth, started to speak, and then shrugged.

Alyssa paced in place. If her father didn't appear in one minute she would charge the plane, rules be damned. Then there he was, an ashen figure wheeled down the ramp by a male flight attendant. "Daddy!" Alyssa wanted to run, but she didn't want to alarm him, and besides, she wasn't Cara or Sabine's age. She wasn't a little girl anymore, even if she felt like one. She admonished herself to act her age. Her father needed her now, an old maid whose sole purpose was to take care of her elderly parent. Would that make her mature? Alyssa had no idea. And there wasn't time to figure it out. She'd just have to fake it, pretend she was a grown-up.

"Fay! Fay!" Alvin's voice was hollow and breathy. His whole body trembled.

"Daddy," Alyssa repeated. She wasn't sure he'd seen her.

"Oh," Alvin said, searching her facing. Did he recognize her? "Hello Alyssa. You're here."

"Yes, Daddy."

He looked at each of them and said, "Old age is not for the faint of heart."

"Always the philosopher," Fay chimed.

"Fay?" He squinted like he was studying an insect under a microscope.

"Right here, darling. Waiting for you." Alyssa noted that Fay didn't move closer to the wheelchair.

"Daddy, I'm going to take care of you."

"About time," Gretchen muttered. Alyssa took this in, but refused to overtly acknowledge the slight. She motioned the attendant to leave and started to wheel her father down the long hall.

"The flight was the worst I've ever experienced," he moaned. Alyssa couldn't remember that last time she had heard her father complain.

She patted his shoulder and kept pushing the chair along. "We're going to get you checked out, Daddy."

"Lorraine? Ken?"

"They'll be here. We're all going help you together." She said the words she'd discovered in Terry's office. She hoped saying them out loud to her father would make them true.

"Good. That's good," he said. Then he sighed and deflated into the wheelchair, like a puppet from which a hand had just withdrawn.

When Alyssa reached the elevator to ground transportation, she turned around. She expected Fay and her brood to be right behind them. Instead, a family of six stared back at her, the parents' eyes blank with exhaustion. They crowded into the elevator together. Alyssa counted to stave off the claustrophobia: 3, 6, 9, 12. The elevator doors opened. Alyssa saw the blue and white ambulance parked outside and sighed with relief. As the ambulance attendants loaded her father into the van she confirmed the destination, "Georgetown University Medical Center." She took one more backward glance. No Fay. No family. They had vanished like a mirage.

"Alyssa?"

She sat next to him and picked up his cool weightless hand. "Right here, Daddy."

"Take me home."

12

"Who's the President of the United States?" Doctor Cabot asked Dad.

Ken surmised that the doctor, a sixtyish man whose white hair neatly framed reddish skin, was Irish. Certainly not Jewish. His father had never been under the care of a Gentile doctor before. An odd choice for Fay to make; she was usually so cognizant of ethnic distinctions. The young woman who accompanied Dr. Cabot introduced herself, Dr. Snelling from neurology. She peered intently at his father and, after the introduction, ignored Ken, which was just as well. He couldn't seem to calm his stump, and was trying to knead it without calling attention. What he wanted was a hot bath, and a rubdown. Ken shook his head, disgusted with himself. His father was in the hospital and he was thinking about a massage.

The phantom pains and real muscle spasms happened whenever Ken entered a hospital. The anxiety he'd experienced when Josh was born had been so severe that the second time around he lobbied Priscilla for a home birth. His free-spirited wife, usually amenable to such back-to-basics thinking, looked at him like he'd lost his mind. Then she got it. "Oh! Of course," she said, embracing him, her bulging middle pressed against his hip. "You'll be fine." But he wasn't. The day of Stella's debut he resurrected his cane, hobbled into the waiting room to give Priscilla's parents the happy news, still unable to stop the darts running up and down his thigh.

Dad searched Dr. Cabot's face. It was almost five, not his father's best time of day. The hazy summer sky filtered through the room's smudged windows. His father squinted. Did he remember the doctor, let alone the current commander-in-chief? He turned to Ken. For a moment Ken wondered if his father recognized him either.

"Kenny, Kenny." A plaintive incantation. A request for help. Ken wanted to remind him of their heated debate, over the phone, long distance, about Oval Office indiscretions. Though a lifelong Democrat, his father was not inclined to excuse the President's affair, and thought he should step down. Ken was more forgiving. But now he kept silent. No coaching allowed.

"What city are we in?" the doctor asked.

"Washington."

"Yes. And do you know where you are now?"

Again, his father surveyed Ken's face, as if the answer might be written on his forehead. Dad shook his head.

"Georgetown University Medical Center," the doctor supplied. Dad nodded.

"One more question Mr. Segal." His father sighed. "What is today's date?"

Ken watched him bite his lip and squeeze his eyes shut. "It's summer. June or July."

"Yes. Friday, June 2nd."

"Oh." Dad hung his head, ashamed not to know such basic information. Ken could hardly bear it.

Then Dr. Snelling handed him a piece of blank paper and a pencil. "Mr. Segal? Would you please draw a circle for me?" Dad proceeded to scrawl long jagged lines resembling an EKG. The young resident took the paper, touched his father's hand and said, "Thank you."

Dr. Cabot jotted notes on his father's chart and flipped through the folder's pages.

"Is Mrs. Segal here?"

"No. But you can speak to me," Ken said. The medical proxy hadn't been signed yet, but he had to take charge.

The Doctor shifted uncomfortably. He glanced down the hall, as if Fay might appear at any moment. "Well then. The preliminary test results indicate Parkinsonism which may account for the sundowning, halting speech pattern, hand-eye dis-coordination, and tremors."

"Parkinsonism?"

"Parkinson-like symptoms brought on by a series of TIA's–"

"Transient ischemic attacks, small strokes." Ken needed to let this doctor know he was up on the medical terminology.

"Yes. The ones he had in the past few months seem to have resulted in end of day confusion and body tremors."

"What's the treatment?"

"L Dopa. Same as for Parkinson's. We'll put him on it immediately. If he responds, we'll know the diagnosis is correct."

"If not?" Ken didn't want the answer.

"His dementia will continue."

The drug had a near miraculous effect. The next morning Dad was up early, hungry and talkative. Ken was exhausted, but relieved. He had spent the night on a cot by the bed.

"Oatmeal. I want oatmeal," his father demanded, no sign of hesitation in his speech. "And a newspaper, *The Post*."

"I think that *is* oatmeal, Daddy," Lorraine said. "I'll go get the paper for you."

Anything to escape the room, away from Ally, who was leaning against the doorframe—her favorite spot for a quick exit. Lorraine didn't acknowledge her sister as she left. Ally looked at the floor.

"Everything okay with you two," Ken asked.

Ally shrugged.

By the time Lorraine returned, Dad had answered the morning residents' questions, substituting a doctor's, "You are a lawyer" with, "Was. I'm retired." Ken thrilled to his father's familiar precision. Then he watched Dad demonstrate his physical improvement with firm steady steps to the bathroom, all signs of the previous shuffle gone. When Ally asked one of the doctors if their father could come home soon, Ken assumed she meant to her house, not Fay's. The doctor said Dad would need rehab for his coordination, a couple of weeks, tops.

"Lazarus returns," Dad quipped.

Lorraine dropped the newspaper on the bed, and kissed the top of his head. "Glad to hear it." Then she motioned Ken and Ally to follow her into the hall. "Be right back, Daddy." Lorraine took a big breath. Ken held his. "I just overheard Fay talking to Dr. Cabot. She was lobbying to have Daddy declared incompetent."

Alyssa gasped. Ken marveled at Fay's warp speed change of tactic. Only yesterday she and that lizard lawyer of hers had left in a huff when Ken refused to let them near Dad with papers that were surely meant to reverse the stop order. Boy was she pissed that she couldn't get his presumably competent signature. Today she was ready to declare him a vegetable. Well, it wouldn't work. "Let's not overreact," Ken said. "He's a long way from incompetent. The medication is working."

"I know, but I just don't trust her," Lorraine went on.

"Me neither," Ally said. "What if she takes him off the stuff?"

Now his sisters were in sync, backing each other up. But Ken would have to tamp down the paranoia before it got out of control. "Fay can't do that. Not in the hospital at any rate."

Ally refused his reassurance. "He can't ever go home with her. Not ever again." Then she tugged Ken's sleeve like she was five. "Shh! They're coming."

They all turned. Fay hung on Dr. Cabot's arm at the far end of the hallway. The doctor saw them and extricated himself from her grasp. Ken motioned his sisters back into their father's room. They positioned themselves around his bed like sentries.

"Alvin darling, you look sooo much better!" Fay pecked his cheek. Dad did not put down the paper. "And catching up on the news. Back to your old self! That's wonderful."

Dad didn't answer. He tilted his head towards her. "Where were you last night?" he asked.

"Why right here, dear, into the evening, until I had to get some sleep. Can't very well take care of you if I don't take care of myself."

"You left at four, Fay, long before evening," Ken said. It was a pleasure to call her on her bullshit.

"Four *is* evening. Why in Florida everyone eats dinner at five! You forget how old I am, Kenneth," Fay tittered, as if she'd made a joke. It was true her advanced age had thrown him off at first, but now that he was onto her, Ken found her scheming all the more despicable.

"How are you this morning, Mr. Segal?" Dr. Cabot asked.

"Fine."

"Good. May I ask you some questions?"

"I've already answered all the questions I'm going to answer this morning. For the other doctors." It was great to see Dad stand up for himself.

"I see." Dr. Cabot looked at the chart and nodded. "I'll come back later when you feel more like talking."

"And–" Fay prompted.

"No visitors besides family."

Ken had scheduled Todd Grayson for eleven. He couldn't keep putting him off. Documents had to be signed. "Why not? My father's doing well. It would be good for him to have visitors."

Cabot looked at Dad, who was still perusing the news. "Perhaps one at a time."

"Thank you, Doctor." Ken was glad to see that Fay didn't have this physician in her pocket on every point of contention.

Fay, bristled at the doctor's rebuff, then moved around the bed to the IV attached to her husband. "What's this for?"

"Mr. Segal's sodium level was low when he was admitted."

"Oh, I have just the solution." Fay pulled a plastic grocery bag out of her satchel.

"You can remove this contraption." She flicked the drip pouch so it swayed like a flag. "All he needs is a V8!" Inside her bag was a six-pack. She pulled a can out of the plastic loops and handed it to Dad.

Dr. Cabot frowned. "If that were enough, he wouldn't need the IV."

Fay ignored what she didn't want to hear. "Or salt pills! I have plenty," she said, riffling through her purse. "Don't worry dear," Fay continued. "I'm not going to let them overmedicate you." Ken suppressed an urge to shut her up.

"Let us do our job, Mrs. Segal. Your husband needs the sodium drip." The doctor nodded to Ken, brushed by his sisters, and left.

Ken exchanged glances with Lorraine and Alyssa. Ally studied her shoes and Lorraine stared out the window. Their silence seemed a conscious attempt at self-control. Or was it simply that the absurdity of what just transpired had left them speechless? V8? This would have been a hoot, if it weren't so horrifying. Ken wondered if it was too late for a restraining order. Ally had been right all along. Dad could never be alone with this woman again.

"Kenneth, Lorraine, may I speak to you for a moment?" Fay pointedly excluded Alyssa, who seemed relieved not to have to deal with her. Ken followed into the hallway, and thought about the strange reversal that took place in hospitals. The patient's room was public space, a way station for family, friends, colleagues, and medical staff to gather, make small talk, drop bombshells, and leave before the full extent of the destruction was clear. The halls were private conference rooms where truths, pain, and strategies collided in all their untidy glory.

"I won't have your father in my house if he can't walk stairs, or go to the bathroom alone. I won't turn my living room into a hospital. I don't trust health care workers. And you can forget about our renting an apartment. I'm not leaving my house unless Alyssa is willing to let both of us back into hers." Fay blurted all this in one breath. While she ranted, Ken noted that her black eyes widened behind her magnifying lenses and took over her face. When she stopped speaking, they went dead, like someone had flipped the off switch.

Lorraine gave Ken a tiny signal. She shifted her weight onto the foot closest to Fay. Ken was glad to let his big sister take over. He disliked confrontation. "Fay, no one said anything about turning *your* home into a hospital. Dad still has a way to go before he's out of the woods. He'll be here for a couple more days and then he needs to stay in a rehab facility for at least a few weeks. We have time to work out *where* he'll go after that." Lorraine waited for Fay to absorb this.

"Fine. So long as you children understand my position."

"Oh, don't worry. We understand perfectly." Lorraine moved away from Fay. Ken turned to go back into the room.

Fay wriggled her torso. She seemed unsatisfied by Lorraine's quick agreement. She raised her voice. "And another thing–"

"What?" Lorraine hissed, glancing over her shoulder at Dad's bed, but Fay refused to be shushed.

"You should know that I'm still mad about what happened last month. My lawyer, Izso Small–" Fay intoned his name as if Ken and his sisters should quake at its mention, "–is a wild dog. You can't bar us from Alvin's room, Kenneth." Fay's saliva sprayed Ken's face. It was all he could do not to wipe it off. "Small has papers for Alvin to sign and your maneuvers won't stop him. And he wants to fight for *everything*. Don't think he won't!"

Ken looked at Lorraine. Fay was going after the house. Alyssa would have a fit. Worse still, the woman talked as if their father were already dead. Ken summoned his most commanding voice. "This is neither the time nor the place, Fay. Our only concern now should be Dad's health." Ken bristled at his own hypocrisy. He, too, was concerned with legal documents. He, too, wanted to maintain control. Grayson would be there in an hour. Ken told himself that this was necessary, to protect Dad, but he knew his own motivations were not so pure or simple. He was also protecting himself. They all were. Just like Fay.

Then in a sudden switch Fay simpered, "Of course, an *apology* would go a long way towards holding him off." Lorraine's mouth tightened, a sure sign she was furious. Ken wanted to take Fay by the shoulders, push her down the hall and out of the building.

"We'll talk," Lorraine said and darted into their father's room, leaving Fay to stare at Ken. He had nothing more to say to her. She was no longer a person to him. Her threats had turned her from his father's companionable partner into an obstacle to his well-being. And theirs.

Lorraine had spent herself on the hallway confrontation and Ken encouraged her to go out to dinner with Ally, "Fill her in." Lorraine rolled her eyes, but did as he asked.

He wanted to handle the legal stuff himself, even with Fay in the room. Ken had decided to proceed with the Grayson meeting, and risk her wrath. It was important that she witness Dad's continued mental competence.

As soon as the lawyer arrived, Fay harangued that Dad wasn't "capable of knowing what he was signing," Grayson looked her up and down, asked Dad what he wanted to do. He said nothing, struck dumb by the sheer force of his wife's opposition.

Grayson picked up his briefcase and walked Ken to the door. "Don't worry," he said, "This was useful. She's obstructing your father's conversations with his attorney. Very revealing behavior."

Ken felt stomach acid rise to his throat. "But Todd, we did the same thing to her and her lawyer." He had a hard time addressing this man as a peer, though they were more or less the same age.

"And that's good. You don't want them to undo your father's intentions. I'll be back soon. When the time is right we'll handle the rest of the paperwork. Alvin needs to recuperate. Trust me. I've seen cases like this before. It will all work out." Grayson's words alarmed Ken. So now this was a *case*?

After Grayson left, Fay kissed Dad on the cheek, gathered her things—shopping bags in various sizes and shapes—and swished past Ken. She thinks she's still calling the shots. When they were alone, his father lay back against the pillow, eyes closed. Ken smoothed the wispy gray hair over his father's shiny pate. "I'm going now, Dad. I'll be back tomorrow."

Eyes still shut, his father said, "She's up to something, isn't she?"

Ken patted his father's veined hand. "Nothing for you to worry about. Everything will be fine."

Dad opened his right eye and focused it on his only son. "We'll see, Kenny. We'll see."

13

Lorraine slid her tray down the stainless steel railings of the hospital cafeteria. A few feet ahead of her, Alyssa stood behind a group of doctors in the cashier line. It was early evening. The vast space—more mess hall than restaurant—filled with physicians in white lab coats, nurses in flowered jackets, and orderlies in green and blue scrubs. To Lorraine the entire hospital was a war zone: the medical staff, the military, and the patients, innocent casualties. Their relatives—she and her siblings among them—were bewildered refugees wrenched from familiar soil onto an alien minefield of potential demise. Lorraine searched the faces for camaraderie. Were they shell-shocked? Numb with grief? Stoic or about to fall apart? She couldn't tell. No one made eye contact. No one *expressed* anything. She imagined each one suspended within a personal interior hell.

Lorraine dreaded being alone with Alyssa. This meal would be the first time since the weekend in her sister's house. After she saw how Alyssa lived, Lorraine thought it best to stay at the Holiday Inn. But this dinner seemed to mean a lot to Ken, who had practically shoved them out of their father's room—the same way he used to shove them out of his own room when she and her sister would pile on his bed to listen to the latest Bob Dylan record. He allowed them one song and then out. Sometimes she'd linger, ear to his door. Little Ally would tug her away. Ally had been afraid of their brother's anger, of getting into trouble with Mother and Daddy. She was still afraid. Lorraine resolved to try with her sister, but had qualms of her own. She didn't think she could handle another rejection.

Alyssa paid for her food—a spinach salad and some chocolate pudding. Not much after a long day. Lorraine understood. None of the choices in the lighted shelves looked appealing: the sandwiches sealed in cellophane, the over-cooked pasta, the Styrofoam meringues. Even her sweet tooth had gone underground, dormant in the presence of this food museum of the theoretically consumable. Her hollow stomach groaned. Her body was hungry and she had to feed it. Lorraine took a tuna salad sandwich, a banana, and filled a large disposable cup with lemonade. Then she followed her sister to a corner table. Alyssa was totally focused on her plate, stuffing one plastic forkful after another into her open mouth.

"How is it?" Lorraine asked. She put her own tray to the side, placed the sandwich before her, and began to unwrap it. The filling—more mayo than tuna—oozed out of the bread and onto her fingers. She wiped her fingers on the paper napkin, but the smell stayed.

Alyssa wrinkled her nose. "Okay, I guess," she said, and then sighed.

Lorraine waited for more but Ally said nothing. "What is it?"

Ally cast her eyes to the fluorescent ceiling. "What are we going to do?"

Lorraine wondered whether she was asking her or some higher power. "What do you mean?"

"About Dad?" Ally looked at her for the first time that day.

Lorraine put down her sandwich and ran her tongue over her teeth, wiping off the fishy glaze. She wanted to reach across the table and take her sister's hand, but couldn't. "We're going to take care of him," she said.

"You mean *I'm* going to take care of him." In a flash Alyssa's eyes went cold. "Because I'm the one who lives here, I'm always the one."

Lorraine absorbed this unfair reference to their mother's last illness without flinching. She had spent long weekends at her mother's bedside, but the stakes were too high now to risk trying to correct her sister's faulty memory. "I know you feel that way–"

Alyssa bristled. "Because it *is* that way!" Lorraine knew she was, at least in part, right. She did live here. Her house was still Dad's, if he needed it. Alyssa was under the most pressure. How could she tell her sister about Fay's latest threat? It would send her on another rampage. But to say nothing was withholding, and there had been enough withheld between them over the years. Best to get it over with.

"Fay said something today."

Ally snapped to attention. "What? What did she say?"

"That she couldn't take care of Dad in her house."

"Meaning what exactly?" Lorraine leaned in, about to form the answer when Alyssa slapped the table. "Oh my God, she wants *my* house, doesn't she?"

Lorraine nodded. "She *implied* that she and Daddy could move in with you."

"Over my dead body." The couple at the next table glanced at Alyssa and then hunched over their food.

"We won't let that happen. Anyway, I'm pretty sure she's bluffing."

Ally didn't seem to hear this. "What am I going to do?"

"Ken and I are here now. We're going to help Daddy, and you."

Alyssa put her purse over her shoulder and brushed the hair off her forehead. Lorraine noticed the graying roots and felt foolish continually picturing Alyssa as the baby. "How? You have your *lives*."

"We'll figure something out." Lorraine knew her response was inadequate.

"I'm tired. I have to think." Alyssa stood and pushed her chair back. "I'm going home." Lorraine watched her dump the remains of her dinner into the designated garbage slot, then tap the tray three times and place it on a stack of other empty ones. Ally's shoulders slouched. She hesitated before disappearing through the swinging doors. Lorraine wanted her to come back to the table, talk it out. Why did Alyssa retreat into herself? Why couldn't she share her turmoil? Lorraine would understand. Brad often accused Lorraine of projecting her feelings onto others, of assuming that their reactions matched hers. But this was her sister, the same DNA. Of course she projected. She preferred projection to the helplessness that welled within her in the face of her sister's impenetrable mystery.

Brightview Rehabilitation Center overlooked the highway on an artificial rise surrounded by immature cherry trees. A winding driveway linked the road to the front *Welcome* entrance, and to a *For Ambulances Only* side entrance—the one Dad had entered five days before. The main building seemed to Lorraine like a country inn, with its high-backed chairs upholstered in navy and cream brocade, except for the uniformed attendants in their white shoes and cheery smocks. Brightview was both state-of-the-art rehab facility with hotel-like suites, sunny sitting rooms, and wide art-lined halls, and a full-time nursing home, whose pine-scented hallways masked the ever-present odor of urine, and rang with the sound of moaning, half-conscious residents who could never leave.

Since the rehab wing was not yet open for business, Daddy was first installed in the nursing section. Lorraine had read about such places and knew this was a good one, but still, the surroundings shocked her. She paced the stale halls with Ken and Ally and tried to focus on her father's care, but couldn't concentrate with the atmosphere so rank, so depressing.

When her father moved into the new wing Lorraine was relieved that it was clean and the assumed stay temporary. He'd be here until he got better. And then…? Her conversation with Ally at the hospital made it clear that Alyssa felt trapped into taking charge of their father. And with Fay breathing down their backs about the house, it seemed less and less wise to take him back to Essex Street. They didn't have to decide yet, Lorraine told herself, before she entered her father's room. Daddy sat next to the window, staring down at the plaid blanket covering his legs.

Lorraine forced a smile. "How are you today, Daddy?"

"I can't find my glasses," he said.

"Oh, I'm sure they're here somewhere," she said and glanced around the room for the errant case. "Here they are." She pulled the large trifocals out from under the bedside table and handed them to her father.

"Thank you," he said, putting on the glasses. "Lorraine?"

"Yes, Daddy."

"When can I leave? I hate this place."

"Soon, Daddy. I know this is difficult, but it's so much better than the other room and you're getting stronger each day. Then you'll be out of here."

He shook his head. "But where? Where will I go?"

"What do you mean, Daddy?" Could Ken have told him? Or Fay herself?

"I can't go back to her. I trusted her, and she double-crossed me. How could she?" Her father removed the glasses and wept.

"It'll be all right, Daddy," Lorraine said, though she wasn't sure it would be. He didn't want to go back to Fay and she didn't want him—the extent of their agreement. When she finds out that he'd signed a new medical proxy naming Alyssa and Ken, and a co-trusteeship designating Ken, she would go through the roof. The fallout worried Lorraine, and the fact that once again she was left out of any official duty in relation to her father's care. Didn't anyone trust her? She was the oldest. She should have a role.

Lorraine watched her father sink into bewilderment. "But she was so happy when I gave her the money! How could she do this?" Tears rolled down his sagging cheeks, onto the pilled gray sweater he wore every day, even in summer.

Lorraine took his hand between hers and kissed his fingertips. All she could do was offer some distraction. She opened her purse and took out the day's newspaper. "Would you like me to read to you, Daddy? I brought *The Post*. There's an article on Harlan Fineman."

At the mention of his old friend her father straightened. "Oh yes. Please. You know, Lorraine, Harlan's the greatest lawyer in the land." He grinned when he spoke Harlan's name, the biggest grin she'd seen in weeks.

Brad handed her the phone. He'd just stepped out of the shower, and was dripping all over their bedroom carpet. Lorraine took the receiver. What now? It was almost midnight. Lorraine had taken the last train home to New Jersey and all she wanted to do was soak in a hot bath and go to sleep.

"I can't do it." Lorraine could hear her sister's shallow breathing through the receiver.

"What do you mean you can't do it?"

"I just can't. It's not going to work here."

"What? What's not going to work?"

Ally paused. "Daddy. Here. My job." Then she exploded. "You've got to do this. You've got to."

"Calm down, Alyssa. Got to do what?" Lorraine felt an inexorable pressure closing in.

"Who's that?" Brad asked.

Lorraine mouthed, *Al-y-ssa*. Brad's eyebrows jumped. He grabbed a pair of striped pajama bottoms, and went back into the bathroom.

"Don't tell me to calm down! You don't know what it would be like. I know you think this is what I'm here for, that I don't have a life, but with him I'll never have one. There's no place to put him. The study is too cold, the upstairs hallway too narrow for a walker, and I can't allow that awful woman in my house. I just can't." Alyssa was gasping for air.

Her rant chilled Lorraine. "What are you asking me?"

"Take him. You've got to take Daddy." There it was.

"Of course. Of course I'll take him." Lorraine marveled at her lack of hesitation. She hadn't even stopped to think.

Dr. Upala, Dad's rehab physician, had suggested the very same thing just days ago. "His wife said she can't care for him and your sister's a bit high-strung," she told Lorraine in her lilting Indian accent. "Your father needs a calm environment to heal and someone strong to oversee his recovery." Lorraine had been flattered that an outsider saw her as she would like to be seen: the mature competent one. She nodded at the doctor's hypothetical solution, and refrained from explaining why she wasn't part of the plan. Until now. In the face of Alyssa's domestic inadequacy, Lorraine would make the save. Not ask questions. She wouldn't mention Alyssa's deal: house forever, Dad home whenever he wanted or needed. What would be the point? The deal, the trade-off, was bogus, because its premise was false. It presupposed that Alyssa could handle her part of the bargain. Daddy had been deluded regarding his youngest. Alyssa wasn't cut out for caretaking. Even the doctor had seen that. But with Fay lying in wait for the house, Lorraine couldn't blame her sister for running.

"You will?" Alyssa's voice shrank down to little girl size. Brad came out of the bathroom. He must have overheard. He glared at Lorraine in disbelief.

"Dad has to agree, of course," Lorraine said, as if that might postpone the inevitable. She knew her father would say yes to anything she suggested.

"What about Fay?" It wasn't enough that Lorraine had just agreed to sign her life away, Alyssa had to worry the thing to death.

"Fay?" Brad emerged again from the bathroom and drew his finger across his throat. "Well, she won't be living with me."

Alyssa sighed. "Thank you, Lorraine. Thank you."

Lorraine's head throbbed. She hated car trips and the combination of a sleepless week and the long dull stretches of turnpike rendered her woozy with despair. At least Brad liked to drive, so she could indulge in her stupor from the passenger seat. Jamie sat in the back spotting license plates.

"Ohio," he called, then added the state to his list.

"That truck has multiples," Brad said, indicating a huge semi passing them on the left.

"New Hampshire, Delaware, Maryland!"

Lorraine sank further into herself. She usually enjoyed the timelessness of their travel games—Jamie became less adolescent and more little boy. She usually played along, but today she couldn't bring herself to participate. She had been on the phone all week with home health aides, medical suppliers, and friends, doing her best to prepare her home and herself for her father. The house was the easy part: a bed, railings, improved lighting, no scatter rugs. She was the problem. The pressure that had been building since Alyssa's request would have been unbearable were it not for the image of her father's trusting face that she kept before her. He needed her and she could not fail him. So here she was, on the way down to Maryland, to rescue her father from the clutches of a mercenary woman and from her sister's panic. Lorraine swallowed hard. No matter how she justified the necessity of her actions, rage, frustration, and fear churned within her. She pulled her sweater over her shoulders and folded her arms.

"Cold?" Brad asked.

Lorraine shook her head.

"You okay?"

Lorraine nodded. "Thank you for doing this. I owe you," she said.

"It's kind of fitting really–on Father's Day."

"Is there a grandfather's day?" Jamie asked.

"Don't think so, Bug," Brad said.

"There should be!"

"Damn right."

Lorraine hugged herself harder. Every day from now on was going to be grandfather's day.

"What's wrong, Mom?"

Lorraine's eyes blurred. The highway's speeding hues ran together like her mother's watercolors. Her cheeks were damp.

"Lor? Are you sick? Do you want me to pull over?"

Lorraine shook her head in a motion so violent it wrenched her neck. She rested her head against the glass and tried to close her eyes, but they were too wet for her lids to shut. She closed her mouth and bit the inside of her cheek. Then she swallowed the sickening sweet taste of her own blood. Lorraine heard herself moan.

"Mom, Mom what's wrong? Why are you crying?"

Brad reached over and patted her left thigh.

Lorraine keened, rocking back and forth. She strained against the seatbelt, without which she would have gone through the windshield. The sound escaping from her mouth vibrated through her whole body.

"Hon–"

"Mom!"

Her throat opened and a wail filled the car. It silenced her men, and shrank the universe down to one humiliating truth: she was no more adequate to the task at hand than Alyssa.

14

The man on Alvin's left held his hand. It felt warm and familiar. His blurry face leaned over to repeat what the lady doctor had just said. "Who's this, Dad?"

Dad? "Oh *Kenny*, boychick!" Alvin wished he could see his son. "Where are my glasses?"

"We'll find them, Dad."

"Mr. Segal, who is this?" The lady doctor—Alvin couldn't remember her name—pointed to a younger woman next to her.

A young woman, dark eyes, round face, like his mother. "Alyssa?"

"Yes, Daddy, it's me." His daughter. He had more than one.

"Good, Mr. Segal. And who is this?" The doctor moved to the other side of Alyssa, to an older woman with a hat on her head.

Alvin hesitated. "My other daughter."

"Lorraine's not here yet, Daddy," Alyssa said and handed Alvin his glasses. He put them on and peered at the assemblage surrounding his bed. Three woman—one with a white coat, two on either side of her, one older, one younger, Alyssa—and Kenny.

"Mr. Segal–this lady, who is she?" The doctor stepped closer to the older woman. The woman clasped and unclasped her hands. Alvin knew her, and yet did not know her name. It lingered around his mind's periphery, like a dream image elusive after waking.

"My other daughter," he said and sighed. The women and Ken each echoed his sigh. He had gotten it wrong. Alvin was mortified. He had disappointed them.

"He's worse," the older woman said. "I won't bring him home in this condition." Home. Whose home? Alvin looked at the blank blue walls. This room was not home.

"He's not quite ready to leave," the lady doctor said. "I think the confusion is from improperly administered medication. He should be taking it on an empty stomach, otherwise, it's ineffective. That's why he's sundowning." Sundowning? Alvin pictured himself on the porch in Puerto Rico watching the sun set over the ocean.

"And what about the catheter?" the older woman asked. "It has to be removed."

The doctor stopped and turned to her. "But Mrs. Segal–" Mrs. Segal? Mother?

Estelle? No. "Mrs. Segal. He's incontinent," the doctor said. Why were Ken and Alyssa looking out the window?

"He's incontinent because of the catheter. I insist that you have it removed!" The older woman's voice got higher and louder.

"No, Mrs. Segal. He's incontinent, period. I'll look in on him tomorrow morning, to check on the medication adjustment." The doctor left.

The older woman picked up her purse and moved to the door. Ken and Alyssa did not turn around. They don't like her. Alvin could tell. She put her hand to her mouth and blew across it. "Bye, sweetheart. See you tomorrow. Don't worry. I'll get you out of here." When she was gone, his children sat on the edge of his bed. Alyssa patted Alvin's leg. Ken rubbed his thigh. Ken shouldn't stand so long.

"That woman?" Alvin asked, not sure he wanted to know.

"Don't you worry about her," Alyssa said. "She's not taking you anywhere."

"But she's my, my–" Alvin lay back against the pillow, exhausted.

"It's okay, Dad. Rest now." Ken kissed his forehead and Alyssa pulled the covers up over his waist. He didn't have the energy to tell her he was too hot.

After they left, Alvin forgot his fatigue and pushed off the blanket. He swung his legs over the side of the bed. His pants were wet—no matter—the cartoon bubble with the answer to his question had risen to the surface. His bare feet hit the carpeted floor. *Wife.*

"Happy Father's Day, Papa!" Jamie wrapped his arms around his grandfather and squeezed. Alvin didn't want to let go, but couldn't breathe with his head jammed against the boy's shoulder.

"Thank you," Alvin said, and extricated himself while still clasping Jamie's hand. So big now. Almost a man. He reached for his son-in-law's hand. "Happy Father's Day, Brad. Thank you for coming."

"We're glad to be here, Alvin," Brad said and retreated to the corner to watch the Sunday morning news shows. Was that *Meet the Press*?

"Daddy?" Lorraine knelt by his chair. Her mother's hair and eyes. "Do you remember what we talked about last time I was here?"

Alvin thought for a moment. "Yes, I do."

"About coming to live with us?"

"In New Jersey." Confirming this aloud made Alvin sad. He had spent most of his life in Washington, and didn't want to leave. But it seemed that the choice had been made for him. Maybe Lorraine knew best. He would have to trust her. After all, he couldn't very well trust Fay—not ever again.

"Yes, we've got a room ready for you and have arranged everything you'll need. The doctor said you could probably leave in a couple of days." Lorraine was talking about her home. Alvin realized he didn't have a home of his own anymore. His wife wasn't acting like a wife. And for some reason, Alyssa wasn't going to bring him back to Essex Street. Perhaps that was for the best. Alvin didn't think he could live in that house without Estelle.

"We put a radio and a TV in there for you," Jamie said, with such enthusiasm that Alvin wanted to cry. Don't. It would upset them.

"Here. This is for you." Jamie handed him an envelope. Inside was a handmade card with a picture of a family: mother, father, and boy standing in front of a house. Their arms were open, as if they were about to burst into song. In the front window was a face—no hair, large glasses, big smile—Alvin recognized himself. Above the house it said, "Welcome home, Papa. We're glad you're here." Inside it said, "Happy Father's Day!"

"Oh, Daddy," Lorraine said, dabbing his cheek with a tissue. Alvin bit his lip. He hadn't been able to control himself. So this was how it would be now: uncontrollable leaking from one end or the other.

Alvin turned off the television set and pushed the roller cart of unappetizing dinner food away from his chair. He stood up on the third try and walked to the window. It felt late, but the sun still shone, blinding him. He reminded himself that it was

June; the sun set late. Was it the equinox? No. It was Father's Day. He had never spent a holiday outside his house. He had never been left alone in a strange place before. What kind of Father's Day was this? They showed up. Then they left him here. More like Abandon Their Father Day.

Alvin edged his way from the window to the bathroom. The rough industrial gray carpet made a scratching sound as he shuffled along. He used the narrow passage between the bedroom and the bathroom like railings, pressing his hands one at a time along the walls for support. His children had arranged this private room for him, but Alvin wasn't sure that was a good thing. Company. He wanted company, even the bedridden or wheelchair bound kind he saw on the way to physical therapy. He'd never been much of a talker, but he preferred the possibility of conversation to this enforced solitude.

When he reached the bathroom he seized up with claustrophobia, the constriction of the walls, and his own skin. He couldn't bear the shoes and socks on his feet, or the dampness of his pants. He took them off, and the infantile diaper. He wasn't a child. Alvin removed his plaid cotton shirt and the thin undershirt as well. For a moment, or what he thought was a moment, he stood frozen in the bathroom, surrounded by limp piles of clothing.

When he opened the bathroom door, the room was dark. The shades were still up. Pinpricks of light from the parking lot below splashed the windowpane. It was night. How long had he been inside the bathroom?

Alvin walked out the door and down the hall towards the nurses' station. The closer he got the faster he ran. "Call my wife!" he said.

"Mr. Segal. It's late. You should be in bed." The night nurse had a broad face and smooth black hair. She glowered at him like he was a naughty child. "And where are your clothes?"

"I want to go home. Now!" he said.

"Calm down, Mr. Segal. We're going to help you." But she didn't. Instead, she pressed a buzzer next to the telephone on her desk.

"I have a right to speak to my wife," Alvin said.

"Yes, you do," the nurse said, "but first we need to get you back to your room."

"NO!" Alvin ran around the cubicle wall and picked up the first telephone he could find. He started to dial. An orderly appeared, a heavy-set man twice as large as Alvin. A bouncer. The nurse and the orderly exchanged glances.

"Mr. Segal," the orderly said. "Let me help you back to your room." Then he placed fingers as long as Alvin's entire arm, on him. The man wasn't going to let go. Neither was Alvin. He clung to the receiver. The phone rang and rang.

"Hello?" The reedy voice startled Alvin. He still expected Estelle's rounder tones.

"Fay! Fay, take me home. Please. I can't stand this place anymore."

"Alvin, it's the middle of the night."

"Fay, please. I've had enough. You've got to get me out of here. Tonight."

"I don't see how I can do that, darling. I'll come see you tomorrow. We'll talk about it."

"NO! Now. If you don't come now, they'll take me to New Jersey!"

"New Jersey? I don't know what you're talking about. You must be dreaming, Alvin. Go back to sleep, dear." The receiver went dead.

Alvin slammed the phone into its cradle. The orderly edged him out from behind the desk. Someone, the nurse perhaps, put a blanket over his shoulders. He didn't realize he was cold until the soft acrylic enveloped him. Then he shivered until his teeth clacked. In his room they washed him. It was humiliating. Alvin hated strangers touching his private parts. Another reason he had to get out. But no one listened. They shushed him as they eased his legs into his pajamas and tucked him into bed. But he wouldn't be shushed. "Pack my bags," he said. "I'm leaving tonight."

Fay stared at the phone. Her head ached and her feet were cold. She hadn't been sleeping. First his children bar Izzy from Alvin's room, then they sneak that Grayson fellow in. Upala, that officious rehab doctor, had so enjoyed telling her she didn't have medical power of attorney, all while Alvin hardly knew who he was or where. And now this. New Jersey? My God, they were going to snatch Alvin right out from under her nose. If he went to New Jersey she'd never recover the money. Fay tugged on the string light in her closet and put on her terrycloth robe and lavender plush slippers. Her mouth tasted like tin. She walked into the bathroom, filled a cup with water and drank. The water didn't wash away the metal. How could she have been so stupid? She should never have let the Segals know she didn't want him here. She should have pretended. Like they did.

What now? How was she going to stop them from taking her husband and with him, her due? She would have to act immediately. For once Alvin was right. There was no time to waste. Fay picked up the phone. "Gretchen? Listen to me. Wake Pablo."

Pablo stood at the night nurse's station and hit the call button again. Where the devil were they? He yawned and stretched his arms over his head. He couldn't believe he was doing this, but what choice did he have? He'd lost another bundle at poker and Louis had tanked their latest venture. Gretchen was giving him the cold shoulder in and out of bed. Fay was still the only fallback position. Whatever she wanted he would do, though he was beginning to think she had rocks in her head. How in hell was he going to take Alvin from here? The idea was ridiculous. The minute the Segals got wind of it they would cry kidnapping, sic their lawyer on them and they'd never see a nickel.

"May I help you?" The nurse sidled up to him. Pablo was in no mood to flirt. Besides, she wasn't his type. Too broad, too old.

"I'm Alvin Segal's son-in-law. I'm here to take him home."

"It's two a.m. Mr.–"

"Diaz. I know it's late, but he needs to be with his wife. He called her."

"Yes, I was there. We had to restrain him. He's asleep now. You can discuss his release when the doctor gets here–around ten." She returned to her desk, her back to him.

"I'd like to see him," Pablo said. "Make sure he's okay."

The nurse turned around. "I'm sorry. Mr. Diaz. It's way past visiting hours. You'll have to come back."

Pablo pinned her with a gaze halfway between seduction and command. "I'm not leaving until I see him."

The nurse looked him up and down. Pablo stretched to his full height, towering over her. "All right, but you can't stay long." Pablo followed her swaying hips and heavy legs down the hall to Alvin's room. "Don't wake him," she said. "I'll be back in a few minutes." She left the door ajar.

Pablo put his hand over his nose to temper the putrid mix of urine and ammonia, and moved closer to the bed. Alvin was on his back, his arms at his sides, his wrists tied to the railings in Velcro restraints. His face was relaxed, neutral. How to move him without disturbing him? What if he cried out? What if the nurse came back too soon? Pablo noted the wheelchair in the corner near the window. He unlocked the brakes and rolled it next to the bed. He would have to unhook the IV. He eased the needle from the old man's hand; the vein didn't bleed. Then he removed the wrist straps and lowered the bed railing. Pablo slipped his right arm under Alvin's back, and his left under the legs. It took more effort than he had anticipated. He clenched his teeth. Half his size, but dead weight. As he lifted him, Alvin's head dropped back, jaw open. Still holding him, Pablo put ear to mouth. Nothing. Fucking Christ.

Pablo put Alvin back on the bed, careful to prop his head so that his mouth would close. Then he reattached the restraints, pulled the covers over Alvin's chest, pressed the alarm button on the headboard, and waited.

The nurse ran in. Pablo realized he'd forgotten the IV, but he wouldn't have known how to put it back anyway. The nurse checked Alvin's pulse and called, "Code Blue," into the intercom on the wall. Pablo retreated to the window. A doctor, an orderly, and another nurse barreled in with the crash cart.

"Such bad timing," Pablo muttered, as he watched them try to jumpstart his father-in-law's lifeless body.

PART IV

Orphans, Widow

15

"Come with us, Kenny," Alyssa pleaded.

"Call if you want me to pick you up," Lorraine said. Ken knew his sisters were worried, probably watching him as they drove away. He began to walk faster. It was at least two miles from the hospital to Ally's house. It crossed his mind that Lorraine didn't want to be alone with Alyssa, but he couldn't help that. *He* had to be alone, to think, to sort out what to do next. He didn't know what to feel. This must be shock.

Ken passed the locked stores, illuminated by piercing nightlights and garish neon signs. Suburban Bethesda looked nothing like the quiet village of his childhood. Quaint one-story shops and specialty markets had been replaced by block after block of national chains, high-end boutiques, motor lodges, and the ubiquitous Starbucks. He walked by the shiny exteriors and well-tended curb pots lush with marigolds and geraniums, and longed for the understated comfort of his childhood haunts. Where was the Farmer's Market with its row upon row of local produce, the Five and Dime with the quirky Halloween masks, the Maryland Diner he and his friends took over after school? So much for history. No wonder most of Ken's students had little interest in the past. This country his father had been so proud to call his home had become a giant uni-burb. For all the enticing displays, there wasn't one 24-hour establishment open where Ken could sit. He looked at his watch. 4:40. One hour since he stood in the emergency room of Suburban Hospital, leg aching, and heard the attending doctor say what he and his sisters already knew. "Your father had a heart attack...weakened by infection…died in his sleep."

The words echoed in Ken's head as he trudged past the meaningless, crude, affluent sprawl. His leg had stopped hurting. The pain had merged into the deeper wound at the core of his being. He felt both hollow and full, naked and shrouded, a little boy, an orphan, and a man taking his father's place. With both his parents gone, the magical barrier between him and his own demise had vanished. Unprotected, he pushed on, inhaling the cool summer air and gasoline fumes from the early morning traffic shooting by in the opposite direction.

No. No. The doctor was wrong. Fay did it. Fay killed him. She and her accomplice, her sleazy son-in-law. Ken began to perspire. What was Pablo doing in his father's room so late, well after visiting hours? Should there be an autopsy? Fay flashed before him: in the rehab center directing the removal of his father's IV, salting his food at Passover, breezing into the room loaded down with packages, throwing her outrageous travel plans in their faces. Neglect, abuse, murder by proxy, or by default. Fay wanted him dead, of that Ken was sure, but it didn't mean she killed him. And it didn't mean she didn't.

Ken wiped his brow, larger each year as his hairline receded. Like his father. The minutes ticked by. He trudged on, becoming more and more his father's son, morphing into his skin, carrying on the best qualities, jettisoning the weakest—the ones that had fueled this dreadful predicament.

He pictured Pablo placing a pillow over his father's face, and stumbled over the uneven sidewalk in front of a fur salon. He caught himself. Get a grip. Gorge rose in his throat. If only Lorraine had been able to take Dad to New Jersey sooner.

Ken reached the fire station—twice the size of thirty years ago—its main building still identifiable by the ornate limestone arch that framed the garage doors. Whenever he and his family had visited, Josh loved to stand outside the building with Papa, watch the trucks move in and out, and scream, "Fire truck!" Papa would nod and pat the little boy's head.

Ken wiped his eyes, and swallowed the salt that had reached the corner of his mouth. He turned onto Dorset's main boulevard. The faint hum of the avenue receded. His energy leaked out over the sidewalk forming an invisible trail behind him, leaving him weaker, older. Where was his marathon runner strength now? The pronounced slope of Essex Street's familiar hills strained against his body. Almost there.

Maybe it was the beam of the lone light at Alyssa's door, or the memory of her anguish as they huddled at the payphone to call Lorraine in her hotel room, or the imprint of his father's unlined face on the gurney, or maybe it was his tendency to avoid conflict at any cost, to tough it out, that suddenly pushed the darkest visions of revenge from Ken's consciousness. He carried his doubt and outrage up the front steps and left them there.

When Alyssa opened the door and threw herself into his arms, he said nothing. Inside the house, Ken kept to himself the sickening images of Fay and Pablo, the accusations of criminal conduct. What would be the use? His sisters would freak, and his gut told him there would be no proof. No way to nail the bastards. Not for murder.

Ken followed Ally to the kitchen, past Lorraine, curled up in a blanket on the couch. At least *they* hadn't killed each other. Ally handed him a glass of water. He drank it in one gulp. Then he wrapped his arms around his little sister. He couldn't remember the last time she'd offered no resistance. Still entwined, his chin on her head, Ken thought about what his father would want for himself, for his children: peace, justice.

Yes. There had to be another path. There had to be a civilized solution. He stroked his sister's chestnut locks. He had no answers, though faith and resolve filled his veins with a sweet power, his or his father's, he could not say, but a righteous power nevertheless.

The spongy ground was damp, soaked with last night's thunderstorms. The gray sky, heavy with clouds, hung close. Ken walked up the low rise flanked by his sisters, Priscilla and the children, and Jamie and Brad. Ken had instructed the limousine driver to park as close to the plot as possible. About one hundred yards ahead Ken could see the single row of chairs, the sheltering maple, the makeshift tent covering the gaping earth, the simple pine casket, and next to the hole, a huge mound of dirt. For later.

Only one of the chairs was filled. There, at the end of the row, sat Fay, enveloped in black from wide-brimmed hat to opaque stockings. Gretchen emerged from the gathering under the tree and sat next to her mother, buffering her from their approach. Lorraine flinched. Alyssa pulled closer to Ken, edging out Priscilla who, with characteristic consideration, ceded her rightful place next to her husband to the bereaved sister. As Priscilla dropped behind with the baby, Ken felt his wife's gentle hand on his shoulder. There weren't enough chairs for all of the extended family, so Priscilla remained at his back. He held his breath and settled on the cold metal, a few seats down from Fay. Brad positioned himself behind Lorraine and Jamie, who fumbled with the program of psalms and brushed back bangs falling into his eyes. To avoid Gretchen and Fay on his right, Ken busied himself with Josh next to him on the other side. The boy seemed to sense the solemnity of the occasion, while Ken adjusted his son's blue blazer and clip-on tie, and sat in rigid silence. Such a little man. Alyssa shushed Josh, though he hadn't made a sound. Preemptive correction, signaling nerves.

A dozen others stood behind Priscilla: cousin Reggie, who'd put on considerable weight since the last time Ken had seen him at Mother's funeral, Dad's law partners in expensive suits, hands behind their backs, like Irish step dancers. Ken shook the absurd image from his mind. He was punchy from lack of sleep. Consuelo and her younger sister, both in dark cotton shifts and summer shawls, stood off to the side. A trio of old biddies—Fay's coven in matching beribboned hats—backed her. Their hands pressed her granddaughters' shoulders, as if the girls might float way. Pablo stood next to them. Ken flushed at the sight of him. Pablo murmured something to the crone nearest Sabine, or was it Cara? How could that smirking snake have been the last person to see his father alive?

The rabbi began. Ken repeated the prayers, mouthing Hebrew he didn't understand. He held Lorraine's hand and put his other arm around his son. Alyssa keened. Fay and Gretchen sat in icy silence, without a twitch. They weighted the row like the fat kid holding down one end of a seesaw.

Then Ken stood and faced the assembled mourners. He had been up all night writing and rewriting his eulogy. Since the rabbi—Fay's rabbi—didn't know his father, except from the wedding, it was up to Ken to convey his essence. "My father, Alvin Segal–," he began, unable to control his quivering voice, "–came to this country from Poland, an immigrant with a worthless law degree. He knew no one, not even the ancient uncles who paid his passage. He started over. Sold shoes. Went back to school. Became a lawyer again, this time an American lawyer. While in school he met the love of his life–our mother–the beautiful Estelle." Alyssa sobbed. Jamie hung his head almost to his knees. "He fathered three grateful children." Ken took a deep breath. "After he lost his life partner, he was thankful for the companionship of Fay Cohen."

Fay sniffed into her handkerchief. Gretchen reached for her mother's hand. "Thank God!" one of the biddies boomed. A shudder ran through the group. Heads turned. Feet shifted. Ken was not surprised. Everyone knew about the rift. They all assumed or feared that Ken wouldn't mention his stepmother. Her friend's outburst shouldn't have happened—Fay's rude gaggle, shaming him graveside. Disgraceful. He hated having to speak her name, having to give her any credit. He had struggled with this tricky point, but decided to rise above her level, to give her a minimal, gentlemanly acknowledgment. It's what his father would have wanted, in spite of her wickedness, in spite of her betrayal. Ken had decided that it couldn't be avoided.

Lorraine nodded at Ken to continue. Just get through it, he told himself. "Alvin Segal's fortitude, his discipline, his loving kindness, his courtly Old World grace, his fine intellect brought him all he could have ever wanted. He was the very definition of a civilized human being. You triumphed, Dad. We will always love you. We will always miss you."

When Ken sat again, he was shaking. Lorraine touched his sleeve. Priscilla bent down to kiss his cheek. Stella rubbed her nose on his ear. Josh leaned on his arm. Alyssa bobbed her approval, not taking her eyes from the ground.

The rabbi instructed them each to take a white rose and place it on the coffin, along with a handful of dirt. Gretchen steadied Fay, while she leaned in to drop the last flower. "Farewell, sweetheart," she said, pressing her gloved fingers to her lips and flinging the kiss over the grave in a final grand gesture.

After the last prayer, the rabbi announced the separate shivas, Fay's and theirs. The mourners broke into two groups, warring factions in retreat. Ally rushed to the car. As Ken approached the limo, he saw Pablo linger beside it. Lorraine circled back, trying in vain to avoid him. "I'm sorry for your loss," Pablo said, blocking her withdrawal. Then he pecked her cheek. Brad, who had been talking to their cousin, rushed toward them. Ken inserted himself between his flushed sister and Pablo. The man took a step back. "I'm sorry things are so strained between us," he said, still addressing Lorraine, who recoiled without a word.

"What the–?" Ken wanted to smash that phony solicitude off his face.

"Everything okay here?" Brad asked, and put his arm around Lorraine.

Then Fay, who had hung back with Gretchen, observing the scene, glared at Ken, Brad, and Lorraine, piercing each with a stone cold stare. She turned to Jamie. In practiced fashion, she softened and addressed the adolescent. "Goodbye, James," she said. Ken wondered what her calculation was. Why target the boy?

"Bye Jamie! Bye Jamie!" Two squeaky voices echoed their grandmother. Sabine and Cara, Cara and Sabine. Ken could never keep Fay's grandchildren straight. They worshipped their step-cousin with an innocence that belied Fay's pretense. Jamie answered Fay with a short jerk of his head. Then he flashed a tight smile at the girls. Ken watched the young man negotiate the awkward encounter. Poised, just like his mother, who put her arm around her son and whisked him into the limousine.

Priscilla touched Ken's elbow. Stella gurgled. Josh tugged at his sleeve.

"Bye, baby!" the little girls called. Stella cupped her hand and flapped her fingers in response. It occurred to him that the looming battle pitted grandchildren against grandchildren. If Fay prevailed, her progeny and their children would inherit everything, and Jamie, Josh, and Stella would be left without the bequests their grandfather had intended. He imagined these girls tearing Stella's hair, kicking Jamie's shins, and knocking Josh to the ground.

Ken motioned his family into the car and raised his hand to let the driver know he needed a moment. He straightened his jacket and walked up to Pablo, stopping close enough to force the man to lean back. Ken waited. Pablo tensed every muscle, ready to slam into the invisible electrified wall that separated them. The man wouldn't dare. Not here. Then, loudly enough for Fay and her gaggle to hear, Ken sprayed Pablo with an unmistakable spit-laced warning, "Stay away. All of you. Stay away from my family."

16

Alyssa watched Lorraine sort through the leftovers dotting the dining table Lorraine had forced her to clear. She didn't like moving her things, even for this most obligatory occasion.

"This'll keep for at least a week," Lorraine said.

Alyssa sighed. Her eyes roamed over the half-eaten spread. A disemboweled poached salmon did double duty as beaten-up centerpiece. Assorted cheeses with their purple and orange rinds, along with an oozing brie, surrounded the fish and flanked baskets of broken crackers and rolls—pumpernickel, seedless rye, and sourdough. Didn't anyone eat bread any more? Fruitless stems straddled unattached grapes. Stray olives banked partial bowls of cashews and almonds. A Lazy Susan, fanned with vegetables and dips, anchored the table's far end. Comfort food, a mourners' feast.

Alyssa didn't want any of it. She had no appetite, except for the sweets. The cookie tray on the sideboard was almost empty, but its remaining glazed shortbreads and miniature chocolate chips beckoned. She bit into a petit four and closed her eyes. The mixture of smooth icing, yellow cake layers, and buttercream filling stopped her from sinking further into the black pit this day had become. Her therapist had once noted that darkness was her habit. Blinds closed, a closet full of black outfits. At least today—funeral day—her mood was appropriate.

Alyssa had found the reception suffocating: hands pressing hers, mouths brushing her cheeks, a pat on her shoulder or back, a long soulful look, and worst of all, the swallowing embrace. Alyssa disliked being hugged. She remembered Mother's command issued from her hospital bed, "Hug, girls," as if the order would fix everything. Alyssa had submitted to Lorraine's too tight grip, but couldn't bring herself to hug back.

Everyone who stopped by after the service—Martin, the lawyers from Dad's firm, the secretaries, cousin Reggie, who could be counted on for family mourning, but little else—had murmured condolences in soft somber voices. Even Josh and Stella, had maintained an unnatural quiet in response to the grown-up atmosphere of sad respectful silences, though Stella burbled a little and drooled on the sofa. Alyssa made a mental note to have Consuelo clean it next week. She didn't want to say anything to her now. Consuelo was clearing the kitchen, just as she had done after Mother's funeral. Alyssa wanted her to be a guest today, but Consuelo had insisted.

With her mouth full of sugared solace, Alyssa opened her eyes, looked at her sister, who was busy putting celery and carrot sticks in ziplock bags, and said, "All I want are these." She pointed at the tray of walnut brownies.

"Are you sure?" Why did Lorraine always second-guess her? Why did she assume she didn't know what she wanted?

"Yes," Alyssa said. "There's a homeless shelter on Bradley. Let's take it all there."

"Okay, if you're sure." Lorraine continued packing the sliced roast beef and accompanying sauces: horseradish, country mustard, mayonnaise. "We'll need a box."

Without a word, Alyssa went to the utility closet and retrieved a cardboard box she'd used for extra soaps, batteries, and emergency supplies. Lorraine followed. Alyssa watched her sister focus her widening eyes on the floor to ceiling shelves that held neatly stacked items in groups of three. "What's this? Getting ready for Armageddon?"

Mother was right: Lorraine was such a drama queen. Alyssa shuddered, almost dropping the box. Lorraine blocked the narrow entry. She said nothing more, but in her reticence was all-too-familiar judgment. Alyssa felt a defensive edge creeping into her voice. "I like to be prepared."

Lorraine mouthed a whistle and backed out of the doorway.

"What was that for?" Alyssa followed her back into the dining room.

"What was what for?"

"The whistle."

"I didn't whistle," Lorraine said, opening Tupperware.

"You did, except without sound."

"Ha! Neat trick."

"You don't approve?"

"Of your supply closet? Sure I do. It's a little fin de siècle, but nifty none the less."

Alyssa threw a dirty cocktail napkin at her. "You're mocking me!"

"Oh lighten up."

"What's that supposed to mean?"

"My God, Alyssa, not today. I'm exhausted. You're exhausted. We've got a lot ahead of us." Lorraine moved around the table and handed Alyssa a ginger snap. She popped it in her mouth. The cookie's crisp spiciness had the desired effect.

Alyssa replayed Lorraine's words. "You think it's not over, with Fay?"

Lorraine gave her the incorrigible child look Alyssa hated. "Of course not."

"But Martin said–" She knew she was indulging in wishful thinking.

"I know," Lorraine interrupted. This drove Alyssa nuts. "I know what Martin said. 'Ninety-eight per cent of these cases settle before they ever get to court.'"

"Then he said we were in good hands."

"Meaning Harlan Fineman?" Lorraine paused. "He's right. Any lawyer who wouldn't attend his best friend's funeral to not contaminate our potential lawyer-client relationship is totally on top of this."

"He's brilliant. Daddy always said so." Alyssa clung to the rock star adoration her father had for Harlan Fineman.

"You know Ally, we're getting ahead of ourselves. She hasn't actually sued us yet."

"That's what I said to Martin."

"And he responded?" Lorraine asked with a hint of anxiety.

Alyssa found it comforting to know that her sister worried too. "He said, she will." Alyssa flopped on the sofa and flung the back of her hand on her forehead; a Victorian swoon was in order, never mind what Lorraine thought. "What can we do?" Ally pressed her fingers to the bridge of her nose. She felt a headache coming on.

"Nothing," Lorraine said.

"I'm not good at doing nothing."

"Yes you are."

"Lorraine!"

"Look at this place!"

Alyssa put her finger to her mouth. She didn't want Consuelo to think Lorraine was criticizing her competence. "Consuelo comes every other week," she hissed.

"To do what exactly?" Lorraine began to count the book piles they'd shoved against the wall to make room for the visitors. "I've never seen such chaos."

Alyssa needed to explain to sister, and to herself as well, that the way the house looked wasn't her longtime housekeeper's fault. "Consuelo cleans the bathrooms and the kitchen. I handle the rest."

"Or not," Lorraine said under her breath.

"You don't understand."

"No, I don't. Mother would be appalled."

How dare Lorraine speak for Mother. The old anger welled up, a reminder of how quickly things could disintegrate between them. Alyssa wouldn't let that happen. She was tired of fighting with Lorraine. And besides, they needed solidarity for the bigger battle to come. She wanted her sister with her now. It surprised her how much. "I can't get rid of any of this. It feels like I'm losing Mother all over again."

Lorraine softened. "I'm sorry," she said.

Alyssa sat up. She couldn't recall Lorraine ever apologizing. Her sister seemed to mean it, but Alyssa had a hard time trusting her ears. Still the sound of Lorraine's voice, thick with regret—so much like Mother's—made it even harder to resist falling under her powerful spell. Suddenly, she wanted her big sister to lead the way, to fix everything. "We have to *do* something," she said, referring to the suit.

Lorraine flung her bag over her shoulder. "Grab your purse. We have food to deliver."

Alyssa went to the kitchen, where Consuelo was still scouring the stovetop, and stacked containers inside the box. A cold sweat of foreboding washed her. "Lorraine?"

"Hmm?"

"And what do we do after that?"

"You're always ahead of yourself, aren't you?"

"I'm serious. I can't just sit on my hands and wait for the ax to fall."

"You'll be too busy."

"Doing what?"

"Cleaning up." Lorraine waved her arms in an all-inclusive circle. Alyssa didn't know if she would ever be ready or even willing to undo the history of her mourning that lined the rooms, carpeted the stairs, and padded the walls in a crazy quilt of grief. But she knew for certain that she couldn't address it alone. Then Lorraine answered her unspoken plea. "I'll help you," she said.

What could Alyssa say to her sister's generous offer? *Thank you? Maybe when the time was right?* Lorraine already had a plan, a plan to rearrange her things. Alyssa wondered where she could find velvet ropes to cordon off her private spaces. And a sign: *Look, But Don't Touch.*

"Well?" Lorraine folded her arms and cocked her head. "What do you say?"

Alyssa picked up another petit four, hoping its sweetness would dissolve her ambivalence. The possibility of actual change made her want to flee. She shrugged. She couldn't make any promises.

17

Consuelo took a sponge to the sink. The caterers had left a mess. Spills and crumbs coated the counters and floor. Crumpled paper napkins and cups overflowed the garbage can. The burners oozed caked-on hollandaise. Although Alyssa told her she was not to lift a finger, she couldn't help herself. She had to do this out of respect for Mr. Segal, just as she had done four years earlier. But she was tired, much more so now than then. Four years seemed like ten to her fifty-five year old body. Mrs. Segal would have appreciated her willingness to pitch in. Consuelo still felt her presence.

Consuelo hadn't expected to stand during the graveside service—she'd gotten a seat when Mrs. Segal passed—but there weren't enough chairs this time and she wasn't family. So she stood behind Mr. Warner, Lorraine's husband, and tried not to think about all the things she needed to do at home: laundry, Sunday dinner for her nephew and niece, replace missing buttons on her favorite blue wool cardigan, pay bills. She tried to think about Mr. Segal and how kind he had been, but looking down at Mrs. Segal's plot pulled her mind back to when it was a deep hole. At that first funeral she had no trouble thinking about Mrs. Segal and how much she would miss her. This time though, her feet hurt and her back ached. She was glad when the rabbi directed each of them to place a rose on Mr. Segal's coffin. It meant they could leave.

Consuelo removed the oversized green rubber gloves and rubbed her neck. Pain had crept up her spine. Then she put the gloves back on and swabbed the counter. Much like her mother, Alyssa expected order in the kitchen, if nowhere else. Consuelo knew Mrs. Segal would have been horrified at the state of the rest of the house. She had trusted Consuelo to make things right, at least regarding housekeeping. But how could she, when Alyssa wouldn't permit her to do her job?

Maybe now that Lorraine and Alyssa were speaking again, this would change. She overheard Lorraine suggest "cleaning up." Consuelo held her breath and waited for Alyssa to explode. She didn't. Good. Consuelo didn't think she could bear to witness another fight.

"You bitch!"

Consuelo could hear Alyssa's pinched high voice from the studio, Mrs. Segal's studio.

"Oh, *I'm* the bitch." Lorraine's voice was lower and heavy with sarcasm.

Consuelo began scrubbing the stovetop with a scouring pad. Why did these girls—women, if only they would act like it—why did they revert to name calling, today of all days?

"Stop it. Stop this. Lorraine, Alyssa–" Mr. Segal's gentle sound inflated into a desperate roar. He was broken. Consuelo was sure of it.

She had watched Mr. Segal sit by his wife's bedside day after day, when the doctors, unable to do more, released Mrs. Segal from the hospital. Everyone knew it was the end, everyone but Mr. Segal. Each morning Consuelo would prepare his breakfast and hand him a can of supplement to be poured into the tube in his wife's stomach.

Every morning she asked the same question, "Would you like me to handle this, Mr. Segal?"

"No, no. I want to." He responded the same way each time before ascending the stairs. She understood. It was something he could do.

Then one morning he took the can and held her hand. He had never done this before. "Consuelo," he said, cocking his head, trying to look her in the eye through those thick glasses of his. "Tell me, do you think she's getting better?"

Consuelo felt the tremor in his cool grasp and saw in his foggy spectacles hunger for a different story than the tragic one he told himself. "Mr. Segal, I don't know. I hope so."

"Yes, yes," he said, letting go of her hand.

"We all love her," she said.

He nodded and left. That was a day before Mrs. Segal died, in bed, after walking the halls "for exercise" prescribed by the health aide. Consuelo had wanted to ask why. Couldn't they see she was dying? Couldn't they leave her in peace? Well, at least she no longer suffered. Her family was another matter. Consuelo heard the crazed voices rise and fall.

"You both ought to be ashamed." Ken was soft-spoken like his father, and the effort of trying to corral his sisters into a truce was evident in his throaty rebuke. "Grow the fuck up!" He almost choked on the curse word.

Consuelo didn't like swearing. How could a family like the Segals use such words, even in anger? Her mother had raised her never to swear. "It diminishes you in the eyes of God." As a teenager in the Dominican Republic, she had scoffed at her mother's conservatism, but the vaccination against profanity took.

"Stay out of it, Ken," Lorraine said.

"You never loved Mother," Alyssa said.

Lorraine shot back, "You think your sniveling dependence is love? Never making a move without her approval. No life of your own. You're thirty-six-years-old for crying out loud."

"I have a life! I have a job!"

"A job isn't a life. A family is a life."

"Stop it. Stop it now!" Ken shouted.

Consuelo wiped the counter where cocktail sauce had left a gelatinous glaze. She had sisters. She understood the competition, the love and hatred, the need to be as good as or better than, though she would never be as pretty as Damita with her big eyes and perfect figure, or as smart as Tia with her college degree, or as fertile as either of them. The oldest, Consuelo made up in status what she lacked in schooling; her sisters bowed before her judgments, and she, in turn, doted on their children. But she never quite escaped her own envy. Still, hard as it was to compare and find oneself wanting, a family had to stay together, especially after a loss as big as this one.

"You're a coward," Lorraine, the loudest, bellowed. "You're afraid to be honest with yourself."

"Where *were* you?"

"When?"

"Just now. With Ken."

"At the copy shop. Not that it's any of your business." Consuelo heard shuffling. One of them racing into the dining room.

"Don't you walk away from me," Alyssa screamed. Bodies banged into the table, a chair crashed to the floor.

"Alyssa! Lorraine!" Mr. Segal pleaded.

"Don't you dare publish those poems."

"What are you talking about?"

"Mother left them for us, not to exploit for profit."

Lorraine, "I have no intention of publishing them. As if anyone would actually *buy* them. You're completely cracked, if you think I'm out to make money."

Once, when Consuelo went upstairs to change the sheets, she caught Mrs. Segal scribbling in a marble notebook, her hand shaking from effort. When she saw Consuelo, she quickly put the book down and leaned forward to slide off the bed and into the neighboring chair, while Consuelo put on fresh linens. Mrs. Segal had loved clean towels and sheets and Consuelo was happy to oblige. It was something she could do for her tormented mistress. Though she could no longer speak, Mrs. Segal seemed to sing her approval of the tucking, folding, and smoothing by a rhythmic wheeze through the tube in her throat.

"Why are you pushing me away?' Lorraine sounded teary now.

"I don't need you."

Oh no. Consuelo stopped drying the coffee pot in her hand and listened. She prayed Alyssa would take it back.

"What about Jamie?" Lorraine sounded horrified. "Don't you want a relationship with your nephew?"

"I don't really care," Alyssa said in the flat tone with which she had relayed her mother's orders to wash the bathroom floor or iron Mr. Segal's shirts. Mrs. Segal had always smiled when she spoke to Consuelo. Not Alyssa. Consuelo didn't take it personally. Alyssa's unhappiness had nothing to do with her.

"About Jamie?"

"Yes."

Consuelo began repeating, *Alyssa doesn't mean it. Alyssa doesn't mean it.*

"My God." Now Lorraine's voice flattened too.

"He's not my kid."

Consuelo shuddered. This should not be happening. Consuelo's composure, the professional surface she was barely conscious of, but which carried her daily through her numbing duties, was about to shatter. Her eyes filled. The pans, immersed in soapy water, blurred before her. Then a thud. Someone had fallen. Or been pushed. A sob. Alyssa?

"Stop this!" Ken.

"Girls, girls, please!" Mr. Segal in a choking whisper.

Should she go in? Help them? No. It was better not to see. Bad enough hearing. She could not bear to witness this family crumbling.

"I never want to see her again," Alyssa spat.

"Lorraine, do something!" Mr. Segal.

"I'm sorry, Daddy. She's made her decision."

Sisters, who share so much, so far apart. Mr. Segal weeping. Then silence. Creak, creak. Someone climbed the stairs in slow motion. Someone else slammed the back door. Consuelo gathered the dish towels to put in the washing machine, but that would mean she had to enter the hall, maybe run into one of them. Instead, she left the folded clothes piled on a chair. She could finish tomorrow.

"Consuelo?"

She turned. It was Ken. His shirt was rumpled and perspiration dotted his forehead.

"Yes, Mr. Ken. Can I get you something? Water? Tea?" Before he had a chance to answer, Consuelo moved to the stove, picked up the kettle and began filling it from the tap.

"No. No thank you. Please. Sit down."

"Mr. Ken, I should be going."

He shook his head and pulled out a chair. "A moment."

Consuelo sat. It felt good to rest her legs, but she was alarmed. Was he going to fire her? Because she knew too much? No, she told herself. Ridiculous.

He cleared his throat. "I'm sorry about–" he gestured behind him.

"No, no need. I understand," she said.

"You may understand, but I don't," he said. "I wish you would explain it to me." Then he slumped in the chair beside her. The breakfast nook was so small that their knees touched. Consuelo was aware that Mr. Ken might need extra room. She adjusted her chair so that her legs pressed against the underside of the table. She was bigger than the Segals. At the end of her life, Mrs. Segal barely reached her shoulder.

Consuelo looked up at the window. The sunset had almost faded. It would be dark when she caught the bus. She should call her sister, let her know they should eat without her. Perhaps Mr. Ken would offer her a ride. He looked at her with such bewilderment. All at once, she wanted to comfort him, to tell him what his mother might have.

"They are filled with grief," she began. "Grief makes people say things they don't mean."

"I don't know. It isn't just that. They've always hated each other."

"No, no. They don't hate each other. They're afraid."

"Of what?"

"Of life without your mother."

Ken sighed. "It feels like a broken home." She wanted to reach out and pat his shoulder, but she did not. "It's true. Mother kept us together, at least on the surface. Now it's every man for himself."

Consuelo wanted to lighten his despair. "Give it time," she said.

"Time will only make it worse. They're very stubborn, those two." Consuelo nodded. She didn't like passing judgment on Lorraine and Alyssa, but Kenneth needed her agreement, and he was right. They *were* stubborn. He rose. "You'll stay, won't you? My father needs you now more than ever. We all do."

Consuelo flushed with embarrassment at her misplaced concern. Mrs. Segal had promised more work, but with her gone and the family in this state Consuelo hadn't been sure they would honor the offer. She should have known she could trust them. "Of course, Mr. Ken," she said.

"Thank you, Consuelo." He started to go, then asked, "Need a ride?"

She smiled and nodded. Such a gentleman, just like his father. "Will Mr. Segal be all right?"

"I hope so," Kenneth said, sounding doubtful.

Consuelo wanted to reassure him. "He's strong. He'll find his way."

Consuelo folded the faded boxer shorts, ragged socks, and threadbare undershirts and placed them in the cardboard box. Only two days after the poor man's funeral and already this wife was getting rid of his things. Consuelo had never understood why Mrs. Fay—Consuelo refused to call her Mrs. Segal; there was only one Mrs. Segal, may she rest in peace—didn't replace Mr. Segal's worn out clothing, why she let him wear fraying pants and suits when he was such a distinguished man.

Consuelo reached for the cartons on the top shelf of Mr. Segal's closet and pulled them down to the floor. Sweaters, some moth-eaten, some not. The cashmere pullovers were in good shape. Mrs. Segal used to give her clothes in good condition. Consuelo would send the men's garments back home to her uncles. The imperious Fay did not so much as offer.

As soon as Consuelo walked in that morning, Fay ordered her to "sort the contents of all his drawers and closets, then pack them. I can't bear to have his belongings here another day." Consuelo was certain that this widow wasn't getting rid of her husband's belongings out of anguish over his loss. Her own mother had not set foot in her bedroom for weeks after Papi's passing. She would sleep on a foldout couch in the living room and weep each time she looked at his picture on her dressing table. Not this one. No tears, except at the grave, for the benefit of the assembled. Not at the shiva, where Consuelo had helped to serve coffee. Not in private, after everyone left. No tears at all. *Congelado.*

Consuelo pushed the boxes into the hallway. She would have to carry each one separately. She didn't want to trip down the stairs. Consuelo could have told Mr. Segal that this woman would not take care of him, would not love him. She saw it in her new mistress's eyes—hard black beads of selfishness. She knew it the moment Mrs. Fay walked past her without a glance. Something Mrs. Segal would never have done. Mrs. Segal treated her with respect. It wasn't long before this woman walked past Mr. Segal himself without looking. He was better off. Sad for the children and grandchildren, but for him, a blessing.

Consuelo brought the last box down the stairs and out to the garage where she'd been told to store them. She turned to go back inside. There was Mrs. Fay, standing next to the automatic door, dressed in magenta loungewear. She must have followed her. In the past few weeks she had behaved as if Consuelo was at best an unnecessary irritant, at worst, a spy. Sure, she heard things. She had heard Mrs. Fay on the phone that very morning. "I want it all," she had said. "After what they've put me through, I deserve it." She was up to something ugly.

"All done, Mrs."

"Good," Fay said.

It did not surprise Consuelo that the woman didn't even bother to thank her. "I'll go now."

Mrs. Fay pivoted so that she was no longer facing her. "Consuelo, I will not be needing your services any longer. Here–" She reached into her pants pocket and handed Consuelo an unsealed envelope. Consuelo had been expecting this. She welcomed it. In fact, if Mrs. Fay hadn't let her go, she would have quit. The woman made her uneasy. She wasn't worried about the money. Alyssa had promised her extra days if she ever needed them, like her mother, who always made sure that Consuelo had enough work. Of course, if Mrs. Segal were alive, none of this would be happening.

Consuelo took the envelope and said, "Thank you." Mrs. Fay followed her up the stairs to the front door. Consuelo gathered her things and left. She heard the door lock behind her.

Outside, Consuelo hurried toward the corner. The bus couldn't come soon enough. She inhaled the damp air. Washington summers reminded her of home, without the ocean breeze. She was glad to be out of that house, where she couldn't breathe. At the bus stop, she opened the envelope and counted the bills—a week's salary plus twenty. She shook her head. At least it would cover the plumber's fee for her own dripping faucet.

18

Izzy Small checked his watch. 11:30. She should be here. Fay hadn't visited his office in years, not since she came in with Barney to make sure the house was in her name and couldn't be taken away by the nursing home, if it came to that. It did, and Izzy handled everything. Like he would now.

Izzy prided himself on living up to his given name, Izso, Hebrew for God's salvation. He wasn't about to stand in for God, but he appreciated that Fay needed the salvation only an attorney could provide. The document he'd drawn up to negate the stop order died with Alvin. Before his demise, it had been impossible to execute, not with the man's children standing sentry around his sickbed.

Izzy hadn't spoken to Fay since the day after Alvin's passing. He'd mumbled something perfunctory and told her to take her time before contacting him again. The money wasn't going anywhere. But the very fact that she'd insisted on scheduling this appointment only five days after burying her husband suggested the situation was urgent.

His stomach growled. He unwrapped the roast beef sandwich he brought for lunch, stood, and looked out the window. His old office had been downtown, a few blocks from Dupont Circle, but rents had climbed, and with work slowing, he'd made the decision a year earlier to move to this strip mall on the outer perimeter of Rockville. The view of the parking lot and suburban shoppers going about their daily rounds depressed him. He used to go out for lunch every day to Duke's or another tony Washington steakhouse. He relished his proximity to power—the politicians, lobbyists and, of course, the lawyers in their thousand dollar suits. Duke didn't seat him in the main room, but Izzy could still glimpse the action, smell the deals, and drink in the heady cocktail of money and influence. Here, the neighboring Chinese restaurant wasn't up to snuff, and other than the donut shop next door and the coffee bar two stores down, there was no place to eat. He missed the downtown scene.

Izzy bit into the mustard, meat, and spongy rye, and mulled over Fay and her family drama. Along with the condiment's tang and the hint of blood in the sliced roast, Izzy tasted the possibility of a big case, a fat retainer, and a nice cushy settlement. One well-handled opportunity could turn things around.

He peeked out the door. "Mona?"

His receptionist looked up from her magazine. Mona had maintained her crisp efficiency throughout their long history together, even as her perfect beehive thinned and her over-tanned skin came to resemble cracked leather.

"Yes, Mr. Small?"

"Any word from Mrs. Segal?"

"No, Sir."

"I'll be back in a moment." Izzy retrieved the key from Mona's desk and slipped down the hall to the men's room. He trained himself to hold his breath to block out the nauseating scent of ammonia, mold, and synthetic carpet that permeated the passage.

Inside the bathroom Izzy exhaled and washed his hands in the small basin. Then he inspected himself in the mirror. He had lost a couple of inches in his seventh decade, but he was still tall, taller than most—a helpful characteristic when leaning over a witness stand. He buttoned his jacket. Too loose. His ex-wife used to tease that he was a walking stick figure, one of those drawings children created before their hand-eye coordination put flesh on bone. Have the suit altered, before the next trial.

When he reentered the office, Fay Segal was seated on the Naugahyde couch. She wore a purple two-piece outfit and propped her purse upright on her knees. She looked smaller and harder than the last time they'd met, as if she'd been freeze-dried. It was difficult to tell if she had slept. Huge pouches under her eyes said not. She's old, Izzy reminded himself, older than me. Good for the case. Old ladies don't seem like gold diggers.

"Fay! Come in, come in." Izzy took her fleshy hand between his bony ones and pressed. Step one: comfort. "No calls, Mona."

Inside the office Fay sat, knees together, hands clasped on her copious lap, an overgrown child in the principal's office, waiting for reprimand.

Izzy perched on the edge of the desk and leaned in, inches from Fay's impassive mask. "So. Tell me. How are you doing?"

Fay looked down and said nothing.

"It must be difficult. So sudden. So unexpected."

"It was sudden, but not unexpected. He was ill."

"Well, you must take care of yourself. The loss of a spouse–"

In an instant Fay threw back her shoulders and snapped into business mode.

"I'll be fine as soon as this matter is settled."

Izzy moved behind his desk and opened the folder before him. "That could take some time. They haven't answered my calls. When I tried to reach Kenneth, he left a message referring me to Harlan Fineman."

"Harlan Fineman? He's big, isn't he?" A hint of worry streaked her brow.

"Yes," Izzy said. "Very." He'd never met the legend, but had often glimpsed him from afar, seated at Duke's best table, an eccentric man dressed like a nineteenth century detective. "I'd say that's good for us."

"How?" Fay had begun to shred the tissue wadded in her palm.

"They hired the biggest gun they could find in anticipation of our next move. They're scared. They're not taking any chances."

Fay licked her upper lip, smearing red around her mouth. "Alvin worshipped him, like he was a legal god. He said Harlan Fineman never loses." Fay begged for reassurance that Izzy was happy to give. He wasn't about to be cowed by some fop past his prime.

Time for step two: champion. "We would have to go to trial first. That will never happen. You'll see. They'll settle."

"How do you know?"

"No one wants a courtroom fight. Especially not three siblings who don't get along."

"The *girls* don't."

Details. He hoped to bypass the family dynamic, but if he could exploit it, he would. "A relatively small amount in dispute."

Fay bristled. "Not small to me."

"An elderly ill man manipulated by his mercenary children into denying his faithful wife her due."

"Yes, yes." Fay relaxed at this, and sat back for the first time.

"You have to decide whether you want to wait–see if they come to their senses and release the transfer–or go ahead and sue."

"What do you recommend?" Fay was positively deferential.

Izzy turned away from her for a moment to sneak a look at his watch. It was almost noon. Time to talk money. "Well, Fay, I recommend that you file the suit. It lets them know you mean business, that you're not intimidated. It'll shake them up. Make them fold. I can handle the whole thing for a modest retainer–" He scribbled a figure and passed it to her. Good. She didn't flinch. "–towards forty percent of the settlement."

"Forty percent!"

"That's standard. Don't worry. We'll ask for more than the transfer amount. We'll go after half the estate."

Fay pursed her lips. "I signed a prenup."

"I was there, remember? But it's not ironclad. It doesn't preclude your receiving gifts. Besides, this is just a tactic to get them to cave."

Fay smiled and unsnapped her purse. She took out her checkbook. "File the papers."

Izzy folded the check, slipped it into his jacket pocket, then once again, took Fay's hand, warmer now. "Don't you worry about a thing. I'll get you what you deserve."

PART V

Served

19

"Lorraine Segal Warner?" The man stood just outside the screen door. He wore a dark blue suit and carried an envelope. Lorraine thought the business attire odd. Was he a door-to-door salesman? *Were* there door-to-door salesmen anymore? Sweat dotted his upper lip. Eleven a.m. and the humidity was already unbearable. Waves of steam hit Lorraine as she pushed open the door. She wanted to retreat back into her air-conditioned home. She hated New Jersey in July.

"Yes, I'm Mrs. Warner." Strange how rarely she used Mrs. or her husband's last name. The only regular exception was with Jamie's teachers. Legally she was still Lorraine Segal. But lately she felt Warner was protective, a cloak over her more vulnerable birth identity.

The man held the envelope at arm's length. "You are served. Sign here."

The man's pen almost slipped out of Lorraine's fingers, but she managed a wobbly facsimile of her signature.

"Good day," he said without the slightest irony.

Lorraine couldn't look at him. She knew it was irrational, but she disliked this person all the same. Kill the messenger. Her body shook. She closed the door against the sultry draft and the awful reality it brought. Then she sank onto the hallway's cold tile floor. She and Brad had had endless tiffs over what to do about the ugly yellow linoleum it replaced. They finally settled on Spanish tile in terra cotta streaked with salmon. Now the warm hues seemed garish. Lorraine needed cool, soothing blues and greens.

After the funeral, Lorraine reeled from her father's sudden death and her own guilt; her grief had been laced with relief, which she admitted only to Brad. She was off the hook. She would not have to upend her life to take care of her father. "What if he somehow knew no one really wanted him?" she asked, weeping into her husband's arms. "What if that killed him?"

Brad lifted her head and brushed back the hair falling into her eyes, "No, no Lor. Don't do this to yourself. Your Dad knew you loved him. If anything, it was Fay who drained the life out of him." Lorraine was not convinced.

She looked at the envelope. Open it. Why? She knew what it held. Why did she have to look at the contents? Reading the words would make the nightmare real.

Lorraine slit the seal with care, and pulled out the packet of documents. "Fay Segal, plaintiff vs. Lorraine Segal Warner, Kenneth Segal & Alyssa Segal, defendants." Then, "fraud," and "conspiracy to commit fraud." Her eyes blurred. Breath rushed through her. Lorraine had expected this for weeks. She had anticipated it every time the doorbell rang. But even so, she was not prepared to be assaulted, nor to defend her roll as a daughter, her integrity, her father, her life. Lorraine squeezed her eyes shut and tightened her muscles from head to toe in a painful reversal of the relaxation exercises she had mastered as a performer. With each contracting sinew she rued the day she gave that woman her blessing.

Her father had said to meet them at the restaurant.

"Fay loves this place, and she's hard to please." He sounded giddy.

Lorraine remembered introducing Brad to her parents. Now with the roles reversed, she had the same power over her father. Her ability with one negative comment, to crush him—the way he and Mother had once crushed her—weighed on her. *He needs me to accept this woman.* Lorraine guessed, though she didn't know for certain, that Ally had already rejected the relationship. Ken wouldn't care. But Lorraine was Daddy's girl. It was up to her to make him happy. Or in this case, to let him take his happiness wherever and with whomever he could find it.

The restaurant, a chic little bistro called Chez Pigalle, was the kind that had transformed Washington from a surf 'n turf town into a sophisticated world capital with cuisine to match. Lorraine stepped down to the ground floor entry and passed through wrought iron doors into an intimate, amber lit space. Dancing girls and accordion players kicked their way across the mural-covered walls in undisguised homage to Toulouse-Lautrec. The maitre d' led Lorraine past tightly packed tables for two—smiling, whispering tête à têtes—a gauntlet of flirtation and romance. She missed Brad, but they both understood that her father's invitation to meet Fay had been extended only to her.

Lorraine approached the back corner booth. Her father, dashing and expectant, rose to meet her. This was how she used to picture him, proudly giving her away at her wedding—the fantasy that had never materialized. "Sweetheart!" He kissed her forehead and Lorraine drank in his familiar strong aftershave. "This is Fay Cohen. Fay, my daughter, Lorraine."

She held out her hand. Fay leaned forward to peck her cheek. A whiff of stale breath forced Lorraine to pull back. At least she wasn't some inappropriately young thing. Her layers of costume jewelry clanked as she grabbed Lorraine's hand. Fay's face was heavily powdered, the only color, scarlet lipstick. Her teased poof of platinum hair gave her an extra inch. She worked at what she had. Lorraine would give her that.

"Oh Lorraine, I'm so happy to finally meet you. Your father talks about you and Jamie non-stop. Alvin–" Fay pressed into him. "Your daughter is even prettier than her pictures." Dad beamed. Lorraine wondered if he expected her to be flattered.

They sat, ordered, and engaged in convivial chatter, throughout which Lorraine caught every wink and titter between the two aging lovebirds. The handholding was the least of it. During dessert, in the middle of the chocolate mousse, Lorraine bent over to pick up her napkin and caught Fay's fingers on her father's inner thigh. When Daddy excused himself and headed to the men's room, Fay quickly confided, "I'm so in love with your father!"

Lorraine knew they'd dated only a month, but she and Brad had fallen in love faster than that, and at her father's age there was no time to waste. Even so, Fay's ardor seemed a bit extreme, more schoolgirl than twice-married senior. After Daddy returned, Fay said, "Such a marvelous meal. I'm very picky, you know. I thought your father would be mad when I walked out of two restaurants the other night, but he just laughed and said, 'You're so like Estelle.'"

Lorraine winced. True, her mother had exited fine dining establishments over a smudged glass, lack of towels in the restroom, or any hint of shoddy service, but she had real taste. This woman was a pretender whom Lorraine would have to excuse for Daddy's sake. She hadn't seen him this happy since her parents' fortieth anniversary party.

Over coffee they made plans to meet again. "Bring Jamie and Brad. I want you to meet my Gretchen, and Pablo, and the girls." Fay flung snapshots on the table. Cute children held aloft by a tall man and a billowy-haired woman.

Lorraine nodded and said, "That would be wonderful," straining sincerity. The sheer novelty of her father involved with another woman had exhausted her. No wonder Ally couldn't cope.

The waiter put the check on the table. With one swollen finger, Fay pushed it across to Alvin. The deliberateness of the gesture struck Lorraine. "Thank you, Alvin," Fay said. Then she winked at Lorraine. "He spoils me so." Again, doubt flared and Lorraine tamped it down. She looked at her father. He glowed.

After they dropped Fay at her house—Lorraine averted her eyes while her father gave his lady friend a goodnight kiss—Daddy returned to the car and asked, "Well, what do you think?" The nakedness of his vulnerability touched Lorraine. She knew exactly what he felt. She knew what rejection would do. She could still hear the words her father so pointedly pronounced sixteen years before–*ugly in every way*–each syllable a devastation, and a violation of her trust in her beloved Daddy. That cruel, unfair assessment of her fiancé—born more from her father's fear of Gentiles than Brad's shortcomings—implanted itself on her heart and nearly destroyed her relationship. Her marriage survived the parental curse and evolved into a tough, self-sufficient partnership, but sometimes the damage surfaced, and the barrier between Lorraine and her parents transformed into a barrier within herself. It was hard for Lorraine Segal to expose her own vulnerability to anyone, including her husband. She vowed never to do the same to Jamie. Any bride short of an axe-murderer would be fine with her.

Of course, the last thing she expected was to have to assess her *father's* choice. Despite the unnecessary anguish he had inflicted on her, or perhaps because of it, she had no desire to dampen his enthusiasm. He'd been through too much. And really, Lorraine had no reason to reject Fay. The woman appeared to be a fine companion—cheery, vivacious, and smart. Lorraine thought that any doubts had more to do with Mother's ghost than Fay herself. Comparison was inevitable. She didn't dislike Fay. She just didn't know her. In time she would. "Are you happy, Daddy?"

"Yes, yes. You don't know. After your mother died, I couldn't get out of bed. I was so lonely. And now, Fay–she's not your mother, but–" His voice trailed.

"I'm happy for you," Lorraine said, and it was true.

He exhaled. "Thank you, sweetheart. It means so much that you approve." Lorraine let it pass that she neither approved nor disapproved. It was his life. And she was glad he once again had someone with whom to share it.

"Mom, Mom! You okay?" Jamie's shaggy bangs grazed the bridge of Lorraine's nose. He peered at her. "What are you doing on the floor?"

"Nothing. I'm fine." Lorraine stumbled to her feet.

Jamie held her up. He was as tall as she. "What's that?" He pointed to the envelope still in her hand. Lorraine looked down at the crushed manila. She wanted to take it downstairs to the shredder in Brad's office and cut its contents into confetti. But that wouldn't change anything. She wanted to tell her darling boy, staring at her with such concern, that it was nothing, but she couldn't lie to her son—her baby, who wasn't a baby anymore. After all, it was Jamie Fay wanted to rob.

Jamie stood before her, waiting for reassurance. "Mom? What's going on? You can tell me." He straightened. "I can take it." How sweet her boy's resolve to be strong, but she kept quiet. Lorraine could hardly handle this assault. How could he? "It's Fay isn't it?"

Throughout these weeks of anticipation, Brad reminded her that they didn't really need the money, that she had a choice: she could let it go, give Fay what she wanted. "No. It's wrong. And what about Ken and Alyssa?" she would ask.

"They're adults," Brad said. "They can take care of themselves." Adults. Not how she saw herself or her siblings these days. The turmoil had returned them to childhood. The crisis had so muddled Lorraine's self-perception that Jamie seemed more grown-up than she or Ken or certainly Alyssa. But she had one clear intuition: in order to answer Fay's challenge, she and her brother and sister would have to fulfill their potential. Finally.

"Mom! Talk to me." Jamie placed his insistent face inches from hers, all of *his* potential manifest. He would graduate high school, leave home, go to college, travel, have a career, find a partner, start a family—her grandchildren—and carve his place in the world. Life would carry him off. Lorraine would wave to him in wider and wider swoops as he receded into his own complex existence. Fay could not stop this. Fay was a temporary obstacle. Fay or no Fay, her son would be fine.

Lorraine nodded. "Yes, honey, it's Fay." She lifted her right arm—Jamie still held her—and put it around her son's shoulder, a gesture that would soon be impossible. She would enfold him as long as she could. One day she would have to let him go.

Alyssa wrapped her robe around her waist and stared at the stack of boxes piled high in her tiny foyer. She tried to suppress a yawn, but couldn't. She'd been working the night shift all week, and was utterly exhausted. Now this. The shipment had arrived days before from Fay—book rate, of course. Alyssa knew what it contained: everything Fay didn't want, wasn't going to fight for, the discards among Daddy's belongings. Alyssa couldn't bring herself to open a single box. Whenever she got ready to rip off the packing tape, she hesitated. Instead, she sat on the staircase and guessed: too small to hold the oriental rugs, the Eames chair, or the rosewood coffee table, but big enough to hold her father's watch, his good cufflinks, and the tie-tacks that she and her sister and brother gave him every Father's Day. Except she knew Fay had kept the jewelry. They would never see any of it again. Alyssa seethed. She pictured Fay, Pablo, and Gretchen dancing around a bonfire of discards and smashing her mother's paintings. "No!" she said aloud.

The doorbell rang. Alyssa peeked through the peephole she installed when she took up residence. She didn't answer the door if she could help it. But something about the stiff neck and impassive expression of the man at the door sent a shudder through her entire body and demanded a response.

"Alyssa Segal?" he called.

Alyssa closed her eyes and counted to three, but there was no avoiding it. Fineman had warned them to expect this any day. If she ignored the man, he would follow her to work and she couldn't take the exposure, even though her co-workers all knew the situation. Alyssa had cried in Paul's office—her boss passed the tissue and listened to her rant. She'd sulked through meetings, after which the local anchor or another producer would take her aside and the whole sorry saga would spill out again. She had to get it over with. She had to open the door.

" Did you get it yet?"

"Yes, a half hour ago," Lorraine said.

"Why didn't you call me?"

"Because I knew you'd call *me*." Lorraine's smugness irritated Alyssa.

"Have you talked to Ken?"

"He's not answering his cell–must be in class," Lorraine said. Alyssa let it pass that her sister had called Ken first. Lorraine went on. "I told Brad. And Jamie."

"How did he take it?"

"Jamie's fine. He knows we'll handle it."

That made Alyssa's nephew a step ahead of her. "I can't believe this is real." She wanted to crawl in a hole, and if not die, hibernate, until the whole thing was over.

"Oh it's real all right." Alyssa wanted more from Lorraine, more than this flat confirmation of trouble.

After she hung up, the fury tying Alyssa up in knots, paralyzing her, preventing her from doing anything but shuttle back and forth to the station, suddenly broke free. She ran to the kitchen, pulled open the top drawer under the phone cabinet, and grabbed the scissors. In the hallway she tore into the highest box, nearly toppling the ones below. Alyssa tossed the crumpled newspaper cushioning the contents and dug in.

She unearthed pair after pair of faded, stained, frayed boxer shorts—plaid and pale blue, flannel pajamas with missing buttons, and socks. My God, that woman had actually sent socks, holes and all. If she thought they were going to settle, because she returned his socks she had another thing coming. And what was this? His home blood pressure gauge? Alyssa pictured it wrapped around her father's scrawny upper arm. A thermometer? Alyssa saw her father open wide to expose his brown jagged teeth. Band-aids? Alyssa flashed to her own five-year-old knee, and her mother—or was it Lorraine?—placing a strip over the stinging gash. Then Alyssa removed a bottle of St Joseph's baby aspirin. For a moment she thought it was hers, a long lost remnant of childhood fevers. She could still taste the orangey pill on her tongue. Why had Fay sent it? To remind Alyssa that Daddy had been so old that he took children's medicine for his heart?

Alyssa looked inside the almost empty carton. At the bottom sat a black leather glasses case. She sighed, opened it, and took out the spectacles. Then she ran her finger around the tortoise shell frame. She tried to look through the heavy lenses, but the prescription was so strong it gave her vertigo. She put the glasses back in the case and clutched it to her chest.

"You're home early," Priscilla said in a stuffy, mucus-clogged voice.

"As promised," Ken said. With most of the faculty gone, and summer school a real drag for everyone—teachers included—he could leave whenever he liked.

His wife's legs wobbled and Ken grabbed the baby whose nose was a crusty, barnacle. "Pris?"

"I'll be fine. I'm making tea." Priscilla's hazel eyes were puffy and ringed with green-black prizefighter circles. She swayed into the kitchen and put a kettle on the stove.

"You need to take something," Ken said, aware of the futility. Priscilla was a hardcore vegan, and didn't believe in putting anything non-organic into her lovely body. She'd gone three nights without sleep, sans decongestants, and it showed.

"No, I'll be fine," she sniffled.

"You're keeping both of us awake, you know."

"We'd be awake anyway. Josh is napping now, so he'll be up all night. And this one–" Priscilla chucked Stella under her chin, glazed with goop.

"Pris?" Ken didn't know how to start.

"What?" Priscilla's voice dropped an octave.

"It came today," he said, handing her the packet. He suppressed the urge to toss it like a grenade, like the man had done. *You are served*. What? Served? Ken imagined himself in the cafeteria receiving a plate of over-cooked spaghetti. The absurd image erased the man's exit.

Priscilla stopped. "Oh dear."

"Yes." He rubbed his thigh. Then the familiar tingling surfaced. He watched his wife's eyes widen as she opened the envelope and read the names. Nothing phantom about this.

"Did you call Lorraine? Alyssa? Your lawyer?"

"Not yet." He'd gotten four messages—one from Lorraine and three from Alyssa. "I wanted to talk to you first."

"Okay," she said, and took the baby from him. Stella settled her damp head on her mother's shoulder. Priscilla sat on a stool and slumped against the counter. "Talk."

"I–" Why did he have to say the words? Ken was sure his wife could read his mind. But Priscilla just sat there in weary misery waiting for him to unburden himself. "I don't know if I'm up to it."

"Up to what?'

"This. A lawsuit, a trial, a fight."

"It's the children's future."

"No. *We're* the children's future."

Priscilla tipped her head away from Stella's curls. "Teacher's salary. No savings. We can't take a second mortgage, because we can't afford a first one. Escalating college costs, two overlapping tuitions. You do the math!"

Ken's guilt, the load he carried daily, had grown in a geometric progression since the birth of the children. Any glitch in their family circumstances—minor illness, a flat tire, an unexpected bill—set off an argument. No matter the catalyst, the fights were always about money. Since his father's death, Ken and his patient wife bickered a lot. "They're smart kids. They'll get scholarships, loans. And you'll work again."

Ken knew Priscilla hated it when he brought up her work. A shrill whistle of steam ended round one in their repeat bout. Ken poured the hot water and dunked a bag of lemon ginger tea in a mug. He slid it across to her, and she passed Stella back to him in one seamless motion. This was the part they were good at—the ordinary moves, the mundane parental dance. The rest, what was ahead, he wasn't so sure.

"*Someday* I'll work again. You know how I feel about being a part-time mom."

"Lots of women do it. Half the faculty–"

"I don't care what half the faculty does! What do they have to do with letting this woman rob your children? Is that what you want?"

Stella stirred and lifted her head from Ken's chest—one eye open—her mother's daughter. Ken shook his head. No, it wasn't what he wanted. He didn't want Fay to get away with anything. He wanted to push her off a cliff and watch her fall. *No, too fast*. He wanted to see her suffer *slowly*, wring her flabby neck until her veins popped out of her head and her insufferable whine choked into permanent silence. Or if quick, it had to be spectacular: sneak down to her home in Washington, turn on the gas, stand across the street and watch it explode in a blaze of fiery revenge.

"Ken! Did you hear me?" Priscilla was close to him now, tugging his arm, her eyes watery with illness and concern. "You have to fight this. You have to!"

Like the death of a parent or the moment a child is born, there was no possible preparation. The past few years had demanded of Ken large, unpleasant emotions, feelings he had shut down since his accident. Priscilla. Mother. The children. Then Dad. Love, death, birth, more death, had opened him up. He had resisted. He had never wanted to become an adult, if adult meant facing his fears and responsibilities. Now this. Served. A lawsuit. A trial. Loss or gain, gain in loss.

Ken put his free arm around his exhausted wife and inhaled his baby girl's feverish warmth. "I know I do."

20

Harlan Fineman's office was his sanctuary. Never one for false modesty—a mode he considered antithetical to truth—Harlan readily acknowledged his prowess in matters of justice and décor. In order to maintain such sway he created a cave in which his brilliant legal mind could recharge itself each day. As the senior partner of Fineman, Jellnick & Sayles he had his pick of suites. His colleagues were amused, but not surprised, when he bypassed the coveted corner rooms with stunning views of the Capitol for the windowless study at the epicenter of the floor. "Just like Harlan to choose the broom closet," they joked. And so the entire firm dubbed it, "Harlan's Closet"—a name he relished—placing it on the door under the more formal *Harlan Fineman, Esquire.*

The room was lined floor to ceiling with books—row upon row of legal tomes, as well as Dickens, Trollope, Plato, the complete works of Elmore Leonard, and stacks of Harlan's own writings, not all of them legal briefs. Harlan's genius—the word most commonly used to describe him and a designation he embraced—extended beyond the law, where he was reigning monarch, and into elaborate mysteries, ditties, and odes, which his friends and family begged of him to mark every milestone event. At that moment, while waiting for the Segal children to arrive, he was polishing a limerick for Sayles' retirement party:

There was an old man from Hoboken
Whose manner was very soft-spoken,
Except when in court
Where he boomed his retorts,
That deceptive old man from Hoboken.

Harlan put down his pen and sat back in satisfaction. He looked forward to the laughter and applause when he intoned the witty lines in his best Southern gentleman drawl. This joy in holding forth had come in handy in his chosen profession. He could command any courtroom with a well-chosen inflection and the lift of an eyebrow.

Harlan drummed his fingers on the edge of the desk. He was anxious for the day to begin. The desk was the heart of the tiny office. He had buried its vast surface in papers, creating little hills of legal conflict held down by globular paperweights of swirling kaleidoscopic glass. Open volumes scored with multiple leather bookmarks banked its perimeter. Harlan reveled in his wizard's workshop of crystal balls and spells. He loved to play presiding warlock, bending over the legal cauldron, cooking up recipes for courtroom victory.

His familiar—a giant stuffed owl given by his wife for his sixtieth birthday a dozen years before—sat on a pedestal behind him. When Harlan unwrapped the creature and stared into its eyes, his wife clapped and dubbed the bird, "Your twin." Harlan enjoyed watching many a client squirm in anxious awe, glancing from him to the owl and back again. Did they actually imagine that the bird would alight on his shoulder if he gave the command? The thought made him chuckle.

Yes, he was an owlish presence, and quite liked it. As a young man, Harlan had been merely odd looking. Now his bushy white eyebrows, high unlined forehead, chiseled nose, and deep laser eyes gave him presence. And the Holmesian tweed cape he sported in cold weather lent him an intimidating air. The quirky persona he developed to deflect the anti-Semitism of 1940's Alabama had served him outside of the stifling South. To this day, Harlan preferred being called an eccentric, rather than a Southerner or a Jew.

He lifted a glass egg and opened the file underneath. Grown children, grasping stepmother, addled father—tricked, manipulated, and recently deceased. He wasn't comfortable thinking of his good friend Alvin as such, but the facts were clear. The man had been duped.

Harlan's mouth twisted. Even applied to Alvin, he couldn't restrain the perpetual amusement with which he viewed the human follies parading past him day in, day out. It was just such a ridiculous and poignant situation that got him out of bed in the morning. He reveled in the muck of other's mistakes. Sometimes his amusement got him into trouble. But he no longer explained himself as he used to. He didn't apologize for being distant or insensitive. Harlan had long ago earned the trust of clients, partners, friends, and family, though none of them could read him all of the time. This amused him further. Inscrutability suited him.

Harlan surveyed the room, nodding to himself. He was about to invite the children of his oldest friend into his inner sanctum. He inhaled. The dark, warm, sedimentary space had the archival smell of dust and leather. He exhaled, wishing he could still smoke cigars. He hoped Alvin's progeny would appreciate the enclave's unique amalgam—one part whimsy, two parts intellect—and its paradoxical window into his personality.

Why did he care what Alvin's offspring thought of him? Because they were related to a man he respected and missed? Why even take them on with his backlog of briefs? Harlan Fineman was much in demand. He'd made a name for himself winning unwinnable cases for Washington's political elites—bipartisan victories that kept him in the public eye no matter which administration happened to be in power. Because he never took a case he couldn't win, he never lost. If he had any doubt about his chances, he turned the job down.

Why indeed? Harlan answered with the simple logical responses he expected of his clients on the stand: because he cared—Alvin's children were extended family—and because Alvin had been his dearest friend, he couldn't refuse them. Once in a long while he took a case like this one, not to challenge the big guns, or to prove the pundits wrong, but for personal reasons, out of love and loyalty. Such was the case of Segal v Segal.

"Sit, please." Harlan gestured to Lorraine and Alyssa to take the worn leather chairs in front of his desk. The Segal girls—he couldn't help thinking of them as teenagers—did as they were told. Lorraine was the image of her mother, the striking Estelle. Alyssa's pallor alarmed him. A health food enthusiast himself, Harlan silently prescribed spinach and an iron supplement.

Kenneth followed his sisters into the office and positioned himself behind Alyssa, leaning heavily on her chair. Harlan remembered Alvin's anguish in the aftermath of his son's accident. "Here," he said, plucking a folding chair out from behind the easel he used to prop visual aids during opening and closing statements, and on sunny days for drawing in Lafayette Park. Ken thanked him. The three sat, eyes drinking in the room. Harlan noted their wonder and avoidance, the vain attempt to distract themselves from their reason for being there, the tension, and the interior cries of "Save us! Save us!" timed to the ticking of his ancient wall clock.

"This is an amazing room," Lorraine said. "I particularly like the owl."

Harlan smiled. "Good, because he'll be assisting me in assisting you."

Lorraine laughed.

Alyssa sighed. No sense of humor. She wanted to get on with it. "I can't believe we're here," she said.

"Do you think Fay's serious?" Ken asked.

Lorraine overlapped with, "What can we do to stop this?"

Now, now, calm yourselves, Harlan wanted to say, but he knew better. A client's desperation was most palpable during the first visit, when shock and denial coursed through them. Though the Segals sat before him like needy supplicants in the presence of their savior, Harlan preferred to think of himself in less religious terms. He saw his job as a legal guide, a spokesman, a retriever of justice, if justice could be found. He was not a rabbi, therapist, or father—though God knows these three middle-aged orphans wanted one—but he could be the facilitator of the best possible outcome. For them. And for Alvin. "A lawsuit is always serious. Although this may be a bluff on her part, we have no choice but to take the action seriously. It must be answered. And there are a number of ways to do that."

"What ways?" They chimed in unison.

Lorraine held a pen and pad, poised to take notes. Good, otherwise they wouldn't remember a thing. Bright as Alvin's offspring were, turmoil had dazed them. Lorraine pushed the writing implement across the page in mechanical efficiency. Harlan understood that the purposeful activity prevented her from jumping out of her skin. Alyssa folded and unfolded her hands. Ken's gaze drifted around the windowless office, looking for escape.

"First countersue. Then wait. See if they make an offer. Her lawyer, Mr. Small, should, if he knows his job, counsel her to do so. She wants money. A long drawn-out proceeding will cost her."

"We're not giving her a thing. She's charging us with fraud," Alyssa said.

"And conspiracy," Lorraine added.

"Criminal charges in a civil suit. Quite unusual," Harlan said. This lawyer, Izso Small, and Alvin's widow were a fascinating combination: incompetent and over-reaching. Any judge worthy of the title would dismiss the fraud count. He wished he could promise the Segals as much, but promises at this point would be unwise. There was always a chance plans could go awry, and accepted procedures falter. Harlan had practiced long enough to know that once a suit was brought, anything could happen. And he relished the fact. His affection for Alvin's children notwithstanding, he loved the greedy drama. This was law at its seediest and most intriguing, exposing humanity, irrationality, and moral defect. Fineman identified with the naked need on both sides. This was his strength and he embraced it. "Your stepmother wants it all, doesn't she?"

"You mean the house? She can't take it, can she?" Alyssa rattled with raw anxiety.

Harlan would not lie to them. "She can try. This is an interesting case, and somewhat problematic."

Lorraine stopped writing. Ken cocked his head.

"What do you mean?" Alyssa gulped air along with the words.

"Your father's intention at the time of the transfer is the critical point in question. Because he is not here, the case is essentially your word against hers."

"What about Martin Patras? He blew the whistle on her and facilitated the stop order," Ken said, coming out of his stupor.

"Martin could be useful, or a problem himself. What he did–" Harlan was loath to disparage another lawyer, especially one whose heart was in the right place. "What he did, if examined, could be seen as impeaching his professional credibility."

"But without him, she would have gotten away with the entire sum!" Lorraine said.

"True."

"A lawyer who breaks confidentiality might not be a reliable witness on the stand," Ken said.

Give that boy an A+. "Yes, quite so." Harlan remembered Alvin bemoaning Ken's flight from law school. Perhaps he hadn't wanted to compete with his accomplished father, like Harlan's own son, the carpenter.

"On the stand!" Alyssa's hands were blotchy from wringing. "Do you think we will go to trial?" The question of the hour, the one every client asked.

"I don't know," Harlan said, careful to modulate each syllable. "The goal is always to settle out of court."

"Martin said only two per cent go to trial," Lorraine said.

Martin again. "Percentages don't mean anything here." Harlan watched his words render each of them motionless. He went on. "It depends on how delusional she is, and how strong you are. She can make a lot of trouble."

"She already has," Lorraine said.

"Quite so," Harlan said. Give them something to hold on to. "With your permission, I'm going to delay awhile. Let her wonder what we're up to. And then file the countersuit."

"Calling her bluff," Ken said. "I like that."

"And after?" Lorraine asked, poised on the edge of the chair.

"We wait for her to answer us."

"We can win this, can't we?" Alyssa asked, her voice wispy with apprehension.

Harlan recalled Alvin's words when they tried a nasty malpractice case together. Alvin had a softer demeanor than he did, but he was the only attorney Harlan had ever considered his superior. Alvin had a quality Harlan couldn't hope to acquire. Perhaps his immigrant past made Alvin so good with the wounded and terrified. Harlan didn't know how to coddle. He preferred fighters. He didn't know whether these three were fighters or victims, but he repeated Alvin's words when his friend took the dying woman's hand. "Step by step. Step by step."

Lorraine and Alyssa traded glances. Kenneth nodded in recognition, "Dad used to say that."

"Quite so." Then Harlan rose and picked up three golden balls. "Watch this," he said, launching them into the air. He juggled before his dumbstruck audience and plotted his next move, recalling what Woodrow Templeton, one of his brash young associates, had once said to his face, "You're the unknowable wise man, Harlan, at home inside your formidable head." Daring of him, and Harlan admired daring. The balls circled, three pairs of eyes widened. Lorraine and Ken applauded. Alyssa giggled. If the case came to trial, Templeton might make a good second chair.

Harlan let the balls drop one by one into his hands. "Do you have a moment? I need your opinion on something." The three stood at attention, under his spell. "What do you think of this?" Harlan cleared his throat and began to recite, "There was an old man from Hoboken–"

21

Outside the tiny terrace of their two-bedroom Virginia cape, Pablo struck a match, lit the cigarette hanging from the corner of his mouth, and inhaled. He sat on a molded plastic chair and put his feet up on the matching green table. The chair legs buckled under his weight and the tabletop took his heel's imprint. Gretchen had gotten this junk at a neighborhood yard sale last summer. She was always scrounging for bargains. Just like her mother.

Pablo swatted away a stubborn mosquito dive-bombing his ear. Most of them avoided the smoke. As did his wife. Gretchen had laid down the law. If he persisted in the filthy habit, he had to at least follow some rules. He kept his coats in a separate closet, and was not allowed to smoke in the house or car under any circumstances. On an August evening like this one, obeying the stricture posed no problem. Pablo enjoyed combating his nightly insomnia with private time on his suburban patch. In the winter though, clad in pajamas and a parka, he longed for the island. It was then that he wanted to share a cigar with his father and listen to the waves endless rush.

Just as well that he was here and not in San Juan. The thick waterlogged air closed in on him. Its oppression matched the pressure inside his head, a pressure he could not share with his father. Pablo and Louis had not recovered from their recent bust. Carlos hadn't understood his son's partnership with a man he called, "an obvious reprobate." He had a blindspot common to fathers; he couldn't or wouldn't see Pablo's failings. His father didn't understand or accept what Pablo knew about himself, that he and Louis were twins—twin schemers—and lately, twin losers.

And then there was Tina, who hadn't answered any of his calls. If he were in San Juan, he wouldn't be able to resist hanging out at the casino, monopolizing her table, demanding attention. No, it was better to stay here with only the homely humiliations of domestic life to bring him down.

Pablo took another drag and flicked the ash on the ground. He scratched his bare ankle. Damn. The insect attacker had its way. An itchy welt rose and reddened under his nail. He thought about returning to bed for a few hours of shut-eye, or of staring into the dark, ticking off unpaid bills, while Gretchen snored beside him. He reached into the chest pocket of his pajama top and pulled out a half pack.

"How long have you been out here?" Gretchen slid the screen aside and stepped onto the flagstone.

Backlit by the hall lights, her hair looked like a flaming dust ball, and her legs silhouetted through her nightgown reminded him of the notorious photo of Princess Diana in all her pre-regal innocence—may she rest in peace. It had been a long time since Pablo first admired his wife's colt-like limbs. After each birth black and blue varicose roads paved their way across her calves, behind her knees and up her thighs, creating a complex highway, which ruined forever Pablo's favorite landscape.

"Go back to bed," Pablo said, lighting another cigarette.

Gretchen turned and walked up-wind. "I can't sleep."

"Join the club."

Gretchen stood very still and swallowed twice. The walk lights circling the patio reflected on her freckled throat, giving her skin a mottled amphibious quality. She seemed ready to swallow a fly. "I talked to Mom today."

This in itself was not unusual. Gretchen and her mother spent hours yakking on the phone about clothes, the girls, recipes. Pablo often wondered how, when they first got together, he could have ignored the squeaky nasality that drove him nuts and made Gretchen a junior Fay. He figured he had just blocked out the sound by obsessing on Gretchen's spectacular breasts, now sagging in the moonlight.

"About what?" he asked.

"About us. About the house."

"Christ, Gretchen! You told her about the bank?" Pablo hated it when his wife went behind his back, especially to Fay. It was one thing when he borrowed money from the woman. He could spin it so she felt magnanimous and he maintained his manhood. He had always paid her back—with interest—up until this point. But Gretchen couldn't spin, couldn't lie. Not to her mother.

"What choice did I have? They're going to foreclose any day now. You're not working. I can't support us on a sales clerk's salary. I have to think of the girls, even if you won't."

"Keep it down. You'll wake the neighbors."

"I don't give a damn who hears me. I'm tired of pretending we're okay. I'm tired of pretending you're something more than a two-bit con artist."

Pablo wanted to slap that big mouth of hers, wipe the scorn off her weary face. "What do you want from me?"

Gretchen paused and sat opposite him. "Mom had a suggestion."

"I'm listening."

"We rent out this house. Consolidate our debts. Or file Chapter Thirteen."

"Bankruptcy?" Atlantic City flashed in front of him. One big score could turn things around. No, forget it. Gretchen wouldn't let him walk around the corner, let alone go away for the weekend, not since he maxed out all their credit cards.

"We can start over."

"Where? Where will we live?"

"With her." Pablo imagined himself inhaling the powdery smell of old lady on a daily basis and suppressed the urge to gag. Gretchen went on, "Just temporarily. It could be good for all of us. She's lonely, and she's having trouble taking care of the place."

"She let go of that housekeeper?"

"Consuelo? Yes. She had to. The woman works for Alyssa. Anyway, Mom needs the help. At least until the estate is settled."

"I thought Izzy was handling that."

"He is," Gretchen said. "It could take some time. Alvin's children are stubborn." Pablo remembered loco Alyssa's outburst in his mother-in-law's living room and her useless brother and sister just standing there. They'd fold. He was sure of it. They were no match for Izzy. Gretchen nudged his arm. Her nails were bitten to nothing. "Pablo? What do you think?"

"I don't know." Pablo dropped his cigarette, and ground it under his slippered foot. Then he kicked the stub into the boxwood at the edge of the terrace. Gretchen disapproved, but he knew she wouldn't reprimand him when she needed agreement on a larger issue.

"It's our best option," she said, looking away from the boxwood.

Pablo considered the angles. It would be a comedown, an admission of failure, living with his mother-in-law. But he could see the possibilities: proximity to Fay and her potential windfall. Alvin Segal was worth a bundle. The prospect of a big payday excited Pablo. It gave him hope that he could wipe out everything he owed, and have a shot at starting over, away from here. Maybe west. Arizona or New Mexico. Fay couldn't, wouldn't deny her daughter, her grandchildren, a share—not if they were all under one roof, taking care of her, comforting her through the ordeal. Then he could escape. Yes. It might be worth the musty odors.

Pablo patted the pack inside his pocket, compressing it flat. He put his arm around Gretchen, a gesture long withheld, and inhaled the pre-dawn air. It was light, clear, all humidity dissipated. "Okay," he said, steering his wife inside. "Tell her we'll come. Tell her thanks."

Fay sat in the sunroom, put her hand to her pounding forehead, and yawned. Four in the afternoon and she wanted to be in bed. Ever since Gretchen and her brood moved in ten days ago, Fay had been beset with fatigue and pains. Yes, it was her idea. In theory, having Gretchen and the girls here was a huge help. Fay hadn't replaced Consuelo, and dust and dishes piled up daily. In fact, they were a nerve-racking annoyance.

A nap would guarantee she'd be up all night. She had enough trouble sleeping before the family invasion. Her mind lit up as soon as she lay down, and ran through a list of *what ifs* concerning the conflict with Alvin's children. *What if they don't settle? What if she never sees even the prenuptial money? What if the whole thing goes to trial?* Izzy had promised her that wouldn't happen, but the situation had already gone too far. She'd been forced to take the little savings she had to pay Izzy's retainer. She'd been forced to file suit.

Now the waiting was killing her. Why hadn't that fancy lawyer of theirs responded? Was it some kind of strategy testing her will? If so, it worked. It was almost Labor Day, at least six weeks after the Segals had been served. Since Alvin's death she thought of his children as the Segals and herself as Fay. Just Fay. She would only use his name to get justice, then never again.

Fay looked out at the overgrown annuals in her garden and the burned-out grass comprising the lawn. She had fired the gardener shortly after letting Consuelo go. Ask Pablo to clean up the yard. It was the least he could do.

"It's mine!"

"No, mine!"

The children were at it again. Everyday after Gretchen picked them up from camp—a forty-five minute drive each way—Cara and Sabine came running in the door screaming like banshees. Over what? A doll, a sweater, who'd get the last cookie in the jar Fay had to constantly refill? Girls fight too much. So competitive. So mean.

"Stop it now. Both of you. No cookies if you don't stop now!" The fatigue and desperation in Gretchen's voice made Fay thankful she was only the grandmother and not responsible.

The commotion ceased. Fay thought about going to greet them while their mouths were still full of milk and baked goods. No. They'd find her soon enough. Instead, she picked up the lavender-scented eye pillow, a gift Mabel brought to the shiva. Fay rested her feet on the rose covered cushions of the wicker chaise and placed the green silk pillow on her eyes. The perfumed darkness was supposed to relax her. Placebo effect, Fay thought when her friend first explained. Fay didn't care, so long as it diminished the throbbing. She breathed in the vapor and the magic began.

"Grandma's asleep with that funny beanbag on her eyes!"

"Shush, Cara! You know you're not supposed to wake her up!"

"Shut up, Sabine. You're not the boss of me!"

"Girls, leave her alone. The woman can come back later."

"What woman?" Fay brushed off the pillow. No point feigning sleep. She looked at her granddaughters' upside-down faces inches from hers. Their breaths smelled like chocolate milk.

Gretchen started for the door. "I don't know, Mom. She asked for you. I'll send her away."

"No, no," Fay said, pulling herself upright, the throbbing in her temples a mere residue now, but she sensed that the slightest stress could bring it roaring back.

"Are you sure? You should rest." Gretchen fluttered when jittery, and this nameless woman at the door made her jittery indeed.

"I'm sure," Fay said, passing her daughter. She approached the front hall, and saw a serious-looking lady in an ill-fitting suit, not more than twenty-five. She carried an envelope.

"Fay Segal?"

"Yes," she said, attempting to straighten her back despite the widow's hump.

"You are served."

After the woman left, Fay didn't remember taking the envelope, or opening it, but she must have.

"The pigs," Gretchen said as she gathered and skimmed the fallen papers at her mother's feet. "Pablo! Where is he when we need him?"

Need Pablo? Fay couldn't imagine what for. She was disgusted with herself for allowing him to con her the way he had conned Gretchen all these years. What could Pablo do about this? What could anyone?

"Sit down, Mom. You look pale. Sabine! Get your grandmother a glass of water."

Fay did feel a bit faint. And ridiculous. She'd been expecting a return volley for weeks. Why fall apart now? No. She wouldn't. As Gretchen eased her into the one hallway chair no one ever used except to pull on or take off winter boots, Fay sighed. It was better to know they were going to fight than to remain in limbo.

"Bend over, Mom. Put your head down. Sabine! Where's that water?"

"I can't find a clean glass, Mommy."

"I'll be right there! Cara, stay with your grandmother. I'm calling Izzy."

Izzy? Izzy got her into this. He'd acted like it would be easy. Fay felt her granddaughter's tiny hand on her shoulder, and the false relief vanished, replaced by fear. As she rested her head on her chest—impossible to bend over completely—the vise behind her eyes tightened. She'd need more than an eye pillow to survive this.

22

Alyssa stood in the middle of her study. It was early Saturday morning. Winter light streaked the blinds and gave the contents of the space a radioactive glow. She had beaten a path through the piles of books, cartons, and furniture that Lorraine had pushed into the room the day before. Her sister was still asleep. Alyssa relished the time alone, before her things weren't hers anymore, before the inexorable process of deconstruction began. Alyssa had invited Lorraine to stay during the depositions, knowing full well that she would take it as permission to launch into clean-up mode.

All through the fall, Alyssa fended off Lorraine's not-so-subtle hints about the house. She hadn't been ready for this or any other sisterly demands. Alyssa made excuses for saying no to Thanksgiving dinner in New Jersey and to the Hanukkah celebration at Ken's—work and work again. Then they offered to come down for New Year's brunch at her favorite restaurant, but she still hadn't recovered from the funeral reception. The mere thought of so much family togetherness made Alyssa edgy. She had to acknowledge though, that Lorraine was right about the timing. They were due in Harlan's office Monday to give their sworn depositions to Fay's lawyer, and what better distraction than to tackle mounds of clutter together? The sound of water pipes and the steady whoosh of shower spray filtered down the stairs. Lorraine was awake.

Alyssa pulled a piece of notebook paper out of her robe pocket. When Lorraine had offered to help her, she felt both thankful and overwhelmed: thankful that she wouldn't be alone, overwhelmed at the massive task. The pressure to decide what to keep and what to discard paralyzed her, but whatever assistance Lorraine could give, she couldn't be the one to make these decisions. It had to be Alyssa's choice, and fear of making the wrong one—throwing away something she might need later, holding on to stuff she'd never use—kept her from making any choice at all. Whenever she felt this stressed out, she asked herself what Mother would have done. Sometimes the answer was hidden. This time it was clear. She'd have made a list.

At the top of the frayed page, its edge jagged from having been ripped off the notebook's coil, Alyssa wrote: *Things that must be let go.* Number one: Mother's clothes. The boxes of frilly nightgowns, silk dresses, cashmere sweaters, feathered fedoras and satin turbans sat stacked against the study's far wall. In the weeks after Mother died Alyssa had managed to pack and carry her mother's personal effects out of her closet and down the stairs to this room, where they stayed, waiting. For what? A garage sale? She didn't have a garage, and besides, she refused to put a price on Mother's belongings—garments that had touched her warm body. Alyssa waved away the subversive image of a bonfire, hissing and sputtering with wool, cotton, silk, and fur. She couldn't bring herself to give away or to wear a shred of it. Mother's taste screamed flamboyant—way flashier than her own—and Mother's figure, before she got sick, was considerably curvier. Maybe Lorraine would take the clothing.

Number two: the mail—six years of it. Time to get rid of the coupon packets, bills, magazines, donor solicitations, all with "Estelle Segal" in the address window. The piles, bolstering each leg of her desk and covering its perimeter, had to go. When was the last time she had space to write a check? Every piece of paper out. Except the *National Geographics*. Maybe Jamie would want them for his collection. Lorraine said he was into history, like Ken.

Then there was the lawn furniture—wire bistro chairs on which she and Mother had sat many a summer evening sipping homemade sangria, Consuelo's recipe. The chairs leaned against the corner opposite the clothing cartons. Alyssa hadn't used the patio since an awkward barbecue that Zeke had insisted on throwing, their first and only fourth of July together. His friends hung around the grill; hers stayed in the kitchen, their incompatibility a fatal sign.

And the painting portfolios—dozens of them that had, until last week, filled Mother's studio. Hundreds of canvases organized by year, never to see daylight. The extra sets of dishes, the pots and pans. Alyssa didn't cook, never would. The rolled up rag rugs made by Lighthouse for the Blind, Mother's preferred charity. The boxes of books—most nights Alyssa was too tired to read. On weekends she might leaf through a *Time* or *Newsweek*, to keep up appearances at the station. But crack a book? Too daunting. Any volume she started, she felt compelled to finish. Better not to begin.

Alyssa sighed. This was only room one. There was more in every unused bedroom, bathroom, and closet. Alyssa sank to the epicenter of the space, a patch of floor, three by three. She pictured herself, an object among others, hardening into a mummified version of her former self, unearthed one day, in the distant future, by a domestic archeologist studying the strange habits of late twentieth century haute bourgeoisie. What would such a student surmise? That one American woman had buried herself in an avalanche of possessions; that there must be others entombed like Alyssa Segal.

The staircase creaked under Lorraine's galloping footsteps. Alyssa crawled out of the room, and brushed the dust clinging to her pajama pants. Lorraine bounced into the room, wet hair flying, determination in her eye, a power bar in her hand. "Let's get going," she said. Her energy, which Alyssa had always found off-putting, demanded that little sister pull herself together.

Grabbing this sliver of opportunity to take the reins, Alyssa waved toward the dig site. "We're starting here. I have a list."

"What do you think?" Lorraine dressed in one of Mother's fifties circle skirts, spun herself into a whir of color, like soft ice cream layering from the machine onto the cone.

"Looks good. Keep it," Alyssa said. They had succeeded in emptying the room of all but the clothes, which Lorraine had moved, against Alyssa's objections, back up to the master bedroom to try on in front of the full-length mirror. It was noon. Alyssa was hungry and tired. "I need a break. Want anything?"

Lorraine pulled a rainbow sweater over her head. "Nothing for me," she said, the sweater muffling her voice. "I want to keep going."

"Overachiever," Alyssa mumbled, and went downstairs to get a yogurt. When she came back, Lorraine had moved on to the nightgowns. Alyssa shuddered. She's not going to try those on, is she?

"These go in the donation box," Lorraine said. Thank goodness. "Have you gone through the vanity drawers yet?" Lorraine sat on the red velvet stool and had the center drawer open before Alyssa could answer. "Whoa! What a haul!"

Alyssa bit her lower lip. The drawer had samples of hand creams, concealers, glosses, blushes, and shadows that make-up counter clerks showered on Mother every time she bought a new lipstick. Alyssa couldn't touch any of it. She watched in horror as Lorraine opened tube after tube, dabbing her lips and cheeks.

"I'll do you, if you'll do me," Lorraine said, pointing with an eye pencil.

"I don't know," Alyssa said.

"Come on. You said you needed a break. It'll be fun." Lorraine continued to primp and paint. Alyssa couldn't remember the last time she and her sister had had fun together. "Remember when you were five and I dressed you up in those cute costumes and took pictures with my Brownie camera?"

Alyssa couldn't help smiling at the image. "The Gypsy and the harem girl?"

"Yes, yes," Lorraine said, steering her to the bench and holding a cream blush to Alyssa's cheek. "My favorite was the flapper. You looked so adorable in Mother's string pearls. They hung down to your knees. It was hilarious. And the high heels, three times your size."

"You crimped my hair in marcel curls," Alyssa added.

Lorraine leaned over her shoulder. "I could do it again."

Alyssa looked at both of them in the mirror of their mother's vanity, heads together, women now with different lives, divergent points of view. She wanted to believe that they could play together again, but to do that she would have to remove the last item from the list, the one written in invisible ink, the one she was least inclined to part with, but which she knew Lorraine would insist upon: her decades of resentment.

"What do you say?" Lorraine asked, brush in hand.

Alyssa took the brush, tapped it on her palm three times, and put it back on the dresser. "Maybe later," she said.

"Okay. Whatever you want," Lorraine backed away from the mirror. She was hurt—Alyssa could tell—though she covered by sorting handkerchiefs. Mother had called Lorraine over-sensitive, but the years had leveled her off. Alyssa envied

Lorraine's distance, the cavalier way she could rifle through and discard Mother's things. Now Alyssa was the anxious one. Lorraine continued arranging the dainty squares on the bed in white, blue, and lilac stacks. "Anything else on that list of yours?" she asked without looking up.

Alyssa pretended to read; the final item was still there, to be unloaded later. Or never. Letting it go would take more than a box and some packing tape. The *Goodwill* truck couldn't take it away. "No," she said. "We're done for now."

23

Fay entered Harlan Fineman's offices accompanied by her son-in-law. She and Pablo would be deposed one after the other. Izzy had told her not to worry, it was yet another ploy in a long series of bluffs. They'll cave, he said. Long before trial, long before the situation gets out of hand, long before her money runs out. But Fay was losing faith in Izzy, now when she needed him most. This was already out of hand. Look where she was: in the enemy camp, about to be deposed. She had never been deposed before. The term got mixed up in her mind with dethroned. She pictured herself being forcibly removed from a large velvet and gold dais, thrown down its carpeted steps, and spit upon. Where *was* Izzy anyway?

Fay looked around the reception area—both sumptuous and understated—nothing like Izzy's bare mall anteroom. Though her nose was blocked from a cold that started on New Year's Day, almost a week ago, she could smell the hearty leather of the black and red couches and the tall fronds on the receptionist's desk. Eucalyptus in January. Fay had hoped to have this all behind her, to begin the year without baggage.

"You'll see, Mom," Gretchen said that morning over coffee as she rushed the girls off to school. "Just do what you have to today and it'll be over in no time." Fay found it difficult to believe her. All through the fall Fay had witnessed close-up the daily strain marching across Gretchen's brow, a younger mirror of her own face, no less harried. Money was all any of them thought about.

Pablo jiggled his foot in a continuous rapid twitch. Fay wanted to slap him. His inability to take care of his family, made this situation all the more loaded. She wasn't fighting only for her own survival, but theirs as well.

"Sorry I'm late," Izzy said as he plowed through the door, coat askew, wispy gray hair plastered on his forehead from the wool cap he stuffed into his pocket. He murmured to the perfectly coiffed woman behind the desk.

She didn't look up. "Mr. Fineman will see you now."

Fay rose. Her face flushed and her legs wobbled. Oh dear. This was no time to fall.

"Are you okay, Mother?" Pablo asked.

She hated it when he called her Mother. "I'll be fine as soon as this is over."

"Let's get this show on the road!" Izzy said. His glee disoriented Fay. Lawyers. They lived for trouble.

"Did you intend the transfer on May 12th to be a gift to you in addition to the amount mentioned in the prenuptial agreement, so that you would get double? Is that what you intended?" Harlan Fineman didn't waste any time. Izzy had warned Fay that Fineman was a master. He warned her not to volunteer anything, not to rush, and to answer the question as asked. Show their side that she would make a formidable witness on the stand.

Fay glanced around the conference table. Sets of male eyes bored through her: Izzy's pale gray, Pablo's black and impenetrable, Fineman's second—Templeton, was it?—bespectacled and earnest, and Fineman's own sharp lasers.

She looked away. The only women in the room were the stenographer, who pretended invisibility, and Alyssa Segal. When Fay first entered, she wondered why in heaven's name Alyssa was there. Fay had no intention of sitting in on the Segal children's testimony, of subjecting herself to their scorn and their lies. Then she realized. Alyssa Segal was there to intimidate her. Well, she was doing a poor job of it, sitting in a compact lump at the end of the long table, coat on as if she might bolt at any moment.

"Mrs. Segal?" It was Fineman again. And then Izzy's inquiring hand on hers.

"Yes?" Fay began. "I mean no. *My* intentions had nothing to do with it. It's what Mr. Segal intended that is important." Izzy withdrew his hand. She was on track.

Fineman pressed. "Are you telling us *you* didn't intend it?"

"It was a complete surprise to me."

Templeton slid a paper across to Fineman who placed it in front of Fay. "Have you seen this before?"

Fay examined the sheet. "Yes," she said.

"Who wrote it?"

"I did."

"Why did you write it?"

Careful. "Because Mr. Segal asked me to."

"Did you read it to him after you wrote it?"

Maybe she did. Maybe she didn't. Fay couldn't remember. "No. He read it himself."

"Did Mr. Segal use the word gift in that letter?"

"No."

"Did you think it was a gift?"

"Yes." No hesitation.

"Did you tell anyone about the money Mr. Segal gave you?"

Fay didn't want to implicate Gretchen. Bad enough her unreliable husband had to testify. "No. No one. Mr. Segal told me not to tell his children."

"But you did have a discussion with the Segal children about the transfer of funds?"

"Yes."

"Where and when?"

"The Monday after Mother's Day, last year, in my living room. Mr. Segal was present." Fay saw Alyssa shift. Good, make her squirm.

"And how do you suppose they found out about the transfer?"

"I don't know. From Mr. Segal?"

Fineman placed his palms on the table and spread his long fingers like a pianist about to play scales. "You said Mr. Segal didn't want them to know. Why not?"

Fay pulled herself up and said in the strongest voice she could muster. "Because Ken, Lorraine, and Alyssa didn't think I should have any gift, or anything at all." Alyssa flinched.

"Did they say that?"

Fay paused. "Not in so many words."

"Then why do you say they didn't want you to have any gift?"

"Because they questioned my right to the money, and they interfered." Fay wanted to direct this at Alyssa, but restrained herself.

"Interfered how?"

"I don't know how. I just know that once they voiced objections the money was held up."

Then Harlan Fineman stood and read from another paper. "You are aware that in your complaint, your suit against the three Segal children, you are accusing them of, and I quote 'conspiring to deny Fay Segal any benefit of the gift made to her, to seize the gift, returning it to their father's trust fund so they would benefit from it upon his death.' Conspiracy. A very serious charge. A crime. What part did each of the children play in this conspiracy that you've sued them over?"

Fay swallowed and looked at Izzy who was rereading the suit. Help! Nothing. Not a flicker of encouragement or direction. "I don't know exactly what they did. I wasn't there."

"Where?'

"At Alyssa's house. Actually at *Alvin's* house." Alyssa crossed her arms. "It was still Alvin's house at the time. Martin Patras was there. And another attorney."

"Were Mr. Patras and this other attorney co-conspirators?" Fineman laced the question with such contempt, it sounded ridiculous. Izzy wrapped himself in an oblivious cocoon. Alyssa loosened up, tipping forward.

"I don't know," Fay answered.

"If there was a conspiracy," Fineman's silky voice hardened, "I need to know what you are basing this charge on. Were the lawyers Mr. Segal hired part of the alleged conspiracy?"

"I wasn't there."

"So you are charging conspiracy and you don't know what took place?"

Fay was getting weary. "I know the result. The gift was blocked."

"Did you pay gift tax?"

"No." Fay wanted to rotate her neck, stretch the kink that shot an arrow through her skull. Instead she willed herself not to move, not to betray any weakness.

"But you thought it was a gift?"

"Yes."

"Did you tell Mr. Segal that the money had not been transferred?"

"No. By that time he was very ill. I didn't want to burden him."

"When Alvin, as you say, was getting very ill, had this been a gradual process? His going downhill?"

"No. It was sudden."

"So when you took him to Puerto Rico were you concerned about the effect of the trip on his health?"

How dare this man. "His doctor, Dr. Cabot, had given us a clean bill for the vacation."

Fineman paused to look down at his notes. "You remember being in the airport when Alvin fell on the airplane, and they took him out in a wheelchair and Alyssa was there?"

Fay wasn't going to give this person anything else to use against her. "The wheelchair was for me. He came off on foot." Alyssa cleared her throat. Izzy rolled his pen between his fingers.

Fineman sat back. "Did it occur to you then that Mr. Segal might someday have to be put in a nursing home?"

"Yes, it occurred to me."

"Was your previous husband in a nursing home?"

Barney's jolly blank countenance danced before her. "Yes." She thought a lot about her second husband these days. At least he hadn't *wanted* to deny her.

"Did it ever occur to you that if Alvin went into a nursing home all his money would go to the facility? Did that thought ever occur to you?"

Fay's insides began to solidify as if Fineman had poured cement down her throat. Of course it had occurred to her. She wasn't an idiot. But she wouldn't give this predator anything. "I don't recall."

"Did it ever occur to you that it would be nice if you could take the money before it was used for a rest home?"

The cement turned molten and flowed out of Fay's mouth. "Not only did that not occur to me, but if I had any money of my own I would have given it to him for any care he needed. I would have gone out and scrubbed floors for him. I was that much in love." Fay knew she had lost control, but the aria satisfied the seething that had simmered within her these many months. The nerve of this proceeding, questioning her loyalty to Alvin, her right to the fruits of their marriage, in spite of his insistence on the damned prenup and his betrayal. He chose his children over her. She would never forgive him for that.

Izzy cocked his head. He seemed to be gauging the effect of Fay's outburst. Alyssa coughed and tugged at the strap on her shoulder bag. Pablo stared at the ceiling. Harlan and his henchman leaned in so she couldn't look away. "Did you ever discuss with Alvin why he was going to give you exactly the same amount you would receive upon his death?"

"He said he wanted to take very, very good care of me for the rest of my life. He said that over and over."

"In front of whom?"

"Me."

"In front of the children?"

"No."

"Did you ever say to Alvin that this additional money would affect his children's estate?"

"No, because he never talked about it again. I thanked him profusely and he smiled and I said I was happy. Then he said he was happy I was happy. He was a very generous, loving, considerate husband, and I let him know that I appreciated it."

"So you felt entitled to half the estate for two years of marriage?"

Warning lights flashed before her. "I never said that."

"But that's what it amounted to."

"It was what he wanted."

Fineman drew himself up and said, "Let's be clear. You have no witness who would corroborate that Alvin said he wanted to give you the alleged gift?"

Fay sank back into the chair and covered her eyes. She wanted all this to fade, for this horrible man to stop badgering her, but she knew her only means of escape was to answer the question. She removed her hand from her face and whispered, "No. No witness."

Harlan Fineman pressed his palm on the notes in front of him, as if embossing a seal. "No further questions."

As soon as he was released from interrogation, Pablo fled Fineman's building and darted into the first bar he could find, an Irish pub a block north, whose faded shamrock banner beckoned. Inside, the walnut paneling meant reliable oblivion. Pablo parked himself on a cracked vinyl stool, lit a cigarette and inhaled. He tapped its tip onto the heavy glass ashtray the bartender had shoved in front of him.

The bastards. All of them were bastards, especially the lawyers, who had fired condescending questions at him for what seemed like hours.

"Are you *currently* employed Mr. Diaz?"

"I'm *self*-employed."

Fineman's sidekick, Templeton, smirked. Pablo had expected as much from Alyssa Segal, who had punctuated his responses with little sucking sounds as she worked a lozenge around that big mouth of hers. Even the stenographer, stone-faced through Fay's deposition, moving only her fingers to record every syllable, had raised an eyebrow.

"Has Mrs. Segal ever given you or your wife financial help?"

"Yes. For our daughters, her grandchildren's school tuition." Pablo had dared them to react. His children had as much right to a fine education as the Segals' privileged brats. The stenographer looked about forty-five, divorced, no kids due to plumbing problems. She thought his kids belonged in the subpar DC public schools with the children of drug dealers. She probably thought he was a drug dealer. They had all been intent on trapping him in the lies he had been forced to tell. Because of Fay. Yes, Fay was a bastard, too, although she had saved his ass on more than one occasion.

"Where do you live Mr. Diaz?"

The question echoed in Pablo's head. He rolled his shoulders in a vain attempt to shrug off the answer, one of the afternoon's degradations.

"You took an elderly man in fragile health on a trek in the rainforest?"

The insinuation made Pablo's temples throb.

"You know a good deal about your mother-in-law's finances, Mr. Diaz."

"She counts on me to help her. I'm an entrepreneur."

"An entrepreneur." Fineman's upper lip curled as he shot Pablo's self-description back at him. This from an attorney in second-hand clothes, retro tweed and spats, which made no sense to Pablo. The man was at the top of his game. Why not dress the part? No matter what straits he was in, Pablo took care to look prosperous. Today he had worn his bespoke Prada suit bought for the dotcom launch.

"What were you doing in the rehab center in the middle of the night?"

Pablo answered that Alvin was unhappy and Fay wanted him home immediately. Pablo took pleasure in Alyssa's gasps and wheezes as he described Alvin's condition, blue and still. Under different circumstances Pablo would have assumed she had hiccups.

"Mr. Diaz, did Mr. Segal ever discuss money with you?"

A full glass appeared before Pablo. He downed it, and savored the sharp after-burn coating his throat, which wiped away the last of the day's script. He slid his glass toward the bartender—a burly young guy with thick eyebrows in permanent glower. Ash covered the bottom of the receptacle. He crumpled the empty pack. Smoking made Pablo's head pound. He emptied the second shot, and looked up at the clock above the bottle-laden shelves. It was nearly five. He wanted another drink, but he would have to go home, face Gretchen's barrage of recriminations, explain the mistake, which Izzy had slammed him for just as he was about to escape into the elevator.

"What were you thinking?" Izzy grabbed Pablo's upper arm. "You just contradicted Fay's testimony, which you witnessed!"

Pablo shook off the old man's grip. Why did Fay have any faith in this geezer? Izzy struck him as inept and dishonest, a fatal combination. "She's elderly. Confused. It's understandable she might forget who she told." He pressed the red down button.

"The confusion was yours," Izzy said, and walked away.

Pablo slapped a wad of bills on the bar and headed out the door. It was almost dark. Bitter cold cut through his overcoat. He extended his arm to hail a taxi. Once inside the stale compartment he imagined directing the driver to the airport, where Pablo would catch the next flight to Vegas. If he'd had the cash he would have done it. If he had the cash he wouldn't have been there at all.

24

"Fascinating," Harlan said, tossing the adjective over his shoulder to Templeton, who raced out of the conference room and down the hall to catch up.

"Yes," said Templeton, huffing and puffing—too young to be in such poor shape. Harlan reached the door to his office. Templeton skidded to a stop next to him, and looked expectantly at his hand on the knob, but Harlan had no intention of letting the young associate in. He'd spent quite enough time with people for one day. And besides, Harlan knew that Templeton only wanted to pick his brain when it would be so much better for him to work out his own theory of the case. Builds confidence. The world didn't need any more Harlan Finemans. If that was even possible.

"So bold," Harlan said, throwing Templeton a bone. "She's not unintelligent."

"No," Templeton agreed, eager for any morsel from Harlan's mouth.

"Brazen. What interests me is the personality flaw." Templeton cocked his head. Harlan went on while fully blocking the door. Templeton got the message and stepped back. "The delusion, the sense of entitlement, the right to run roughshod over everyone to get what she wants, even little children."

"Quite extraordinary," Templeton ventured, "almost sociopathic." He waited, knuckles clenched on the case file, for Harlan's agreement.

Harlan wondered if he could steer Templeton into a Yoga class to relax the fellow. "Yes," he said, "and the theatrics. I loved the bit about scrubbing floors."

Templeton chuckled with appreciation and passed his hand across his already thinning pate. "A real diva, that one."

"And here's where we are in luck," Harlan said.

"How so?" Templeton gulped, taking a half step forward.

"Divas tend to overplay, to milk the audience's response," Harlan paused. "Useful in the long run." He turned his back to Templeton, opened the door, and stepped inside, careful to close the door quickly behind him.

Just before he had clicked it shut, Templeton, panting for a last word, asked, "What about the son-in-law?"

Harlan wished his colleague hadn't asked, but preferred not to be rude. He cracked the door. "You mean the liar?"

Templeton jumped at the word and backed down the hall. Harlan closed the door and sat at his desk. He hadn't meant to shame the poor man. Templeton was a good lawyer—potentially a great one—but when there was nothing to say about a subject, say nothing. End of lesson. He'd made a split-second judgment not to call Pablo on his blatant contradiction of Fay's testimony. The deposition record would be quite enough to hang them both. Harlan picked up a pad and began a thumbnail sketch of Pablo Diaz. The flashy suit, the facial hair. Above all, he hoped to capture the feral look in his eyes when he fell into the trap.

Alyssa dashed into the station, barely acknowledging Arnold—the security guard with whom she usually exchanged pleasantries—and headed straight for Paul's office. She had to restrain herself from pounding on the door, but her timid, insistent knock didn't register. He had to be in there. Paul always left his door open when he was out and closed when in. Alyssa needed to see him immediately. Ever since Mother's illness and death she had relied on Paul as more than a sympathetic boss. He was a father-therapist-friend. He'd seen her through the worst time in her life, never failing to calm her. She knocked harder.

"Come in," Paul said in his familiar bass.

Alyssa looked back as she closed his door behind her and noticed heads turning away in studied obliviousness. She knew the station staff talked about her. She knew she didn't fit into their world, though she did her job well. When she first came to work fifteen years ago, she tried hard to join the coffee break chatter, but soon found she had little to contribute. Her responses to jokes and gossip were off; she laughed too much in a voice too loud, or she looked blank rather than enthralled at the juicy tidbits. Eventually she stopped trying. Alyssa didn't care what they thought of her. Paul and her best friend, Zelda—a single producer like Alyssa—were all she needed.

"You won't believe what they said," Alyssa told Paul before she'd managed to sit down. "Under oath!"

Paul sat back in his chair and smiled that toothy grin of his. Alyssa appreciated the way his eyes rested on her, without judgment. He was the busiest man at the station, but he always had time for her. She loved him for it. Not that way. He wasn't her type, with his portly frame and stubby fingers. And his wife of thirty years was a real dear.

"So?" he said.

Alyssa proceeded to recount Fay's protestations of devotion to her father and Pablo's tall tale. Every so often Paul would interject "slow down" in response to her rapid-fire gulping as she spilled the story. During the depositions Alyssa had made a huge effort to suppress any reaction to their outlandish statements, and in so doing had quashed every automatic response including inhalation. In the safety of Paul's office Alyssa could breathe again.

"That's it. What do you think?" Alyssa fell back into her chair, winded.

Paul grinned. "I think it's great news."

"Why? They're not giving up. We have to give *our* depositions next week. I'm so freaked out."

"Great news, because if they are resorting to declarations of love and outright lies then they don't have a case. They'll settle. After the hash they made of the depositions, their lawyer will insist on it."

"But he's an imbecile to have encouraged them this far."

"Don't worry, he's just going through the motions. You'll see. It will all work out." Alyssa wanted to be convinced by Paul's take, but she wasn't. She realized as she drank in her boss's common sense, thirsty for more, that no reassuring words could make this travesty acceptable. Nothing would make it okay except its end. Paul went on, "What do Lorraine and Ken think?" Alyssa nibbled her lower lip, avoiding Paul's gaze. "You haven't spoken to them today?"

She shook her head and felt the muscles around her skull shrink like those awful swim caps she had worn at camp. She wanted to go home, pull the curtains in her bedroom, and lie on the bed, forever. When she volunteered to attend Fay and Pablo's depositions, she hadn't anticipated the anxiety it would create. Sure, she'd assumed nerves, but nothing like this. Her body seized from her toes upward. This must be what ALS feels like, she thought, and then was ashamed at the comparison. She was not going to die. This wouldn't kill her.

"You should talk to them," Paul said. He often reminded her to reach out to someone else, not to depend only on him, her cue to thank him and leave. But she wasn't ready.

"I know, but Ken's at work and Lorraine will–"

Paul raised a finger. "Ah, ah, ah, don't project. You don't know what she'll say."

Alyssa stood. "Right." But she knew. Lorraine would try to take her mind off the day, and expect her to play more "bag and toss," the cleaning game big sister had invented. Despite Alyssa's initial efforts at control, Lorraine had taken over. She'd become intent on emptying every shelf and corner. She even had her own list, and was probably working her way through Alyssa's closets at that very moment. Alyssa's head hurt. "I think I have to go home. I'll do the 6 a.m. shift tomorrow."

"Not a problem." Paul waved his pudgy hand.

On the way out, at the station entrance, Ally made a point of talking to Arnold, the doorman she'd breezed by earlier. She asked him about his children, his wife, how Christmas had been, and watched him beam the moment he answered. Her own hollowness crept in; she wanted to flee this man and the wholesome life reflected in his face, a life full of loved ones. Even Fay and Pablo managed to live together, though after what she'd witnessed today she knew their relationship was a calculation.

Alyssa pictured her living room, and her sister clearing it with ruthless efficiency. Energy pulsed through her. She wanted to go home, cancel the dumpster; she hated that it took up her whole driveway and sparked the neighbors' curiosity, a further invasion. They walked by with their children in strollers and on bikes with training wheels, heading to the elementary school playground for a Saturday afternoon on the swing set. "Renovating?" they asked without waiting for an answer. She watched these self-satisfied parents proceed up the hill, and was certain that they talked about her, like her colleagues did. So what? Who cared what any of them thought? Lorraine included. Alyssa resolved to take everything out of storage, everything her sister had forced her to remove. Fill the empty spaces. Reclaim her house.

25

Lorraine had experienced flop sweat once before, when performing her one-person play, *Women in Extremis,* Off-off Broadway in a tiny basement cabaret before an audience including Brad, her parents, and theater and television producers, who had the power to lift her career out of the underground theater netherworld. It was her big break and she knew it. The perspiration, an inadequate term for the wet film, which coated her forehead, dripped into her eyes, ringed her mouth with salt, and prevented her hands from being able to grip her props, gave her the sensation of being an urban waterfall, one of those hard stone walls washed with a perpetual sheet of water that were supposed to relax tightly wrapped office workers. Except on that stage no calm could be found. It was too intimate. Lorraine had been inches from everyone in the audience. They could see her shine, watch the droplets scatter whenever she moved her head. Like now, across the table from Small.

Harlan darted into the hallway, and came back unaccompanied. Where the hell was Ken? He should have been here an hour ago. Now she'd be next and she wasn't ready. Alyssa glanced at Lorraine, then disappeared. Lorraine couldn't blame her for not wanting to be there any longer than necessary, but she felt abandoned. If Ally could sit through their accusers' testimony, why couldn't she sit through her sister's? Alyssa's own deposition had been amazing—cool, unflappable. Couldn't she stay and beam a bit of her glow onto Lorraine?

She repeated her theatrical mantra: *stay in the moment.* But it didn't help. While listening to Alyssa's forthright answers to Small's nasty questions, she began to panic. No matter how much Harlan or Brad or Ken or even Alyssa tried to spin this—*it's a formality, just be honest, don't worry, you'll do fine*—Lorraine became more and more convinced the closer deposition day got that she wasn't up to the task. Her lack of professional experiences, her private nature, felt like distinct disadvantages. Alyssa gave firm, steady responses, and Lorraine saw the world turn upside down. This must be how Alyssa was at work: efficient, no-nonsense, competent.

When Lorraine woke up that morning, she was stunned to find a new book tower smack in the middle of the living room. She didn't dare ask why. *That* Alyssa, the one whose control issues manifested in piles of junk and the sudden reversal when she made Lorraine put every ragged towel in the linen closet back where she'd found it, had been dormant today. Thank goodness. Whatever Alyssa's shortcomings, she had been masterful here. Lorraine's competitive hackles rose and her marshmallow insides sloshed. Do not throw up. She forced her attention on Small's thin lips. She found the man repulsive. She would have to use all of her performer skills to face this mercenary.

"What was your father's mental condition the day he signed the letter rescinding the transfer?"

"He was alert."

"How did you know that?"

"He clearly communicated his intentions to me, my brother, and sister, and to Mr. Patras."

"Was he your father's attorney?" Lorraine knew Small wanted to pin Martin with malpractice for setting this in motion.

"He was my father's advisor."

"Was he your father's attorney?"

"Asked and answered," Harlan snapped.

"On that day was he your father's attorney?"

"I'm not sure." Harlan and Templeton exchanged glances. She was such a dope. She had made more trouble for Martin. All Small did was persist, push her, and she broke. Lorraine opened her purse and removed a tissue. It would have been too obvious to dab her forehead, so she settled for the run-off around her lips. One bead slid along her nose. She tipped her head to direct it across her cheek. Too late. The globule landed on the legal pad in front of her. Harlan said to write down anything that struck her as important. The paper was blank and wet.

"You have stated that it is your contention that your father did not make Fay Segal a gift. On what basis?"

"He said it was not a gift."

"Were there witnesses?

"Yes, in Fay's house the day after Mother's Day last year. Fay, her daughter, and son-in-law, my sister, my brother." Lorraine rubbed her slick palms on her thighs. The wool pants resisted the moisture, so she wiped one hand at a time on the upholstered chair seat.

"Did you visit your father often in his last year?"

"Uh–yes."

"How many times?"

"I don't know."

"Two, three?"

"More than that."

"Half a dozen?"

"I spent time every week with him during his last illness."

Small's marble eyes held her. "Before or after the subject of this suit came to light?"

Lorraine wanted to walk out. This man was playing on the guilt she carried every day, the guilt that she had not taken better care of her father, the guilt that she had not stopped him from marrying this woman, and the fear that she and her siblings, along with Martin, had somehow, in trying to correct a potentially devastating error, made an even bigger one.

"After." She sniffed back the rivulets, which ran out of each nostril.

"I'm sorry, I didn't hear you."

"After," she croaked.

"Mrs. Warner, did you consider your father to be a generous man?"

"Yes."

"Even when he chose to leave the bulk of his estate to your sister?" Small had asked Alyssa if she lobbied for the house. She bristled and denied it. Even so, Lorraine wondered if it might be true.

"Yes," she said.

"A gift which amounted to half of his estate," Small continued. Gift. The word stabbed Lorraine, a wound that hadn't closed since Martin revealed her father's plan.

She swallowed. "Yes, he was generous."

"Still, that must have been difficult for you. The inequality."

Harlan placed one hand on the table. "Objection. Opinion, not question."

"Was the inequality difficult for you?"

Lorraine's eyes stung. Sweat? Tears? All one. Like the curtain call in which her soaked costume stuck to her as if she'd been caught in a downpour, Lorraine forced herself to finish, mortification or no. "My father knew I was settled in my marriage, that I had what I needed."

"That will be all," Small said. Harlan put his cool, dry hand on her shoulder and ushered her out of the room.

Ken followed the heavy aroma of beef, thyme, and tomatoes to the kitchen. Stew. The smell alone could have sent him plunging decades back, to childhood winters. That, and the sight of Lorraine bowed over the iron kettle, her wavy hair so like Mother's, reminded Ken how much he missed the family that used to be.

Lorraine lifted her head and tapped the wooden spoon against the pot's rim. "Hey, how did it go?"

"Yes, how was it? How did you do?" Ken hadn't even noticed Alyssa sitting in the corner, her head framed by hanging pans. Well, his sisters were together. There was hope. When Ken left Harlan's conference room, he'd imagined that he'd tell all, including his gaffs—his confusion over dates and places, his stammering, the number of times he asked for questions to be repeated, because his brain, both shut down and hyperalert, couldn't withstand Small's interrogation. But despite her industrious cooking or maybe because of it, he suspected that Lorraine was in worse shape than he, and revealing his screw-ups wouldn't reassure her.

"I got through it," he said. "What about you two?"

Alyssa perked up. "I thought I really held my own against that scumball!"

Lorraine nodded glumly. "Alyssa did great. Strong, firm, she'd didn't take any crap. I on the other hand–" She shook her head.

"It couldn't have been that bad," Ken said.

"Where were you anyway?" Lorraine asked. "You were supposed to sit in on my testimony. In fact, you were supposed to go before me."

"Sorry. I didn't allow enough time on the interstate." Ken knew this was a poor excuse. The real reason was worse. He'd left late, because he hadn't wanted to come at all. "Harlan said it didn't matter what order we went in."

Lorraine glared. "It mattered to me. It really threw me that you weren't there. I was terrible."

Ken turned to Alyssa who was tapping Morse code with a fork. "Ally? Is she exaggerating? Tell her she did okay."

Ally put down the utensils and shrugged. "I wasn't there. I had to go back to work."

"Well what exactly did you do wrong?"

Lorraine sniffled. "I got Martin into trouble."

Too much self-blame. "He got himself into trouble. Besides, he's a lawyer. He knew what he was doing when he spoke up." Ken said this out loud as much for himself as for his sister.

"And I sounded as uncertain as I felt," Lorraine went on. "It was like I didn't know how to be myself."

"But you told the truth?"

"Yes, but I *sounded* like I was lying."

Ken looked at his sisters. When had they switched insecurities? Ally all bluff and bravado, Lorraine all whine and whimper.

"What did Harlan say?"

"He told me not to worry, which meant I stunk." Lorraine was so hard on herself.

"Harlan's precise." Ken wanted to temper her self-flagellation. "When he says not to worry, he means it."

Lorraine twisted her lip, unconvinced. "I don't know how I could ever take the stand."

Ally huffed. "They'd be bigger fools than we think they are if they push this to trial. They've got no case. Just a lot of trumped up charges. Conspiracy! Give me a break!"

Ken cleared his throat. Ally's bluster concerned him. It was dangerous to get too cocky. "Small asked about the recordings."

Lorraine's eyes widened. Ally stood. "The ones we did in the rehab center?" Lorraine asked.

"Yes."

Ally inhaled. "What did you tell him?"

"He wanted to know what they contained and who had them. I told him they contained our father's statements of intention regarding the money and that Fineman had the tapes."

"That's good, right?" Lorraine seemed unsure.

"I don't know. Small's building a case that we put thoughts in Dad's head, that we were running the show, preventing Fay from getting her due. The tapes could be damaging."

Alyssa bristled. "Why? Daddy said what he said."

"But remember how we had to draw statements out of him?"

Ally jumped out of her chair. "Come on, Ken. Conspiracy?"

"I'm just thinking like a lawyer." Ken had enjoyed preparing for his testimony more than actually giving it.

"Small's more jackass than lawyer," Alyssa sneered.

Lorraine turned down the burner. The flame flickered and went out. "Ken's right. Better pray Fineman can keep them out of Small's hands." She opened the cabinet above the stovetop and pulled down three large soup bowls. Ken noticed large gaps in the dish stacks, and nothing on the top shelf. Must be due to the cleanout his sisters were working on. Come to think of it, the house did seem different. The walls had odd rectangular spaces where paintings and photographs used to be. The halls, nearly impassable last year, echoed.

Lorraine ladled the stew in generous portions, and Alyssa placed the bowls on the table. They sat in their historical places, and although their bodies were larger, for Ken it might as well have been parents' night out, with big sister in charge. Only now big sister was shaken, little sister was hyper, and it was up to him to soothe them both.

Lorraine blew on a spoonful of steaming broth. "What happens now?"

Ken had asked Harlan the same thing, and repeated his words verbatim. "We wait for them to decide if they want to proceed or settle."

Alyssa bared her teeth, and tore into a roll. "What do you think?"

"I don't know." Ken paused. He patted his lips with the napkin. Foreboding mingled with the savory aftertaste of childhood comfort food. "It's already gone further than I ever anticipated."

26

Izzy folded the white carton lid and licked his left forefinger. A hint of orange sauce hung under the nail. He ran his tongue around his mouth picking up a trail of chicken and ginger. Sesame seeds caught between his crowded teeth. He would have to floss later. After he reviewed the transcripts. He looked at the clock. Better get to it. Fay would be waiting by the phone.

Every morning since the depositions a week ago, Fay called to harangue him. "Find a way to settle this. I need to get out without spending any more money." Her voice pierced his eardrum. He wanted to hang up on her, but he restrained himself. After all, she was his client.

"I don't want to go to trial!" she squawked that very morning.

"I'm aware of that. Their inadequacy can be used against them."

"How?"

"As leverage."

"But that lawyer of theirs–"

Izzy shuddered at the mention of his adversary. Being in the same room as the great and powerful Harlan Fineman had been a thrill, a sort of lifetime achievement, but by the time Izzy returned to his mall office, the buzz had worn off. In retrospect he felt only Fineman's disdain, like a sticky residue, which no amount of scrubbing could remove. Or perhaps it was worse than disdain; it may have been disregard. From the way he had raised his chiseled chin every time he objected, Fineman made clear that he did not consider Small worth thinking about. Izso Small would show him.

"Don't worry, I'll handle him," Izzy bluffed, not sure what he would do. "The deposition transcripts just arrived. I'll call you after I read them."

Izzy combed each page twice. It was all there: Fay's inability to offer a witness, Pablo's direct contradiction of that fact, the potential for Martin Patras' disbarment, Alyssa's curtness, Lorraine's nerves, Ken's waffling. He admitted to himself that his assessment of the Segals' testimony involved a great deal of reading between the lines. Their poor demeanor, which he was convinced would prejudice a judge or jury against them, had been palpable, even if absent from their actual statements. He trusted what he had seen more than what he was now reading. The salient question: did their failings outweigh his own clients' gaffs? If so, he would certainly push Fay to continue, right up to the courtroom door. He wasn't about to let Harlan Fineman's mere reputation derail him. A win here would mean more than money, which he needed—his ex had been nagging him to pay for her new roof. A win would lift his practice to a different and superior league. Beating Fineman could send shock waves through the legal community, elevating him to giant killer. At the very least, it would propel him out of the mall.

"They can't stand up to this process," Small told Fay a half hour later. "They'll make lousy witnesses in their own defense."

"What do you mean?" she asked.

"Ken bumbles. Lorraine was terrified."

"I thought that was Alyssa."

"Alyssa is cold, unsympathetic. I'm thinking like a juror now."

"This could be a *jury* trial?" Fay's surprise registered in a louder than usual blast.

"As plaintiff, the choice is yours. The prospect of a jury trial will scare them silly. Enough that they'll fold."

"Hmm," Fay salivated, then asked, "What about Pablo?"

"Minor player. His impact will be minimal."

"I'm worried about Consuelo."

Izzy had forgotten about the housekeeper. Fay was right to be concerned. Who knows what the woman overheard? "Let's not get ahead of ourselves."

"But she was there, in the house, that day with Alvin on the phone."

"How good is her English?"

Fay paused. "Fair."

"Good. As long as it's not excellent, I can discredit her." He'd play the language card. The woman couldn't fully comprehend whatever she'd heard. He could depose her, but didn't think it was necessary, not when there were incriminating tapes. Fay's breathing accelerated. Slow her down. "But we're still a long way from the witness stand."

"It's your job to keep me out!"

Izzy didn't like it when Fay—or any woman for that matter—took a tone with him.

He knew his job. His job was to ruin Harlan Fineman's perfect record. "I will. Let the Segals stew a little longer. The depositions traumatized them. They'll cry uncle. Just wait."

Fay hung up without another word. Izzy piled the depositions at the corner of his desk. Where was the cellophane-wrapped carrot cake he'd bought at the deli that morning? Ah. Squished under the file for a man who'd been hit by an ambulance. That one would be a piece of cake. Izzy bit into the iced crumbs and chuckled at his mouthful of cliché.

PART VI

Court

27

Lorraine, her brother, and sister followed Woody Templeton into the chamber. He wore his earnest competence like an expensive suit, pride that unsettled Lorraine. Or was it his constant sniffing? She wasn't sure. The past few weeks had been so disorienting she no longer trusted her impressions of people, places, or events. The trajectory from her father's death last June to this day of reckoning had been so rapid, so surreal, it had distorted her sense of time. It was early spring, not even a year later, and Lorraine could not stop asking, *how could she be here, about to defend herself in a court of law?*

"Wait here," Templeton said, motioning them to sit in the first row behind the defense table. Then he turned his back, put down his briefcase, and began organizing accordion files.

Lorraine sat. Ken put his crutches on the floor and lowered himself next to her. Harlan had insisted that Ken leave his prosthesis at home, in anticipation of Fay's accusation that he had "carried Alvin from the house." Harlan wanted the jury to think, *those poor children,* and then, *that evil woman.* His careful staging both comforted and alarmed Lorraine. She was in good hands—the best—as her father reminded her repeatedly during his last days. She told herself, *here you are, now deal with it.* Alyssa slid in beside Ken. These days they moved in birth order. No one touched, or made eye contact. It wasn't necessary. They were tied together as surely as if they had been bound, gagged, and thrown as one flailing mass into the ocean.

Lorraine looked up for a sliver of sky. She needed to escape the atmosphere of contained expectation, but there were no openings, no windows—just like a theater. She had spent her life—before suburban motherhood took over—in theaters, from the grungy Off-off Broadway spaces that hadn't met a code they couldn't violate, to regional stages designed by master architects. The suburban courtroom was more the latter, with its deep mahogany wood trim lining forest green walls, crimson cushions on the jury chairs, and an autumnal blend on seats for onlookers. Would there be any? Lorraine imagined the space could have been a screening room or cabaret, if not for the judge's podium, the witness box with its high-backed La-Z-Boy, and the two long tables for the legal teams and their clients. The room triggered familiar theatrical suspense, its dramatic silence containing stories held mum inside the panelled walls. The same butterflies and adrenalin that she experienced waiting in the wings before a first entrance tumbled within her. Lorraine glanced at Alyssa, slumped in dejection. Ken sat stiffly and stared at the empty judge's chair. Lorraine concentrated on her breathing, preparing for what could be a more difficult labor than delivering Jamie into the world.

"Where are they?" Alyssa asked.

"They'll be here. They have no choice," Ken said.

At this, Templeton turned and bent over the railing separating them. "Once they arrive, the lawyers will meet with the judge to discuss final offers for settlement."

"We're not–" Alyssa said.

Templeton raised his hand, and Alyssa sank back. "Most cases settle in the eleventh hour. The judge will encourage this. Harlan and I will bring their offer back to you, and you will decide whether to accept it, or go forward."

Lorraine and her brother and sister took a collective breath.

Templeton continued, "We are fully prepared, whatever you decide."

Then the doors behind them opened and a piercing cackle punctured the room. "I can't believe we're here!"

Lorraine used her peripheral vision to watch Fay waddle into the courtroom, followed by Gretchen and Pablo. Fay was dressed in her best—a black and gold tunic and long skirt—a gaudy contrast to Lorraine's navy wool dress, the most conservative thing she owned. Gretchen looked drawn and skeletal in a suit whose too short skirt, revealed her bony knees, and Pablo, in his beige linen jacket, could have been a cruise director. They sat across the aisle behind the plaintiff's table.

Templeton waved to Harlan, who had entered behind Fay's offspring. Lorraine wanted to smile at the sight of him, clad in vintage sienna tweed—and were those spats?—but her mouth resisted. This was no day for amusement. She raised her chin in his direction. Harlan dipped his head in response, and shook Ken's hand. Alyssa thrust hers forward and Harlan cupped it between his.

A moment later Izzy Small inserted himself between them. "Judge Naylor is waiting for us." Alyssa recoiled. Ken studiously ignored the man. Lorraine turned away.

After the three lawyers exited to the judge's chambers, behind the podium, Lorraine slumped as the simmering animosity descended around her, raising the temperature in the courtroom, rolling down its walls, and transforming this legal theater into a furnace set to incinerate and resolve, one way or the other, the charade of the past ten months.

Lorraine tried to swallow, but her throat had gone dry. Her body ached, immobilized by days of sleepless preparation for the unthinkable now come to pass. She and her siblings faced the judge's podium, shoulder to shoulder, refusing to acknowledge the adversaries across the aisle. Somehow, over the years, long before Fay entered the picture, Lorraine had sensed that it would come to this—a public spectacle. Her parents' love carried conditions. They needed her to be strong, so she was; they needed her to be capable, so she was. But, in light of recent revelations, Lorraine felt that her very strength and independence had been used against her, to dismiss her needs—so much like Ken's and Alyssa's—to be cherished and cared for, like any other child, notwithstanding her forty-five years. All she wanted was to be treasured without requirements.

Ken tugged at his pinned pant leg. Alyssa, whose pale face had a clammy sheen, fixed her gaze on her lap.

"What an attractive courtroom!" Fay brayed, "Somber, yet not depressing." Gretchen's mop head bobbed in sympathy. "I really can't believe we're here!" Fay repeated, full blast this time for their benefit—Lorraine was sure—her own thoughts out of Fay's mouth. But the woman had brought this on herself, as Harlan often reminded them: Fay was the aggressor.

"It'll be all right, Mother. This is just a formality," Gretchen said. Her wraith-like figure swayed.

Ken shifted, and murmured, "bullshit" under his breath.

"I certainly hope so," Fay said, pitch rising. "As soon as this farce is over, let's go to lunch. Something festive. Maybe Mexican!"

Ally cleared her throat and looked at Lorraine. They were both thinking the same thing: the brazen idiot, counting her chickens.

"Look," Fay went on, "Lorraine's husband isn't here." Lorraine's cheeks burned. How dare that woman use her family as a psych out trick? They'd agreed that Brad should take care of Jamie. "Wouldn't Alvin be appalled?" Fay cackled. "I do miss him so. He was something. His feet may have been cold, but the rest of him was HOT!"

Gretchen giggled. Alyssa lurched forward. Ken's back flinched in awkward spasm, as he tried to block his sister's head from hitting the railing. Lorraine grabbed his arm. She wanted to charge Fay's red cape like a bull and rip the woman's tongue out, but knew this tasteless desecration of her father's memory was just a desperate ploy. That knowledge though, didn't quell her outrage.

Alyssa, upright, muttered, "Bitch."

Ken patted Alyssa's thigh. "Don't let her get to you."

Then the lawyers reentered, Fineman in the lead, with Templeton trotting behind. Small trailed—he seemed to be avoiding his opponents' wake—and hustled Fay and her family into the anteroom. After they left, Fineman approached the railing. Lorraine froze. This was it.

"The conspiracy count is dropped," Harlan announced.

"Thank God," Alyssa said, falling back as if everything was done.

Harlan went on, "Should we go to trial and lose–"Alyssa gasped "–there will be no punitive damages." Lorraine felt her brother's and sister's relief in the combined nod-shrug that passed from one to the other down the bench. But *she* was not relieved. Templeton shifted behind Harlan, about to pounce. Lorraine had to remind herself they were on her side.

"And we have a final offer," Harlan added. The room seemed to darken. Lorraine glanced at the ceiling lights; they were still on, despite her imaginings.

"What is it?" Ken whispered, as if he couldn't bear to know.

Harlan spoke in measured tones. "They want half the prenuptial amount and this is over." Lorraine couldn't tell from his deadpan delivery what he thought, but she was aghast at the nerve of this woman.

"In addition to the transfer money?" Ken asked.

"That she tried to steal," Alyssa said.

"In addition, yes," Harlan said, bypassing Alyssa's outburst. Something in his owl eyes as he peered at each of them told Lorraine that he was reading them, gleaning their stomach for the fight ahead if they didn't take the offer. The amount dangled before them like bait, or a final bluff, an indication of Fay's complete and utter misreading of the Segals. The woman didn't understand who they were. Their pitiful deposition performances had left the impression they couldn't withstand a trial—the meek children of a timid man, pushovers, who will fold rather than face a public battle—emboldening Fay and her reptilian attorney. But they were wrong.

Lorraine realized in this decisive moment that neither she nor her siblings had been able, until now, to take their own measure, to know for certain, that they would or could fight this battle to its resolution. At this moment, in Ken's quiet inscrutability, Alyssa's controlled wheezing, and Lorraine's own clenched jaw, they adopted their father's qualities: his strengths—integrity and determination—as well as his weaknesses—passivity and fear of confrontation. Unlike his friend Harlan, Alvin Segal had not been a trial lawyer. He preferred briefs and filings to active courtroom drama. He preferred to hide.

And yet—Lorraine watched Harlan and Templeton as they patiently paused for an answer, a signal to stay or go—her father had proven that he too was a fighter. He'd fought his way into American society, and though he'd long lingered in the shadows, he did, ultimately, take his rightful place at the pinnacle. He overcame his limitations, and set a standard, one which Ken had more than met when he fought his way back after the accident, and which, even Alyssa, in her pain and confusion, had fulfilled in a solid career. Now it was Lorraine's turn.

"Prevail," Daddy had said, the day before he died, looking up at her with his milky half-blind eyes.

"What do *you* want to do?" Harlan asked only her. He had read her thoughts, respected her status as oldest, and gave her the decision-making power.

"We don't have the money to give," Lorraine said.

"We do if we take care of the college costs ourselves," Ken said. "We never really expected Dad to pay for that, did we?"

True. She hadn't expected anything, until she heard the contents of the will from Martin. Then she expected everything and more, every nickel, including Jamie's trust, knowing even that would not make up for the unequal shares. "I don't know," Lorraine said. She had to step carefully. She could feel her brother cracking. She looked over at her sister. Too quiet.

"Maybe we should just let it go. Go out to lunch, be done with all this," Ken said, copying Fay's plan.

"Ally?" Lorraine tried to rally her sister from her stupor.

"It's too much," Ally said. "It's robbery."

"Not unless you agree," Harlan corrected. "We're prepared to go to trial. My sense is they aren't."

"A bluff?" Ally asked.

"It wouldn't be the first," Woody added.

"This is so awful," Ally said.

"It will be a hundred times more awful not to stand up for what's right," Lorraine answered. She looked at Harlan. His smooth forehead and receding hairline reminded her of Daddy.

Then Ally spoke, reaching for Ken's hand. "It's your decision, yours and Lorraine's. They're your children."

Lorraine smiled a thank you. Then she realized that Alyssa's house would not be in jeopardy if they settled, but she couldn't walk away on that basis. "Ken, listen to me. We haven't come this far to give up now."

"It's a risk," he said.

"Your brother's right," Templeton said. "A trial always involves risk."

"We can't cave out of fear," Lorraine said.

"We'd still be left with something," Ken said. Who was he trying to convince, Lorraine or himself? She paused to let Ken's rationalization dissolve, replaced by her long-standing indignation. Harlan's eyes focused on her. The insecurity she'd entered the courtroom with that morning had vanished. She spoke directly to him as if he were indeed channeling their father.

"No. No. It just won't do," she said, her voice steadier than her body, which shivered with a righteous fever. Jamie's college fund was the least of it. This judicial stage would determine her place in this family, and most importantly, what the Segals would be from now on: a family that stood up for principle or one that let an outsider roll over them. "We haven't come this far, been through this much, only to let her rob our children, and mock our father's wishes. We won't be able to live with ourselves if we give in. Daddy told us to fight. He wanted Harlan to help us. There isn't enough to give her what she wants and to take care of the grandchildren. It would be a travesty of what our father intended."

"Are you sure?" Ken asked.

"Yes, yes I am," Lorraine said, as resolve solidified within her. "I couldn't live with myself if I didn't take this all the way. It's what Daddy wanted us to do."

Harlan spoke. "So your decision is?" He wanted her to spell it out. Like the meticulous Alvin Segal, who expected precision in the most mundane verbal exchange and drove their mother crazy correcting word choice at the breakfast table, Harlan wanted absolute clarity. Her brother and sister turned as one and waited for Lorraine to speak. Their deference surprised and pleased her. They had followed Harlan's lead and given her back her place.

"We fight," Lorraine said.

Harlan nodded, his eyes flashing approval. He clapped his hands. "We proceed." Templeton grinned his litigators-love-to-litigate grin. And with that, the two left to deliver the news.

Lorraine felt her brother and sister straighten beside her, their spines lengthening as if her rallying cry had stretched them beyond their ordinary stature. It took a moment before they could move. Lorraine handed Ken his crutch, Ally slid aside. They stood. Ready. Together.

Fay sat in the empty courtroom in stunned disbelief. Despite Gretchen's pleadings to "come out for a bite," she had lost her appetite the minute Izzy returned with the Segals' refusal. There would be no celebratory lunch of enchiladas and sangria. Instead, a trial would begin—Fay glanced at her watch—in twenty minutes. A jury trial. The very scenario Izzy had assured her over and over again, was only a ploy, to alarm Alvin's children, to force them to settle. Now the bluff had been called. How dare they go this far! How dare they spit in the face of her most generous offer! Had they accepted, she would have gotten only three-quarters of her due. Now she would have to submit to this dreadful public action, spending money she didn't have to hold on to money she deserved. She would have to undergo more grilling from that lofty attorney of theirs, as well as the scrutiny of a jury. Now she was the one scared silly, not those greedy Segals.

Fay checked the time again. Fifteen minutes until the room would fill and jury selection would begin. There was no going back. She felt dizzy. Perhaps Gretchen was right; Fay should have eaten, fortified herself against the coming onslaught.

A clerk entered, positioned himself next to the judge's podium, and clasped his large hands together. The sight of this guard jolted Fay. The flutter in her upper chest drifted down into her empty stomach. The man did not acknowledge her. Fay hated being ignored. She noted the firearm on his belt, and the handcuffs chained to his pocket. What he would do if she suddenly started screaming? If only her voice had any power to stave off her imminent exposure. Fay wondered if Izzy knew what he was doing. He had misread the opposition. Was he capable of trying the case? He'd been so sure they would take the offer. Had he even prepared for the alternative? He certainly hadn't prepared *her*.

Fay studied the guard, whose steady professional glare aimed past her. If she vented her rage, attempted to destroy this hall of justice, he would bark on his walkie-talkie for backup, then wrestle her to the ground, embarrassed to be tackling a woman of advanced years. Then she would be the defendant in a case of criminal vandalism. This seemed to Fay's overwrought brain, preferable to what was about to happen.

Alyssa surveyed the forty-two faces seated on the defense side of the aisle. The judge had instructed her, along with Ken and Lorraine, to move to the plaintiff side—a few rows from Fay, Pablo, and Gretchen—so that he could fill the opposite seats with potential jurors. These people seemed to Alyssa like space aliens, not a jury of her peers. They may as well have sprouted antennae and wings. Alyssa's nerves distorted their human characteristics. She was afraid to identify with anyone who was about to pass judgment on her.

After the judge heard a few excuses—no childcare, unforgiving boss, hourly work—he dismissed a young woman with hair cascading down her back, a stocky grumbling lady, and an elderly African American man who leaned heavily on his cane.

"I'm going to ask the defendants in this case to stand and face the jury pool," the judge said in clipped, businesslike tones.

Then he called each of their names, and Alyssa stood, hoping she wouldn't faint. Templeton had instructed them to maintain a neutral expression, to look the jury pool in the eyes, but not to stare. After all, he said, "It's a civil trial, so, nine of them will be your jury."

"If any potential juror recognizes any of the defendants, their attorneys," the judge continued, "or has had any past history with the defendants' father, Alvin Segal, or their mother, Estelle Segal, please raise your hand." Alyssa shuddered at the unexpected mention of Mother's name. It violated a boundary, dragging her into this obscene proceeding. But even if the judge hadn't named her, Mother was there, inside Alyssa, crying out to stop this.

A middle-aged man wearing wire-rims raised his hand. "I recognize Harlan Fineman." *Natch*. Harlan was by far the most famous person in the room. Out of the corner of her eye, Alyssa caught him turn and face the man. He welcomed scrutiny in a way she couldn't. He was used to it.

"From personal experience?" the judge asked.

"From the newspaper," the man said.

Alyssa heard Small clear his throat. He must hate this. No one recognized *him*.

"You are free to go," the judge said. Then he instructed Alyssa and her siblings to sit, and had Fay and Pablo rise. Fay clapped her hands together. The veins bulged. Alyssa pictured her keeling over. Pablo lifted his chin as if for a photo op. No hands went up. No one knew either of them. The judge read a list of witnesses, and one woman with hennaed hair said that Dr. Cabot had treated her aunt. The judge released her. Then he asked if anyone had personal experience of conflict over a will or estate. Three people raised their hands; each was excused.

Alyssa counted and re-counted the heads before her: 3, 6, 9, 12, 15, 18. Counting calmed her. Six of them would decide the case, plus three alternates. Multiples of three. Good.

She began to scrutinize the faces for signs of empathy—softness around the eyes, kindness seeping through their pores. It was hard to discern humanity when they were trying to be invisible, bodies rigid, faces blank. Understandable. Who wanted to serve on a jury? Alyssa found herself begging them—the promising ones, the ones with a maternal or paternal aura—to stay. But the longer the lawyers questioned, the more candidates they dismissed, the less Alyssa could uncover a strategic pattern. She figured Small wanted older women who might identify with Fay, but he challenged two gray-haired women. Harlan had said he wanted younger jurors who would see themselves in the Segal children's plight, but he rejected four, to Alyssa's mind, presentable professional types. Perhaps he was concerned they would sneer at Martin's ambiguous ethics, or look down on Lorraine's lack of steady work. They might feel superior to Ken, the high school teacher, or judge Alyssa herself deficient, because she lived alone.

And then, one by one, individuals agreed upon by both sides—old and young, male and female—began to take their places in the jury box. *Our jury,* Alyssa thought, chilled by the reality. She tried to memorize their faces, this time searching for intelligence. Warmth was good, but in a crisis, brains trumped feeling. Mother and Daddy had taught her as much. How else would these people be able to sort the arguments, the contradictions? Alyssa looked at the man in the front row at the far left. He had a full head of hair, which had begun to recede. She guessed he was about Ken's age. Did he have common sense? The woman next to him was young, barely out of school. Was she mature enough to comprehend their loss? In the second row sat a housewife—Alyssa didn't know this for sure—but she had said she worked at home, a euphemism for Lorraine's situation. Alyssa studied each face, finding them more and more impenetrable.

Only the woman at the near end of the back row, the one with the gray-streaked ponytail, gave her any acknowledgment. A slight tip of her head towards Ally, or was it Ken? The woman had softened when Ken adjusted his crutches to stand before them earlier. She wore oversized glasses and a loose white blouse, and gave off a faintly bohemian air, which reminded Alyssa of Mother. She might be an artist. Alyssa sent her a telepathic message: *make things right*.

The woman looked past her, unavailable like the rest. Frustrated, Alyssa retreated into her comfort zone, the fantasy world where people were collectables, like the dolls in her bedroom, or the magazines Lorraine had insisted upon removing. Alyssa pictured each juror sitting obediently on her shelf, unable to take any action that might harm her, unable to take any action at all.

Izzy shuffled the index cards before him, then rested his right hand on his bulging file as if it were a bible. Swear to tell the truth, the whole truth. Thank God lawyers didn't have to swear such an oath. His job was merely to point out *possible* truths: that the Segals were greedy, detested Fay, and did everything in their power to persuade their addled father to rescind his most generous gift, all to their collective benefit.

Fay sat at their plaintiff's island, fuming, furious at the failure of their eleventh hour play. Perhaps he had exuded too much confidence in suggesting the final offer. *A slam dunk…they'll fold like a house of cards.* He should have given her the straight story: one never knows what a defendant will do under pressure. He had to admit, at least to himself, that this one caught him by surprise. Why hadn't Fineman pressed his clients to settle? He couldn't possibly want to put them through a full-on court proceeding. Or did he? Izzy checked out his adversary. Fineman had such a serene presence. If his eyes were closed, Izzy would have sworn the man was meditating. Fineman, the legal wizard of Washington. He probably thinks he can pull this one out of a hat. The thought rattled Izzy.

"Mr. Small? Are you ready to begin?" the judge asked.

Izzy absorbed the jurors' expectant attention, and that of the clerks, Fay, Pablo, Gretchen, the defense table, and two court watchers in the seats behind him. The room hummed with anticipation. His temples throbbed. Ready? He'd slept too soundly the night before. He'd assumed an easy paycheck. He should have, at the very least, outlined an opening. Izzy cleared his throat. Here goes nothing.

"This case revolves around some nasty business," Izzy began, speaking into the ether. He smoothed his jacket lapels and reminded himself to face the jury box. It had been a long time since his last jury trial—six, seven years, he couldn't recall—but he figured trying a case was like riding a bicycle. "A family dispute," he continued, and then proceeded to tick off the main points in the mental checklist he'd formulated on the fly: Alvin's gift to Fay, the Segal's influence on their fragile father, the significant dates of Alvin's phone order, the letter taking back the money he wanted her to have, and the trust change naming Ken Segal co-trustee. The jury took this in with impassive concentration. Izzy despised juries. Who were they anyway? Random citizens required to perform their civic duty. Sheep. Find one to address; the rest would follow. His eyes settled on an older balding woman he thought might identify with Fay.

"It's important for you to keep in mind throughout the testimony you are about to hear, that Alvin Segal was so far gone when his children got hold of him, that he didn't know what he was doing." Izzy zoomed in on the woman's exposed scalp. He drifted, musing whether or not she had, as he had done, considered implants. He drifted back, "You will hear expert testimony from a board certified gerontologist to that effect."

Izzy moved toward the jury. The front row recoiled. He pulled back. Don't push them. Save it for the closing. "And most importantly, you will hear, especially from the defense, that the amount in question is identical to the amount named in the prenuptial agreement. That might raise eyebrows. I see some of yours lifting. It certainly gave me pause when I first heard of the situation. I ask you to remember that the prenuptial agreement between Alvin Segal and his beloved Fay says explicitly that Mr. Segal could, at any time, give Fay gifts. The agreement did not preclude them, even in the same amount."

Izzy waited while the jurors scribbled his words on their notepads. Power surged through his chest, like a jolt from paddles used to revive heart attack victims. He might make it through this after all. He was capable, convincing, a force to be reckoned with. Then he realized that the one point he had most wanted to make had been rendered moot in the judge's chambers. Fineman had bested him. He couldn't shout conspiracy. He had to settle for the milder *undue influence.*

"Finally, I will ask that you recognize the Segals' manipulation of their father–" Izzy said, pointing for the first time during his opening, towards the defense table. "You'll hear tapes exposing their actions. And I'll ask that you repudiate their calculated attempt to rob Alvin Segal's wife of her dear husband's gift."

He relished the bulging vein in Kenneth's temple, Alyssa's fixed mouth, and Lorraine's hard stare. They certainly looked guilty. Anyone could see it, even a reluctant jury. Then he sat. Fay listed towards him, but said nothing.

"Mr. Fineman?" The judge motioned to the defense table.

Fineman rose, buttoning his natty tweed jacket. Did he think this was a tea party? Izzy checked the jury, hoping they would think him a buffoon, but instead he saw that they were intrigued. "If the court will permit, a moment while we set up," Fineman said. Set up? Set up what? Then Templeton lifted a huge poster board and placed it on an easel in front of the jury.

Izzy craned his neck. "Your Honor? May I stand near the jury box to follow along?" The judged waved him over. Izzy moved next to the woman with the zebra-striped ponytail—one of Fineman's picks—her face the most animated of the lot. Her eyes narrowed at his proximity. Or perhaps she was having trouble reading the chart. They had gone to the trouble of creating a timeline. Izzy's back tightened. God, Fineman was putting on a show, a production with visual aides. Izzy should have seen this coming. Fineman was known for entertaining and instructing a jury like a star professor before awestruck pupils. Damn. No sooner had Templeton, that flunky, positioned the board, than the jurors—working as a unit now—leaned in, alert, pencils erect, ready for the defense attorney to lead them through it. He could see by their eagerness that Fineman had won the opening duel without having even addressed them. The simple act of showing an outline primed them to believe his theory of the case. Notes or no notes, they wouldn't credit a thing Izzy had said.

The top of the chart, in big bold letters, read: *Fay Segal, plaintiff v. Alyssa Segal, Kenneth Segal & Lorraine Segal, defendants.* Below, a timeline began with *1938–Alvin Segal comes to America from Poland.* Ken didn't have to look at the chart. He knew its contents by heart. For the past three months—at Harlan's request—he had put together the sequence of events, starting with a brief family history, then the incidents in dispute. At first Ken approached this assignment with dread he didn't dare reveal to Harlan. After all, the man was saving them money and for that Ken was grateful.

"You can do this, can't you?" Harlan had asked, more as a formality than an expression of doubt. Harlan, a man of supreme confidence, expected the same from those around him, even vulnerable clients.

"Yes, of course," Ken had answered.

But he wasn't sure. He was a high school history teacher, not a lawyer. How would he know what to include, what to leave out? Once he began though, his insecurity dissipated. Night after night—with Priscilla begging him to come to bed—Ken reviewed the twists and turns leading up to the present. He matched his notes with his sisters' to give Harlan the most complete picture possible. No detail was too small: not Fay's dismissal of Alvin's hearing problems months before the call to the broker, not her desire to put her husband in a nursing home the minute he had any physical difficulty, not Consuelo's presence in their home. Harlan dropped the reference to Alvin's deafness—Dad's frailties could work against them—and decided to play up Fay's nursing home plans, and the housekeeper's knowledge. Ken didn't know what Consuelo would say, but Harlan had placed her in a far more central role than Ken could have anticipated.

Sleep deprivation aside, Ken had relished the job. As it turned out, he was good at it. He understood the logic of the case. He was able to put it in order, think like an attorney, see the other side, which his sisters refused on principle to do. They acted as if justifying Fay's actions, even for the sake of their own strategy, was family treason. But for Ken it was a satisfying game. He used to beat his sisters at chess, because he was better at thinking three or four steps ahead, the very skill he used to help build the case. Why, he asked himself while he watched the jury study his work, had he resisted so adamantly his father's pleas for him to go to law school? Ken saw now, after having acted as Harlan's client/paralegal, that not only was he made for the law, he would have enjoyed it.

Ken listened to Harlan, with his masterful demeanor, take the jury through the contents of the revised chart. His chart. Ken claimed it with pride. Harlan's freewheeling style awed him, his ability to improvise from whatever Small had dished out. "Mr. Small indicated in his opening that his own eyebrows raised at the coincidence of the prenuptial amount and that of the transfer on May 12th. Exactly my reaction, and it should be yours." Harlan was not above telling the jury what to think. "The amounts are the same, because Mrs. Segal was looking to double her money, half the estate for two years of marriage. Not a bad haul."

Harlan was much looser on his feet than in the privacy of his office. The courtroom was his element; it freed him. Like a great performer, Harlan Fineman blossomed in front of an audience. He was on. "The case is about someone who will never testify–" Harlan continued, immediately conjuring Dad, "–Alvin Segal, a dignified, discreet person, a careful person, who carefully drafted an estate plan meant to provide for his children and grandchildren." Ken wondered what Dad would have thought of his old friend's description. He would have been flattered, but also mortified that his second marriage had resulted in such public disclosure. "This case is about his intention, about what Alvin Segal wanted," Harlan went on. Not this. Not this display.

"What Alvin Segal wanted was to take care of everyone in his family, fairly and equitably. The plaintiff has acknowledged in her deposition that he never once called the transfer *a gift*. It is our contention that in order to care for his wife, and at the same time protect money for his grandchildren's education and his three children–" Harlan turned and gestured in their direction, introducing each of them like game show contestants. "–Lorraine, Kenneth, and Alyssa Segal–in order to preserve his original unchanging intentions towards his beloved family, Alvin Segal sought only to *advance* Fay Segal the prenuptial amount. "

At the mention of his name, the kernel of fear lodged inside Ken burst open. Just sitting in these seats, sweat gluing his pant leg to the upholstery, trying to hold himself together for his sisters, for his wife, for his children, was all he could manage. The reality sank in; he was being introduced as prelude to testifying. He stared at the witness stand. How would he cross from here to there? How would he maintain any sense of propriety, hopping on one foot, crutches under arms, as Harlan requested?

Ken had long ago rejected the role in which he was now cast—tragically crippled son—though he understood the necessity. He had worked hard to function normally. He had perfected the use of his state-of-the-art prosthesis. No one who saw him stroll down the street, guiding Josh's tricycle while carrying Stella on one shoulder, or running in the town marathon would ever pity him.

This was his favorite ride, the seamless drive from Austin to San Antonio, midday Mondays. Ken jumped on his bike—a 1974 Honda CB550, bought for pennies, because it was twelve years old—and cruised along I-35, words and images percolating through his brain. He had escaped the Northeast a year earlier, after a horrendous fight with his father, who refused to accept that his only son would not wise up, stop wasting his time, and go to law school.

"I'm a writer," Ken shouted and slammed the door to his parent's home. He knew he sounded deluded, but didn't care. He was sick of compromise. As an undergraduate he had wanted to major in literature. His parents vetoed the choice with a word: impractical. So he settled on history, and rationalized it as good background for a novelist.

Now, bombing down the blinding highway, Ken felt free. The fact that he was broke didn't matter. His odd jobs, from bartender to security for the Laguna Museum to Barton Springs lifeguard, paid the rent on his crummy studio in downtown Austin. The jobs numbed him, but demanded no real commitment, leaving his mind open to fill notebook after notebook. The writing—character sketches mostly—hadn't yet coalesced into stories. Ken felt sure they would. One day.

With the sun directly overhead Ken realized he was late. He'd promised to meet Nan for lunch at noon on the River Walk, next to the outdoor café where they met. She said she had to talk to him about something—mysterious woman, Nan, several years his senior, her maturity the main attraction. Ken was sick of clingy college girls, leaning on him when he couldn't yet lean on himself. Nan was self-sufficient; she'd supported herself for years as hotel manager for a Hill Country B & B. She wanted nothing from Ken but a good time.

Don't keep the lady waiting.

He gunned the engine. The speedometer hit 97. Nan's face, her dune blond hair and the freckled mosaic that fanned across her nose, filled Ken's mind as his front tire blew, and hurtled him and his motorcycle upside down on the four-lane stretch at Live Oak.

"Mr. Segal? Mr. Segal?"

Ken wondered why the voice was calling his father. He opened one eye.

A man lifted his lid, and stabbed Ken with a beam of light. "Mr. Segal? Can you hear me?"

Ken realized *he* was Mr. Segal. He tried to speak, but his tongue wouldn't move. Nod, he ordered himself. He willed his head forward and searing pain inflamed his back and neck.

"Good, he's waking up," the man with the gizmo on his forehead said.

A doctor. Of course. Ken opened both eyes into a protective squint.

"Boychick!" The real Mr. Segal covered Ken's hand with his. Shadows with hair at differing heights surrounded his bed. Dad, Lorraine, Brad, Nan. Nan was here. Adrenalin surged, but nothing moved. His body was not at his command. He wanted to ask if he was paralyzed, but the words wouldn't come.

"Can you feel this?" The doctor poked Ken's left arm.

Ken nodded, welcoming the pain. Not paralyzed. His body throbbed underneath a thick cloak. Layers of padding separated him from his senses.

"This?" Right arm. Again, fire.

"And this?" The doctor moved to the end of the bed. Left foot.

Ken rasped, "Yes." His mouth tasted of blood. His throat burned.

"Is he going to be okay?" A voice from the shadow in the corner. Mom.

"And this?"

Ken heard the doctor and saw him touch a white object at the end of the bed. Then he noticed that his right leg was swathed, hip to toe in bandages. The object was his right foot.

"Kenny?" Lorraine approached his side.

The doctor waited for his reply.

Ken closed his mouth. He refused to answer. Instead he forced his head away from his family's pleading gaze and rested his cheek on the starched hospital pillow.

"Well then," the doctor said, after a clinical pause. Even through the fog of pain Ken sensed that the physician just wanted to get on with it. Do what had to be done. "Mr. Segal," the doctor continued, "you're very lucky."

"What?" Luck didn't put you in the hospital. "How long have I–?"

"You've been unconscious for thirty-nine hours."

Thirty-nine. Ken's logy brain struggled to translate the number into days. One. And a half. Plus three. Then he noticed Nan, standing in the doorway, like she couldn't decide whether to stay or go. This reminded Ken of Ally. He surveyed the faces. No Ally.

"Now that you are awake, we have to deal with the leg," the doctor said.

"What do you mean by that?" Lorraine asked, the only one who hadn't moved.

"We have to decide whether or not to try to save it." Ken watched his father and mother turn ever so slightly away from his bed.

"What do you recommend?" Lorraine again. Her voice was firm, too firm. She's steeling herself, Ken thought. He couldn't connect with the conversation. What were they talking about? His leg. They were talking about his leg.

"A complete resection," the doctor said, overlapping Lorraine. No hesitation.

"Resection?" Lorraine pressed for clarity.

Don't explain, Ken begged silently. Don't make it real.

The doctor put his hands together and dropped to a hush. "Amputation."

Ken heard his father exclaim, "No!" Then his mother gasped and stumbled out of the room. His father's hoarse cry, "Estelle, Estelle!"

Brad wept and left. Nan stepped into the room—more a traffic maneuver to avoid the exodus than a sign of commitment—her glance darted between sister and brother.

Only Lorraine stayed put, and held his hand while she shot question after question at the doctor—*surgeon,* Ken corrected—a surgeon who had planned this all along. His big sister was doing the job no one else could, least of all Ken. He fought to remain present, not to float down the hall to embrace his distraught parents.

"Is there any chance of saving it?"

"Very little."

"Give us a percentage?"

"Ten percent."

"What if we wait?"

"Gangrene."

"How much do you have to take?"

"Above the knee."

"How many of these procedures have you done?"

"Hundreds."

Ken let the volley between Lorraine and the surgeon lull him, like watching a game whose outcome was fixed.

"When?" Lorraine asked.

"Tomorrow morning, first thing."

Lorraine rubbed his arm. Ken saw her face was wet, though her voice remained steady. The doctor patted the wrapped leg, as if putting it on hold for later purchase.

"Can I stay?" Nan knelt next to him, and stroked his hair. Hers curtained her eyes. She made no attempt to part it. "I'll stay all night. You shouldn't be alone."

"Yes," Ken said. He didn't recognize his own strangled voice.

Lorraine kissed his cheek. "I'll be back in the morning. I love you."

Ken's lips wouldn't pucker, so he squeezed her hand.

Nan stayed the whole night, as promised. She cooled his forehead with wet washcloths, and sang Simon and Garfunkel to him in her wobbly soprano. Ken couldn't tell her that he hated "Bridge Over Troubled Water," or that he was out of his mind with terror. He couldn't tell her anything. It would be their last night together. After the operation Ken hardly saw her. Weeks later, when he had learned to operate his prosthesis well enough to hobble down the hospital's rehab corridor to make a call, Nan let him know that she was sorry, but she'd intended to break up with him that day. Ken understood. It wasn't anyone's fault, certainly not hers.

Or his father's. Dad came each day to prop him up during physical therapy, but Ken found himself doing the reassuring. "This is my fault," Dad said, over and over. "If only I hadn't driven you away."

Ken would steady himself against his father's short sturdy frame and shake his head. "No, Dad. You're wrong. You had nothing to do with it. I drove myself." When he said this, his father would sigh, unconvinced by the literal. He refused to let himself off the hook. The accident had crushed his father's spirit just as the motorcycle had crushed Ken's leg.

Neither he nor his father knew then that Ken would recover, meet Priscilla, have a life. He would move on, except for a part of himself that remained arrested at age twenty-nine. In this hour of reckoning in a Maryland courtroom, middle-aged Ken was stripped once more of the able-bodied persona he'd fought valiantly to assert. He was reduced to the physical, undeniable truth of his condition, the whole truth and nothing but: amputee, the man with the missing limb. That's all he would be today, an image, a powerful symbol of need, and a sympathetic foil for Fay's treachery. How could she deprive this unfortunate man? The totality of his adult achievements—devoted husband and father, respected teacher, responsible member of the community, even his small but critical contribution to their defense arsenal—would count for nothing next to the absence of his right leg.

28

Day two—plaintiff day—a day that would, from Harlan's vast experience, undoubtedly be filled with falsehoods and distortions. He trusted Templeton to cross-examine Dr. Cabot's standard brand of medical arrogance. The physician had testified that it was impossible for Alvin to have been both clearheaded on May 15th, the day he signed the advance letter, and "a zero"—as the good doctor loudly proclaimed—on the mental status exam he administered the following day. Templeton offered their good days-bad days theory of Alvin's condition, and extracted the doctor's grudging admission that in *some* cases that was true, but not, he was certain, in this one. Harlan's young colleague went on to ask why, if Mr. Segal was in such bad shape, had the doctor okayed the trip to Puerto Rico. Cabot's shoulders twitched—an involuntary distress signal Harlan hoped the jury caught--and said, "He trusted Mrs. Segal's judgment." Then he added, insisting on the last word, "Mr. Segal could not have been fully oriented on the fifteenth."

Templeton returned to his seat and whispered, blowing his metallic breath into Harlan's right ear, "Couldn't budge him." Harlan made a mental note to recommend green tea with honey, but wasn't worried about Cabot—his intransigence a pebble in his shoe—annoying but trivial.

Harlan glanced in his clients' direction. Cabot's adamant testimony had rattled the trio. They craved animal comfort, but

Harlan knew his job: to give them something better and more lasting than a hug, to give them a victory—worth more than a fatherly embrace. Harlan noted Lorraine's rigid jaw, Ken's rapid blinking, and Alyssa's pallor. He reminded himself that they were like any other defendants. Just because they were Alvin Segal's progeny didn't make them immune to the anxiety engendered by a hostile expert witness.

Small called Jimmy Stackwell. Harlan relished this misguided choice. Stackwell was, after all, the broker who along with Martin Patras, had blown the whistle on Fay. His sympathies were with Alvin and the children. Why then had Small called him for the plaintiff? Harlan watched Small sidle up to the witness box. He managed in the course of the first five minutes to fire off one leading question after another to which Harlan had the pleasure of voicing repeated objections.

Small thrust his head toward the stand. "Did you have any reason to believe that Mr. Segal did not know what he was doing when he transferred the funds?"

Stackwell, a handsome man with a boyish face and unruly blond locks, more aging model than stockbroker, answered, "No," before Harlan could again interject—

"Objection!"

When Templeton took over, Stackwell's affection for Alvin–"one of my favorite clients" and suspicion of Fay–"she succeeded in subverting the estate plan to get what she wanted" came to the fore. Harlan watched the Segals relax, their chests rising and falling in unison.

"Is it fair to say that Fay was upset with you?" Templeton asked.

"Yes. She accused me of spilling the beans."

Fay sat in stony denial, unreadable behind shaded glasses, listening through the Court-supplied headset for the hard of hearing, like Eichmann in the glass booth.

"She was doing an end-run around the prenup. She didn't want anyone to know," Stackwell went on.

"And was the word 'gift' ever used by either Alvin or Fay in regard to these funds?"

"No. Never."

"No further questions, Your Honor." Templeton sat, more pleased than after grilling the doctor.

Small jumped to his feet eager to redirect. He had to reclaim his witness. Harlan's curiosity peeked. How would he do it? "Was the word 'advance' used in reference to the money in question?"

"No. Transfer," Stackwell said.

Then Small picked up a document and approached the witness stand. "Would you please read the last sentence in your notes?"

Stackwell reached into his jacket pocket and pulled out tortoise shell glasses at odds with his good looks. "They are meeting with Alvin to try and convince him to stop the money transfer."

"*They* meaning who?" Small asked, in a thin whine.

"Alvin's children."

Point for Small. Harlan was glad to see the man had something in his arsenal. He preferred an armed opponent to one who threw himself under the tank. He glanced at his clients. Enjoy the game, he wanted to say, but the last exchange had punctured them. All three flattened into a slouch, like airless balloons. It wouldn't do to have them on the stand in that condition. Harlan made a mental note to inflate them with a joke or a Watergate story or something current, though he was tired of talking about the President's personal life. Political tales needed to age, for their full import to transcend gossip.

The judge called a lunch recess. The jury filed out. Small and his crew vanished. Harlan looked back at the Segals, who hadn't moved. Ken puffed his cheeks like a blowfish. Alyssa had her head in her hands. Then Lorraine stood in slow motion. Tell them a fable. That should do the trick.

Alyssa wished she could appreciate Harlan's attempts to distract them over salami on rye, but tales of Washington skullduggery circa 1972 didn't cut it. Alyssa forced a grin when he finished regaling them with insider details of the Watergate apartments. Who cared if the carpets were shoddy and the views overrated? She dumped her uneaten sandwich in the cafeteria trash. Ken and Lorraine had worried about running into Fay, et al., in the court building's lunchroom, but Templeton said they had headed outside.

Alyssa watched Lorraine wolf her turkey wrap, chasing it with a brownie. Her sister's ravenous intake made Alyssa queasy. How did she keep her figure with an appetite like that? How could she eat at all? Ken, ever the moderate, had finished half his salad, and left the off-color fruit cup alone. He caught Alyssa checking out his tray. "Want it?" he asked, offering her his leavings. She shook her head. She wouldn't be able to keep anything down.

On the way back to the courtroom, through the judicial building's tunneled hallways, wending their way behind Harlan in a *Make Way For Ducklings* —Alyssa's favorite children's book—single file line, she imagined Fay's chortle at Jimmy Stackwell's damning notes, and the doctor's intransigence.

Once back inside, Alyssa saw she was right about Fay's surging confidence. Her double chin stretched upward as her son-in-law, chest swelling, put his hand on the bible, and swore to tell the truth. Alyssa's unfed insides rumbled. They believe they might get away with this. Small asked Pablo to recount his discussion with Lorraine about Daddy's care, implying she and Ken had neglected their father by not visiting enough. Alyssa had thought the same many times after Mother died. She resented the burden of being the closest child, on call 24/7. She resented her siblings' excuses: children, distance, lives. But how dare these predators try to prejudice the jury this way? As if her sister and brother did not deserve what Mother and Daddy wanted to give them. Just as she did. Alyssa looked at Lorraine, her hands folded in her lap, knuckles red from squeezing. She must be smarting from Pablo's insinuations.

Then Small asked Pablo if he knew what perjury was. What kind of lawyer puts that idea in the jury's head? Alyssa should have been grateful for this blatant gaffe, a sure sign of his incompetence, but the smarmy tenor of Small's voice disturbed her. Her head throbbed as she listened to Small extract the concocted revelation that Fay had announced her husband's "generous gift" while they were visiting Pablo's parents in Puerto Rico, and that the identical nature of the prenuptial amount gave Pablo pause, so much so that he spoke privately about it to Alvin. How convenient. Alyssa looked over at the jurors, who remained expressionless. They couldn't possibly buy this jive. Alyssa began to question her chances. What if Lorraine was wrong? What if confronting Fay blew up in their faces? What if they lost, and she had to sell the house to pay the legal bills, to pay Fay?

Then Harlan stood to cross-examine Pablo. "You said that only two people were present for this conversation, you and Mr. Segal?" Harlan began.

"Yes."

"And Mr. Segal is dead?"

"Yes."

"So you are the only one who can say what happened in that conversation now?

"Yes."

"And you said to Alvin you were concerned. What is Fay going to do if she exhausts this money?–" Pablo nodded, "–and then Alvin dies. 'And then Alvin dies.' That is what you said to him?" Harlan's voice deepened with the galling picture of Pablo confronting her father with his own demise. "Alvin took care of all expenses, so why would you be concerned that Fay would not have enough to live on, that she could go through all that money?"

Pablo paused. "Fay is extremely generous."

"To you." Alyssa sat forward. Harlan wasn't going to let him get away with anything.

"To everyone."

Then Harlan picked a file off the desk. "So when your mother-in-law testified at this litigation's deposition to the question, 'can you give us the name of any witness that Alvin said he was giving you a gift?' and her answer is 'no,' there are only two possibilities: either she is mistaken or this conversation never took place—isn't that correct?"

"No." Pablo's body jolted. Alyssa pictured him in an electric chair.

Harlan kicked into high gear, pushing Pablo to the wall. "This conversation that you have just testified about never took place, did it?"

"It did."

"Why didn't you tell Fay about the conversation to give her peace of mind?"

Pablo's silky baritone began to crack. "I didn't think it was necessary."

"Isn't it a fact, sir, that the reason you are testifying here today that you never mentioned this conversation that you had with Alvin in which he told you it was a gift is because you know Fay Segal testified in a deposition three months ago that there were no other witnesses who heard Alvin Segal say that the money in question was a gift? Isn't that a fact?"

"No. That is not a fact, and I resent your accusation!" Pablo's indignation splattered against the transparency of his lie and didn't stick. He was finished. Alyssa wanted to jump to her feet, but didn't move, mindful of Templeton's instructions not to react to anything pro or con.

"Nothing further, your Honor," Harlan said, returning to his seat. Alyssa admired his economy, the way in which, with a quick turn, he dismissed Pablo from consciousness. Harlan Fineman didn't wasted an ounce of energy, unlike Alyssa, who was forever draining herself with doomsday scenarios. Pablo stepped down, shoulders slumping, vertebrae compressed. Harlan had deboned him like a fillet.

Alyssa sighed. After witnessing Harlan's prowess she felt safer, but not yet safe. Her mind raced ahead. What would Fay say? What lies would she tell? Would age give her a free pass? Alyssa wanted to follow Lorraine's admonition: stop projecting. Then she glimpsed her sister's face. Her color had returned, but her eyes darted all over the room, like beams scanning the night sky before the Blitz.

Lorraine didn't want to look at Fay, let alone listen to her. But there she was, hoisting her tubby form with the aid of Small, her decrepit henchman.

"Mrs. Segal, whose idea was it to get married, yours or Mr. Segal's?"

"Mr. Segal's. He was a very ethical moral man. He wanted to set a good example for our grandchildren." A good example of what? Jamie had adored his grandfather, but Lorraine should never have allowed her son to spend a weekend with this woman.

"Would you tell the jury a bit about your life together?"

Fay smiled. Only the lower half of her face moved. Her eyes remained fixed. "We had a wonderful life style, Alvin and I. We were very much in love. Because Alvin was on a special diet, I prepared special foods for him. I'm an excellent cook." Lorraine pictured Fay pouring cupfuls of forbidden salt into Hungarian goulash. "We had candlelight suppers in front of the fireplace, sharing Alvin's favorite red wines. We ate out, we went to concerts, lectures, movies, the theater." Lorraine remembered waiting on the stairs for her parents to come home from a show, eager to hear their assessment of the actors, the sets, the play. "We traveled to beautiful places." An image surfaced: Jamie walking with Daddy and Fay, holding their hands, combing the Cape's shoreline for shells. Lorraine had invited them, right after they began dating.

"I wanted all my friends to meet him and threw dinner parties often. He took me to his office party and gala black tie events, where he introduced me to his colleagues. He was very proud of me, and I of him. Then we would dance the night away." Fay's breezy manner stunned Lorraine. What would the jury make of her?

"Would you recount what happened on Mother's Day of last year?" Small asked, finally zeroing in on the matter at hand. Lorraine braced herself.

"I remember it quite clearly, because that's a big holiday in my house. My daughter, my son-in-law, and their children were there. We were about to have brunch when Alyssa and Ken came to the door–" Fay paused. "They insisted on seeing Alvin, on taking him for a drive to their mother's grave, they said. I invited them to stay for the meal first and then we could all go, but they seemed in a hurry to get him out of my house, such a hurry in fact that—I can picture it vividly—Ken lifted Alvin off his feet and carried him out." Ken's thigh nudged Lorraine's at the bold invention.

"Had you ever told the Segal children about the money Alvin gave you?"

"Oh no. Alvin made me promise not to ever talk to the children about any of his gifts. He was afraid they would be jealous." Fay's claim riled Lorraine, both because she would certainly not have begrudged his new wife presents if that wife hadn't turned out to be so grasping, and because Lorraine was indeed jealous, not of Fay, but of her sister and the gigantic gift she had received.

"Did you ever have any concerns that you expressed to Mr. Stackwell about Alvin's income?"

"I had some concerns. I'm an old lady. He was an old man. I was hoping, in spite of our advancing ages, that we would be able to continue our lifestyle."

Lorraine propped her hand under her chin to keep her jaw from dropping at Fay's staggering performance. She sounded both reasonable and calculating. She displayed her blatant materialism in such a matter-of-fact manner that it seemed perfectly justified. Lorraine's desire to have her father taken care of had clouded her early perceptions of Fay. She hadn't understood the woman at all. Fay was smart and persuasive, a practiced schemer. Please God, Lorraine prayed, don't let the jury fall for her the way Daddy did.

Small inched closer to the stand, as if he were about to share a juicy piece of gossip with his client. "One more thing: tell us about Alvin's and your relationship with Alyssa Segal." Oh. Lorraine couldn't see Alyssa with Ken between them, but at the mention of her name, her sister's dread passed through her brother to Lorraine like a muffled message in a game of telephone.

"Well," Fay began in a low simper, "Alyssa was very sweet and considerate towards us. She brought little gifts of food and fancy soaps."

"Did you visit Alyssa's house?"

"It was Alvin's house as long as he lived." Lorraine leaned forward and saw Alyssa's hands kneading her skirt.

"Alvin's house then. Did Alyssa invite you over?"

Fay stiffened. "Alyssa is a very private person. She didn't like to entertain. In fact, she rarely stayed more than a few minutes when she came to visit *us*. And she often broke appointments, which upset Alvin."

"How so?"

"Once, after the third or fourth broken dinner date, he got so angry that he threatened to take the house from her. He said she could live in a shack for all he cared." Fay huffed this last statement in a lame imitation of Daddy's anger. Lorraine wanted to put her hands over Alyssa's ears.

"Did he act on this threat?"

"No, I talked him out of it." The hell she did.

"Alvin, I said, Alyssa's a nervous person and can't handle much contact with people. That's why she's barricaded in that house."

"Barricaded?"

"Yes, it wasn't just the missed engagements that set Alvin off, it was the condition of the house." Lorraine bit the inside of her cheek. "The house was a shambles. The one time Alvin and I went over to pick up some packages we were appalled. Piles of junk everywhere. You couldn't see the living room furniture or walk up the stairs. It looked like a warehouse." Shut up, just shut up.

"How did Alvin react when he saw the house?"

"He was shocked. He told me Alyssa couldn't handle the responsibility, that maybe he should rethink the estate." So that was the point—to give the jury permission to consider a finding that would force Alyssa out of her house and hand Fay the long-sought windfall. Lorraine looked at the jurors scribbling on their pads. As much as she had resented being last on her parent's list, she couldn't and wouldn't begrudge Alyssa the one thing that grounded her, the one thing that kept her from spinning out of Segalla forever.

Fay rested her head against the seat and closed her eyes. She needed to shut out everything, including the back of Pablo's head, and the annoying way he drove with only one hand on the steering wheel. The backseat of Pablo's Taurus was comfortable, except in hot weather when the vinyl stuck to her thighs. But this was an unseasonably cool March. She sank back into the cushions. She wanted this day over, and was glad Pablo and Gretchen weren't speaking. She couldn't bear to hear a dissection of her own testimony, let alone his. The tape looping through her brain was bad enough. Fineman's face with its chiseled bones and penetrating stare flashed before her.

"Is it true that Alvin put up all the money for the many pleasurable activities you undertook?"

"Yes," she had said. Alvin had provided everything, including this ordeal.

"If someone looked at the letter you wrote for Alvin could they tell whether it was a gift or an advance?"

"No."

"Did you take Alvin on a trip to Puerto Rico the day after the Segal children confronted you with the money transfer?"

"Yes, but the trip had been planned for months."

"Do you remember saying to one of the children, 'Alvin is going to have to go to a nursing home?'"

"I didn't phrase it like that." Then Fineman invited her to tell the jury what she did say. "I am an old lady. Alvin would lean on me to get up the stairs, to go to the bathroom in the middle of the night. I was worried I wouldn't be strong enough to continue meeting his needs. I had no intention of putting him in a place where he wouldn't be taken care of."

Fineman conceded the reasonableness of her point of view, but asked if she would reconsider her testimony about Ken carrying Alvin out of the house. Fay admitted she might have been mistaken. "I am an old lady. Sometimes I do not remember things precisely. Sometimes I do."

I'm an old lady. Fay rubbed her forehead and neck. Too much bouncing. Pablo drove fast, like they were making a getaway. But they would all have to return tomorrow to sit through the defense's distortions.

"You were angry when you accused Stackwell of 'spilling the beans' weren't you?" Fay was angry now, as she held on while Pablo swerved around corners. "Why didn't you, after the questions as to his intention arose, simply ask Alvin to write a note—he was a lawyer after all—saying that this money is a gift, and you were going to get an additional equal amount upon his death?"

"I would never do that." Now Fay wondered why she *hadn't* sealed the deal? She had underestimated the people in Alvin's world, from Patras to Stackwell to his avaricious children. Even Consuelo.

Fineman quizzed Fay about her relationship with the housekeeper. "We'll see what Ms. Marti says." Then he let the subject drop.

Fay couldn't remember what Consuelo might have witnessed. Her mind jumbled with dates and images: Alvin in his plaid pants struggling up the stairs, Alyssa scowling at her, spoiling her Mother's Day, Ken waving the forgotten prenup in her face, Lorraine holding Alvin's hand in the hospital, whispering in his ear, then pulling back when Fay entered the room. She couldn't remember much, but she knew they were after her from the beginning, hiring this hotshot to humble her under oath.

"You kept a very good secret, didn't you?" he asked, rendering her promise to Alvin not to tell the children anything financial some kind of dirty trick.

Pablo slammed the brakes. Fay opened her eyes. They were in her driveway, home from battle. Pablo's long legs took the steps two at a time. He acted as if he had some place to go. Fay knew he didn't. Gretchen opened the car door and reached in. Fay grabbed her cold hand. She wanted to rub it like she used to when her daughter played in the snow, gloveless. Instead, Gretchen stroked Fay's stiff fingers, and pulled gently to ease her out of the vehicle. "Ugh," Fay groaned. She hadn't realized she'd made a sound until she saw concern cross Gretchen's brow. These days the sound inside her head was one long groan.

"Are you okay, Mother?"

Fay let go her daughter's hand, waving her off. "I'm an old lady," she said.

Even so, she could walk the few feet to the front door by herself.

In the attic bedroom of Fay's cramped colonial Pablo settled himself in bed beside his snoring wife. He didn't want to wake her, not out of courtesy—that had vanished from their interactions—but from an instinct for self-preservation. He didn't need Gretchen haranguing him over his botched testimony. She'd held herself in check the whole way home. Gretchen didn't like fighting in front of her mother, making the past six months increasingly tense. They suppressed their normal bickering over the laundry or over shuttling Cara and Sabine to and from activities, containing their marital struggles in a steel drum labeled *Contents Under Pressure*. Pablo knew if he tapped his wife on the shoulder in the semi-privacy of their bedroom, her anger would explode all over the house. What would be the point? He was well aware of the impression he'd left—predatory son-in-law hoping to catch the runoff should the jury rule in their favor. Pablo smiled in the dark. His stint on the stand was one of the few times he'd actually shown his true self. Fine time for honesty. He wanted a smoke, but didn't relish descending two flights of stairs and standing outside in the mud just to light up. He needed a fix, something to ease his gnawing apprehension.

Tina. He could call Tina. It was 1:45, the same time in San Juan and her night off. Pablo slipped from under the quilt, careful not to disturb Gretchen. He took the phone from the nightstand and crept into the bathroom. The warped door stuck as he eased it closed. Then he waited, listening for stirrings. Nothing. He sat on the closed toilet seat and punched in Tina's number.

The phone rang and rang. What if she was out on the town? What if she didn't want him anymore?

"Hola?" Tina's humid alto aroused him.

"Tina, cara mía!" A shiver ran through Pablo as he spoke his daughter's name. Why had he and Gretchen named their eldest such a common endearment?

"Pablo! Mi amor, que pasa?"

Pablo moved from the toilet to the floor, back and butt against the smooth chilled tile, and whispered the day's indignities to his distant lover, who received the litany without comment, only the occasional sympathetic grunt—the same sound she made during sex. When he was done, drained of some frustrations, still rigid with others, he asked her to talk. She obliged. Her silky tones slid over him—her words guiding his hand, his hand, her words. He imagined her fingers and legs in place of vowels, his ear the conduit for her body, until he was spent. Then Tina asked when she would see him again.

Pablo didn't answer. He didn't know, and he was tired of lying. He was tired of making promises he couldn't keep. He was tired of women, their constant demands, their predictable recriminations, when all he hoped for was sweet oblivion. "Sleep well," he said, reverting to English, as his eyes refocused outward on the hard white light of Fay's bathroom fixtures.

29

Ken ordered a Venti latte, and moved to wait in the prep area for his order. A line of caffeine-deprived strangers stretched behind him to the door. He had been up all night, running through his testimony. Lorraine suggested that he visualize himself on the stand. He imagined the faces of the jury, riveted or bored, with him or against him. He told himself that holding their attention, persuading them to side with him and his sisters, would be akin to standing in front of a classroom of resistant tenth graders and capturing their interest in the Battle of Waterloo. He sketched a map of the troops on the chalkboard, acted out the fighting, played both sides, with whoops, hollers, and shouts of "Charge!" eliciting giggles from the girls and embarrassed grins from the boys. At that point he had them. He was good with captive audiences, but the thought of this one petrified him. In the courtroom Ken knew there would be no laughter, and he prayed that the smirks would be directed at Small's inevitable attempts to trick him and not at his anxiety-induced stammer.

Ken placed his crutches by the nearest table, hoping that the inscrutable guy in the business suit would take the hint, hurry, and finish his drink so he could sit. Fineman had convinced him that they needed to use every weapon in their arsenal to enlist the jury's sympathy. He dismissed Ken's protests. "Think of the trial as theater and the crutches as a necessary prop." Ken didn't argue. No one won an argument with Harlan Fineman. That's why they hired him. Ken smoothed his pant leg over his thigh.

He would remove his prosthesis when he got to the courthouse. Back at the counter, he studied the barista, all fuchsia bangs and piercings. What was taking her so long?

"Venti latte," she called, and pushed the tall hot cup across the countertop to Ken. He pulled a wooden stir out of the nearby holder and looked around. Still no seats. He swished the milky liquid and checked behind him. He wanted to sit in one of the far corner booths, away from the incessant traffic. But the booths were packed with bleary-eyed mothers, tiny babes strapped to their chests and grazing toddlers hanging on their knees. Ken missed his kids. He'd spent far too much time shuttling between home and DC, prepping for this watershed day, like the day he met Priscilla, the day they got married, or the days his children were born, a day when he must be a man, an adult, "put away childish things," to quote Edna St. Vincent Millay. A defining day.

Ken turned, picked up his crutches and the coffee, and pushed towards the front of the café to a table for two facing the front door, vacated by an elderly couple in matching running suits. He sat and sipped the scalding liquid. His mouth blistered. His mind raced. *I swear to tell the truth, the whole truth, so help me God.* Harlan repeatedly reminded him and his sisters to make clear that they were simply carrying out their father's wishes, that there was no coercion whatsoever.

"Move aside, move aside, coming through." A lanky African American man with a Rastafarian knit cap and tangled dreadlocks pushed down the line to the cash register.

"These people were in front of you. You'll have to get in line, Sir," the barista said.

"No coffee for me. I'm here to deliver my message for the day."

The man threw open his arms. He was draped in a baggy coat, multiple scarves, a torn down vest, and stained red wool sweater, all wrong for spring in DC, a sure sign of schizophrenia, Ken surmised. The man's fingers peeked through half gloves, which must have been green, but were caked with mud or worse. He looked up at the recessed lights and arty coffee posters. He stretched to his full height, stamped his feet twice, ascending an invisible podium.

Again the man spread his arms. "My people!" A woman near the door sniffed, pivoted, and left. The businessmen in line pretended to ignore him. The baristas behind the counter shrugged and went on serving. "My people, hear me!" he said in a beautiful baritone. Ken wondered if he had been a singer.

A burly guy in running shorts barked, "We hear you. Now shut up!"

"Heed the message of the day. Today will be a day of reckoning."

Ken froze.

The man went on. "Today will be a great day for the truth." Then he bowed.

Ken wanted to resist the message; the guy was nuts. But he found himself drawn in. The man pulled his coat closed and began to move back along the coffee line, smiling and patting cringing customers, all the while bellowing, "Have a great day! Have a great day!" When he reached the door he whirled on his heel, almost knocking over an annoyed high school student. He pointed at Ken. Up until this moment the man had addressed only the people in line.

"YOU!" Ken wanted to disappear, but the entire room turned their attention to him. He locked eyes with the man. "YOU–" The dirt-encrusted finger continued pointing. "You, my man, will have a GREAT, great day today. Mark me. Mark my words. They come from above."

Ken didn't move. The man stared. He was waiting for Ken's acknowledgment. Ken resisted, but the man wasn't going until he'd completed his mission. Ken wanted to go back to sipping his coffee in anonymity. He wanted to ignore the unhinged angel with his insane message. He couldn't. He needed it too much. The angel had called him, "my man," as if they were father and son. Ken swallowed. The man's finger shook.

A low hissing began in the room. Customers stared, egging him on. *Say yes. Get rid of him.* Ken straightened. The man threw back his shoulders in response. Then Ken dipped his chin, giving the slightest of nods. *Yes.* Message received.

The man curled his pointing finger back into his palm, tipped his head, and left the shop.

Ken darted into the men's room, leaving Lorraine, Alyssa, and Priscilla staring at him with mouths agape. The story he just told them of a messenger, an "angel" in street person clothing, was incredible—more than that, considering the source. Lorraine's brother was not given to otherworldly encounters, but his crushing grip as he relayed the incident said he was in earnest. Lorraine noted the bruised circles under his over-bright eyes. He and Priscilla were staying with his college friend, Neill. Out of Alyssa's earshot, he'd told Lorraine that he couldn't spend one more night at their old house. "It spooks me," he said.

"Me too," she said, knowing she wasn't going anywhere. Ally couldn't be left alone the night before their testimony on Day Three. Defense Day.

Now Ken was seeing angels. Of the three of them, Lorraine had always thought him the most analytical, the least prone to religious, mystical, or psychic signs, but he was past exhaustion, running on adrenalin—like she was. Fatigue and strain left him open to support from all sources, even from above. When he returned, hobbling on crutches, pant leg pinned, he kissed Priscilla, and handed her a large satchel. His wife looked drawn but stylish in her usual black and grey. Lorraine wanted to know what he meant, but was afraid to ask.

Alyssa stepped up. "Do you think it was Daddy?" Lorraine hadn't heard a peep out of her all morning, not over their half-eaten eggs, or in the car. Lorraine would have preferred to drive–Alyssa was insecure behind the wheel on a good day—but chose not to ask anything of her sister this morning, especially not a change in routine. The ride was bumpy, Alyssa's heavy foot riding the brake, like she didn't trust her ability to stop.

"I don't know. All I know is he had an important message," Ken said.

"They're settling?" Alyssa said, ever in wish-fulfillment zone.

"No. Not like that. A message from–"

Lorraine swallowed. Was her agnostic brother going to say *God*?

"Above," Ken said, and grabbed Lorraine's hand as if to arrest her doubt. Whoa.

They stepped out of the elevator and steered through a crush of potential jurors with day tags stuck to their jackets. Lorraine wanted to sit, but the guard hadn't arrived to unlock the courtroom yet, and the hallway benches were full of other plaintiffs and defendants awaiting trials in the neighboring chambers. She leaned against the wall nearest the windows, looked out the smudged panes, and tried to concentrate.

All night long she had rehearsed her testimony. She paced Alyssa's house, sorted the guest room closet—there was still so much to get rid of—and recited the bullet points. She would be first, assigned to set the tone: direct, honest, loving. Look the jury in the eye. Be forthright. Don't flinch. She would tell her father's story, the family story. Fineman coached her like a seasoned director. Only this wasn't a play in which the consequences were only fictional. This was reality with the possibility of loss to follow.

Lorraine held the maroon silk scarf she had draped over her collarless jacket. The long matching skirt made her look smaller than she was—a good thing according to Fineman. "Tasteful, vulnerable. That's what we're going for." But of course, her performance on the stand mattered most. Ever since her deposition testimony, she had wanted to redeem herself. Now she would have the chance.

Ken motioned to his wife and Alyssa, who hurried to his side. In the huddle, Lorraine felt Ally's warm breath on her cheek. Ken bent in close, his graying curls almost brushed her forehead. "Just remember, he said I would have a great day!" Lorraine couldn't quite believe the magical thinking, but she wouldn't undermine it. Whatever got Ken through the trial was fine with her. He needed his sign. And she needed her brother. "Don't you see?" He went on, triumph turning teary. "That means it's going to be okay. I know we can't really know it now, because we have to live through this, but we're golden. All of us. I can't have a great day unless we *all* do. So we will. We're all going to have a great day!"

"Wow," Alyssa said, and gazed up at her big brother. Lorraine watched her sister transform into the four-year-old who'd snuggle against Ken while he read her a fairy tale with a perfect ending. Lorraine still didn't buy the connection between homeless prophet and their plight, but she'd take a shot of Ken's faith, no matter where it came from. She smiled. If he could find a hopeful sign in a coffee shop, she could find one in him.

Alyssa wrapped her bleeding cuticle in tissue and squeezed. She'd been so good all year—no biting—but the strain of the past couple days sent her back to old habits. She looked down at the paper. The red-brown stain soaked the fibers, its scalloped edges fanning away from the nail. This better dry up before she testified.

She glanced at Harlan, Woody, and Small, all locking horns with the judge. At the end of yesterday's testimony Woody told them that he and Harlan were going to try to get the whole thing dismissed on the basis of "no stated gift." Lorraine, ever the cynic, kept saying this would go all the way to judgment. Alyssa hated it when her sister acted holier than thou with her dire conclusions.

The lawyers split off from the judge. Harlan and Woody returned to the defense table without a word to Alyssa or her siblings. Small adjusted his jacket and turned his chin in Fay's direction. The motion had failed. Lorraine fixed on some distant focal point. Ken sighed. Alyssa wondered where his angel was now.

She wanted nothing more than to get this over with. She wanted to go back to work, to sit in Paul's office, tell him all the gory details of her courtroom saga, and to laugh with Zelda over Fay's comeuppance. Most of all, Alyssa wanted to go home. Each day it was more difficult for her to get up, get dressed, leave her bedroom sanctuary, and go downstairs to Lorraine's chirpy greeting. Alyssa wasn't used to houseguests. It would have been easier to have a complete stranger stay than any relative, particularly Lorraine. Her sister's imposing persona, the way she pushed until Alyssa gave in, infuriated her. Why did Alyssa accede to Lorraine each and every time she walked into a new room and began dismantling it? Why couldn't Alyssa stand up for herself? She wanted her sister to leave, to leave her alone. She wanted her house back, all of it, even what Lorraine called junk. But something about her sister's bulldozer drive paralyzed Alyssa. And now the house itself was in play, thanks to Fay's despicable claim that Dad had been mad enough to consider withdrawing it, Alyssa didn't have the energy to fight both her stepmother and Lorraine.

During the nursing home doctor's testimony, Alyssa hung on the sympathetic physician's words. No matter how hard Small pushed, she maintained her assertion that their father was, "so brilliant, that even two-thirds of his mental capacity was more than enough to understand his finances." Then Alyssa's mind would drift home, unpacking boxes of Mother's old records, placing Dietrich and Chevalier back on the study shelves Lorraine had emptied. Alyssa didn't want to be fully present until absolutely necessary, until she had to rise, swear, and testify. Harlan had promised she would go last, which meant she wouldn't be burdened with telling the whole story. That was Lorraine's job, thank goodness. Lorraine liked to talk.

Alyssa looked up at Martin Patras on the stand. When had the doctor stepped down? She licked her lips, dry from nerves. Martin, Grayson, Lorraine, then Ken. Four to go. Martin didn't carry himself like an attorney, let alone a courageous one. His shoulders slouched, his eyes shifted. If Alyssa were on the jury she would have thought the man was hiding something. Where was the forthright warrior who'd fallen on his sword for their father? Without Martin blowing the whistle on Fay's scheme they would have had no chance to put things right. Whatever attraction Alyssa had felt for Martin disappeared in the face of his sheepishness. He mumbled. The judge asked him to speak up. Small accused Martin of resigning his position as their father's lawyer because he had, "breached attorney / client privilege" and was now, "trying to cover up. "

Martin sputtered, his voice hoarse, "No, not at all."

Harlan attempted to save this lame display by prodding Martin to recite the estate plan figures, and the "sizable change" the transfer made. "Nothing for Ken. Nothing for Lorraine. The house at risk." It wasn't what Martin said, but the craven way he said it that worried Alyssa. If she was not convinced—and she *knew* the truth—how could the jury be?

Alyssa looked down at her hand. Her finger throbbed. The blood had crusted over the nail. She rubbed the cuticle three times. Flakes dusted her skirt.

"What's this?" Lorraine hissed, and held up the bloody finger.

Alyssa withdrew her hand. "It's nothing."

Lorraine rummaged in her purse. "Here," handing Alyssa a Band-Aid. She hesitated. She didn't need Lorraine playing nurse, and wanted her to forget the finger, focus on herself. Her sister's damp face glowed. The blush she'd applied that morning stood out like hives. "Take it," Lorraine ordered, still waving the strip between them.

Alyssa didn't want to further upset her, so she wrapped the adhesive around her nail. "Thanks." She hoped a maternal Lorraine meant she would get through this, that they both would.

Harlan was delighted that Todd Grayson, dapper in a gray suit and pink shirt, more than made up for Martin Patras' poor showing. Harlan had concentrated on preparing the Segals and assumed that a lawyer—any lawyer—would have prepared himself. Never assume. From the self-contradictory statements and confused timeline, it appeared Martin hadn't even reread his deposition. Grayson, on the other hand, sailed through. Harlan could tell from the jury's collective posture, upright and forward, that the man impressed them. They liked a guy who made no bones about his expert status on elder law and estate planning. They loved that he had "spent hours with Alvin, getting to know him, making sure his wishes were honored." Grayson was a lawyer with heart and confidence, a combination the jury ate up. He made quick work of Small's feeble attempts to discredit him. "This is my specialty, making sure a man at the end of his life is protected from undue influence." Grayson stared Small down until the man had to back away from the stand. "No one stood over Alvin Segal's shoulder. The changes he made in his estate plan were of his own free will. Of that I am sure."

Harlan turned to Lorraine and whispered, "Ready now?" She had concerned him. Martin's botch rattled her, and her deposition performance had been weak, a surprise. Wasn't she a trained actress? He'd read that even Olivier had incapacitating attacks of stage fright. Now her color had returned. All she needed was a good curtain warmer, which Grayson amply provided. She nodded, beaming. Harlan rose. "The defense calls Lorraine Segal."

Lorraine stood, edging past her brother and sister, whose necks stretched, like chicks waiting for the mama bird to drop a worm down their throats. She raised her right hand, took the oath, entered the witness box, and faced the jurors with a direct open gaze. Good girl. Harlan took a deep breath. Now for the main attraction.

The stand was a world within a world. Lorraine had spent most of the previous two days anticipating this moment. She projected herself into its isolated position in the courtroom spotlight, imagined all attention on her, but hadn't expected the power emanating from this perch. There she was, poised on the slight elevation, below and to the left of the judge's mountaintop, within striking distance from him, but poles apart. Even if she had still felt like fleeing—a desire that vanished with Grayson's masterful testimony—the judge's stare alone would have locked her in place. This four by four platform was a tiny country she had never before visited, and please God, would never visit again. She was there to post her flag and leave.

Her proximity to the jurors startled Lorraine. She swiveled the high-back witness chair to face them. From the floor the jury looked far away, but here they were right in front of her, like the neighborhood welcoming committee come to deliver gift baskets. Lorraine looked each of them in the eye, some more available than others. The young man in the front row scribbled, though Lorraine wondered what he could be writing. She hadn't said a word yet, except to swear to tell the truth. Perhaps he was writing *Lorraine Segal will tell the truth.* She guessed they must be eager for the other side, to weigh her story against what they had already heard. As Harlan approached her, Lorraine settled on the ponytailed woman at the end of the first row, the middle-aged one with big red rimmed glassed, in whom Alyssa and Ken had also placed their hopes. All through the plaintiff's testimony this stranger had maintained a look of intense concern. Speak to *her.*

"Tell us about your father," Harlan began.

Lorraine adjusted the microphone attached to the right corner of the stand. Though she trusted her natural volume—unlike Martin or Ken, she was not soft-spoken—she wasn't taking any chances. She had to be heard. Lorraine bent the flexible coil inches from her mouth, and then looked at the woman, who responded with a slight smile. Perhaps it was only everyday pleasantness, nothing personal. No. The woman was sending her a special acknowledgment. They were in this together.

"My father was an immigrant to this country," Lorraine said. Her body pulsed like in performances past. But this was real, Lorraine and her family exposed. Her whole being worked to sort the sensory input into the necessary—the jurors, Harlan—and the unnecessary: the packed courtroom, the blurry heads of Ken, Priscilla, and Ally, the looming judge, Fay at the plaintiff table. Lorraine forced herself to block them. Ken and Ally would rattle her with their sibling empathy. Lorraine didn't trust herself to look at Fay and her relations. Their animosity might incite her own, and she couldn't afford to let anger pollute her testimony. Harlan's parting instructions: stay calm; focus on your father; it's all about what he wanted.

So Lorraine poured out the story of her father's escape from Poland, the loss of his family during the war, his starting over alone in a strange land, his journey from shoe salesman to esteemed lawyer, meeting their mother in the cafeteria of the University of Minnesota, their long marriage.

"Would you describe for us your father's personality and how people responded to him?" Harlan asked. Lorraine pictured her father, his bald head shining under the courtroom lights, his trifocals magnifying his soft brown eyes, his unlined face, like a baby with a five o'clock shadow. "My dad was respected for a number of reasons, his fine mind, and I think more than that, his principles. He was a highly principled person. People responded to him immediately. They would look at his face and say what a very sweet person he was, as well as a brilliant lawyer."

"When your father announced he was going to marry Fay, how did you feel about that?"

"I was happy for him. He had been devastated by my mother's death and was extremely lonely. He and Fay were really good companions for each other. I thought it was great." Lorraine knew she was laying it on thick, covering the Segals' complicated history of family judgments. She couldn't help wondering what her father would have said if he'd had to swear in a court of law to his feelings about Brad.

"Prior to the current controversy, which has brought us before this jury, had you ever discussed your father's estate plan with him?"

"I did not know its details. He told me it was equitable, with something for everyone. That was all I needed to know." Hearing herself quote Daddy and affirm her trust, she realized he hadn't meant to slight her.

"After your father became ill, did you discuss his care with Fay?"

"Yes. She called me and said, 'You know, I think your father needs to be put in a nursing home.' I didn't understand, because that statement seemed to come out of the blue."

"What was your father's condition during the two months before his death?"

"He had good days and bad days. He'd talk politics with my son and follow the news closely. Sometimes he'd tire in the afternoon and go to bed very early. He had trouble walking."

"Sunday May 14th, Mother's Day of last year—why did you come to the Washington area that day?"

"I came at my brother's and sister's request. Martin Patras had asked us to be present when he discussed with our father the transfer of money he'd made on the twelfth."

"What was your attitude about this transfer?"

"I didn't know what to think. I was just waiting to hear my father express his intentions."

"And if your father had said that he wanted to give Fay this additional sum?"

Lorraine swallowed. Now was no time for ambivalence. "So be it. It was his money to give and use as he pleased."

"Did you have any concerns about the need for this money to cover a nursing home or other medical expenses?"

"Of course. My father was a very proud and independent man. His uncles had lived into their nineties. He wanted to cover his own expenses, not be a burden."

"And the concern was that this money was going to Fay?"

"It was a big chunk of money to be taken out of this fund while he was ill."

"When Mr. Patras and Mr. Grayson arrived, what happened?"

"Mr. Patras asked my father if it was his intention to give Fay a gift during his lifetime and then another equal amount as a death benefit? My father answered, 'No, the estate is too small for that. There wouldn't be enough for the grandchildren.' Then Mr. Grayson read my father a letter clarifying the transfer and asked my father if he agreed and if he would sign it. My father said 'yes' to both and signed the letter."

"What happened the next day?"

"We brought Daddy back to Fay's. On the way over to her house he said, 'Fay knows this is an advance.' Once we arrived my father said the same to her. Later, over lunch, out of earshot of my father, Fay said to me, 'You know, Alvin can give me half the estate if he wants to,' and I said, 'Of course he can. It's just a matter of what he intends.'"

"Did you have any discussion with Fay in the next few weeks at the hospital or the rehab center?"

"Yes, after their trip to Puerto Rico, he went immediately to the hospital. She spoke to us there, demanded an apology, and said, 'My lawyer wants to go after everything.' I didn't know what to say, so I answered, 'We'll talk.'"

"Nothing further," Harlan said and nodded to Lorraine. Did he wink?

Small sidled to the center of the room. "Mrs. Warner," "Is it true that you are a trained professional actress?"

"Yes." Lorraine stiffened. The nerve. "That is true."

Small's lips flattened. "And you worked on the New York stage?"

"Yes, in hole-in-the-wall theaters. Never on Broadway." Lorraine realized she was volunteering information; she couldn't help herself. Defensiveness was her usual fallback regarding her failed career.

"You are a member of Actors' Equity, are you not?"

Woody rose to his feet. "Objection. Relevance."

"It goes to her credibility, Your Honor."

The judge nodded. "I'll allow it."

Did no one believe her? That couldn't be. She was telling the truth. Lorraine wanted to think that her initial testimony had been so strong that Small had no choice but to try to lessen her impact, even with transparent attacks at her profession. "And the plays that you performed in were productions sanctioned by that professional actors' union, were they not?"

"They were unpaid Equity showcases. I know what you are implying." Small's eyes were empty black dots. Lorraine focused on his forehead. "I am *not* acting now." This came out too loudly, echoing all over the room.

Small pivoted on one foot and turned back to her. "You testified that your father was very happy to see all three of you together at your sister's home."

"Yes."

"Isn't that because the three of you rarely if ever got together?"

"No. That is not true." Lorraine swallowed. Her first lie under oath.

"Isn't it a fact that you were estranged from your sister Alyssa?'

Lorraine willed herself not to look in Ally's direction. She addressed the jury as if they were understanding friends who had overheard a private fight. "Alyssa and I did not speak after our mother died. We were deeply sad at that time and we took our grief out on each other. It was very painful." The jurors softened. They were with her.

"Did your father and mother attend your wedding?"

Lorraine flushed. "No. They didn't."

"Isn't it a fact they would not talk to you for nine years?"

The muscles at the top of Lorraine's head tightened. "No. That's absolutely untrue and outrageous. Immediately after my wedding my brother had a terrible accident and we all, Brad and I, and my parents, came together to support him, and had been together ever since."

"But they did not go to your wedding?"

Bastard. Exposing her abandonment in order to discredit her.

Woody jumped up. "Asked and answered."

Small retreated a step. "Was there a plan in place, once your father came home from the hospital, for you to take him home with you to New Jersey?"

Lorraine pulled herself up and this time met Small's gaze. "You mean after Fay brought up the idea of putting Daddy in a nursing home?" Small did not react. "Yes. As soon as she mentioned this notion, my sister called me, alarmed. I said 'He will come to New Jersey before I see him in a nursing home.' And when I spoke to Fay about it, I reiterated that Daddy could come live with me. She asked if she could come along too. And I said, 'Of course.'" The truth about a necessary lie.

Small faced the jury. "Isn't it a fact that what really happened is that you planned to spirit your father away, so that you would have control over him, and that Fay would not permit him to be taken from her."

Lorraine took a deep breath. "No. That is not at all what was going on. In fact, no decision had been made. I offered to have him come with me after treatment, an offer he accepted, but unfortunately he died at the rehab center."

Small went back to his desk and hunched over his files. Then he turned back. "Nothing further." The light in the room shimmered. Lorraine saw stars. She had given her all.

"You may step down, ma'am," the judge said. Lorraine didn't like being called ma'am, but here, in the court, it meant she was an adult—a mature, regular, even ordinary person—and not a thwarted artist, an eccentric housewife with laughable ambitions. Here she was simply Alvin Segal's daughter, who had done her best to plead for understanding and recognition.

Lorraine walked the short aisle back to her seat. For the first time she looked at Ken and Alyssa. Her brother's shoulders had relaxed, as had her sister's expression. Ken patted Lorraine's back, then Woody called him to the stand. At the mention of his name, Ken hoisted himself onto his crutches. Priscilla put out her hands, then withdrew them. Lorraine could see her torment; she wanted to help her husband. But Ken had to do this on his own. It was a relay. Lorraine had done her stretch, pulled ahead, and passed him the baton.

Ken thrust his crutches out in front of him. Thrust, hop, thrust, hop. The distance between the defense seats and the witness stand couldn't have been more than twenty feet, but it might as well have been a marathon mile lined with onlookers. Instead of cheering crowds rooting for his success, the plaintiff table sent hostile rays, and the jury voyeuristic stares. Ken knew it was their job to be curious about him and his family, but they weren't going to get answers about his private misfortune. When he reached the stand, Ken paused to anchor both crutches firmly on the step before lifting himself up. A slip here would ruin Harlan's choreography.

"Do you need some help?" Woody asked.

Had Harlan and Woody planned this? Given that Ken had to appear capable as well as broken, there was only one possible answer. "No thank you, I've got it," he said. *It,* his body.

Ken put the left crutch behind the witness chair and leaned heavily onto the right as he repeated the clerk's words. His armpit ached. Ken braced himself against the top of the chair, put down the second crutch, and lowered himself onto the seat. Display over. Unlike Lorraine, he couldn't address the jury directly. He was afraid if he made eye contact with any one of them he would break down. Instead, he looked at the water pitcher and cup next to the microphone. No witness had taken a drink, but the exertion of mounting the stand on top of his nerves, had left Ken parched. He reached for the pitcher. His hand shook.

"May I?" Woody said, and poured the water into the paper cup. So much for self-sufficiency. More than anything, Ken did not want to appear pathetic—sympathetic yes, pathetic no.

Ken took the cup, gulping its contents in one swallow. "Thank you," he said, almost choking.

Then Woody launched into a series of questions, which hammered home Dad's intentions, the coincidence of his father's illness with the transfer of funds, the impossibility of fulfilling the intended estate plan if Fay doubled her money. Throughout this litany Ken's confidence returned, but not his voice. Woody chided, "You're going to have to speak up."

Ken cleared his throat. "Sorry." He moved closer to the microphone, like he was entering a special zone uniting him with everyone in the chamber.

"When you heard about the transfer in question, what was your attitude towards it?"

"I was confused. I could not believe that Fay would do anything like that, and I wanted to get to the bottom of it."

"On Mother's Day of last year, did you carry your father out of Fay's house to attend a meeting with Martin Patras?"

Ken shook his head and for the first time looked at the jurors. "No. Alyssa picked up Dad on Mother's Day. I wasn't there. And even if I had been, I couldn't have lifted him and carried him down the steps."

"Was your father comfortable with so many questions about money and his death?"

"Dad was matter-of-fact and articulate. He was very clear that he wanted his original plan left in place, and signed a letter to that effect."

"What happened next?"

"We brought Dad back to Fay's, and he said, as soon as he walked in the door, addressing Fay, 'I need to speak to you.' Then he told her about the letter and Fay said she wanted all the copies. My father repeated that the transfer was an advance on the prenup. Fay didn't remember signing a prenup, so I showed her a copy. Then she sent her son-in-law out of the room to call Mr. Small, and announced that she and my father were going to Puerto Rico the next day."

"What did you think about that?"

"I was flabbergasted."

"Nothing further."

Ken knew what his father must have felt during his last rollercoaster days. As soon as Small stood to cross-examine him, Ken's energy waned, as his father's must have after their prodding. No wonder Dad had failed Dr. Cabot's tests.

Small took a bound volume from the plaintiff table, flipping the pages. "You said in your deposition that although you were your father's co-trustee, you knew nothing of the estate plans until Martin Patras relayed them to Alyssa?"

"That's correct."

"Your father kept financial matters to himself?"

"Yes."

"Isn't it true that once he was ill, it was your idea to remove Fay as co-trustee, giving you sole control over your father's assets?"

"No, the change was my father's idea. He ran his own affairs until the day he died."

"In your deposition you stated that you tape-recorded your father while he was in the rehabilitation facility."

Ken knew where this was going. "With his expressed permission."

"For what purpose did you record your father?"

"In anticipation of the possibility of these proceedings." It gave Ken a charge to spout fluent legalese, not to mention matching Small move for move.

Then Small veered towards the judge. "Your Honor, I would like to introduce tape number one from the exhibit list." Ken's throat went dry. The judge nodded, pointing to the recorder on a table near the jury. Small placed his index finger on the button and turned a dial. Must be volume. Disembodied voices filled the courtroom.

"Why are you whispering?" Alyssa. "We have to tell Daddy he's being recorded."

"I know." Ken heard his own cracking voice and cringed. "I guess this feels underhanded, even if it isn't." Small glanced at the jurors.

"We're protecting ourselves." Alyssa again.

Then his own voice. "Doesn't it feel shady to you?" The jurors were watching him now. Ken wanted to sink through the floor.

Alyssa, "We have to do what we have to do."

Small pressed a button again, and a new voice, a softer one billowed forth.

"I, I can't remember. What was the question?" The hint of accent, the halting, breathy sound of his dead father. "There's a problem. I, I don't know what it is." Small had cherry-picked only the most confused section, removing Dad's clarity about Fay's betrayal. He had called it "premeditated." *Play that,* Ken wanted to say, *play that for the jury.*

Instead, they heard Lorraine prompting their father. "Do you mean with Fay, Dad? Is Fay the problem?"

"Uh, uh–"

Small snapped off the recorder in a triumphant flourish. Then he paused as if to size up Ken. "Do you work out, Mr. Segal?"

"I beg your pardon."

"Do you lift weights, exercise?"

"Yes."

"You said you couldn't carry your father, but you helped him up the stairs and into Fay's house the following day, didn't you?"

"With my sisters."

"Were you wearing your prosthesis that day, Mr. Segal?"

Heat flushed Ken's neck. "Yes, I was."

"Mr. Segal, don't you usually wear a prosthesis?" Breathy gasps rippled through the courtroom.

"Yes," Ken said. What did this ambulance chaser think he was doing?

"Why aren't you wearing one today?" The jury's faces formed a collective scowl.

Woody jumped to his feet. "Objection! Relevance?"

"Goes to credibility, Your Honor," Small simpered as he addressed the judge.

"I'll allow it." Then the judge turned to Ken. "Answer the question, Sir."

Ken cleared his throat. "Sometimes my–my–stump–" the word Ken never used, landed like a bowling ball on concrete, "sometimes it's sore, and I am unable to put pressure on it." A trickle of perspiration slid down Ken's forehead into his left eye. He tried not to blink it away, aware that rapid blinking looked dishonest. Ken was not lying, but he was not telling the whole truth either. He looked at the jurors. They squirmed right along with him.

"Nothing further." Small sat.

Ken reached for his crutches and heaved himself up and over the witness box steps. He vaulted to the defense seats in three long strides. Fay and Pablo bowed their heads as he passed. Even they appeared sickened at their attorney's tactic. Ken squeezed in beside Priscilla, who eased him down. He wanted to sink further, put his head on her shoulder, and fall asleep. He closed his eyes. Behind his lids he saw the angel spread his tattered wings.

"You okay?" Priscilla whispered. Ken nodded, eyes open. Lorraine smiled. Alyssa sighed. She was next. She rose to take her turn. He tugged her skirt and mouthed, "Great day."

Harlan gazed at his opponent. Small had fallen into his trap. Only an ogre or a fool would have the gall to question Ken's impairment. The man had failed to understand the most basic principle of jury psychology. Juries believe what they see. Hence the opening charts, hence the crutches. Once the jury saw Ken, they would not only accept his every word, they would want to take care of him, and his sisters as well. Harlan knew that the tape recording had shaken his clients, but whatever the damage, the leg business minimized it. Small lacked fellow feeling. He didn't understand sorrow and pity, because he had none—at least not the latter. Harlan watched Small roll a pen between his fingers, his nostrils flared, his eyes hooded. He must have suffered, but whatever sorrows he may have experienced did not translate into compassion. Or insight. Small did not know he was part of a drama. He did not know how dramas were constructed. Perhaps when this was over Harlan would recommend the man read *The Poetics.* Hell, maybe he'd give it to him as a parting gift.

Alyssa levitated into the witness box. Her body felt light, her head heavy, her feet inaccessible. Were they really inside her black flats? They must have carried her past the plaintiff table and the jury box, onto the stand. She couldn't recall. Her body's heat concentrated in her flaming cheeks.

"Ms. Segal," Woody said, bringing her back to earth, "there has been a suggestion that somehow–were any of the children estranged from your father?"

"No, never." Alyssa looked at Lorraine, so much smaller sitting next to Ken than when she filled the room with her testimony. "As my sister said, there were a lot of hard feelings after my mother died. We loved her very much. May I have a tissue?" The judge waved the clerk to bring a box of tissues. Alyssa dabbed her eyes. "We took it out on each other."

"So the suggestion by Mr. Small that there was ever an estrangement between your father and any of the children was absolutely false?"

"Yes. Absolutely false." Her eyes dried. Alyssa wadded the tissue into her fist.

"And was there ever any suggestion that your father wanted to cut out any of the children or grandchildren from his estate?"

"Never."

"How often did you visit your father in the hospital or the rehab facility?"

"Every day."

"And how did he seem to you during that time?"

"Mostly alert and responsive."

"And he died a few weeks later?"

"Yes, Father's Day weekend."

Woody paused, stepped back, turned, then moved towards her again. "One more thing. We are in the midst of litigation here?"

"Yes." What was Woody doing? Wasn't Small supposed to grill her next?

"And I assume this has not been pleasant for you?"

"No."

He paused again. "Why are you contesting this claim?"

The heat in Alyssa's face spread through her limbs. The interior fire fueled the answer that burst out of her. "Because, because Fay betrayed the most honorable man I have ever know in my life. He loved his children. He loved her, and he was very generous to all of us. And he had no intention of cutting Lorraine or Ken out of his will. He had no–it meant everything to him to leave his grandchildren money for their college educations, and she–" Alyssa shot a laser at Fay, "–she betrayed him. And he knew it, and he told us the last day of his life to fight her with everything we had."

Woody paused and then nodded. "I have nothing further."

Lorraine sat in awe. Alyssa's outpouring, so much more passionate than anything yet heard, electrified the courtroom like a lightning strike. When her scared rabbit little sister had first taken the stand, Lorraine wondered if the jury noticed her tap, tap, tap on the jury box railing, but then Alyssa turned Fay and family into steaming ash. Lorraine could not have revealed herself as completely as Alyssa had done. Lorraine wanted to give her a standing ovation, but Alyssa's testimony wasn't over. Small had to try to undo the damage.

"Ms. Segal, did you attend your father's wedding to Fay?"

"No."

"Why not?"

"I was–I sent them a gift–but after my mother died, it was hard for me to deal with anyone in her place."

"Isn't it true that you hated Fay?"

"No."

"Isn't it true that you resented her becoming your father's wife?"

"No. I was glad he had someone."

"Isn't it a fact that before last May, in the year or more that you lived in your childhood home, your father never visited?"

"No. That is not true."

"When was he there?"

"He came in January to see the new decorative touches I had made."

"Like bags of cast-off clothes, piles of garbage?"

Alyssa gave a quick shudder. "I beg your pardon." No. No. Lorraine could not stomach this henchman's attempt to humiliate Alyssa.

"Isn't it true that you have been in treatment for a condition called hoarding?" *Was she in treatment?* Lorraine wondered if he meant her regular therapist.

Woody jumped up. "Objection! Relevance."

"Goes to her relationship with her father."

"I'll allow it." The judge addressed Alyssa without looking at her, as if to save her from further embarrassment. "Answer the question." Was it Lorraine's imagination, or did the judge sneer at Small?

The deep alto Alyssa had used earlier to vent her indignation dissolved into a strangled soprano. "Yes."

"And isn't it true that your father was extremely disturbed by the condition of his home?'

Alyssa worked her upper lip. "He never said that to me."

"Why didn't you meet your father and Fay at the airport as requested when they returned from Puerto Rico?" Small had pressed his luck, gone too far, back into fabrication. Lorraine watched Alyssa's defensiveness transform into attack. Unlike Small, Lorraine knew that getting her sister angry was a no-win situation.

"What? No! I was there," Alyssa protested. "Fay has it wrong. In fact, I witnessed her very strange behavior when she exited the plane without my father. When a passenger informed us that he had fallen in the aisle, that a stewardess was bringing him in a wheelchair, she didn't even turn around to see. Fay simply stood there, oblivious, showing no concern whatsoever."

Small had overreached again. "No further questions, Your Honor."

Lorraine watched Alyssa return to her seat. Lorraine took a chance and reached for her hand. Alyssa did not reciprocate, but did not withdraw. Ken cupped their fingers between his. "Told ya."

30

Consuelo sat on the hard bench outside the courtroom waiting to testify. Mr. Fineman had explained to her over the phone that she would not be allowed to watch the trial until *after* she had given her testimony. All afternoon she watched men in suits and ties, and women in jackets and straight skirts walk up and down the hallway.

Consuelo smoothed her black dress over her thighs. The material had begun to pill, but she knew not to pick at the clingy fabric. She had borrowed her sister's navy jacket, which was just boxy enough to cover the too-tight silhouette. She hadn't worn this dress since her mother's funeral seven years earlier.

How much longer? This was her day off and she couldn't afford to spend it this way. This was the day she did her own laundry, shopped, scrubbed her own floors. Mr. Fineman told her last week that there was a possibility the trial wouldn't proceed, that the "parties" as he called them, would "settle." If that meant give up, Consuelo knew otherwise. She knew Alyssa, Lorraine, Mr. Ken, and Fay, too, would not back down.

A large man with a holster at his side peeked through the door. "Ms. Marti?"

"Yes."

"They are ready for you." Consuelo rose and followed him inside.

The courtroom's high ceilings and rich colors made her feel as if she had entered a ballroom and not a court of law. Many faces turned towards her. Until she stopped and faced the clerk, who held a bible out in front of her, she did not see anyone she knew. Directly in front of her, at a table, wearing large headphones, sat Fay. Her glasses were shaded, so Consuelo couldn't tell if she returned her gaze. Pablo and Gretchen sat on either side of Fay. Pablo had never addressed her, and Gretchen rarely—only to bark orders. Now they looked flustered, like they didn't understand why she was there, as if it were their private event and she hadn't been invited, as if she was supposed to stay out of sight, serving and cleaning, while the guests enjoyed themselves, not become the center of attention, and certainly not be heard.

On the other side of the aisle, over the clerk's left shoulder, Consuelo saw Alyssa, craning her neck, Ken, his wife Priscilla, and Lorraine, one arm across her waist propping the other elbow, a hand on her throat like she was about to choke. They looked young and defenseless—children in adults' bodies. She wished she could smile at them, but her lips wouldn't comply.

Mr. Fineman stood next to the table in front of the Segals. Consuelo wanted him to come closer. "Tell us your name and please speak to me way back here," he said.

Consuelo did not like addressing strangers, but this was important, so she took a long breath and tried to reach him. "Consuelo Marti." The sound of her own voice in such a vast room startled her.

"Before you began working for Alyssa Segal and Fay Segal, how long had you worked for Alyssa's parents?"

"For over twenty-five years."

"So you knew Estelle Segal, Mr. Segal's first wife, well?"

"Oh yes. She was a wonderful wife and mother."

"And Mr. Segal? Would you say you knew him well?"

"Yes. Especially after Mrs. Segal died. I stayed to take care of the house."

"The house in which Alyssa Segal now resides?"

"Yes."

"And once Alyssa moved into the house and Mr. Segal moved to Fay's house you continued to work full days in both places?"

"Yes. I went to Alyssa's house once a week and Mrs. Fay's house four times a week."

"When you were at Fay's house what did you observe about Mr. Segal, whom you had known for so many years?"

They had gone over this during the session she had with the other lawyer, Mr. Templeton. "After he got sick, he was–" Consuelo wanted to say it exactly as she had practiced. "–he was all right some days and not on others."

"Could you be more specific?"

Mr. Segal's bewildered face appeared before her. "Some days he seemed confused. He would brush his teeth for more than half an hour or shave himself for too long."

Mr. Fineman stepped away from the table and moved closer. "Do you remember Friday, May 12th, of last year?"

"Yes. I was in Mrs. Fay's house doing my regular duties."

"Which were?"

"Washing the dishes from the night before, vacuuming, dusting."

"Do you remember anything out of the ordinary about that day?"

"Yes, Mrs. Fay was very angry."

"About what."

"Mr. Segal had had an accident. She told me to scrub the bathroom and to take up a rug in their bedroom that had been soiled." Consuelo looked down at her lap. She was glad that Mr. Segal was not there to hear this. Bad enough that Fay had humiliated him in front of her.

Then Mr. Fineman spoke more softly. "Anything else?"

Consuelo had to concentrate not to look at Fay's table. "Mrs. Fay told me to watch Mr. Segal, that she would be out for the rest of the day."

"Was this unusual?"

"No. At first she spent most of her time with him, but when he got weaker she would go out more often, go shopping, do other things."

"How did this affect him?"

"He was not happy. He was upset. Sad." Again Consuelo saw Mr. Segal's open round face float in front of her, its many expressions changing like the flipbooks she had entertained herself with as a child.

"What did you observe about their interaction when he got worse?"

"My personal opinion is that I believe she did not want to–"

"Objection."

"Sustained."

Consuelo looked at the jury and silently finished her thought: *Fay did not want to take care of him anymore.* The woman in the middle of the front row, the one with large thick glasses, glanced at Fay, then back to her. She understood. Consuelo was sure. Her years working in people's homes, listening to conversations she wasn't part of, respecting their privacy, never talking about her employers, not even to her sisters, had taught her to trust her instincts. She knew what she heard. She knew what she saw. She understood without being told. This juror did not need to be told either.

"Okay." Mr. Fineman walked to the center of the courtroom. "Miss Marti, is there anything else that occurred on May 12th of last year?"

Consuelo remembered that Mr. Segal had begged to come with Fay. But she didn't say that. Mr. Fineman had said to keep her answers short. And that wasn't what the lawyer wanted from her. "I remember coming back downstairs to get a cleaning product I had forgotten. I had to wait though."

"Why?"

"Because I didn't feel comfortable interrupting the telephone call Mr. Segal was having. It seemed important."

"Where was Fay Segal during this call?"

Consuelo forced herself to look straight ahead. Out of the corner of her eye she could see Fay's face, expressionless like one of the stone monuments that Consuelo admired in Washington's parks. "She was standing behind Mr. Segal with one hand on his shoulder and the other on a piece of paper in front of him. She was moving that finger along the paper."

"What was Mr. Segal doing?"

"He was reading aloud from the paper."

Mr. Fineman turned to the jury. "What was your impression of this interaction?"

"Objection." The other lawyer jumped to his feet. "Calls for speculation."

The judge waved his hand without looking up. "I'll allow it."

Mr. Fineman nodded to her. She swallowed and spoke as loudly as she could. "Mr. Segal sounded like he didn't want to do what he was doing, like he was being forced."

"By whom?"

"By Mrs. Fay."

Again Mr. Fineman looked at the jury. "Miss Marti, did Fay ever to your knowledge do anything to separate Alvin Segal from Alyssa Segal?" Consuelo caught Alyssa twisting her body towards Kenneth, seeking protection.

"Yes. Mrs. Fay suggested to Mr. Segal they should make Alyssa move out of the house on Essex Street, where Alyssa was living."

"Did Fay say anything about Mr. Segal going into a nursing home?"

"Yes. When he was sick. I don't remember the exact time."

Then Mr. Fineman faced the jury. "What did you think of Mr. Segal?" The other lawyer shifted in his seat, but did not object.

Now, when Consuelo had to describe him, Mr. Segal's face began to fade. "He was a gentle man, a nice, generous, very good person."

Mr. Fineman approached the witness box. He stopped about three feet away, the nearest he had been. "One last question: has your testimony here been affected in any way because you worked one day a week for Alyssa Segal?"

"No. Not at all."

"Nothing further." Mr. Fineman went to his table and sat.

The judge said, "Cross-examination."

Mr. Small stepped forward. He was thinner than Mr. Fineman and his skin color was bad. Consuelo could see that he didn't take care of himself. And unlike Mr. Fineman, he moved in too close, so close she could smell his sour breath. "How long did you work for Mrs. Segal after her husband died?"

"You mean Mrs. Fay?"

"Yes," he said.

"A couple of weeks."

"Did she say why she let you go?"

"She said she could not afford to pay me."

"When you said that Fay Segal asked Alvin Segal to make Alyssa Segal move out of the house, did he ever do that?"

"No."

"Did you often listen in on discussions between Fay and Alvin?"

Consuelo noticed the gap between Small's discolored teeth. "Not on purpose. I was in the house."

"You still work for Alyssa Segal, is that correct?"

"Yes."

"As a housekeeper?"

"Yes."

"In your professional opinion, what is the condition of Alyssa's house?"

"I'm not sure what you mean?" Consuelo knew exactly what he meant, but it wouldn't hurt to make him explain, like when Fay told her not to touch the windows, but had expected her to dust the blinds and the sills. And Mr. Templeton said not to be afraid to ask for clarification.

"Is it neat? Clean? In order?"

Mr. Fineman stood. "Objection. Relevance."

The judge shook his head. "I'll allow it."

"Miss Alyssa loves her home–"

"Answer the question."

"The rooms that I take care of–the kitchen, the bathrooms, the bedroom–are in good shape."

"And the rest of the house?"

"I am not allowed–" Consuelo stopped herself. She had already said too much.

"Would you speak louder please?"

Consuelo looked at Alyssa, whose thick brown hair had fallen over her eyes. *So sorry.* "I am not allowed in the rest of the house."

"Why not?"

"Miss Alyssa likes to arrange the other rooms herself."

"Do you walk through the hallway to get to the bedroom?"

"Yes."

"Do you pass the dining room to get to the kitchen?"

"Yes."

"So you see these areas even if you don't clean them?"

"Yes."

"What condition are those areas in?"

"There are a lot of things stored there."

Mr. Small sidled up to the jury box. "What kind of things?" He put his hand on the rail separating him from the jurors, looked down at his shoes and cocked his ear. Listen to *this*, he seemed say.

Consuelo did not want to give this man any satisfaction, but she was under oath. "Books, magazines, clothing, boxes–I don't know what's in them."

"Isn't it a fact that Alyssa's house is overrun with all manner of junk? That since she moved in it has become unlivable?" If only Lorraine had been able to do more, but it seemed that every time she cleared one room, Alyssa refilled another.

"Ms. Alyssa lives there just fine. She likes to hold onto her things."

Small pursed his lips. "When you said that Fay was not happy with Alyssa, is it possible that Alyssa might have done something to cause the problem?"

"It's possible, but–" Miss Alyssa has her problems, but this situation was all Fay.

"And isn't it possible that, because of the condition of the house, Mr. Segal agreed with Fay that Alyssa should leave?"

"No, Mr. Segal would never take the house away from Alyssa."

Mr. Small put his face so close Consuelo could see the bit of food caught between his upper teeth. "How can you be so sure?"

"Because he promised Mrs. Segal, Mrs. *Estelle* Segal."

"Eavesdropping again, Miss Marti?"

Consuelo did not get angry easily, but this nasty man aroused her. "It was when she was dying. In the bedroom. I was there, helping Mr. Segal take care of her. She took his hand, she made him promise to give Alyssa the house." Consuelo exhaled. She saw Lorraine lurch forward, and Kenneth stop her with one hand.

Small cleared his throat, walked a tight circle, and came back to the same spot in front of her. "Do you think it was perhaps a burden on Fay, considering her advanced age, to see Mr. Segal so sick and that, knowing he was in your capable hands during the day, she needed to take a break from the stress of the situation, since she was taking care of him in the evening after you left?"

"It could be." Consuelo's cheeks flushed. This man was forcing her to say things she didn't believe.

"Ms. Marti, could you tell the court where your allegiance is in this matter?"

"My allegiance?"

"Your *loyalty*."

Consuelo straightened. She would not allow this bully to condescend to her. "I know what allegiance means."

"Then please answer the question. You worked for the Segals for many years. You work for Alyssa Segal now. Where is your allegiance in this matter?"

Consuelo looked at Kenneth. He had his father's soft eyes. Then she looked at Lorraine, her brow lifted with her father's dignity. And Alyssa, knotted in pain, holding herself together with her father's reserve. "My allegiance–my allegiance is to Mr. Alvin Segal, and to his memory."

It wasn't enough that the Segals had enlisted Consuelo to slander her, now Fay had to endure a second stint on the stand. After the judge reminded her she was still under oath, Small had her refute the nonsense about ignoring Alvin's needs, taking Alyssa's house, leaving Alvin in the airplane aisle. The longer this obscene trial went on the more confused she became. She couldn't remember dates or details, but she was sure whatever their side said was nonsense. Complete and utter.

"*Alvin* said he wanted to sell the Essex Street house. Not me. In fact, I tried to talk him out of it, but he was so angry he said, 'I'm going to sell that house, and buy a shack to conform to the terms of the trust agreement.' I tried to calm him down. 'Alyssa's a busy career woman,' I said. 'She has a lot on her mind. Don't be so angry.'"

"As to not taking care of Alvin once he got sick–that was all I did. When I went out it was to shop for *him*–his prescriptions, his groceries, his needs. If I was gone longer than an hour I always called to tell him when I'd be back. I knew he didn't like to be alone long."

"And I tried over and over to bring those girls–" Fay paused to force the jury to take a good long look at Lorraine and Alyssa, those spoiled excuses for daughters, "–to bring them together. It broke my heart to hear Alvin say with such pain, 'fractured family'—his words. I tried, I asked them what it would take for a reconciliation, but I never got anywhere with either one."

"And I would never, ever, leave Alvin, my darling husband, in the aisle of a plane. Alyssa is flat wrong about that. I got him a wheelchair and insisted an ambulance be called." Fay didn't care that her voice had grown shrill. She didn't care that the jury saw her agitation. Why pretend calm when her world was crumbling? Let them see what these fabrications were doing to her.

After reversing their testimony, Fay wanted to step down, but Fineman had to have his turn. She could hardly keep herself upright. "Did you use your hearing device when Consuelo Marti was on the witness stand? Did you hear her testimony? Can you tell us any reason why she would have made up a story about what took place on May 12th? Why would she do that?" He fired question after question, not accepting that she didn't know why the blasted woman would say what she said.

"I don't know. She may have been disappointed that I could not keep her employed. I don't know."

"So you have no reason, is that correct?"

"What is the question?" The room began to spin.

"Can you tell us any reason why Ms. Marti would come to the witness stand, take an oath, and describe what happened on May 12th, which is entirely different from what you said when you were under oath?"

Would Alvin still admire his friend if he could see the browbeating he was giving her? "I don't know. I was very surprised at her testimony. I had a good relationship with her, I always respected her, gave her time off when she needed it. I have no idea why she would say the things she said."

"Mrs. Segal, where did Mr. Segal want to go to convalesce after his time in rehabilitation?"

"He called me in the middle of the night. He wanted desperately to come home to me. I sent my son-in-law to get him out of there immediately."

Fineman moved to the tape recorder. "Your honor, I'd like to play tape two from the exhibit list."

Then he pressed the button and Fay heard Lorraine ask, "Daddy, would you like to go home with your wife after this?"

"No." Alvin whispered.

"Why not, Daddy?"

"Because she's not acting like a wife." Alvin sounded like the peremptory lawyer Fay had been so taken with when they first met, admonishing some lesser light. But it was not an inadequate colleague he dismissed, it was she.

Fineman snapped off the machine. He was done with her. Fay returned to her seat, unsure whether or not she had withstood the siege. It was all such a slap in the face. This is what she got for taking care of a sick old man in his last days? To have her motives doubted at every turn? To be picked at like a carcass in the desert until there was nothing left? Where, oh where, was her reward?

Izso Small finished his cold coffee and tossed the cup into the wastebasket beside his desk. The light outside his window had long since faded. He stood, peering through the murky glass. The parking lot was empty except for a security truck and his own car, a fifteen-year-old Mercedes he'd bought after his biggest malpractice case settled. His ex-wife had gotten everything but the car, which she didn't want. Said it was a pretentious reminder of his wannabe status. She was right. After that win, his cases shrank in size and number. Izzy didn't know why. Usually a large settlement attracts new clients. Izzy had long since given up trying to understand. Like a tire with an invisible leak from a nail he couldn't find, the result was the same—the slow and steady deflation of his career.

Izzy returned to his desk and stared at his notes for the closing—twenty-six pages of longhand script on a yellow legal-sized pad. And he wasn't done. If he included every detail, his summation would run at least forty-five minutes, long by civil case standards, long for a four-day trial. He didn't care. Fineman and company had taken the jury's time during the opening with mind-boggling charts delineating the Segals' whole life. He'd been caught short by their scrupulous preparation. He was determined not to let that happen with his last chance to wrest victory from his opponents' fastidious hands.

It was a good sign that Fineman had tried and failed twice during bench conferences to get the case dismissed, first on grounds there had been no evidence that Mr. Segal intended a gift to Fay, then by virtue of the housekeeper's testimony. Izzy countered with Diaz and Dr. Cabot, then the judge ruled in his favor, a small but significant win. There was still a chance the jury would see this his way. The Segals made some mistakes, revealed themselves unfavorably. Alyssa's emotional outburst was an unexpected windfall. Such passion could work against them. Or not. He had tried to use it to push the judge into reconsidering his dismissal of punitive damages, citing "venom and hatred of Fay Segal, obviously expressed."

The judge remained unmoved. "Your objection is noted and overruled."

Damages or no, Izzy knew he had one more chance to move the jury and he was determined to take full advantage. He wished Fay had a softer demeanor and Pablo a less shifty one, but what could he do? He would remind the jury that the Segals were guilty of undue influence. Izzy smiled. He would go for the jugular. He thumbed his notes. He was ready. He didn't care how much time it took.

Izzy looked at the clock. 3:20 a.m. No point in going home. He'd anticipated an all-nighter and had sent Mona out to get his suit from the cleaner. It hung, swathed in plastic, over the door. In the morning he'd shower at the health club at the other end of the mall. Izzy lay down on his couch. The cushions had long since lost their bounce, and the springs dug into his back. He turned on his side. The couch creaked. He put one hand under his rib to protect it from the coils, and the other under his head. Then Izzy Small closed his eyes. On the inside of his lids Harlan Fineman appeared, in cape and ascot, in all his overbearing glory. Izzy opened his eyes. It would be a long night.

31

Harlan Fineman watched Small work his way back and forth across the courtroom floor, like he was creating a trench to hide him. His summation had, so far, taken nearly two hours. Throughout, Fay sat immobile, shrouded in widow's weeds. The jurors, alert and upright earlier that morning, anticipating that the fourth day of Segal v Segal would be the final one, their release imminent, sank under the weight of Small's exhaustive and exhausting retrial of his entire case. Small shuffled his three-inch stack of index cards. He'd better be rounding third, Harlan thought.

"No May-December marriage this–only two senior citizens coming together at the end of their lives. Of course, the similarity between the prenuptial amount and the gift number raised questions." Then Small clapped his hands together as if he were about to swim the breaststroke, and attacked the "hostile witnesses," Martin Patras and Jimmy Stackwell, and their "violations of ethical duty" as Alvin's advisors. Harlan found this rich from a bottom-feeder like Small.

The man struck a halleluiah pose. "Everyone is trying to cover up, some better than others. Remember Lorraine is a professional actress who has performed on the New York stage. And the tapes, the tapes, ladies and gentlemen, were classic undue influence. Let's look at the children's motives. They all got on the stand and swore to the moral high ground." Small's tired voice strained for dramatic effect. "But I submit to you that their real interest isn't principle. It's money. Mr. Stackwell's records prove that the Segals took their father out of his new home to engineer a transfer of money back into their own pockets. And later in the rehab center, Mr. Grayson, yet another lawyer–a smooth operator–brought papers, which Alvin signed making his son Kenneth co-trustee. And who gets the money if it goes back into the estate? I'll tell you who–Ken and his sister Lorraine."

Small paused, took a deep breath, and gestured past Harlan to the row behind him. "And what about Alyssa? You heard her tirade, her seething emotion as she ripped into Fay. Very revealing. Alyssa knew that if Fay prevails she could lose her home to pay for this costly trial. She knew her father wasn't inclined to leave it to her in the first place. A shack, ladies and gentleman, is where he wanted her to live. You finally saw the truth. They hate Fay. That's it folks, they want money and revenge. That is what they are after."

Now, now, Harlan wanted to say to his squirming clients, *never mind the blustering man.* He's worn out himself and everyone else. At Small's, "Thank you, ladies and gentlemen," the courtroom exhaled.

After a short break in which his opponent sat, quite undone, Harlan stood, placed his hands on the defense table like a pianist flexing his fingers before the concert, and said, "I am not leaving, Your Honor."

As soon as the jurors returned to their seats, Harlan walked over to them and began. "Ladies and gentlemen of the jury, first of all I would like to assure you that I will be brief. This is the only time I will have to speak to you. Here is the verdict sheet that you will get in the jury room. It says at the top, *Fay Segal versus Alyssa Segal et al*. The 'et al.' are the two other children. Fay Segal triggered this case. She filed suit. In the closing argument, the children were referred to as co-conspirators. Alvin's Segal's close friend, Martin Patras, was practically called a perjurer. And anybody else who had something to say which interfered with Fay's claim has been branded a liar, and some much worse."

"Why did Mr. Small's closing take so long? Here is why. The Court has read it to you, and I would like to read it to you again. 'The plaintiff–that is Fay Segal–has asserted in this case that Alvin Segal intended to make a gift to her. A party who claims donative intent by another has the burden of proving the claim by clear and convincing evidence: clear in the sense that it is certain, plain to the understanding and unambiguous; convincing in that it is so reasonable and persuasive as to cause you to believe it. But you do not need to be convinced beyond a reasonable doubt. That is the highest standard, for criminal cases only. And this, despite the opposing counsel's debasing accusations, is not a criminal case."

Harlan paused, pushing up his sleeve to look at his watch. "I will not be before you for *two hours*, because the law, the *law* ladies and gentlemen disposes of this case. Mr. Small asked, 'What would Mr. Segal do if he were here, this dignified, discreet, intelligent man? His children called co-conspirators. His whole medical life opened for public display. Everything about his life and his person torn apart over the money she wants. What would Alvin Segal do if he walked into this courtroom and heard the argument just given? He would be incensed about what his wife, her family, and her attorney have done here."

"And now I'm going to speed through this because *he*–" Harlan pointed at Small like a tour guide calling attention to a dinosaur skeleton at the Smithsonian, "–not the defense, must prove his case. As you look at the questions before you it should become clear why he branded several professional people as perjurers, liars, and cheaters. He had to do that, because people just do not give away money. Maybe for an emergency. There was none here. Maybe to a beggar in the street, or to a charity. Otherwise, no."

"You will be given the prenuptial agreement. Mr. Small's signature is on it, as is Fay's. We wouldn't be here dragging Mr. Segal's life all over the carpet of this courtroom if Mr. Small had told Fay 'get this amended or it's going to lead to a lawsuit. You'll be the plaintiff. You'll have to prove your case with clear and convincing evidence.'"

"Every time Mr. Small confronts the fact that her claimed gift is the same as the prenuptial amount, the parallelism is so obvious that he has to say, 'I can understand why you would be skeptical.' Fay has been married twice before. One of her husbands went into a nursing home. She knew if Alvin went into a nursing home, she might never get the money in the prenup. So shortly after Alvin got sick she maneuvered an advance she would later call a gift, while putting neither word in writing. Clear and convincing evidence is often documentary. This prenuptial agreement and the May 15th letter are clear and convincing."

"And they have another problem. Someone who does something wrong often flees. Fay takes off for Puerto Rico with a man who will return so ill he would never go home again. And he paid for the trip. Alvin Segal paid for everything." Harlan paused to let this sink in.

"All the liars and perjurers Small tags–Martin Patras, Jimmy Stackwell, Todd Grayson–professionals who deal with the elderly, with prenuptial agreements, with estate plans–they know the fingerprints when something is suspicious. All the elements were there. Old man. Getting sick. As Stackwell said, 'it was an end-run around the prenup.' And the headlines, ladies and gentlemen: Fay says, 'Maybe he belongs in a nursing home.' She bans Patras from the house. 'Don't bring any papers for him to sign. Stay away.' When Patras discovers what Fay was up to he is branded a liar here in open court."

"What's the estate distribution? The house to Alyssa, a quarter to Fay under their agreement, an eighth in trust to each of three grandchildren–and the remainder, cut in half after taxes, and divided between Lorraine and Kenneth. If you credit this gift to Fay there is nothing left. Alyssa would have to sell her home to pay Fay. Do you think Alvin Segal wanted his children to remember him like that? Of course not."

"Then they add Consuelo Marti to the liars list. The minute she says something different than Fay under oath she is branded, along with the rest. Fay is a serial witness killer, ladies and gentlemen. She knocks off anybody who gets in the way."

Harlan approached the plaintiff table, stopped, right in front of Small, and stood with his back to his opponent. "I was very interested to see how Mr. Small would spin the most damning testimony, Stackwell's notes, that Fay said he'd 'spilled the beans.' He kept repeating that money was the motive for the case. He was right. He just got the sides wrong. This is Fay Segal versus the Segal children. She started it."

Harlan moved towards the jury box, inches from the railing. "In closing, ladies and gentleman, it is Mr. Small's burden on each and every count listed on the verdict sheet, and he does not meet one of them: no gift, no incapacity, and no undue influence." Harlan extended his arm to sweep Lorraine, Ken, and Alyssa into the jury's view. "These are Alvin Segal's children. Martin Patras triggered the meeting. The children were passive. They did not conspire to misuse their father."

Then Harlan turned and gestured at the door. "If Alvin Segal could walk into this courtroom today, you would hear an indignant man to the limits of his civility, unable to imagine that, despite the prenuptial agreement, anything like this would take place. It is a cautionary tale to everyone here as you get older, and I–" Harlan paused. He was tired. He hadn't reckoned with how much this summation would drain him. "I am getting older. Some of you have older parents. The truism is good days and bad." For Harlan Fineman, this was both.

Harlan looked at each juror. They were drained, too, but they were with him. "I will not speak with you again. As a personal note, this was a trial that I am glad I had the opportunity–" His voice caught, surprising himself. He took pride in self-control, but invoking his dear friend's image over and over had exacted a toll. "–Excuse me–" He cleared his throat and began again. "I knew Alvin Segal. Mr. Small said he *wished* he knew him. I *did* know him. I have been trying cases for over 50 years, and I never wanted to keep a jury over a half an hour out of respect for your time and service. As far as I am concerned, you are the best judge. You *are* the court. Thank you."

Lorraine wanted to cheer, cry, and kiss Harlan on the tip of his formidable nose. Sitting through Small's interminable rehash had been excruciating. During most of his account Lorraine feared the jury would fold into his pocket. She feared his relentless onslaught would force them to throw up their hands and say, "You win!" Then Harlan rose and swept the place clean of all the muddy thinking and flat-out lies. And he had done more. The unexpected. This cerebral man had revealed his sorrow at her father's botched legacy, his awareness of aging, his humanity. He showed the jury the depth of his friendship and respect. Underneath all the reserve, the superstar attorney mystique, was a truly civilized human being—a mensche—as Daddy would have said. Harlan stood up for her father, and she would be forever grateful. Harlan Fineman had reminded Lorraine what this was really about: not what her father had left her, but her father himself. Alvin Segal. The life he had built with his true love. The life from which the false one tried to profit.

Suddenly, Lorraine missed her father with a longing she hadn't felt since she was seven. *Daddy, Daddy, Daddy*. Lorraine stifled the sob rising in her throat and reached for Ken's hand. Long-delayed grief had her in its grip. There was no postponing it now.

"You okay?" Ken asked.

"I miss Daddy," she said.

Her brother nodded. "Did you see the old man who sat in the back row just before Harlan spoke?"

"A court watcher?" They had a few—retired people, who made a hobby of attending trials.

"He reminded me of Mom and Dad." Ken was still reading signs in strangers' faces, but Lorraine had to grant that the short elderly gentleman had Mother's ruddy cheeks and snowy hair, and Daddy's unlined face.

"The Jewish Santa?" Alyssa said. Lorraine laughed, tears still damp on her cheeks.

The judge sent the jurors out for lunch under the clerk's watchful charge. Then they would be sequestered until they reached a verdict. Lorraine and her siblings gathered their belongings and left the chamber. Now there was nothing to do but wait.

Outside on a concrete bench a few yards from the building, Ken took Priscilla's hand. He had always loved her long thin fingers. A light breeze lifted the sea foam scarf she'd tied around her swan neck. No matter what happened next, Ken knew he was a lucky man.

"Do you want me to get you something?" Priscilla asked. "There's a food wagon around the corner."

Ken was too nervous to eat. "No thanks. After." *After* everything would be different. Or would it? The whole process of defending himself had transformed Ken's assumptions about his life. Before this nightmare began, he assumed he would carry on in his habitual fog. His job, which required only part of him, had seemed a reasonable way to hedge his bets. And the accumulating debts, despite Priscilla's frugality, were the price he paid to live in a neighborhood with fine schools to send Josh and Stella to when they were old enough, which was now. Josh would be five soon, ready for kindergarten. Marriage, first child, second child, tenure. Ken clicked down the dead bolts on the high security door of his commitments. He had been deathly afraid of being locked in too early. He loved Priscilla. He loved the kids, but nothing had brought him face to face with the man he needed to be until this trial. Since college he had walked backwards into adulthood, looking over his shoulder so as not to bump into anything or hurt anyone. Backwards until the force of Fay's assault whipped him around, face to face with his mature self, the one who realized that he had hurt himself by hiding from his deepest ambitions.

"Well, *I* have to eat." Priscilla stood and kissed him on the forehead. "Oh," she said, already a few feet away, "Do you want this?" She held up the tote bag. The outline of the prosthesis inside looked like a torpedo.

"Not now," Ken said. "After."

"I'm not staying." Fay rose, steadied herself on Gretchen's arm, and pulled on her coat. She couldn't linger in this awful place a moment longer.

"Mother!" Gretchen planted herself in front of her.

"It's been three hours. I don't understand what's taking so long, but I'm not waiting around to find out." Fay started towards the elevator.

Gretchen blocked her path. "At least wait to talk to Izzy."

"What about? What's done is done." Fay remembered Alvin saying this in Puerto Rico. "I'm tired." Gretchen patted her mother's arm. Fay pressed the down button. "Where's Pablo?"

"He left an hour ago. Said to call him when the jury came back."

As if her son-in-law cared. Fay was sick of him, sick of everyone, even her big rag doll girl, still hanging onto her for dear life. Their dependence sapped her. She resented them all, even God help her, her grandchildren. They expected too much. If this didn't work out, it wasn't her fault. The elevator doors parted, revealing Izzy, briefcase in hand, head bowed. In defeat or thought, Fay didn't know. He lifted his head and looked Fay and her daughter over like he'd never seen them before.

"I'm leaving," Fay said.

"Shouldn't she stay?" Gretchen overlapped.

Izzy shrugged. "It's not necessary."

Fay turned to her exasperated daughter. "See. Now let's get out of here," she said, entering the elevator.

"I'll let you know," Izzy said, his face narrowing in the closing door.

Fay stared at the floor numbers, flashing their descent, and silently answered, *no need.*

Terry repeated his therapist mantra, "slow down," but Alyssa couldn't stop spewing three days of pent-up apprehension into the receiver. Terry had promised her he would be available throughout the trial, whenever she needed him. And now she really, really needed him to do his job, reframe—as he liked to say—the potential for pain that grew with every passing minute.

"But it's almost five o'clock. They've been in there all afternoon and Woody came out and said that they–"

"The jurors?"

"Yes, the jurors asked the judge for another definition of 'undue influence.' They're considering the possibility we're guilty of it!"

"It's their job to consider *all* the possibilities. The fact that they asked the question means they don't want to make a mistake." Terry spoke in the measured tones Alyssa had come to rely on; the even sound had gotten her through Mother's death, Daddy's wedding, and now would have to get her through this. "Where are your brother and sister?"

Alyssa peeked around the corner and saw Lorraine still standing by the window nearest the courtroom. She hadn't moved in hours. How was that possible? Alyssa couldn't stay put. She'd gone outside only to count to three, turn around, and come back in, all the while with the phone to her ear, calling Zelda, Paul, and now Terry. This phone session would cost her a fortune. She didn't care.

"Lorraine is here. I don't know where Ken and Priscilla have gone, but it can't be far. Woody told them to stay close, that the verdict could come at any moment."

"Why don't you go sit with Lorraine?"

"You know why." Alyssa watched her sister lean like a broken statue against the window frame.

"I thought you two were getting along."

"I guess. I don't know. I'd rather talk to you."

"How do you feel?"

"Out of control."

"That's understandable. The jury is in charge now. You can't do anymore to affect the outcome." Terry had a way of shifting from salve to punch without warning. But she had no time to grasp his statement's full import. Ken and Priscilla came up the stairs. Woody entered from the anteroom next to the chambers, and motioned her to come over.

Alyssa's insides twisted. "Something's happening. Gotta go."

She turned off the phone, cutting Terry's "good luck," to "good lu–" and brushed the moisture from her eyes.

"The judge wants this wrapped up today," Woody said. "He sent a note to the foreperson and got a message back. They believe they'll be able to finish soon."

Soon. Soon they would know if they had done enough. Soon this would be over. Soon this would be a story to tell. But until soon was *now*, it might as well have been tomorrow or next week, or next year. Alyssa couldn't think beyond an awareness of each agonizing second clicking toward a resolution for good or ill. She wanted to call Terry back. Say she couldn't bear another moment. Instead she did as he suggested, and approached the windowsill next to Lorraine, who tucked her skirt under to make room. She was still too quiet. Alyssa felt stranded. The sill was dusty, but she sat. More than her clothes would need cleaning after this.

"Ladies and gentlemen of the jury, have you agreed upon your verdict?"

Lorraine and her brother and sister took their places one last time, standing at attention behind Harlan and Woody, both of whom had their hands folded, a formal honor guard. Next to Lorraine, Ken rested on his crutches, and Alyssa twitched like a broken windup toy. Priscilla took the row behind them. It was close to six o'clock. The jury had deliberated for over five hours.

"Yes, Your Honor," the foreperson said, a small, soft-spoken man, in a sweater vest and a plaid shirt. Lorraine couldn't read him or any of the other jurors.

Woody had said, "If the jury looks at you when they enter it's a good sign." They did, but Lorraine didn't trust signs as much as her brother. She reasoned they had nowhere else to look. Small stood alone on the other side of the aisle, and who would want to look at *him*? Fay's table was empty. It hadn't occurred to Lorraine that Fay and her family might not stay.

"Who shall say for you?" the judge asked.

"I shall," said the foreperson. The clerk asked him to stand. He was tiny, like Daddy. Lorraine held her breath.

"Do you find by clear and convincing evidence that on May 12th Alvin Segal intended to make a gift to Fay Segal?"

"No."

Lorraine exhaled. Alyssa leaned against Ken, who wrapped his arm around her while pushing aside the crutch.

"Do you find by a preponderance of the evidence that on May 15th Alvin Segal did not have the mental capacity to understand the contents of the letter of the 15th and to agree with the statements contained therein when he signed that letter?"

"Capacity."

Lorraine began to nod in unison with Ken. Alyssa curled into herself.

"Do you find by a preponderance of the evidence that the defendants–" Lorraine and Ken and Alyssa, so named, swayed together accompanied by Alyssa's rhythmic moans. "–either individually or in concert exercised undue influence over Alvin Segal on May 15th to get him to sign the May 15th letter?"

"No."

Relief swept through them. Lorraine gripped Ken's hand. Alyssa convulsed in sobs. The clerk asked two more questions about the trust agreements, but Lorraine didn't hear them. She could only listen for the answers. Before they entered, Lorraine silently chanted the mantra of favorable responses: no, capacity, no, capacity, no.

"Capacity," the foreperson answered, echoing Lorraine's inner voice.

Last question.

"No," he said, and restored justice to its rightful place.

Priscilla put her hand on Ken's back. Lorraine touched his cheek. "It's over," he said. Alyssa picked up her head and smiled, though her crying had taken on a frightening life of its own. Small asked to poll the jury, and once they confirmed the result, snapped his briefcase shut, attached it to a cart of stacked case files, swiveled his body like a top, and rolled out.

Lorraine wanted to run to the jurors, hug them, and in the European manner, kiss each on both cheeks. Instead she clasped her hands over her heart and bowed. The foreman bowed in return. Woody passed Alyssa a tissue, and Ken, after repositioning his crutch, extended his hand to Harlan. "Thank you."

"My pleasure. I enjoyed working with you," Harlan said, as if her brother were second chair and not a client. Then he held Lorraine's fingers between his. "You did the right thing." Lorraine nodded.

Outside the judicial building, the eggshell of childhood cracked open as Lorraine, her brother, and sister stepped into the early spring twilight. No more false protection. No more illusions of a champion to the rescue, Harlan's prowess notwithstanding. Lorraine knew they had saved themselves. They hadn't retreated. They'd fought and won. Lorraine had discovered within her wounded child, a valiant adult, whom a jury of her peers had found credible. She had faced a public reckoning and survived. The complicated resentments she'd carried for so long dissipated in the wake of an actual, palpable victory. Lorraine had proven herself, and laid an inner foundation from which to carry on.

PART VII

Leavings

32

Pablo put down the receiver and ascended the stairs to Fay's room. She hadn't said a word all the way home, retreating to her bed with strict orders not to disturb her "under any circumstances." When Gretchen asked what if Izzy calls, Fay repeated the directive, adding only, "I'll speak to Izzy when I'm good and ready."

She knew. Pablo wondered how.

When he reached her door, Pablo took the piece of paper, on which he had scribbled Izzy's message, folded it and slipped it under, careful to make no sound. He stood a moment to listen. Silence. Then he walked down the hall to pack. Gretchen was in the kitchen preparing tacos for the girls. He could be out before dinner.

Between folding his shirts and sorting his socks, Pablo told himself that leaving was inevitable. Even had Fay won, he and Gretchen would not have recovered from his failure as a husband, father, and provider. A victory would have cushioned them for a few months, but eventually he would have had to admit that it was no longer acceptable to depend on Fay, and by extension on Alvin Segal, to use them to mask his deficits. Tina's shiny world beckoned, with its chips, cards, and wheels, a world Pablo still believed would one day yield his worth.

Fay held onto the armchair beside the door and slowly lowered herself. A sharp jab shot through her knee as she picked up the paper. She sank into the chair. Its well-worn cushions hugged her sore thighs. She would not rise any time soon. Then Fay read: WE LOST—all in caps, like a ransom note. The Segals and their high-priced legal team had kidnapped her future. Now she would have to pinch pennies, worry. Forever.

At least with a kidnapping, the ransom brought your loved one back. But nothing was coming back to Fay. Why? Because she had the misfortune of marrying husbands who left—plane crash, dementia, heart failure—not of their own volition, but with the same result. Each had left Fay with a parting gift: children, house, the promise of care 'til the end of her days. None of these gifts panned out. Gretchen and the house were burdens, the promise, broken.

Tabor, Cohen, Segal. She resented these men and their two syllable names. Perhaps she would go by Fay from now on, like Madonna or Cher. After all, she was alone, without resources, except her frayed resilience. Each marriage had rubbed it raw. This last had nearly finished her off. She was on her own. Again.

With Alvin dead, his legacy inaccessible, Fay would have to take the seething within her and use it to fuel yet another rebirth. Tired as she was, she would not go down like this. She rested her throbbing head against the chair back, closed her eyes, and forced herself to picture some place sunny and warm. She had always loved the ocean. She concentrated what was left of her energy and began to drift with the waves. The saltwater supported her. She floated. For the first time in four days, Fay smiled.

"More Champagne." Ken snapped his fingers and the waiter appeared with a second bottle. Alyssa and Lorraine clinked their flutes, giddy from only one glass, their stomachs empty all day. He wished Priscilla were there to share the victory party, but she had taken the next train to make it home for the kids' bedtime.

"What the hell, pass me the rolls," Lorraine said.

"Butter?" Alyssa helped herself and pushed the dish stacked with ruffled patties towards Lorraine. Ken loved seeing them united, even in diet sabotage.

Lorraine slathered the creamy chunk onto the roll in her hand and put another on her plate. "Mmm," she said, mouth full. Ken too, wanted to gobble every hors d'oeuvre in sight—the thick pâté, the salty smooth caviar, the slippery oysters, the rich fois gras—and then the entire tasting menu, multiple entrées and double desserts.

"To us," he said, lifting his glass.

"To us," they cheered.

Other diners turned and stared. Ken didn't care. This was their night, and it was their right to crow. He wanted the whole room to join the party. Tonight he loved everyone. These strangers might have been his jury out on the town basking in a job well done. Ken wanted to treat them all.

"A toast," he said. "To Harlan and Woody, without whom we could never have gone through this and come out the other side." Ken had invited the attorneys, but both politely declined. Sitting with his sisters he understood why. The relationship was professional. Harlan had revealed his deep connection to Dad in his summation, but that would be the extent of it. Ken wondered if he would see him again. He was glad Harlan acknowledged, "working with" him. Ken relished their collegiality, the glimpse it had given him of his father's world.

"To Harlan and Woody."

Lorraine and Alyssa lifted their glasses. "To Harlan and Woody."

"And to Dad."

"To Dad!"

"And to my sisters," Ken paused. Lorraine's cheeks flushed with alcohol. Alyssa's eyes were glassy. "May they always be as close as they are today." He grabbed Lorraine's right hand, sticky with butter, and placed it on top of Alyssa's to seal the pact. "Promise me," he said, "promise *yourselves* that you'll never leave each other again."

Lorraine nodded firmly. Alyssa, after a long pause in which Ken recognized her habitual ambivalence, bowed her head once.

"Out loud." Ken believed in the power of oaths.

"I promise." Lorraine's strong voice covered Alyssa's "promise" without the pronoun. It would have to do.

"Good," Ken said, releasing their hands. "Let the feasting continue."

Alyssa dabbed her mouth with her napkin, trying to maintain her composure, while Lorraine, freed by Ken's intervention, launched into a litany of coming family events. "There's Jamie's eighth grade graduation—that's right around the corner—and the annual trip to the Cape. You guys are coming right? And Jamie's Bar Mitzvah in September. It'll be so great to be together."

Another list. Lorraine didn't stop for breath or answers, but ticked off the dates, like a metronome set at presto. The speed and enthusiasm of her delivery swamped Alyssa, threatening to drown her in future demands. Such scheduled closeness made Alyssa claustrophobic. She looked at Ken, who basked at his dream-come-true-reunited family. How could she disappoint him or her benevolent dictator of a sister? How could she not do her part to make this new and happier chapter in the Segal saga a reality? She looked down at her dessert plate, ran her finger over the smudge of chocolate drizzle still remaining, and licked. Its sharp bitterness coated the roof of her mouth.

Alyssa forced a smile at Lorraine, wishing she wasn't returning to the house for one more night. She wished her sister would go back to her family, leave her be. All Alyssa wanted was to go home, lock the doors, soak in a lavender-scented bath, and then sleep on fresh sheets, alone.

Lorraine untied the portfolio's frayed black ribbon, and laid it open on the floor of the studio. The large rough Italian paper fell to either side of the case. Lorraine spread the paintings out one by one, creating a floor mural. The thrill and exhaustion of the day, not to mention the gigantic meal, had kept Lorraine awake. Alyssa had gone to bed without a word, as soon as they returned to the house, but Lorraine couldn't calm down. She hoped looking at her mother's work would help.

She studied the soft yet precise brushstrokes, and the rich though subdued colors of her mother's signature style. The contradictions defined the abstracts and her mother. Her shy persona masked someone with definite ideas, as quick to judge a person as to decide what color goes where before the watercolor could dry. Her smooth sensuous hands knew what they thought and so did she. Her mother could be wrong, as she was about Brad. Even on her deathbed she had a hard time admitting the mistake that had damaged their relationship.

Lorraine could still conjure her mother's once zaftig form and face aglow with merriment and rosacea, sunk into folds, motionless on the hospital bed, like a giant Shar-Pei waiting to be petted. She would never forget how her mother tilted her head back and submitted as Lorraine swabbed the oozing hole, which surrounded the white plastic tracheotomy tube, and cleaned the cylinder of mucus blocking her mother's airway. Lorraine had been surprised and proud to discover that she could handle these grim duties.

I'm sorry you have to do this. I do love having you here. You make me feel good–better than anybody—this on a piece of yellow paper, one of the many that Lorraine had scooped out of the trashcan, when her mother wasn't looking. *I wish I was a tree… tell that doctor to go to hell…The nurse told me that when she walked in I was almost blue…of course, my favorite color is blue.* When her mother caught her with a torn note sticking out of her jeans pocket she felt foolish and stubborn, a familiar juxtaposition in Mother's presence, but she couldn't bear to destroy these communications, no matter how mundane or soaked in fluids.

"Is it okay with you, Mom?"

Mother picked up her pad and blue felt pen and wrote in the thick, even script Lorraine envied: *I don't know why I'm trying to say anything. Shakespeare said it all.* Then came the admission that Lorraine would never forget: *I know I disappointed YOU so many times.*

Disappointed. What an understatement. Lorraine knew how difficult it had been for her mother to own up to any failing, especially a parental one. The belated acknowledgment that Mother knew her withholding had put distance between them, barely penetrated Lorraine. For years she had waited, longing for such words from her mother's mouth. Instead, Mother pretended that nothing had happened, and even embraced Brad. Lorraine knew after so much time, there under the frosty hospital room lights, a glancing confession would have to suffice.

She picked up the paintings, one at a time: greens and blues rippling down the page; yellows and oranges dancing with each other in feathery swirls; a slash of black separating red globs. She paused at a bold splash of rose and violet spheres, colliding with each other. The clash of strong, deep colors spoke to Lorraine of the tension between herself and Alyssa. Lorraine put the painting down. What had Mother expected when she set their troubles in motion, pitting the one who stayed against the one who left, then reinforcing the divide in her final act?

Consuelo's revelation had jolted Lorraine. She hadn't imagined that giving the house to Alyssa was her mother's idea. This was the last piece of the puzzle, the one Martin hadn't known. Now it all made sense. Daddy had been too passive to take an action that radical without a push from his wife. First Mother, then Fay. The truth stung, but not as much as it would have if the trial gone against them. Public vindication gave Lorraine something her parents could not, a sense that she had been seen and found worthy. The victory made it possible for her to forgive. She understood her mother's impulse to protect Alyssa, even at the expense of her two older children. A mother has to answer the greatest need, which wasn't Ken's or Lorraine's. Her portion of the proceeds—the smallest, but at least something—would pay for Jamie's music camp and a long family vacation.

The studio walls were lined with black cases. Lorraine wondered if Alyssa would mind if she took a few paintings back to New Jersey. Maybe she could frame some, or find a New York dealer to take them on consignment. It seemed a shame that, with the exception of a few private sales and small gallery showings, Mother's work had not gone out into the world. How many cases were there? Lorraine began to count. "One, two, three, four, five–"

"Thirty-nine."

"What?" Lorraine whirled around. Alyssa stood in the doorway, wrapped in terrycloth, her eyes bloodshot.

"There are thirty-nine cases and one thousand forty-six paintings."

"Oh. Wow." Lorraine should have known Alyssa had counted. The cold overheads cast a bluish tinge over Alyssa's face, unlike the natural light Mother had preferred to work under.

Alyssa stepped into the room. "What are you doing?"

"I couldn't sleep. Thought I'd get a head start on tomorrow's tasks."

"I told you not to touch Mother's studio." Five years later, and it was still "Mother's" studio.

"I just thought it would be a good idea–"

"It's not for you to think." Alyssa folded her arms and planted her legs. She was the gatekeeper and she wasn't letting Lorraine in.

"What?"

"It's my house."

Lorraine didn't need to hear this again, as if they hadn't traveled this distance together, as if the trial had never happened. Her equanimity on the subject, only hours old, was shaken by her sister's blunt declaration. Lorraine didn't need the fact thrown in her face. "I know. I'm just trying to help."

Alyssa looked down. Lorraine noticed that her sister's feet were bare on the stone floor. "I don't need anymore help. Consuelo is coming in the morning. She and I will finish up. Go to bed." An order. Alyssa turned out the light.

Lorraine had sensed something amiss with her sister during dinner, but chalked it up to the fatigue of their ordeal. Now, standing face to face in the dark, she knew her instinct was right. "You know," she began, "Mother wanted me to help you."

"What?"

"In the hospital. At the end."

The note read, *Ally's crying all the time.* There at her mother's bedside, Lorraine hadn't a clue what she was supposed to do about *that.* Her mother had picked up the pad; her even loops turned jagged. *Please cooperate. She's alone. She needs you.*

All these months, cleaning out the house, holding Alyssa's hand through the trial, Lorraine thought she'd found a way. Her sister's rigid posture said otherwise. "She asked me to take care of you."

Alyssa let out a tiny gasp. "I don't need–"

"You do. We both do."

Alyssa turned. "You?"

"Of course. I need you by my side, for the celebrations, not just the crises."

"You have a husband and a son. You did fine without me."

"No. No I didn't. Not a day went by that I didn't think of you. And miss you."

Alyssa hung her head. "I thought of you too. And Brad. And Jamie."

"But thinking–my thinking of you, you thinking of me–isn't a relationship. It's what we *do* together that connects us: the meals, this sorting, what we've just been through. Not what's in our heads."

Alyssa stepped back. "I can't. I can't anymore."

Lorraine could feel Alyssa collapsing into herself. She wanted to enfold her sister in her arms. She wished she could make Alyssa understand that their bond could not withstand another separation. She wanted to erase the ever-widening gulf between them, but she didn't know how. "Let me help you."

Alyssa shrugged. She didn't trust her. And why should she? Lorraine had to admit that she *did* want too much from her sister, a lot more than Alyssa could ever give. She started to leave, her robed body silhouetted by the distant hall light. Then she stopped. "Do you think it's true what they said about us?"

"Who?" Lorraine asked.

"Small, Fay."

What do you mean?"

"That we came together out of greed?"

Lorraine bowed her head. It was a question she'd asked herself. "Not greed. *She* was greedy." Lorraine didn't want to say her name again. "We came together because we had to, because it's what Daddy wanted."

"And if none of this had happened, would we be talking now?"

None of this. Lorraine wondered how far back to go? Mother rebuking her for wearing a short skirt, a tight blouse, pointing to her knees, telling Ally, "Don't ever dress like your sister." The bewildered seven-year-old nodding in fear. "I don't know, but I do know that we can have a future. It doesn't matter how we got here."

Alyssa shook her head. "It matters."

Take care of her.

Lorraine remembered her answer: *Mom, Alyssa won't let me.*

The shadow in the doorway disappeared. Though the door was open, a latch had clicked between them. Lorraine could ram herself against it, try to break the lock, or she could accept that her sister required unlimited distance.

Consuelo picked up the pipe cleaner figures and placed them in a shoe box: the mother with the wild yarn hair, the father with the string tie, the children—a girl with straw braids, a boy holding a plastic dog, and a baby, squeezed into the tiny white cradle. As soon as Consuelo arrived that morning, Alyssa asked her to clean and pack the pink dollhouse. She was glad to do it. After she finished her usual duties, Consuelo had often gone to the spare bedroom—one of the rooms Alyssa had designated off-limits—to study the miniature rooms, topsy-turvy with neglect. She would imagine how she might arrange them if they were hers. She would be sorry to see the house go, though she knew it was a good sign from Alyssa. Perhaps Lorraine had had a positive affect after all.

Consuelo watched the awkward and wary dance between Lorraine and Alyssa before Lorraine left that morning. When the elder sister said, "I'm going to call you, every Sunday," Alyssa didn't answer, but neither did she bite her head off. Progress.

Consuelo dusted the little dining table. Should she polish its mahogany surfaces?

No. Silly. She wrapped its spindle legs in tissue and put it, along with the matching chairs inside another box separate from the doll family. Then she folded the floral curtains from the doll kitchen and bathroom and tucked them next to the doll people. She opened the hope chest at the end of the doll parents' bed, marveling at the pretty cross stitching on the handmade faded yellow quilt, the knit rugs in bold reds and blues from each doll bedroom, and the corduroy throw pillows on the worn living room couch. Such a shame no one would enjoy them now.

"How are you doing?" Alyssa asked.

Consuelo held up a tea set the size of her palm. "I've finished the furniture. I just have the china and breakables to wrap."

"Thank you."

Consuelo looked up at Alyssa. Her eyes seemed bigger than usual, like she hadn't slept. "You're welcome. Do you want me to put the house in the attic when I'm done?"

"No, I mean thank you for what you did. In court."

Consuelo looked down again. "You don't have to thank me. I was glad to help."

"You did more than that. You saved us."

Consuelo shook her head. She didn't feel comfortable accepting such gratitude for what anyone in her position would have done. Alyssa started to leave. "Did you want me to store the house for you?"

"No." Alyssa turned to face her. "I'd like you to have it."

Consuelo almost dropped a thimble-sized pitcher. Alyssa had given her many things over the years—new clothes with the tags still on, extra sets of dishes, books for her nieces and nephews, even jewelry, including a delicate ivory cameo that was Mrs. Segal's, as well as generous yearly raises and Christmas bonuses—but somehow this seemed too much. "No, no, I couldn't."

"Please." Alyssa's voice had gone dead. "You'd be doing me a huge favor."

"But it's your house."

"I don't need it anymore." Consuelo didn't understand what Alyssa meant, but knew she couldn't persuade her. Once Alyssa decided something she was immoveable.

"Miss Alyssa, are you sure?"

Alyssa sighed. "I am." She seemed resigned. To what Consuelo did not know.

"Thank you." Consuelo smiled. "I'll take good care of it." She placed the pitcher and the matching handblown glasses, small as fingernails, in tissue paper.

Alyssa bent down and handed Consuelo two wooden bottles, whose white had long since faded to bone. "Don't forget the milk."

33

The deck chair was hard on her back, but Fay endured its broken straps and extreme angle. She needed to be here, in this spot, every day at precisely 11 a.m. That was when Nico took his swim in the hotel pool. They had met at the Manager's cocktail party. Nico stood alone at the far end of the buffet table, and every so often reached down to dip a cheese twist in one of the accompanying sauces. He was tall—she liked that—a refreshing contrast to her previous men, and she guessed over 80. Well-preserved, impeccably dressed in cream linen, and stately, except for the slight hump. He radiated health, which was why she had expressed shock when she learned that his lymphoma of years earlier had reasserted itself.

She approached him, facing the setting sun. "Lovely evening isn't it?" Something innocuous was best, nothing for the gentleman to object to, nothing personal.

He nodded and asked in a thick Cuban accent, "Are you here alone?"

Fay was unused to such directness, but she took it as interest. "Why yes, I am. And you?"

"Yes," he said, taking a long sip of rum.

They had dinner together that night—broiled fish, cheesecake. Floridian establishments knew what customers of a certain age wanted. Fay discovered that Nico—Nicanor Guzman—was a Cuban Jew, who had been in the States for fifty-two years. He had started from nothing and managed to accumulate a small fortune in real estate. He was here in Bonita Springs looking into the possibility of buying up time-shares along the Gulf.

"I was thinking of purchasing one myself, but I wouldn't know where to start," Fay said. "Perhaps you could give me some guidance."

"My pleasure," Nico said, kissing her hand. His wife of fifty-five years had died only weeks earlier.

Sitting by the pool, waiting for Nico, Fay marveled at the turns her life had taken. The events of the past year and a half had almost flattened her. She had never miscalculated so badly. Gretchen told her not to beat herself up. "How could we have known they would put up such a fight?"

"I should have seen it coming, that day in my living room, Alyssa boiling over."

"She looked crazy. Incompetent."

"That was supposed to be Alvin."

After the debacle, Fay was spent, quite literally, but she still had to pay those despicable children and the legal bills. It irked her no end that Izzy's fee reduced what she would have gotten had he advised her properly, to half. She put her house on the market, and after a slow summer, got a bid just large enough to cover her obligations and a fresh start, beginning with this trip Gretchen had insisted upon. "You need rest, Mom." It still didn't seem fair that Izzy made money when she lost, but she tried to let it go. She'd heard that he'd closed that hideous mall office.

So many of Fay's old friends had retired to Florida. She brought Gretchen and the girls along to consider it. Gretchen needed a new start as well. Fay told her she was better off, but her daughter was still reeling, six months after Pablo's desertion. He called to talk to the girls every few weeks, and promised to send money, but his checks bounced as often as they cleared. Fay had complained about having her daughter and grandchildren staying with her in DC, but she would have been lonely without them. Maybe they could all get a condo together. Or rent a house.

She would think about that later. Here, under the palms, the possibilities once again seemed endless. She fanned her fingers and admired the hard gloss of her crimson nails. She ignored the web of bulging veins and the ever-expanding band of age spots that camouflaged her hands. Focus on the assets; her nails had never looked better—long, sharp, shiny. Fay watched Nico cross the courtyard, puffing out his brown chest at the sight of her. She couldn't believe her luck.

After his swim, Fay handed Nico a towel and applauded his twenty laps of American crawl. You'd never know he was terminal. They sat together on the pool terrace and ordered Rum Jumbies. When the drinks came, she noted his morose mood.

"What is it?"

"It's been six weeks."

"I'm sorry. I know how it is. I lost my husband last year."

"I can't sleep."

"You need distraction."

"No," he said. "I need to remember."

She paused. She had to tread carefully. "Tell me about her. Tell me about your wife."

"She was my life. I don't want to live without her."

"That's not what she would want," Fay said and tapped his hand lightly. "She would want you to go on and on."

"No chance of that."

"Miracles happen."

"Not anymore. Not without her."

"Everything happens for a reason. Paths cross. Nothing is an accident."

"You think so?"

"I know so."

Nico smiled, shedding his veil of sadness. Was it her words of wisdom or the rum? Fay didn't care. This one would be easy. And she deserved it.

34

"Turn on the TV," Lorraine called from the kitchen.

Jamie was in the family room watching an ESPN re-run, the Yankees winning the '96 World Series. "It's not six yet!"

Lorraine flipped sizzling chicken pieces one by one. She could hardly hear her son over the range hood's blower.

"I don't want to miss the news!" she said, and then added water, rice, sage, and rosemary—their fragrances rising from the pan. She turned the burner down to simmer. Pilaf took about thirty minutes, plenty of time for her to catch Caitlin O'Mara's report from Washington.

Every night for the past four months Lorraine had commandeered the television to watch O'Mara, every night since Alyssa had once again stopped talking to her, shortly after she sent Lorraine huge boxes containing all of Mother's artwork, and one with the blue dollhouse, its contents neatly wrapped.

When the phone slammed in her ear, Lorraine felt sick, nauseated by the near-certainty of her sister's permanent withdrawal from her life. It felt final, and unlike their mutual parting after their mother's death, irretrievable, precisely because Alyssa had made the decision alone. In spite of Lorraine's pleadings not to do this again, not to walk away, not to break the promise they'd both made to Ken that euphoric night, after their triumphant day in court. It was a year ago, but Lorraine couldn't forget the look in her brother's eye—the pain and sadness. Ken couldn't go through this again.

He and Priscilla had been so busy getting ready for the move, Lorraine didn't want to add more disturbance. But as the days of silence added up, she knew she would have to tell him. Ally was closer to Ken—especially now—but Lorraine was sure Ally wouldn't be able to explain this. Lorraine found it remarkable that Alyssa could answer Ken's need in so magnanimous a gesture. When she had suggested to Alyssa that she consider selling the house to make a new start, she hadn't expected this result.

"Mom! It's on!"

"I'm coming." Lorraine wiped her hands on a paper towel and ran into the room, almost tripping over Fred, who was sleeping on the floor.

"Hello Charlie!" Caitlin said, addressing the unseen anchor, her voice perfectly modulated, her hair streaked with expensive highlights. Lorraine remembered when Cate was a dull brunette, chattering over coffee on another network's inane morning show. Odd, how she had grown in stature as a serious reporter, while her coiffure brightened to Hollywood blond. Her head almost filled the screen, but not quite. Behind her: banks of monitors, computers filling the station's DC bureau, and shadowy figures moving in the background.

"There she is!" Jamie's arm shot out of his sleeve, finger pointing to the upper left corner of the screen.

Lorraine moved in closer. She recognized the poof of unruly hair, the shoulders in perpetual slump, the arc of over-ripe cheek. Yes, it was Alyssa. Her sister at work.

Alyssa had never wanted to be on camera. For a brief period when Alyssa first took this job, Lorraine encouraged her to become an on-air reporter. "You're pretty enough. You're smart enough. You're young enough," she said.

Alyssa would shake her head. "I'm too fat," she answered. "And you don't have to be smart to be on camera."

"Cate O'Mara is smart," Lorraine went on, not leaving well enough alone.

"Cate is a star." End of discussion. Ally became O'Mara's producer, comfortable with her role behind the scenes.

Lorraine watched the blurry image of her sister reaching with her right hand. The drone of Cate's voice, drained of content by Lorraine's fierce focus on Alyssa, served as atmosphere for the real story Lorraine narrated: she's reaching for the phone. No. Wait. Alyssa's hand moved back to her mouth. Chopsticks. A carton. Chinese food. The rapid jaw movement was so Alyssa.

"Slow down, enjoy your food," Lorraine used to tell her.

Lorraine knelt inches from the television, miles from Alyssa. This was how it would be now: indistinct glimpses of her baby sister, on a screen, in the background, oblivious to being watched by the one person in the world who she no longer wanted to see; a one way mirror with Lorraine looking in, like a detective reading a suspect for clues, at Alyssa, a faceless figure going about her business unaware of the longing observer. What did Lorraine expect to see each night when she tuned in for O'Mara's segment? Did she think Alyssa would send her a signal like she used to when she'd call to say, "Stay on the phone. I'll be behind Cate's right shoulder. Watch for the head scratch." Then she'd raise her left arm, Lorraine would squeal at their benign subversion of national news, and they'd chatter away for the entire segment.

In her favorite fantasy she imagined Alyssa turning to the camera, walking forward, pushing O'Mara aside and saying, "I take it all back. I'm still here for you. Call me."

But there were no signals. The smoke from Alyssa's fire had gone out. There was no on-air code, no secret sister language. No communication at all.

"Back to you Charlie," Caitlin said. The report ended, replaced with Charlie's head, the New York skyline behind him. Alyssa was gone.

"Mom? Mom, when's dinner?" Jamie asked.

Fred licked her salty chin. Lorraine looked at her watch. "Soon," she said.

Lorraine sighed and returned to the kitchen. As she set the table, she tried to recall exactly what had been said that precipitated this latest rift? She remembered anger, confrontation. Over Ally's absence at Jamie's Bar Mitzvah? Or her last minute cancellation of their spa weekend?

"It's not just that," Ally had said, when Lorraine tried to make her acknowledge the cause's pettiness, tried to prevent escalation into full-scale warfare. But it was already too late. Ally had a list of Lorraine's wrongs, which she trotted out whenever Lorraine pushed too hard. Ancient wounds reopened or never closed, a fatal infection that had spread through the body of their relationship and killed it.

Now only shadow sisterhood remained: one inside the box, one outside peering in, grieving the loss of the living. Whatever she had done or said, Lorraine knew she didn't deserve to be shunned. This was worse than losing Mother and Daddy, worse than Fay's treachery. The estrangement between Lorraine and her elusive sibling, set in motion a needless mourning for separated lives. They had both left Segalia behind.

Lorraine turned down the burner. "It's ready," she called. Brad ambled in, followed by Jamie, and Fred, who sat under the table, tail wagging. Lorraine picked up her fork and stopped, mid-air.

"What is it, Hon?" Brad asked.

For a moment she held chopsticks in her hand.

"Mom?"

Lorraine shook her head, and said nothing. Alyssa's already had dinner.

Ken stood in the front yard of the house he had grown up in and pointed to boxes near the curb. "Those go upstairs and to the left. The master bedroom."

The broad-shouldered sweating young Israeli grunted assent, strapped the cartons together and hoisted them on his back. Priscilla was inside with Stella and Consuelo, setting up the kitchen, and supervising the professional clean-out company she'd insisted on hiring. He had joked about adding a HAZMAT team. Ken could hear Josh's happy yelps as he ran around the new backyard—new old backyard. Ken still couldn't believe he was here. For good.

When Alyssa had called to say she was leaving, and that she wanted him to have the house, he'd been astonished. He'd pictured her year after year holed up like Miss Haversham, disintegrating along with the debris, becoming one with her yellowing heaps. He thought he'd have to dig her out one day.

"I just figured we'd rent for a while," Ken told Alyssa. The money from the estate had made it possible for him to take Harlan up on his offer and pay for school: paralegal at Fineman, Jellnick & Sachs by day, Georgetown Law by night.

"Daddy would have wanted it this way," Alyssa said, "now that you're following in his footsteps."

"But where will *you* go?" he asked.

"I don't know. I'm going to take some time off. Maybe travel."

Ken couldn't picture Alyssa going anywhere, but he didn't say so. The trial had shaken them all to the core. It had realigned them, reshuffled their assumptions about themselves. It catalyzed him into doing something he'd never imagined himself capable of. Perhaps it had done the same for Alyssa.

"But this was your inheritance."

"I'll be fine, she said. "I have a great job, savings, no dependents. You have a family to raise. I want you to have it. Mother would want you to have it."

Mother? Why did his younger sister have to invoke their mother whenever she wanted to justify her own behavior? "Does Lorraine know?" he asked, fully aware the very mention of their sister would rile her. Alyssa walked away, the answer he expected.

Ken mounted the front steps and entered into the empty front hall. Something was wrong between Lorraine and Alyssa. Again. Something he couldn't fix. He was done negotiating between his sisters. He would save those impulses for his new profession. He had to accept the way things were, not dwell on promises broken, the shards of family splintered. This was who they were: two women allergic to each other.

Josh came running in. "Daddy, Daddy there's a bird's nest right outside my window!"

"Come show me."

Josh took Ken's hand and pulled him up the stairs, almost toppling the mover on his way down. When they reached the second floor landing, Josh pushed open the door to his new room, Ken's old one. Ken used to sit for hours looking out at the oak whose branches had housed nest after nest of bird families.

"See, Daddy! There!"

The nest was smaller than the ones Ken remembered, a handful of thatching, twigs, and fuzz that looked like the dust from dryer exhaust. Ken lifted Josh.

"An egg!" he squealed. "Two!"

"Like you and your sister," Ken said. Or Ken and Alyssa. Or Ken and Lorraine. Three broken into twos: a pair and one odd person out.

"No Daddy. We're not birds."

Ken kissed his son's moist forehead and put him down. "You're right. We're not. Go find Mommy. Ask her if she wants pizza."

Josh shrieked, "Pizza," and sped downstairs.

Outside, Ken lifted Josh into the car and secured the strap from the child seat around his son's waist. When Ken stood, a man with a red beard was jogging in place beside him.

"Hey," the man said. "Welcome to the neighborhood. You're gonna love it here."

"Thanks." Ken smiled. "Actually, I grew up in this house."

"Oh." The man stood still. "You're–?"

"Alyssa's brother." Ken thrust out his hand. "Ken Segal."

The man took it and said slowly, as if the response had answered a longstanding question, "Al-y-ssa."

"Yes," Ken said. The man started running in place again. "What's your route?"

The man pointed down the street. "Along the creek path and up Bradley. Do you run?" Ken nodded. "Maybe we could run together once you get settled."

"That would be great," Ken said.

Josh wiggled in the seat. "Daddy! Pizza!"

The man took the boy's cue and pushed off. "I'm Jeff, third house down, the blue Cape. Let me know if you need anything."

"Thanks."

The man turned, waved, and called over his shoulder, "Welcome back!"

In the car, on the way up Essex, Ken drove past his street's familiar landmarks, real and ghost: the Mayor's house with the giant hedge to hide behind, the log cabin that had been transformed into a two story contemporary, the colonial with the wrap-around porch where he and his best friend Tommy used to stage endless shootouts. He was grateful for Alyssa's generosity, for the comfort of having this house still in the family, and for the connection it held, that could never be completely sundered.

"It's too much. You're asking too much."

"Joining your family for an important milestone is too much?"

This exchange and the heated accusations that followed played over and over in Alyssa's head, as they had all through the fall and winter, even though she tried to block them out with pop tunes piping through the headphones the stewardess just handed her.

Lorraine's question, with its implied judgment, had devastated Alyssa. She was found lacking, because she didn't honor what her supreme sister deemed important, The answer meant she had failed. Yes, it *was* too much. The singing, the cakes, the toasts, the extended family, the dear friends, Lorraine's friends, who were closer and more relaxed with her than Alyssa could ever be. She could not bring herself to go to one more party. Lorraine didn't understand how tiring it was, Lorraine with her inexhaustible energy. Even after spending all that time together before and during the trial, Lorraine still couldn't comprehend Alyssa's need for solitude. Lorraine didn't get that too much contact could destroy her. Lorraine refused to accept that Alyssa wasn't built like she was, or like most people for that matter. Though she was often lonely, she craved separation. Though she bemoaned her lack of social life, when given a choice, Alyssa chose to fly solo.

Fly solo. Ha. The day she signed the house over to Ken, Alyssa booked a one-way ticket to California. She'd always wanted to see the Pacific.

Paul told her to take all the vacation and sick days she needed. "I can't remember the last time you took a week off," he said.

Zelda asked her to call whenever she wanted. Zelda had been more uneasy than Alyssa over the house thing. "Are you sure? Are you absolutely sure you want to give it up?"

Alyssa would nod and say, "Absolutely sure." She'd told Zelda about the dreams that had started the night after the trial, the dreams of Mother racing through the house, bumping into things, telling Alyssa to get out while she could, "before it was too late." She left out the parts in which Mother, dressed in a see-through negligee had fought Alyssa to open the curtains, to "let in more light." The semi-nudity creeped Alyssa out.

"They're only dreams," Zelda said. "You don't have to do what they tell you."

"Yes, I do," Alyssa said. In therapy, Terry had once told her that everyone in a dream was you. Ever since the trial, Lorraine had bugged her to sell the house, saying it wasn't healthy to stay in such a haunted place. Then the dreams started, and Alyssa grudgingly admitted, that Lorraine was right. Alyssa had become Mother, a ghost of herself in her childhood home. It was time to go.

Alyssa nibbled the salty nuts and sipped the Chardonnay the stewardess had placed before her. Leaving had been surprisingly easy. Terry talked her through it, and warned, "Once a hoarder, always a hoarder." But it wasn't as bad as she had anticipated. Consuelo helped sort what to give away, what to throw out, and what to keep in storage for whenever Alyssa decided to return, all without the judgment Lorraine had levied. Alyssa was glad Consuelo was going to work for

Ken. They'd always gotten along, and Priscilla needed all the help she could get, with those two babies, and Ken working and studying round the clock.

Alyssa opened her handbag, and rifled through the contents. She pulled out a sketchbook and a set of pastels and placed them on the empty seat beside her. Alyssa was glad she had salvaged them at the last minute. She envisioned herself sitting on the beach at sunrise, drawing sky and water, just as she had done on family vacations to the Delaware shore. Underneath the wallet, change purse, lipsticks, reading glasses, sunglasses, lozenges, tissues, scarf, rain poncho, rain hat, straw hat, cellphone, address book, pens, pad, and sunscreen was a marble notebook containing Mother's poems—the ones she wrote when she no longer had the energy to hold a paintbrush. Alyssa took it out and put in on her lap.

Letting it all go purged the poison that had been slowly suffocating her. Ken must have told Lorraine. She wondered if her sister was proud of her. Though Alyssa couldn't speak to Lorraine, she thought about her every day. And Brad. And Jamie. Lorraine was wrong about thinking. There was energy in it. And what connection would she have if she didn't think about people? It was all she could manage.

Alyssa opened the notebook, traced the heavy strong loops of her mother's hand, and read

My three–
Baby, baby, baby
Peek-a-boo:
Now I am here
Now I am not
Now I am not.

She hoped that Lorraine would one day forgive her, now that she had given up the house. Alyssa didn't believe in telepathy, but she imagined the bond between her and her sister intact though for the time being unusable, like the necklace Mother had left her, the one with too many missing beads. It sat on her vanity tray, until Consuelo found it, and asked if she wanted to throw it out. "No," she had said, "leave it. One day I'll fix it."

The stewardess bent over her. "Pillow?"

"No thank you," Alyssa said. "I'm comfortable as I am."

***

Acknowledgments

I would like to thank director and publisher Kevin Atticks, editorial consultant Margaret Jenkins, designer and marketing advisor Lillian Lane, and the entire publishing team at Apprentice House Press for making this book a reality. I am very grateful to them all.

Like my first book, *Dying in Dubai,* this novel began in Alice Elliott Dark's writing workshop in Montclair, New Jersey. I owe Alice and the members of the group—Patricia Berry, Lynne Cusack, Rachael Egan, Dionne Ford, Kirsten Lagatree, Debra Galant, Cindy Handler, Patience Moore, and Carole Ravin—a great debt for their time, astute contributions, and generosity. They gave me the courage to tackle an unfamiliar genre. The period in which I worked with them—from 2005 through 2009—was essential to the manuscript's development.

Special thanks to authors Marina Antropow Cramer, Martin Golan, and Jenny Milchman for their fellowship over the years, to Gail Goodman and Michael Ettinger for their insights, and to web designer Paul Tsang for his professional expertise.

Finally, I would like to thank my friend Robyn Travers, who never stopped pushing me to get this novel out into the world, my late husband, Jerry Mosier, who always encouraged my creative ventures—if only he had lived to read this one—Shari Coronis, who provided peerless friendship and wisdom, and my dear son, Oliver Blooston Mosier—this manuscript's very first reader—whose love, support, and approval were and are indispensable.

About the Author

Roselee Blooston is the author of *Dying in Dubai, a memoir of marriage, mourning, and the Middle East* (Apprentice House Press, Loyola University MD, 2016)—a Foreword INDIES Book of the Year Winner, and an Eric Hoffer Book Award Finalist. Her plays have been produced in New York, nationally, at the Edinburgh Festival, and over Voice of America, and her short stories, essays, and articles have been published in national magazines, journals, and anthologies. She teaches writing and lives in New York's Hudson Valley.

For more information go to *www.roseleeblooston.com*.

Apprentice House is the country's only campus-based, student-staffed book publishing company. Directed by professors and industry professionals, it is a nonprofit activity of the Communication Department at Loyola University Maryland.

Using state-of-the-art technology and an experiential learning model of education, Apprentice House publishes books in untraditional ways. This dual responsibility as publishers and educators creates an unprecedented collaborative environment among faculty and students, while teaching tomorrow's editors, designers, and marketers.

Outside of class, progress on book projects is carried forth by the AH Book Publishing Club, a co-curricular campus organization supported by Loyola University Maryland's Office of Student Activities.

Eclectic and provocative, Apprentice House titles intend to entertain as well as spark dialogue on a variety of topics. Financial contributions to sustain the press's work are welcomed. Contributions are tax deductible to the fullest extent allowed by the IRS.

To learn more about Apprentice House books or to obtain submission guidelines, please visit www.apprenticehouse.com.

Apprentice House
Communication Department
Loyola University Maryland
4501 N. Charles Street
Baltimore, MD 21210
Ph: 410-617-5265 • Fax: 410-617-2198
info@apprenticehouse.com • www.apprenticehouse.com